HORRO
THE SILVER SCREAM

EDITED BY JOE MYNHARDT AND EMMA AUDSLEY

Crystal Lake Publishing
www.CrystalLakePub.com

Copyright Acknowledgements

TABLE OF CONTENTS

Should every independent film be made in a unique way?
How should a company promote and distribute their films?
How important is timing when releasing a movie?

Entertaining Tidbits and Anecdotes: **375**
    How has the horror movie genre evolved since you started out?
    Does CGI improve or impede on the quality of horror movies?
    Which other careers did you almost join?
    Any advice for newbies?
    What's an average day like on set?
    What's the biggest piece of advice you can give anyone in your
        field?

INTRODUCTION BY JOE MYNHARDT

A CHILD OF the 80s, I became hooked on horror movies and television when I saw *Alfred Hitchcock Presents, Tales from the Crypt, Swamp Thing, A Nightmare on Elm Street, Halloween, Friday the 13th*, and even *Mad Max*. I was immediately fascinated by not only how much these movies offered, but by the minds that had created them. Little did I know back then just how many people are involved in the making of a film.

Who knew I would become an author twenty years later (a time when I did everything possible to watch the classics from as far back as the 50s), and knowing how inquisitive a writer's mind is, perhaps one day I'd like to write and/or create movies. And that's where this book found its origin:

My love for Horror movies.

My passion for creating something out of just an idea.

My interest in the creation of movies.

My fascination with the people who create movies.

And my dedication to the genre.

Early last year I published a collection of On Writing essays by over sixty authors through Crystal Lake Publishing. This was the ever popular *Horror 101: The Way Forward*, where we briefly covered every aspect of being an author, from writing short stories to comics and games, and of course movies. After receiving a lot of feedback from readers about the screenwriting and adaptation aspects of writing, I decided to start putting together *Horror 201: The Silver Scream*.

A lot of work has gone into this book, over a year and a half time-wise, thousands of emails and correspondence, and of course decades of experience. At the end of the book I'll have to thank a bunch of people who helped put this mammoth project together.

I

HORROR 201: THE SILVER SCREAM

There is, however, one person I have to thank right now. Wes Craven, in his absence. Wes was the first person I interviewed for this book, and he was even scheduled to write the foreword and afterword for this book. Unfortunately he passed away just a week ago. From what friends have told me, he still found time to help out people even towards the end. I must thank him for even replying to my requests, since after he joined, everything just fell into place.

What lies ahead is a compilation of essays on screenwriting, novelizations and other movie tie-ins, editing, producing, financing, running a small film company, the horror film industry, the horror genre, and a lot of interesting facts and stories about our favorite movies and film makers.

The goal of this book is to educate, entertain, and inspire.

Enjoy.

Joe Mynhardt
September 12th, 2015

II

THE HORROR FILM INDUSTRY

.

HORROR *IS* CULTURE,
OR THE *CLOVERFIELD* MONSTER IS OSAMA BIN LADEN

KEVIN WETMORE

IN 1999 *THE* Blair Witch Project seemed poised to change the face of horror. It was not the first found footage film (that honor goes to Ruggero Deodato's 1980 film *Cannibal Holocaust*, which admittedly is not entirely found footage but instead features literal found footage in which the producers learn the fate of a documentary film crew lost and killed in the jungles of South America when their cameras are discovered). It wasn't the first found footage films since Deodato's (there had been at least five in the two decades in between, although many of those were more "mockumentary" than found footage—see, for example, *Man Bites Dog* (1992)). It wasn't even the first found footage film of the year it came out (that honor goes to *The Last Broadcast*, an interesting found footage film that [spoiler alert!] suddenly shifts into a narrative fiction film in the last five minutes for no discernable reason). But a perfect storm of marketing and timing made *The Blair Witch Project* the new face of horror in 1999. Featured on magazine covers, playing at Sundance and Cannes, *Blair Witch* was cited as one of the biggest box office ratios of all time—making more money per dollar spent than any film to date. After a decade of ironic horror like the Scream films, *Blair Witch* promised to make horror genuinely frightening again. It inspired many, many parodies.[1]

And no imitators.

There was no flood of found footage horror after *Blair Witch*. Even its sequel, the underrated *Blair Witch Project 2: Book of*

---

1. Although there were at least thirteen found footage films made between Blair Witch and 2007, none received much public attention or would be considered box office successes. To be honest, I'd be impressed if you could name any of them.

Shadows (2000), was a straightforward narrative film, not a found footage film. One of the biggest horror films of the decade, and nobody tried to use the same technique to make other films, not even in a direct sequel![1]

In 2007, *The Poughkeepsie Tapes*, *Paranormal Activity* and *[REC]*, all found footage films, unleashed a flood of imitators: *Diary of the Dead* (2007), *Quarantine* (the American remake of *[REC]*, 2008), *Cloverfield* (2008), *Paranormal Activity 2* (2010), *The Last Exorcism* (2010), *Trollhunter* (2010), *Paranormal Activity 3* (2011), *Apollo 18* (2011), *Paranormal Activity 4* (2012), *V/H/S* (2012), *Paranormal Activity: The Marked Ones* (2013), *The Sacrament* (2014), *As Above So Below* (2014), and *Unfriended* (2015), to name but some of the bigger ones among the hundred or so that have appeared in the last decade. So what was the difference between 1999 and 2007 that opened the floodgates? The answer is simple and obvious.

The world experienced the terror attacks of 9/11, and this event reframed our experience of found footage films.

Now, we could argue that the effect of *Blair Witch* just took a while to develop imitators. After all, 2001 is just two years after 1999, and if there's one thing we know about horror producers it's that they love ripping off the last successful thing. But the popularity of found footage films with audience (which encourages the continuation of the cycle) is a direct development of the experience of 9/11.

Found footage films recapitulate the experience of the terror attacks on 9/11. Except for a handful of folks in New York and Washington, the world experienced the events of 9/11 through media—television and internet reporting. The images were grainy from shaky cameras. Information came in bits and pieces and was unreliable. In addition to the national media, many individuals in New York ran to rooftops with their cameras and began filming. This footage would subsequently be used in documentaries or news stories about the day. Add this experience to the rise of the terrorist video—the use of the video camera as a weapon by which terrorists (whose very name indicates their function—to cause fear) perpetrate acts of violence—beheadings, for example, while their victims kneel at their feet, crying, pleading, screaming, waiting for the violence to begin—and you have a society primed for documentary-style horror films. In other words, the amateur documentaries of 9/11, the experience of 9/11 through mediated reports, and the videos of terrorists filming their own atrocities all combine to create an environment in which the audience had been trained to find the found-footage film terrifying.

Robin Wood, in his seminal *Hollywood from Vietnam to Reagan*, saw *Night of the Living Dead* as an analogy for the Vietnam War. Shot in black and white, handheld, the style was the same as news footage from Vietnam. The film begins with an image of the American flag backwards and, set in the heartland, shows a farmhouse under siege and the people sheltering there killed one by one, as often as not by their own mistakes than by the eponymous living dead. Slasher films from the eighties reflected the ethos of Reagan's America. When the President and First Lady publicly push for anti-drug legislation ("Just say no") and abstinence-only education (another form of "just say no"), is it any wonder that films begin to show teenagers having sex, doing drugs, and then paying the price by being killed by a puritanical serial killer?

Back in 1986, anthropologist David Scruton developed the field of sociophobics, the study of human fears as they are experienced in society. Scruton (and those who followed him) argue that we are taught by society and culture what to be afraid of and how to be afraid. In other words, fear is not just the product of your own psychology but also cultural and social factors. Horror films are thus also a collective social experience that allow us to experience our fears together, with the idea that in doing so we are better capable of dealing with them in the so-called real world.

In short, horror films are rooted in our cultural fears and allow us, as a society, to confront those fears.

Example: The atomic bomb was developed in the United States in the forties and used on Japan in the Second World War. In 1949 the Soviet Union announced their possession of atomic weapons and the arms race began. In the Fifties, in cinema, big bugs and atomic monsters suddenly started showing up. *The Beast from 20000 Fathoms* (1953), *Them!* (1954), *The Atomic Monster* (1955), and *It Came from Beneath the Sea* (1955) were all monster movies in which the creature was either created by or awoken by atomic energy. Note: *The Beast from 20000 Fathoms* was based on Ray

Bradbury's short story "The Foghorn." In Bradbury's story, the dinosaur is summoned by the sound of a foghorn, which it thinks is another dinosaur calling to it (hence the title). In the film, the beast is awoken by atomic testing. We'll come back to this idea with *Godzilla*, below. But at this point you should get the idea: we get atom bombs, horror goes atomic.

The sixties started innocent enough, but the Summer of Love ended in bloodbaths, riots, and the shadow of Vietnam. The Manson Family, the Weather Underground, a decade of assassinations (Kennedy, X, King, and Kennedy), and Kent State made it a violent and dangerous decade. The kids were rebelling and the system was fighting back. Horror left atomic monsters behind and began telling stories of killer kids, of families torn apart, of the inability of the government, the military, the church and the schools to protect and save us and our values. *Night of the Living Dead*, as mentioned above, echoes Vietnam. Let us also remember, however, that Helen Cooper is killed by her own zombified daughter using a trowel. Tom and Judy, the clean-cut young couple that ten years earlier would have been the hero and heroine and survived, blow up in the truck due to their own ineptness when attempting to get fuel for the vehicle. Barbara is dragged off by the zombie of her own brother, and after Ben survives the night by going to the one place he absolutely refused to go, he is shot by a posse out killing the living dead. George Romero tells the story of delivering the print the night that Martin Luther King, Jr. was assassinated, and regardless of why Duane Jones was cast in the role (Romero says his ethnicity had nothing to do with it), one cannot help but see the echoes of the Civil Rights Movement and the backlash against it in Southern states in the film.

The kids are not alright is also a sentiment in the biggest horror film of the following decade. While some of *The Exorcist* is a direct response to the Second Vatican Council (AKA Vatican II), in which the mass was changed from Latin to the vernacular and a number of changes in the Catholic Church were introduced to modernize it (and concurrently conservative forces within the Church pushed back, all of which is on the screen in *The Exorcist*), the film is at heart about a mother who no longer recognizes her daughter. Chris MacNeil tells Father Karras, "You show me Reagan's double, same face, same voice, everything. And I'd know it wasn't Reagan. I'd know in my gut. And I'm telling you that 'thing' upstairs isn't my daughter." But her daughter, who is entering puberty in the film, is part of the "Love Generation." She, and they, are rebellious, overly sexual, disrespectful of authority—especially parents and institutions (like the Church), foul-mouthed and violent. Chris MacNeil no longer recognizes a little girl because that little girl is growing up and doing adult things. *The Exorcist* is terrifying because of the demonic, because of the special effects, but also because of its depiction of a little girl saying and doing things not considered appropriate in middle-class families.

Every culture produces the monsters it needs to explore its own sociophobics, and those monsters change through time. After the American occupation ended in 1952, Japanese filmmakers began working on a film that showed American atomic testing in the Pacific created a monster that began to destroy Japan. 1954's *Gojira* (Godzilla, in English) is very different than its later sequels in which the titular lizard defends Japan against aliens and other monsters in films aimed at children. The first Godzilla is a horror movie. Watch the uncut, subtitled version. This is not a film for children. This is a film terrified of atomic weapons and what they could do to Japan. Not only had two a-bombs been dropped on Japan in 1945, but in early 1954 the Lucky Dragon incident occurred.

The Lucky Dragon was a Japanese tuna fishing boat that was fishing near the Bikini Atoll on March 1, 1954 when fallout from a fifteen megaton atomic test caused radiation burns and eventual radiation sickness, cancer, and death for the exposed crew. *Godzilla* begins with a ship being destroyed and survivors diagnosed as having radiation burns. At heart, *Godzilla* reveals the very real fear of atomic energy and American callousness towards those affected by its testing.

Fast forward forty years. Atomic testing is nowhere to be seen in Japanese horror cinema. But another incident raises sociophobic concerns and sparks a worldwide horror trend. On March 20, 1995, Aum Shinrikyo, a small Japanese doomsday cult, carried out a terror attack known as the *Chikatetsu Sarin Jiken* or "Subway Sarin Incident." The group spilled liquid sarin in Tokyo subway cars during rush hour, resulting in eight dead and thousands hospitalized. The attack was caused by the group's desire to bring down the government, install Asahara Shoko, the group's leader, as the new ruler of Japan and hasten the apocalypse. Aum rejected modernity, but was willing to use the tools of modern technological Japan to end it. In other words, they used modern technology to bring about a spiritual destruction.

Koji Suzuki's 1991 novel *Ringu* was subsequently adapted into a film by Nakata Hideo in 1998 with radical transformation of the source material. The film is very different from the book, and the reason why is the book was written before the Subway Sarin Incident; the film was made after. In the book, Sadako was a hermaphrodite infected with a virus and it is implied she is the child of an ancient supernatural being, none of which shows up in the film. In the film, Sadako is a vengeful spirit who uses television and video to kill. In other words, she is a spirit that uses modern technology to bring about destruction, terror and mayhem. *Ringu* is a film exposing Japanese unease in the face of the Sarin attack.

It is no coincidence then that American remakes of J-horror begin after 9/11. The terror attacks of 9/11 similarly featured a religious group with an apocalyptic terror agenda using modern technology (planes) to attack, kill and cause fear. Gore Verbinski's *The Ring* was released in October 2002, a little more than a year after 9/11. No gore in the film; mostly it creates a dreadful anticipation. It creates terror. The Japanese films that followed *Ringu* and their American remakes half a decade later all combine this same formula of spiritual terror and modern technology: *Kairo* (2001) / *Pulse* (2006) (ghosts using the internet), *Ju-On* (2002) / *The Grudge* (2004) (psychic rage imprinting upon a house and able to follow those who leave it), *Chakushin Ari* (2003) / *One Missed Call* (2008) (ghosts using cellphones), and so forth.

It is also no coincidence that "torture porn" isn't a thing until after the Iraq War began. March 2003 marked the beginning of the American invasion of Iraq. Afghanistan had already been invaded in the months after 9/11. Prisoners from the latter were taken to Guantanamo Bay where they were subjected to waterboarding and other forms of "enhanced interrogation." Prisoners from the former were sent to a prison at Abu Ghraib. Both "Abu Ghraib" and "Guantanamo" became synonymous with torture in the latter months of 2003.

In 2004, the first *Saw* film was made. Six sequels followed. In each of these films, humans were tortured. Bodies were torn apart on screen. Characters were waterboarded. At a time when the nation was struggling with the idea of torture, our horror cinema provided an opportunity to engage with the topic. Admittedly, the script was first written in 2001, before 9/11, and the writer and director were not American, but the film was made in the United States after 9/11, and the audience was more willing to follow in this context than if the film had been made in the nineties. Regardless of the filmmakers' intent, audiences encountered the film in a context in which torture was being publicly debated.

In a 2006 article in *New York* magazine, David Edelstein coined the term "Torture porn" for these films, arguing that *The Devil's Rejects*, *Saw*, *Hostel*, *Wolf Creek* and others engaged in sadistic violence on the human body in a manner never before seen, and directly related to what was happening in Iraq and Cuba. The larger issue Edelstein finds, is the issue of empathy and POV. We are supposed to want to empathize with the victims and the fear we feel is generated on their behalf. But the whole point of going to see the film is to see these people get tortured. No one would go to a film called *Saw* that just featured conversations about the bad things we've done. When you call a film *Saw*, something better be sawn off by the end.

Hostel (2005) clearly demonstrates this ambiguity. It is a horror film. It's an Eli Roth film. We are there for the blood and guts and mayhem. We spend much of the film attempting to figure out who is doing the torturing of these people and why. We finally learn that wealthy foreigners are paying big bucks to torture and kill Americans. So when Pax (whose name ironically means "Peace" in Latin) sees the German businessman who killed his friend in a train station after escaping the torture factory, he feels (and we feel) that he is fully justified in brutally killing that German businessman. Torture is wrong, and people who do it are evil, says the film, until you or your friends are tortured and killed, then the use of brutal violence becomes morally acceptable because "they started it," and anything we do is just payback. *Hostel* is the working out of the morality of torture in horror film form.

Post-9/11 horror films are often occupied with random, violent death—not because of what you've done or who you are, but because of where you were when the killing started. The epitome of this is found in *The Strangers* (2008) when Kristin McKay asks the masked individuals who have broken into their house and are torturing them why they are doing it, one of the killers replies simply, "Because you were home." Unlike the serial killer films of the eighties and nineties, where the killers had a specific motive to target their victims (even if the motive was that the kids were drinking, having sex and doing drugs—see above), after 2001 the victims are determined randomly or because of where they were (Twin Towers, Pentagon), rather than who or what they were.

So, am I just some egghead throwing theories at some of your favorite films which are, after all, just horror films? Maybe. Looking for proof? Remakes prove my contentions.

George Romero's *Dawn of the Dead* (1978) is a satire on consumer culture. Two SWAT officers, a television producer and a helicopter pilot, flee Philadelphia during the zombie apocalypse and hole up in a mall near Pittsburgh. Why are there so many zombies at the mall, one asks. "This place was important to them," comes the reply. The zombies are hordes of literal consumers. Nothing else matters. Very visible among the dead are a nun and a Hare Krishna, also at the mall after death, indicating that both traditional and imported religions are part of the marketplace—commodities rather than spiritualities. The humans are no better. They have everything they could ever want. They own everything in the mall and very quickly they grow bored. Their lives lack meaning. There is no long term satisfaction in living in a mall.

Fast forward to 2004 and the remake, which did not resemble the original very much at all except for the concept, and there is a good reason for that. The mall won. Consumer culture does not need to be satirized again because Romero did that and nothing changed other than we got more comfortable being consumers. The remake is the product of 9/11. The zombies in the original were slow and appeared sad. Their lives were empty. The remake zombies were fast and pissed. When they saw humans they screamed and ran at them, even to the point of injuring themselves so long as they got a crack at tearing apart a living human. This is zombie as terrorist.

The film also explores the failure of relationships—nobody trusts anyone, no relationship survives the film (the first onscreen death is of Ana's husband, who immediately tries to kill her). Parents die, leaving children alone, spouses die, children die—every character is left alone in the end. The film explores economic uncertainty. Virtually everyone left in the mall is working class: a nurse, a church organist, a truck driver, a cop, security guards, and a retail salesman. The only wealthy character, Steve, is a total asshole who abandons his post, videotapes himself having sex, and refuses to help the rest of the group work, insisting that since it's his boat they are planning to escape to, he does not have to do anything else. This is the one percent as selfish villain. Lastly, the film demonstrates the impossibility of happy endings. Most of the characters die during the escape attempt. Only four make it to the boat. Then, the credit sequence (over which plays a song called "These Are the People Who Died") shows the four reach an island with the boat and are immediately attacked by another zombie horde. Everybody dies. Nobody is happy. Even the original ended with two characters escaping in a helicopter, which rises up. The original literally ends up, the remake ends way down. Changing culture means changing mall dead.

More recently, as of this writing, *Poltergeist* has been remade. Again, especially for those of us who grew up in the eighties, the original was a terrifying film about the spirits that infest the Freeling household. It is also a satire of the Reagan era (Steve Freeling reads a Reagan biography in bed), in which a corporation moves the headstones but not the graves in order to maximize profit. It is a terrifying climatic realization in the original.

In the remake, this fact is brought up early in the film, casually at a dinner party. Everybody knows it. What's the big deal? By 2015 we expect corporate and government malfeasance. In the remake, the father has been unemployed for several months and the family has moved to the house on top of the graveyard as part of a needed downsizing to control expenses. This film is the product of recession, of economic uncertainty. The ghosts of the original were angry because their graves had been desecrated. The ghosts of the remake want to (pardon the pun) repossess a house not really paid for.

When making films, we are not just figuring out what scares us, individually, we are also crafting stories and images rooted in the sociophobics of our time. The better horror films, the lasting ones, the ones that still have the power to scare ten, twenty, thirty years later, still work in some cases because the nature of the horror is fairly universal. In some cases, our context has changed but the film still works because there is an element of (here's my big academic word for this essay) transhistoricity. *Night of the Living Dead* may have been shaped by Vietnam, but there is something in it that still works today.

There is universality in the specific. Don't write a general horror film, because they rarely work. The stories that work are rooted in the specific moment. If I may use an example from Shakespeare: *Hamlet*, written sometime in 1599-1600 expresses the concerns in that culture about royal succession (Queen Elizabeth was old and had no children—the last time that happened there was a civil war), about religion (who's right: Catholic or Protestant) and the power of theatre to shape our understanding. No one sees *Hamlet* today and thinks about who will inherit the throne or whether Purgatory is real or not. But we still read and watch *Hamlet* because it speaks to us in new ways about the human condition.

But Shakespeare did not set out to write a play about the human condition, just as George Romero did not set out to create an enduring horror film that spawned remakes, sequels and arguably all of modern zombie culture. In both cases, the artist told a story about right here right now (although in Shakespeare's case the actual setting was Elsinore, Denmark in the middle ages). The universality of these texts is found in their specificity. We, as audience, are able to relate to the moment, the emotions, the fear, even though the context may not be ours. Horror only works in context. A monster just standing there is not actually very scary. A monster under the bed is much more disturbing. A monster under YOUR bed wins the terror award.

The paradox is, though, that even though the scares and the context must be specific, there is a danger in directly writing about the sociophobic topic. Don't write based on the actual thing. There were films made about 9/11: *World Trade Center* and *United 93*. They focused on the heroics of the day and audiences stayed away in droves, preferring fantasy to reality. Steven Spielberg's *War of the Worlds* (2005), on the other hand, was fiction, based on a novel written in 1897, and made seventy-seven million its first weekend and was in the black by its second weekend. It had everything to do with the 9/11 experience, but was not directly about 9/11. It instead recreated the experience of 9/11 in a context that allowed the audience to deal with the fears indirectly. That's the key.

Enduring horror is not about special effects, jump scares and gross outs. It rises from sustained dread because of larger fears linked to the anxieties a society experiences. Don't just think about what scares you. Think about what scares us and your films might just transcend the moment and become a long term frightfest.

Further Reading:

Aviva Briefel and Sam J. Miller, *Horror after 9/11: World of Fear, Cinema of Terror* (University of Texas Press, 2012)

Alexandra Heller-Nicols, *Found Footage Horror Films: Fear and the Appearance of Reality* (McFarland, 2014)

David L. Scruton, *Sociophobics: The Anthropology of Fear* (Westview Press, 1986).

David J. Skal, *The Monster Show: A Cultural History of Horror* (Faber & Faber, 2001)

Kevin J. Wetmore, *Post-9/11 Horror in American Cinema* (Continuum, 2012)

Robin Wood, *Hollywood from Vietnam to Reagan . . . and Beyond* (Columbia University Press, 2003)

SCARE TACTICS

THE EVOLUTION OF THE HORROR FILM & VIEWER DESENSITIZATION

DAVID C. HAYES, MS, MFA

A DOOR CREAKS in the darkened mansion playing across the silver screen and the audience gasps, waiting on the edge of their collective seats. Suddenly, a cat leaps from the door with a terrific yowl and the audience screams at the shock of seeing something, anything! This scenario is, of course, not as common an occurrence in regard to the horror film of today where more graphic and intense imagery is the norm. The viewing audience for any particular genre of film, especially horror, is affected by its own environment. This environment determines the level of effectiveness of the film's intent. In the case of a horror film, the intended effect is to scare, through tension, graphic images, innuendo, etc., the viewing audience. This is, of course, accomplished by cooperation between the filmmaker and the audience. Thomas Schatz writes, "Genre study may be more 'productive' if we complement the narrow critical focus of traditional genre analysis with a broader sociocultural perspective. Thus, we may consider a genre film not only as some filmmaker's artistic expression, but further as the cooperation between artists and audience in celebrating their collective values and ideals." (Schatz 1981: 15) This cooperation is wholly dependent on how quickly or in what direction the audience and filmmaker matures.

THE HORROR FILM INDUSTRY

The horror film has been a mainstay in narrative filmmaking since the very beginnings of the art form (Thomas Edison's 1910 film *Frankenstein* being the most noteworthy), and has been incredibly prevalent ever since. The horror film has persevered throughout film history even as other genres have fallen by the wayside. Glenn Walters's definition of horror is the most succinct. He writes, " . . . the definition of cinematic horror . . . asserts that horror is a fictionalized account designed to evoke terror through the implied presence of supernatural or grossly abnormal forces." (Walters 2008: 2). It is the cooperation between horror fan and horror filmmaker that has allowed the genre to flourish. Both audience and artist have grown as preferences change, as well. Stephen King states that horror films often serve as a, "barometer of those things which trouble the night thoughts of a whole society" (King 1981: 131). Since the audience preference is based on a sociocultural perspective, the genre must grow to fit that perspective or become obsolete. In the case of the horror film, the audience has matured along with world events and the information available as the Earth becomes a global community. Naivety and multi cultural ignorance are no longer the norm. The audience, in every day life, now sees and hears more than their grandparents. In turn, the horror film had to change. "The genre film celebrates our collective sensibilities, providing an array of ideological strategies for negotiating social conflicts." (Braudy & Cohen 2004: 699). In that regard, to keep pace with world events and the effects that these events have on the audience, the horror film had to take a darker edge and become more graphic. The audience continues to become more and more desensitized to tragedy and mayhem simply by repetition from various media outlets. The horror film had no choice other than adapting to this new tolerance that the audience has for the gruesome, or perish itself. Horror is an escapist pastime and if the escapist pastime is nothing more fantastic than what the audience can see on their evening news, then that pastime will become obsolete.

Schatz has determined, in regard to identifying films within a genre, that the following criteria are met:

> *establishment* (via various narrative and iconographic cues) of the generic community with its inherent dramatic conflicts;

animation of those conflicts through the actions and attitudes of the genre's constellation of characters;

intensification of the conflict by means of conventional situations and dramatic confrontations until the conflict reaches crisis proportions;

resolution of the crisis in a fashion which eliminates the physical and/or ideological threat and thereby celebrates the (temporarily) well-ordered community (Schatz 1981: 30).

For the most part, the majority of films generally accepted into the horror genre follow these guidelines in relation to their qualifications for placement within. The only difference between them, as stated earlier, is that they progressively, through the passage of time, grow more and more daring and risqué. Walters has compiled factors specific to the horror genre that speak to a film's relevance, and the creation of fear, in that genre. The first is Universal Relevance. Walters states, "The universal relevance of a film is the degree to which it touches on the ubiquitous aspects of fear and terror, as they apply to the themes of darkness, danger, and death." (Walters 2008: 3). The degree that this is acceptable to a horror audience will vary per time period. The creaking door of an old mansion, for example, would likely not qualify as a danger to a modern audience, although an axe through the creaking door would. Conversely, modern audiences might now be more fearful of the darkened forest than their predecessors, since more and more people are no longer exposed to wilderness. Walters's second points of relevance are Cultural and Historic Fears. He writes, "Based on Skal's societal concern model of horror picture appeal, we can see that horror movies in the United States have reflected a number of cultural changes and historical events . . . " (Walters 2008: 3). Lastly, Walters identifies Subgroup Relevance, dealing with neighborhood or small group fears, particularly those involving developmental trends and Personal Relevance, dealing with an individual's predisposition and psychological make-up as deciding factors (Walters 2008: 3). With Walter's points detailing the relevance of fear in the horror genre, the idea that universal, societal and personal fears drive the acceptance and appeal of films in the genre, it is completely plausible that as the world changes, so does the canonical elements that must make up a horror film.

The extinction of an art form, specifically a horror art form, that does not keep pace with its audience is directly related to the experience of the legendary Grand Guignol Theatre in Paris, France. Although it did not use film as a medium, the Theatre, a performance art based in horror, provides a snapshot of not catering to a desensitized audience. Hand and Wilson write, "The Théâtre du Grand-Guignol in Paris (1897-1962) achieved a legendary reputation as the 'Theatre of Horror,' a venue displaying such explicit violence and blood-curdling terror that a resident doctor was employed to treat the numerous spectators who fainted each night. Indeed, the phrase 'grand-guignolesque' has entered the language to describe any display of heightened, remorseless horror." (Hand 2008: 1). For years the Theatre would run short, terrifying plays interspersed with light comedy. The Theatre ran successfully using the same type and kind of material. In the beginning years, the Theatre was shocking and often censored by the French government. As the audience matured with the world around it and a global community began to emerge, the Guignol no longer provided the level of shock that the audience craved. Agnes Peirron notes, "By the Second World War, the theater was beginning to vacillate . . . The war dealt it its final death blow. Reality overtook fiction, and attendance at post-war performances dwindled." (Peirron 2008: 3). The Theatre eventually closed its doors in 1962 for good. When the predominantly French audience looked for escapist entertainment at The Grand Guignol during World War II, they were in need of something more than they would see in their daily lives. A Nazi occupation and a continent torn by the most horrific war anyone had seen up to that point made the Guignol ineffective. Although theatre is more limiting than film in terms of narrative storytelling, the desensitized audience that flocked to the 'Theatre of Horror' quickly dissolved when the horrors that they would see in everyday life made the Guignol pale in comparison.

Examining two films in the genre separated by many years with similar themes will highlight the effects a maturing world has had on the horror film. Tod Browning's *Dracula* (1931) and Neil Jordan's *Interview with a Vampire* (1994) are both vampire films in the horror genre. They were created 63 years apart and, by all accounts, were received by eager audiences favorably. Based on an amalgam of Bram Stoker's 1890 epistolary novel and the hit Broadway show, *Dracula* was lensed throughout 1930 and released on Valentine's Day in 1931. A particularly large gamble for Universal Studios, the film went on to great acclaim and, in 2000, was officially archived by the National Film Registry. Needless to say the film is pervasive and still a classic in the genre. When released in 1931 the film shocked audiences. Lugosi's portrayal of the Count took the breath away of many audience members, and the idea of bloodsucking vampires roaming the countryside swept the nation. By today's standards, of course, the film seems incredibly tame. The shocking (to the viewing public in the 1930s) sexual innuendo in *Dracula* titillated audiences nationwide. Again, compared to the standards of today, the sheer-clad form of Frances Dade's Lucy Watson apparently was too much for some impressionable audience members, but the same costume would not be regarded as risqué at all. The fact remains that the terror of *Dracula* was so intense that it, for all intents and purposes, made the horror film vogue in the United States and started an incredibly lucrative franchise for Universal Studios that lasts to this day. Shocked and enthralled, *Dracula* made horror fashionable. This happened due in large part to the sociocultural status of the viewing audience in 1931.

The Great Depression had ravaged the country only two years earlier and a majority of the nation was still suffering under the economic downturn. The country was ten years removed from the horrors of World War I but, in an age where information could not be disseminated quickly, that war was not waged on U.S. soil. The country was relatively sheltered. World news rarely affected the average citizen of the United States in 1931 and, being so insulated, *Dracula's* intended audience was not exposed to the horrific images and stories the world over. Watching with glee the opening of The Empire State Building that year, the public was largely ignorant of the Yellow River Flood that took the lives of 900,000 to 2,000,000 Chinese, for example. As pedestrian as modern audiences might find *Dracula* today, it was the pinnacle of terror in 1931. In addition, the year would continue to be monumental for the genre with the release of James Whales' *Frankenstein*. It would receive an even greater reception than *Dracula*.

THE HORROR FILM INDUSTRY

On the other side of the century, in 1994, Neil Jordan's *Interview with a Vampire* is a completely different work. Although the central themes are similar, the film is entirely different, more graphic and more visceral than its progenitor. *Interview* features a great deal of gory effects that would never have made it past the cutting room in 1931. The same idea applies to *Interview*'s homoerotic overtones and even the victimization of a child. Audiences in 1931 would be ill-prepared for *Interview with a Vampire*. Narrative filmmaking in general, even, had evolved to such a point in the 63 years between *Dracula* and *Interview*. The clouded relationship between protagonist and antagonist in *Interview* would probably not play to *Dracula*'s thrilled audience. The world of *Interview with the Vampire* had outgrown *Dracula*; it had seen images more horrific than *Dracula* and would not be satisfied with *Dracula*'s brand of horror. In the interim between films, the United States entered the global community with its entry into World War II, which affected the populace with the horrors reported back. The Cold War, and constant threat of nuclear war, preyed on the minds of average Americans for many years. The Vietnam War found itself on average American televisions on a nightly basis in the 1960s and 70s, forever changing the amount of terror and horror that the average American could become used to. Each of these events further desensitized the viewing audience. Compared to an impeached President, Goldie Hawn's bare breasts on national television (on the variety show *Laugh In*) and being able to watch a war hosted by Dan Rather, the shock and terror of *Dracula* looks positively innocent. *Interview with a Vampire* was a successful release that garnered much the same praise as *Dracula*. Since the audience had 'matured' since *Dracula* and the brutality surrounding them had increased, pushing the norms along with it, *Interview with a Vampire* only followed the specifications set by its placement in history. It needed to be more graphic, bloodier and sexually intense in order to have the same effect on its audience as *Dracula* had. This is evidenced throughout the evolution of the horror film. Even in increments as small as a decade, using films based from the same literary source material (as opposed to those in name only) from Bram Stoker's original novel, a definite shift can be seen. F.W. Murnau's *Nosferatu* (1922) to Browning's *Dracula* made a definite jump in sexual tension and innuendo. The next step lead to Terence Fisher's *Horror of Dracula* (1958) from Hammer Films, which sees an even greater leap in moral latitudes and visceral imagery that begins with partial nudity and more gore. This eventually leads to Francis Ford Coppola's *Dracula* (1994) and a host of other, modern adaptations. Each of these is leagues away from Browning's, Murnau's, and even Fisher's version.

Walters states, "Horror films reflect current societal issues and concerns by denoting how the fear of totalitarianism in the 1930s gave birth to movies like *Frankenstein* (1931), the fear of radiation gave flight to the creature features of the 1950s, the war in Vietnam gave rise to a new breed of zombie movie as represented by 1968's *Night of the Living Dead,* Watergate inspired mistrust for authority figures and films like *Nightmare on Elm Street* (1984), and serial killers encouraged an interest in movies like *Silence of the Lambs* (1991)" (Walters 2008: 4).

Thomas Schatz believes the static and dynamic structure of genre theory is twofold. He has written that the structure is both formulaic and in a constant state of flux. The flux that genres are in are often due to changes in cultural attitudes, film trends, industry economics and the like (Braudy & Cohen 2004: 691). The formulaic aspect that Schatz mentions is precisely what defines a genre, although the formulaic aspect of horror films changes over time with the further desensitization of the horror film audience. A steady increase in violence, gory imagery and sexuality, including nudity, has defined the metamorphosis of the genre. The thematic elements of the horror film have, largely, remained intact. There has been a shift in the narrative elements of the horror film, as well, that tend to mirror the change of content.

Walters's belief that, "Horror films are popular because they speak to the basic human condition, to existential fear, and to people's attempts to overcome their fear belief systems" (Walters 2008: 10) is directly correlated to what the public views as an acceptable horror film. Since these fears change from generation to generation, the horror film itself must change with it. This change has resulted in a higher degree of shocking imagery and violence, sexuality and former taboos proliferated throughout the horror genre. It is not to say that the horror film has desensitized the viewing public, but, conversely, the horror film had to increase its level of imagery in order to survive since the viewing public has already been desensitized.

Works Cited

Braudy, Leo and Marshall Cohen, eds. (2004). *Film Theory and Criticism*, 6th Ed. New York: Oxford University Press

Dracula, 1931. [DVD] Tod Browning. United States: Universal Studios

Hand, Richard J. & Michael Wilson (January 2008). "The Grand-Guignol: Aspects of Theory and Practice" Grand Guignol Online URL:

http://www.grandguignol.com/tri_1.htm

Horror of Dracula, 1958. [VHS] Terence Fisher, Great Britain: Hammer Film Studio

Interview with a Vampire, 1994. [DVD] Neil Jordan, United States: Universal Studios

King, Stephen (1981). *Danse Macabre*. Boston: Viking

Nosferatu, a Symphony of Horror, 1922. [DVD] F.W. Murnau. Germany: Jofa-Atelier Berlin-Johannisthal

Peirron, Agnes (January 2008). "House of Horrors" Grand Guignol Online URL: http://www.grandguignol.com/history.htm

Schatz, Thomas (1981). *Hollywood Genres*. New York: McGraw Hill

Walters, Glenn (January 2008). "Understanding the Popular Appeal of Horror Cinema: An Integrated-Interactive Model" *Journal of Media Psychology*, Volume 9, No. 2. URL: http://www.ccc.commnet.edu/mla/sample.shtml

SCREAMING IN MY EAR

BRIAN PINKERTON

ON SATURDAYS, I drive my daughter into downtown Chicago for rehearsals with the Chicago Youth Symphony Orchestra. She plays the oboe. My musical instrument is the pen. While she spends the day fine-tuning her craft to Mozart and Bizet, I hunker down at the nearby Harold Washington Library to pursue my darker artistic aspirations to follow in the footsteps of Stephen King and Richard Matheson.

One day, quite by chance, I discovered an iconic building from my favorite 1970s television show just one block away. It's the Old Colony Building, a classy slab of architecture that was used as the exterior of the "INS Newsroom" in the horror series *Kolchak: The Night Stalker*. This is where Carl Kolchak (brilliantly portrayed by the rumpled, tenacious Darren McGavin) wrote stories exposing supernatural forces that his boss Tony would inevitably crumple in disgust at the end of each episode. Every week, Kolchak shrugged off the rejection and by the following week he was doggedly investigating a new monster. For a horror writer, the perseverance was inspiring.

Kolchak: The Night Stalker, a spinoff from a pair of very successful TV movies, lasted only one season. But it has since developed a passionate cult following and inspired, among other things, the hit series *The X Files*. When I revisited the episodes on DVD, I enjoyed them immensely all over again. Then I began to analyze why I found them so wonderful. On the surface, it didn't make sense. The show is woefully dated. For the most part, the horror elements are very low budget, relying on shadows, brief glimpses and folklore. There's more aftermath than action. In at least one episode, the menace is entirely invisible. In episodes where the monster is more visible, the makeup is often awkward or borderline silly.

Yet the series remains highly engaging and sometimes genuinely creepy. Around the same time that I revisited Kolchak, I watched a crop of current horror films. The experience was disheartening. The movies all felt bland, even though they had huge budgets and amazing technical resources to realize their ambitions. While the Kolchak series felt warm and involving, the newer, bigger horrors felt cold and remote, like I was observing the action but not along for the ride.

Realizing my attitude might be tempered by nostalgia, I watched a handful of classic horror films I had never seen before. I followed that with newer genre offerings and felt the same response. I tried to analyze the engagement gap. Why did "new horror" leave me dead inside . . . and not in a good way?

Then I fingered a likely culprit.

CGI.

Excuse me while I step on my soapbox now. A real one made of wood and nails, not a digital fakery composed from kilobytes.

Computers are ruining modern horror movies.

One of my favorite horror novels (and hopefully yours, too) is *I am Legend* by Richard Matheson. I'm a fan of the somber 1960s film adaptation featuring Vincent Price (*The Last Man on Earth*), the wild 1970s rendition starring Charlton Heston (*The Omega Man*), and the heavily influenced (and influential) *Night of the Living Dead* by George Romero. Each of these three films is eerie and compelling in its own way.

Now let's fast forward to the 21st century. The Will Smith version of *I am Legend* begins strong with some haunting moments . . . until the monsters arrive. They look like a mob of Casper cartoons. I remember watching in a theater and when those critters showed up, I felt pulled out of the story as swiftly as if someone had yanked me by the collar.

For the rest of the film, Will Smith fights a horde of computer generated animation, barely a step up from the live action/animation mix of *Who Framed Roger Rabbit?* The monsters all looked alike, clinical and obvious, as if someone had repeatedly poked "copy and paste" into the frame from a PC.

The hooded ghouls of *The Omega Man* with their white contact lenses and sneering disdain for advanced civilization may have been cheesy, but they retained a dark core of humanity that made them seductive and ultimately more than a little disturbing. Human actors brought them to life with flesh and blood. We knew Heston wasn't interacting with a green screen.

CGI may be technically superior but it's also distancing. Stephen Spielberg learned the hard way when he re-edited *E.T.* to introduce CGI effects to make the title character appear more polished. It was visually smoother, sure, but blander and less special than the stiff, wobbly critter we all grew up with. Fans complained and Spielberg eventually ditched CGI *E.T.*

Some filmmakers get it. *The Dark Knight* is a superior action film because it relies on real stunts and locations. The chase sequences are captured by cameras, not drawn up in software. When the hospital blows up, it's for real—the film company took advantage of a real building being demolished. The big dramatic scenes focus on the conflict of the individual characters in the midst of the violence. They don't take a back seat to the effects. It earned Heath Ledger an Oscar.

Let's go back almost a hundred years. Silent comic Buster Keaton—that man had some scary courage. He performed all of his own stunts, and it shows with real excitement on the screen. During the filming of one movie, he broke his neck. It wasn't the first or last time he risked his life for a gag. In *Steamboat Bill Jr*, the side of a collapsing building falls on him and he survives by standing in the exact spot where an open, upper-level window lands. The wall weighed two tons. If he had been standing slightly off his mark, he would have been crushed. No studio would permit such a stunt today. You wouldn't even hand it over to a stunt man. You'd draw it up on a computer to make it pinpoint perfect. As a viewer, you'd know it was artificially composed in some SFX studio and fail to register any real threat.

Martial arts star Jackie Chan, inspired by Keaton, used to do all of his own stunts. During the end credit scroll of his movies, they would show outtakes of him getting hurt and battered while filming action sequences. His fight scene choreography is exhilarating.

I'm not saying we need to put our actors and actresses in harm's way to make action exciting. CGI employed sparingly and seamlessly can be effective if the main thrust of the narrative is grounded in humanity. For a good example, check out the 2010 vampire film *Let Me In*. Unfortunately, too many films get giddy with CGI effects and fill the frame with so much visual noise that it becomes a lazy thrill composed out of chaos and clutter. CGI makes it easier to show everything . . . and leave nothing to the imagination.

Many of today's horror movies race to pile up the big effects, rolling through a chain of outlandish sequences like a hyperactive video game. It's an emotionally empty experience. The excitement is forced through fast editing and extreme gore rather than clever storytelling. It cries out for attention with the persistence of a screaming child.

We live in an age of bombardment. Every day, we experience massive competition to engage our tiny, fragmented attention spans. This not only influences the movies we watch but other forms of entertainment. You can see it in the crass, in-your-face obviousness of a lot of TV programming. In music, it appears in the production and re-mastering process. Have you heard about the "Loudness Wars?" Look it up and see if that's the reason your favorite music has lost its impact.

Today's audio engineers have sacrificed dynamic range for a more bloated sound that maximizes everything in the mix until there's no room for the music to breathe. Imagine a fist at the mixing board pushing everything up to "11," ala *Spinal Tap* . . . Drums, vocals, keyboards, guitar, bass, until the instruments lose their separate identities.

If you analyze a wave file of a song re-mastered for loudness, you will discover a solid brick replacing what used to appear as a spikey spectrum of range. The high ends are clipped off and the low ends shoved up. Everything gets muddled together in the middle for a dense, tiring listening experience. It's known as brick-walling to ensure there aren't any quiet moments in the music and it's meant to accommodate the new way we listen to music—compressed digital files dumbed down for cheap mp3 headphones, where the nuances of dynamics are lost. By artificially inflating the sound, online streaming audio can retain a consistent volume across artists, sources and within songs.

Even Metallica fans have complained about the crappy sonic effects of brick-walling, protesting the mastering on the album *Death Magnetic*. And this is a fandom that likes their music LOUD. But loud, brittle and distorted into sludge? Not so much.

Sadly, it's not just newer music. In the past decade, we've seen classic rock re-mastered for loudness, turning up all the levels to create a bloated, bloodless listening experience. There's a reason more people are seeking out vinyl—or in some cases, earlier compact disc editions that remain faithful to the warmth of the original recordings.

Too many movies strive for the same effect: a brick of loud visual noise, dumbed down for wandering attention spans. An iPhone screen is too small to see subtleties, so why have them? Check out the Transformers series or the latest superhero movies. Bricks of noise. You're artificially engaged, but you forget what you saw a week later because it all runs together and never really captivated your heart or mind. It's streaming eye candy on the go, junk food that feels good going down but leaves a trace of indigestion.

Great horror builds from suspense. Study the pacing of the Carpenter's *Halloween*, Hitchcock's *Psycho*, or even the original *Texas Chainsaw Massacre*. You are at the edge of your seat when the climax kicks in because you have been sucked in with artistic finesse.

As a horror writer, the things I value feel quaint and old fashioned: deliberate pacing, emotional resonance, building and releasing tension, an intimate sense of character and setting. I want the reader to fully experience the story rather than observe it from a safe distance.

My novel about rival horror film directors, *Rough Cut*, builds to a frenetic finale but you need to be patient with it. The house of cards must be constructed before you shake the table beneath it. Across online sites and social media, *Rough Cut* received wonderful reader reviews, except for one—someone who gave up after 100 pages, expressing frustration that no one had been killed or maimed yet.

Perhaps I need to revisit my approach to bring it more in line with modern movies and music. MAYBEISHOULDUSEALLCAPSALLTHETIMEANDSTIFLETHES PACESBETWEENWORDS.

THE HORROR FILM INDUSTRY

If horror doesn't scream, is it heard?

After several months of weekly rehearsals, my daughter performed in her winter symphony concert. I enjoyed the experience as a proud papa and music lover. While horror stories and classical music could not be more different on the surface, I am able to enjoy some of the simple similarities. The music goes on a journey and soars when it needs to, a uniquely human composition of pacing and dynamics to stimulate and intrigue. Around every turn, there is anticipation . . . for what awaits . . . beyond the deceptive calm.

FROM PAGE TO FILM
WATCHING MY STORY COME TO LIFE

MICHAEL LAIMO

MY NAME IS Michael Laimo, and I am the author of 8 novels, and over 100 short stories, all of them horror. I've written many articles, and chapters in how-to books. Since you are reading this, then you know I've been asked to contribute to this collection titled *Horror 201: The Silver Scream*. Which, as you know, delves into the art of filmmaking.

It's an honor to be here, because I am not a filmmaker. I am an author, through and through, self-taught and considerably lucky to have reached the level of success I've earned. Which, by any writer's standard, is pretty damn great . . . unless of course you consider how much money I haven't made doing this. I still work a day job, still plug away at my writing endeavors and tuck away most of my work for a rainy day. Or a sunny day. Depends how you look at it. But I am here, and for that I am grateful.

I've written a handful of articles as to HOW I got my movie deals. If you are unfamiliar with my work, I have had two of my novels adapted into feature-length films for NBC's Chiller Network. I've also had four short stories filmed by amateur filmmakers. I've revealed in the various interviews and articles that I pretty much got lucky, that I was recommended to the production company Chiller had hired to film their original features. Word got around and made its way to those in charge, who reached out to me and asked me to submit. Mind you, it was not a shoe-in. My work was being considered alongside many other books, and in the beginning was even rejected. But I held on, and in the end, was offered a deal.

So . . . what happened next? Interestingly, in all the interviews I gave, no one asked me to talk about the development process until now. Maybe it was because I really hadn't had too much of a hand in the creative process. After all, I'm a writer and not a filmmaker. But . . . no one knew my story, my characters, better than me. And that's where I came in.

I was asked to attend a meeting up at NBC, where I met Chiller's program director, general manager, and others who would be working on the *Dead Souls* film. It was an ultimate moment for me, seated in a conference room at a big-ass table with no less than a dozen people discussing my plot, my story, my characters. There was an air of respect toward me as the creator of something they chose to put seven figures into. It was truly gratifying . . . and yet the truth of the matter was that I was in awe of all these people, and of their positions working for NBC. I suppose mutual respect is the right term here.

And we talked. And talked. The screenwriter that was commissioned had read *Dead Souls* and had a copy of the paperback with a shitload of post-its sticking out of it. He had some questions. No, he had many questions. And so did the director. And the producer. And . . . I had the answers. Thankfully, when I received word about *Dead Souls* being made into a movie, I went back and read it because there's nothing more frustrating than when a reader starts asking you questions about your plot and characters, and you have no idea how to answer them because you've forgotten the work's finer details.

The first discussion we had was which story to tell. *Dead Souls* tell two stories—one from the past and one in the present. And the folks working on the movie didn't know which one to focus on. They had been leaning on telling the entire story of the past, but I dissuaded moving in that direction. I felt the present story was a more interesting one that could be developed using flashbacks from the past. There were pros and cons against each idea, but it was ultimately decided to go with the present story after I thought the important aspects of the past (the crazed minister crucifying his family) could be told in the first ten-fifteen minutes of the film.

Once that detail had been finalized, the next issue was how the minister would crucify himself. I immediately raised the idea of having the final nail sticking out from the crucifix so he could swing his arm onto it. This little tidbit made it into the film and the actor's performance is mind-blowing. It's one of the best scenes in the film.

After a few hours discussing, and a nice meal at a local NYC eatery, it was a waiting game. John Doolan, the screenwriter, had about two weeks to complete the first draft of the *Dead Souls* screenplay. This was a job I didn't want. He had to take a very complex story which in truth would need about 6 hours of screen time to adapt as is, and cut it down to fit into a 92 minute film. There would be plenty of scenes cut. It became apparent to me that the script would simply tell the meat and potatoes of the story, and would leave out some characters and scenes. John and I traded many emails discussing how some plot points would be handled. He would also communicate these to the powers-that-be at NBC, as they wanted full input on the story. I suppose if I had my way, I would've wanted those 6 hours (and a mini-series!) to tell my story, but I was at the mercy of Chiller and Synthetic Cinema and let them have free reign of the project. Seriously, who was I to resist? I was simply thrilled to be a part of this exciting process.

I would say no less than 6 drafts showed up in my inbox over the next couple of months. It was very interesting to see scenes come and go, to see the dialogue change, to see the story develop into a darn good made-for-TV screenplay. I had plenty of feedback along the way, and was thrilled to see almost all of my points taken into account.

Once the final script was delivered, the process of casting was set into motion. Another meeting was called and I was again thrilled to be a part of it. I was shown the headshots of many actors, and those that were in the running to play the lead characters. I knew some of the actors that were called upon, including Evan Peters and Noel Fisher. Exciting stuff! In the end I had no say in who was chosen, as it was really up to availability and budget. Ultimately, I was thrilled to see Jesse James in the lead role of Johnny. I'd remembered him from the *Amityville Horror* remake and to this day have kept in touch with him.

A few months later, filming began and I was on set for three full weekends of filming. It was a first for me, being on a movie set, and an ultimate thrill seeing about 60 people working on something I had created. There were many speedbumps, like a fly infestation and unseasonably cold nights. But the cast and crew got through it all.

It was my last day on set, after taking pictures with some of the actors and producers, that I was notified about my novel *Deep in the Darkness* being considered for another Chiller feature. When *Dead Souls* aired, I had a party at my house and received a text an hour before it started from producer Andrew Gernhard that *Deep in the Darkness* was greenlit.

It was a great night for me, and an ultimate moment in my career, watching one of my books come to life on TV, and being informed that another would be made . . . That I would get to do it all over again.

In the end, my involvement on both films was minimal. But, I'd continuously reminded myself that I played the biggest role of all in the creation of these films: that I wrote the stories they were based on.

Many writers have asked me for tips on how to get their works produced into films. I always tell them to write the best story you can, and it will find its way to the right people.

HORROR THEATRE: HORROR FILM'S OLDER, OFTEN SCARIER SIBLING
A (BRIEF) HISTORY OF HORROR ON STAGE

KEVIN WETMORE

HORROR THEATRE BEGAN with the beginning of theatre. Supposedly, at the premiere of Aeschylus's *The Eumenides* in 458 B.C.E. at the City Dionysia, the large religious drama festival in honor of Dionysus in Athens, the opening scene of the Furies waking up and smelling the blood of Orestes caused warriors to faint and pregnant women to miscarry on the spot. The plays presented in ancient Athens featured ghosts, demons, monsters, murders, and all kinds of bodily harm. In Euripides' *Medea*, the title character murders her children, causes her ex-husband's new bride and her father to catch fire and melt at the wedding, and then rides away in a dragon-pulled chariot while laughing at her ex. What is that if not horror?

Indeed, Aristotle wrote in the *Poetics* in 335 B.C.E. that the reason theatre existed in the first place was to raise "fear and pity" in the audience and then purge them of it through catharsis (tangentially, Aristotle was writing in response to his teacher Plato, who in *The Republic* said he would ban theatre as it was a falsehood that had a real effect. People were terrified when Medea killed her children, but no real children were killed, and so real emotions were created by false events, which Plato could not abide. Aristotle took Plato's argument and turned it on its head, saying that the emotional effect was the whole point, thus beginning an argument that is still unsettled today: does watching horrific things make us more or less likely to do horrific things? Platonists say yes, we watch *Friday the 13ᵗʰ* and it inspires us to violence. Aristotelians say we watch *Saw* and work out our violent impulses in the theatre, not on each other).

Fast forward from the Greeks to Shakespeare and his contemporaries. The English renaissance might be the single greatest flowering of horrific stories until the twentieth century. In *Hamlet* (1599), a ghost tells his son to avenge his murder. The son then feigns insanity, drives his girlfriend to suicide after murdering her father, wrestles with her brother in her grave, forges a note that gets his two college friends executed, and then fights a duel in which four people, including him, are poisoned. *Macbeth* (1605) opens with witches plotting something (it is never made clear, other than they plan to go see Macbeth). Within five acts, ghosts and the goddess of the witches show up. Macbeth and his wife murder the king ("who would have thought the old man to have had so much blood in him?"), frame his bodyguards and kill them, send assassins after friends and family, killing at least one child ("Mother, I am dead!" he screams as he is slaughtered onstage), and throw a dinner party haunted by one of their victims. Spoiler alert: She goes crazy and commits suicide and the guy whose kid he killed beheads him in a fight. And we give these plays to high school students and tell them they are the greatest things ever written.

But the renaissance gets so much darker than Shakespeare. In Beaumont and Fletcher's *The Second Maiden's Tragedy* (1611), a young woman commits suicide rather than be ravaged by a tyrant king. When he announces that just because she is dead, it doesn't mean they cannot have a sexual relationship, her ex-fiancée pretends to be a mortician who claims he can make the body seem lifelike and covers her face in poisoned makeup so when the tyrant begins to make love to the dead body, he burns to death from the poison. All this happens on stage in full view of the audience. Similarly, in Thomas Middleton's *The Revenger's Tragedy* (1606), Vendice carries around the skull of his dead lover until he can force the man who killed her to kiss the skull's now poisoned mouth.

In John Webster's *The Duchess of Malfi* (1612), the two brothers of the title character plot to have her and her family killed so that they may inherit her wealth. An assassin kills the children and her husband, and then strangles her inside a coffin he has brought to her bedroom after he has her imprisoned in a madhouse. The brothers react badly to the success of their plan. One goes crazy and believes himself to be a werewolf and the other is killed by the assassin they hired.

Ghosts, witches, demons, devils, assassins, murder, torture, and good old fashioned body horror show up in many tragedies from this period. *The Witch of Edmonton* (1621) involves the title character summoning the devil in the form of a large black dog named Tom, who proceeds to wreak havoc. Christopher Marlowe's *Doctor Faustus* (1594) tells the story of a man who sells his soul to the devil and at the end of the play is dragged off to hell, long before Sam Raimi ended a similarly titled film the same way. The English renaissance was filled with bloody, horrific dramas on stage that easily equal the horror films of today.

Meanwhile, over in Japan, the kabuki theatre presented horrific tales, as well. Plays about ghosts and demons and monsters were presented in August during O-bon, the festival of the dead, the idea being that summer was the best time for stories that chilled you (scary story as air conditioner!). Fans of J-horror would have no problem recognizing Oiwa from *Tōkaidō Yotsuya Kaidan* (Ghost Story of Yotsuya, 1825) by Tsuruya Nanboku IV. Killed in the dark by her husband so that he can remarry someone younger, her dead, wet long-haired ghost appears in mysterious ways through the rest of the play.

Fast forward to Paris and the Théâtre du Grand-Guignol, which presented horror and comedy plays from 1897 to 1962, offering the original splatter stories. Special effects, makeup, skillful performances by star actors who became celebrities (Paula Maxa was the original "scream queen"—she was murdered over 10,000 times in hundreds of plays over a twenty year career, dying by stabbing, rifle shot, strangled with a necklace, eaten by a puma, guillotined, hanged, stung by scorpions, and even cut into eighty-three pieces by an invisible Spanish dagger!), and cleverly structured plays (both original and based on stories by authors such as Poe) all combined to make the Grand Guignol the most successful horror theatre in history. At its peak, on average two people fainted every night at the Grand Guignol. Resident playwright André de Lorde was a librarian by day and wrote 150 plays of torture, murder, insanity and revenge that would give any exploitation film a run for its money. The theatre was so well known for over-the-top horror that its name has become synonymous with splatter and gore.

THEATRE AND FILM

As cinema started to develop, it was shaped and influenced by theatre. In the west, cinema was regarded as a form of photography, and thus early films are pictures of nature and mechanics: the waves at Jersey shore, a train pulling into the station, a horse running, etc. In Japan, cinema was considered a form of theatre, and thus early Japanese films are of kabuki plays. The cinema itself became a form of theatre, the projector placed on one side of the stage and the screen and *benshi* (live narrator) on the other—the mechanics of projection becoming as much a part of the spectacle as what was being projected.

Dominating western theatre at the time was the rise of naturalism, through people like Henrik Ibsen, Anton Chekov and Konstantine Stanislavski, all of whom promoted a realistic form of performance. The first western horror films tended to be naturalistic. They were adaptations of popular texts. Universal's horror films, although claiming literary sources, were actually derived from stage adaptations. *Dracula* was a 1924 stage play from London by Hamilton Deane and John L. Balderston based on Stoker's novel (Stoker, by the way, was a theatrical manager himself, owing his career to the actor Henry Irving, who served as model for the vampire count, so we have theatre to thank for the original novel as well!). The play was on Broadway by 1927 with Bela Lugosi in the title role. When Carl Laemmle bought the film rights he wanted Lon Chaney for the title character, but Chaney passed away. Lugosi lobbied for the role and got it. In other words, Universal's *Dracula* has a theatrical origin, more than a literary one, as does Universal's *Frankenstein*, adapted from Peggy Webling's 1927 play. These two naturalistic adaptations of their source novels became the text that was then adapted into the film version.

Similarly, in the kabuki theatre of Japan, there is a tradition of actors playing heroes fighting other actors in giant monster costumes with no attempt at what the west would consider realism. In *Musume Dojoji*, a woman is revealed to be a giant snake. In

Tsuchiguma, the title character, a giant earth spider, fights the hero. In *Tenjiku Tokubei Ikoku-Banashi* (the Tale of Tokubei from India), Tokubei the magician summons a monstrous, giant, fire-breathing toad to trample and destroy the house of his enemy Sōkan, whose troops must retreat when the giant toad breaths fire at them. Wonder where Godzilla came from? Traditional Japanese theatre had as much to do with it as atomic weapons. The horror cinema is a reflection of the dominant horror theatre of a culture.

At the very least, theatre serves as a source of stories for the cinema. Just as the stage versions of *Dracula* and *Frankenstein* served as the source for their respective films, so, too, do contemporary stage plays serve as sources for cinema. The practice began when *The Cat and the Canary*, the Broadway hit of 1922, became the 1927 silent film of the same title. Tracy Lett's play *Bug* (1996) became William Friedkin's film *Bug* (2006). Stephen Mallatratt's 1987 stage adaptation of Susan Hills 1983 novel *The Woman in Black* became the second-longest running non-musical in the West End before it became the 2012 film. And, of course, *The Rocky Horror Show* became *The Rocky Horror Picture Show*.

Which brings us to . . .

THE CHALLENGE OF CAMP

Much horror on stage today is not particularly horrific or frightening. It has been replaced by camp. I say this as someone who proudly directed *Evil Dead: The Musical* in Los Angeles. Based on all three films in Sam Raimi's Evil Dead trilogy, it is an incredibly fun musical. With song titles like "What the Fuck Was That?," "Ode to an Accidental Stabbing," "Cabin in the Woods" and "Bit Part Demon," the show embraces all the lunacy of *Evil Dead 2* and *Army of Darkness*. We had a splash zone: The first three rows all got complimentary ponchos, because at the end of the evening they would leave the theatre looking like Carrie. They got hit with blood spray every time someone got shot, stabbed, chainsawed or otherwise abused. Oh, and we rained blood down on them from the catwalk, because why not? Fun for all, but not frightening. Gross, but not scary. The play is fun—if you get the chance to see it do so. Twice. But it ain't really horror. It's camp.

I have sat through and thoroughly enjoyed *Silence of the Lambs:*

The Musical, Toxic Avenger: The Musical, Reanimator: The Musical and no less than three different musical *Exorcists*. All were fun and very funny. None were particularly scary. All fell into the trap of camp.

Maybe it is the musical format. Perhaps anytime one takes a horror film and translates it using musical tropes the result must be camp. There are, however, genuine horror musicals that treat the subject matter seriously: *Sweeney Todd, Jekyll and Hyde, Phantom of the Opera*, and even *Carrie*, based on the novel by Stephen King. On film, *Repo: The Genetic Opera* and *Phantom of the Paradise* have their disturbing moments. But more often than not, "horror musical" means *The Rocky Horror Show, Little Shop of Horrors, Bat Boy, Addams Family*, and *Zombie Prom*. Again, all fun, no fear. All of them wink at the audience and roll their eyes as if to say, "We don't take the horror part too seriously and we hope you don't either." They have fun with conventions and tropes, and every once in a while, go for the gross-out. It is because they are afraid they cannot create fear in the audience, so instead they go for goofy fun—"If we cannot scare you," they say, "we can make you laugh, since it is also a physiological response to horrific events." And then we get *Cannibal! The Musical*.

On the other hand, while there is much campy horror on stage (especially in musical form), there are also experiences more genuinely terrifying than most horror films. *The Woman in Black*, as noted above, was a long running play in London, and it was and is terrifying. Audiences regularly scream and jump and begin to dread the next appearance of The Woman. Also in the U.K, Andy Nyman and Jeremy Dyson (of the television series *League of Gentlemen*) wrote *Ghost Stories*, which they describe as a combination of a thrill ride and a scary play, and so it is. Similarly, in the U.S., magicians Todd Robbins and Teller (of Penn and Teller) developed *Play Dead* in Las Vegas, took it to New York for an Off-Broadway run and then toured it to numerous cities across America. Teller directed and Robbins played the lead, a magician who kills a member of the audience, tells the story of Albert Fish and practices what he claims is genuine spiritualism. The show was unsettling, entertaining, and genuinely disturbing.

All three of these plays took advantage of the distinguishing characteristic of theatre, which is that it is live. The actors are in the same physical space as the audience at the same time. Movies are colored lights on a wall with a soundtrack. Theatre consists of the physical body of the actors in close proximity to yours. This allows theatre to often be far more unsettling than cinema. At Zombie Joe's Underground in North Hollywood, they offer an annual revue called *Urban Death*. About 20-30 one to five minute sketches are presented as part of the show. Some are funny. Some are strange. Some are genuinely terrifying. One year the show opened with the entire audience being plunged into utter darkness. Nothing could be seen. Folks laughed nervously. Three minutes later (a very long time in the dark), the lights came up very quickly and before there had been an empty stage, now there was a pile of corpses. We never heard them enter or get into place. They were just suddenly there after all that dark.

They opened their eyes, slowly rose out of the pile and began walking towards the audience, each one locking eyes with and slowly moving towards a specific audience member. Just before the walking corpses reached the audience, the lights went out again and the theatre was plunged into darkness. It was terrifying. In the same show, the lights came up on a naked woman on stage with a look of utter fear on her face, shivering and trying to cover herself. From the center stage door, about twenty feet behind her, an evil clown appeared. He took several minutes to slowly cross to her. The tension in the room was unbearable. We knew what was coming. It was happening right in front of us. We were powerless to stop it or look away. Once he reached her he began to strangle her and again we were plunged into darkness. The actual violence was the button on the build up to it, which took a long, long time. THAT is horror.

CONTEMPORARY HORROR ON STAGE

Large numbers of people and companies are making horror theatre today and the plays they make are proof of Clive Barker's assertion that, "There is no delight the equal of dread." Barker himself, it should be noted, began his life as a playwright, writing such wonderful horror plays as *The History of the Devil*, *Frankenstein In Love or The Life of Death*, and *Crazyface*. In an interview with Lucy Snyder, Barker remarked that his early theatre work has influenced all of his horror writing afterwards, "because making plays makes you very aware of your responsibility to your audience in a way that really no other medium does, even cinema." The plays by Barker and the others discussed here are designed to fill audiences with dread and fear and squeamishness. Wildclaw and Annoyance in Chicago are two theatre companies that specialize in horror theatre. Nightmare New York, Psycho Clan and Vampire Cowboys, among others, make New York's stages just a little scarier. Los Angeles has Visceral, Zombie Joe's Underground, Delusion, The Guignolers, and Unbound Productions/Wicked Lit (the last of whom perform plays in Mountain View Mausoleum and Cemetery—it is especially chilling to watch an adaptation of Poe's *Cask of Amontillado* in a real crypt or Lovecraft's *The Unnamable* in a real cemetery in which you hear things crashing through the woods just outside the fence), among others.

Playwrights, many of whom also work in cinema in various forms, have created a library of horror plays in the past few years. Writers such as Tracy Letts, Conor McPherson, Scott Barsotti, Ian MacAllister McDonald, Don Nigro and David Skeele, among many others, have built up bodies of work rooted in horror. Lori Allen Ohm adapted *Night of the Living Dead* as an effective stage play (when done well) that has been performed all over the world. Stuart Gordon started his horror career as a theatre director and producer and continues to perform these roles (pun intended) despite a lengthy career in film. He rose to prominence with his horror films in the eighties (*Reanimator*, *From Beyond*, etc.). In 2009, though, he directed the one-man theatrical show, *Nevermore . . . An Evening with Edgar Allan Poe* written by Denis Paoli and starring Jeffrey Combs. In 2011, Gordon produced, directed and co-wrote the book for *Re-Animator: The Musical*, which began in Los Angeles and toured to New York and Edinburgh. Likewise, Roberto Aguirre-Sacasa, who wrote the screenplay for the remakes of *Carrie* and *The Town That Dreaded Sundown,* has plays with titles like *Say You Love Satan*, *The Mystery Plays*, *Dark Matters*, and *King of Shadows*, and finds his work as a playwright, screenwriter and graphic novel writer all mutually influence one another. Many folks who make the horror movies you like also make horror theatre.

SO WHAT ARE THE TAKEAWAYS?

1. Know your history. If you want to make horror movies, know what is out there and where it came from.
2. Source material. There are two and a half millennia of drama out there. There is nothing new under the sun, so why not steal from the best. I'm still waiting for a film based on *The Second Maiden's Tragedy* or some of André de Lorde's sick, sick plays (BTW, Richard Hand and Michael Wilson have translated many plays from the Grand Guignol as part of their work in the drama studio at University of Glamorgan—worth checking out!)
3. Reading plays give you lessons in structure, dialogue, character creation and other things necessary to telling a compelling story in a media that consists primarily of visual storytelling with dialogue.
4. There are opportunities to share your work through theatre more immediately. Film is expensive. Mounting a play might be a way to get your script out there AND continue to revise the script because you get immediate feedback in a way that you never could or will with film. The actors can tell you the challenges they face with the script—which lines are difficult to say or make no sense. The audience gives you immediate feedback. Do they jump? Do they squirm? Do they scream? If not, you might need to work on the script. Similarly, things that look good on paper might not sound good or work well when said aloud. Plus, performing your plays live force you to be creative and inventive. There is no CGI. There is no "fix it in post." Either something works or it doesn't.
5. I am not suggesting that theatre exists solely to serve film—it is a great form in its own right and has a huge fanbase out there. There is a genuine audience for horror theatre, just as every October haunted houses crop up all over the map offering interactive horror experiences that even those who do not regularly seek out scary things embrace. Many of the performances of the companies I mention above sell out every seat in the house at every performance. Plus the live horror experience is a fun way to experiment with telling effectively scary stories. A few years back I was invited to turn my university

library into a "literary haunted house" for Halloween weekend, performing a dozen five-minute plays in the stacks for audience groups of ten or so. In one night, hundreds of people walked through the performances and the actors were able to perform each play dozens of times. It was an exercise in minimalism and economy that nevertheless scared a lot of people. We've been doing it every year since. And again, the feedback is immediate. Perhaps one of my favorite moments in my entire career was when a group was watching a brief scene from *Dr. Jekyll and Mr. Hyde* as I stood behind them during my rounds, seeing how each scene was going halfway through the night. As Jekyll began his transformation (a simple but effective theatre trick involving the use of makeup and different color lights), the other performer in the scene turned to the audience and whispered fearfully, "It's Hyde! RUN!" And they did, leaving the actors facing an empty space wondering if they had to finish the scene. You can't top that for feeling like a scaremaster.

THE WASHINGTONIANS

RICHARD CHIZMAR

L**IKE MOST FILMS**, it all started with the story. Or in the case of *The Washingtonians*, it all started with the short story.

Bentley Little's "The Washingtonians" first appeared in issue fourteen of Cemetery Dance magazine. It was Fall 1991 and while that particular issue is best known for the original appearance of Stephen King's wonderful tale, "Chattery Teeth," I have to tell you, I was just as excited to publish Bentley's story as I was Steve's. "The Washingtonians" is *that* good.

While I'm at it, I have to admit something else, too. It's obvious from the opening pages that "The Washingtonians" is a great example of black horror/humor. It will make you laugh at times and it will also make you think quite a bit.

But—and here's my admission—"The Washingtonians" also *scared* the hell outta me. The white powdered wigs. The shiny, old fashioned uniforms. The pale pancake made-up faces. And don't even get me started with the teeth! Those damn wooden teeth. All these things gave me nightmares, and as often is the case, I couldn't wait to share them with the rest of the world.

So, many years later, when I was asked to pitch some story ideas for the second season of Showtime's *Masters of Horror* television series, you can bet that Bentley's story was at the top of my list. I don't remember which other stories my writing partner, John Schaech, and I pitched, and I don't remember much about the entire process, other than a very clear memory of the final conference call with the producers and series boss, Mick Garris, that took place during the college football national championship game.

What I do remember is that once Mick and the producers

expressed initial interest, we turned in a detailed ten page outline, and then it quickly progressed to a series of phone meetings, which culminated in that final conference call. And within a couple days of that phone call, we were given the greenlight and hired to write the script.

John and I immediately set out to write a 60 page script. We both adored the original short story, so staying faithful to Bentley's vision was a given. As for our collaborating process, John was in Los Angeles at the time and I was in Maryland, so we did our usual routine, which involved swapping pages on a daily basis, rewriting each others' work and each of us adding thoughts of our own. Although this was our first foray into writing for television, we had already written several feature films, so the process was a quick one. About three weeks later, we emailed Mick a 59 page draft, and to our delight (and relief), he loved it.

A word about Mick Garris before I continue. As fine of a writer and director and producer as Mick is, he's an even better man. He's generous with his time and advice; he's kind but honest with his critical eye; and maybe best of all, he has the heart of a fourteen-year-old boy beating somewhere in that chest of his. In other words, he still believes in the magic and loves horror and having fun and creating nightmares as much as John and I do; if not more. Mick's passion was infectious and confidence inducing. I'll always be grateful that he gave us a shot with such a cool story and then went out and found us such a legendary director to film our script.

That was the next step in the process. After Mick and the other producers all approved our draft, it was sent out to several directors. I had already heard whispers that there were a couple of holdover scripts from Season One that no one had chosen, so I remember feeling nervous: *what if none of these "masters of horror" like our script enough to want to direct it?*

Okay, forget nervous. I was terrified.

Fortunately, we didn't have to wait long to hear that two different directors had taken a shine to the script—the first being the legendary Ken Russell of *Altered States* and *The Liar of the White Worm* fame—and the night that Mick called to tell us the final decision was a good night, indeed.

Peter Medak. Director of the horror classic, *The Changeling*, starring George C. Scott and that infamous wooden wheelchair at the top of the stairway!

John and I were already huge Peter Medak fans and couldn't wait to see what he would do with this story. His sensibilities seemed to perfectly match the story's dark mood and sense of grand weirdness.

The next week of pre-production turned out even better than we hoped for.

Firstly, Peter truly did love the script and the idea of mixing horror with humor. He also recognized the political slant of Bentley's original story and was eager to see how far he could take it on film.

Secondly, to our surprise, Peter decided to hire John to play the lead role in *The Washingtonians*. John was a well-respected actor long before he ever set pen to paper, appearing in major motion pictures with the likes of Tom Hanks, Harvey Keitel, Gwyneth Paltrow, and many others, but this would mark the first time John had acted in a role he had actually helped to write. We were both thrilled.

But, alas, the honeymoon wasn't meant to last.

John and I were still celebrating Peter's hiring when word came down from above that we needed to make specific cuts to the script for budgetary reasons. Of course, we both understood the financial constraints of a television series shooting on a very tight schedule, but we were still bummed to find out we were losing the entire college campus scene and the car chase that followed (although losing the high speed chase made total sense to me).

But, for me, the worst was yet to come, as we were told that one more scene had to go: the "hide and seek" sequence that came right before the grand finale in the banquet hall.

It was my favorite—and the scariest—scene in the entire movie. Washingtonians searching the night-cloaked woods for our family in peril. Pale faces floating in the darkness, lit from below by swaying lanterns. It was a hold-your-breath scene of suspense, and I was crushed to see it go.

But if there was one thing I had learned in Hollywood it was that you couldn't fight the producers when it came to budget cuts. They were the lords of all creation.

Or could you?

As it turned out you *could* . . . if your name was Peter Medak. A few days after John and I sat down and rewrote the script to accommodate the new scenes, and just one week before the start of filming, I received a frantic phone call from the set in Vancouver. Peter Medak and John were on the other line, asking me to fly out there right away and join their efforts to prevent any further changes to the script.

Now let me be clear that Mick had nothing to do with any of the changes. And let me be doubly clear here . . . the other producers who were asking for (okay, *demanding*) these changes were not the bad guys. They were simply doing their jobs. None of this should be viewed as whining or complaining on my part. Trust me, I know better. This was simply a case of a couple of stubborn writers and a very stubborn director fighting for the integrity of a story they all loved.

In the end, we were able to compromise. We changed the very last scene of the movie to please them, and were able to keep the rest of the script intact, including the magnificent banquet scene, which cost a nice little bundle to film.

A week later, I flew to Vancouver and watched the "house under siege" scene as it was shot late into the night and early morning. I turned down the opportunity to appear in the film as a Washingtonian. I ate more craft services food than any cast or crew member, including a heaping paper plate of hot wings at 2am. And I experienced the thrill of a lifetime watching Bentley's (and our) creations coming to life before my eyes.

My favorite part of the trip was watching John, my childhood friend and writing partner, go head to head with veteran actor, Saul Rubinek, in the role of Professor Harkinson, as they played verbal ping pong with page after page of detailed historical dialogue. It was an astonishingly beautiful and over-the-top performance, and I'm grateful I got to witness it in person.

My only regret—besides those budget cuts; I swear I'm not whining—was that I was unable to get to Los Angeles a few months later to take part in the commentary track for the DVD. Later, as I listened to John and Peter's comments, I realized how special the whole experience had been; how much I had learned from Mick and Peter and John; and how fortunate I had been to be able to help bring a cannibalistic George Washington and his followers to the world's attention.

We had done it; we had changed history.

"SO-BAD-IT'S-GOOD" AND UNDERRATED GEMS

NICK CATO

BELIEVE IT was sometime in the 1980s, when, during the VHS-renting boom, those yearning to make their own horror films discovered a video camera was much cheaper to buy or even rent than an actual film camera. A bunch of shot-on-video horror titles infested local VHS rental stores. Most ranged from unwatchable to so-so, but aside from one or two, they were pure trash. And worse yet, many of them were made bad *intentionally*.

In 2007, directors Quentin Tarantino and Robert Rodriguez's film *Grindhouse* was released to major movie theaters around the world. The film was a double feature of 70s-style exploitation movies, shot with intentional errors and scratches deliberately put onto the film to make it look like an older, worn print. It was a tribute to the drive in/grindhouse films they had both grown up with and been inspired by. And as fun as some of it was (especially the faux exploitation film trailers shown before and between the main features), the film just wasn't the *real thing*. A loving tribute, sure, but not an authentic 70s films, and hence, the genuine charm of a genuine 70s film was not there *in my humble opinion*.

For several years now, the SyFy channel has been making their own "bad" scifi and horror films, most dealing with some kind of giant animal or extreme weather condition. Films such as *Boa vs. Python* (2004), *Magma: Volcanic Disaster* (2006), *Sharktopus* (2010), and *Sharknado* (2010—which amazingly spawned two sequels), have become staples of their Saturday night lineup. These films feature ridiculously bad special effects, horrible acting, and plots that cause one to wonder if they even hire writers. And while these films have a following (at least I'm guessing they do or they

47

wouldn't be making so many), they are *truly* bad films. They're an attempt to create schlocky cult films but instead are cookie-cutter corporate garbage. I'm afraid to see just how much money the SyFy channel has wasted on this nonsense, but it's safe to say if they took some of their funds and made it available to filmmakers who actually knew what they were doing, there's a good chance they just might produce something worthwhile (and it pains me to say this as the legendary Roger Corman, who was responsible for countless, *genuine* cult films, is involved with many of SyFy's lame output).

So what is it that the creators of 80s shot-on-video features, popular directors like Tarantino and Rodriguez, as well as the SyFy channel, are missing? What was it about some of the older, low budget 50s and 60s horror and science fiction films that managed to work in light of everything they had going against them?

Most low budget features of yester-year were paid for independently and created by people who were committed to getting their vision out no matter what the cost (be it financially, physically, and even emotionally). Most of the time these low budget horror/scifi films failed. But on occasion, they worked. And when they "sort-of" worked, it was nothing but pure luck and good timing.

Directors of films that came to be known as "So-Bad-It's Good" films, in most cases, *didn't set out to make a bad film.* Most set out to make their own genuinely scary epic, and still more attempted to make something *different.* Say what you will about a film like *The Toxic Avenger* (1984), but its ability to entertain is second to none (although I'll admit I can't say the same for its sequels). Sure, it's a bad film, but it's a *genuine* So-Bad-It's-Good film, complete with likeable characters, off the wall (and clever) special effects, and plenty of dark humor, not to mention a nice blending of genres. Same for one of the best "So-Bad-It's-Good" classics of all time, 1963's *Blood Feast*, which also happens to be the world's first gore film (at least the first one most horror fans actually saw). While director Herschell Gordon Lewis openly admits the sole purpose he made the film was to make money, he didn't set out to make a bad film, and in the process he inadvertently started a whole new subgenre: the splatter film. *Blood Feast* works on its sheer audacity alone. No one who has seen it cares about the terrible acting or goofy dialogue; the ahead of its time gore scenes never leave the viewer's mind, especially those who saw it when first released. Nothing like it had ever been seen before it, and unlike the mainstream horror films of the time, it managed to shock and jolt people in ways Hollywood films simply couldn't.

The vast majority of So-Bad-It's-Good films were intended to be serious features. They were meant to compete with films like *Night of the Living Dead* (1968), *The Exorcist* (1973), and *Halloween* (1978). There are countless films inspired by these (and other) classics, and others that are complete rip-offs, but only a handful worked. Some of the films that worked are called "Hidden" or Underrated Gems, while others that didn't work became So-Bad-It's-Good favorites, and the rest, unwatchable and ultimately forgotten.

The 1970 film *I Drink Your Blood* isn't nearly as scary as *Night of the Living Dead* (the film it set out to top), but in many regards it's twice as disturbing. Same for the 1974 film *The Antichrist* (a.k.a. *The Tempter*), an Italian, blatant rip off that contains several scenes that are every bit as intense and offsetting as anything in *The Exorcist*. Both *I Drink Your Blood* and *The Antichrist* are low budget horror films that work despite not being as "good" as the films they imitated.

1972's *Invasion of the Blood Farmers*, 1982's *Basket Case*, and 1999's *The Blair Witch Project*, for example, are all low budget films that became classics (and notorious) for different reasons.

Invasion of the Blood Farmers is a simple tale of modern day druids living in Upstate NY. It features terrible acting, non-existent "special effects" and a plot that's beyond dumb. Yet it manages to entertain with unintentional laughs and a weirdness factor that never gets old. It's a "real" So-Bad-It's-Good horror film that gained attention during the 1980s video boom and an article in an early issue of *Fangoria* magazine.

Basket Case is perhaps one of the grittiest offerings of the 80s, and despite the cheap creature effects and less than stellar acting, the film has become a classic in many horror film fans' eyes. It's disturbing, eerie at times, and heartfelt to the core, managing to resonate with horror fans the world over even with an abundance of dark humor thrown in and an incredibly low budget. It's an Underrated Gem if there ever was one.

The Blair Witch Project is a prime example of what can be done when filmmakers put their minds to the task at hand. Love it or hate it, the super low budget film came out when teen-friendly features like *Scream* (1996) and *I Know What You Did Last Summer* (1997) had horror fans thinking the genre was done for. Suddenly there was a renewed realization that Independents could create something better than any multi-million dollar production could hope for. While *The Blair Witch Project* is a bit more serious in tone than *Invasion of the Blood Farmers* and *Basket Case*, it's still a low budget film with amateur acting, a simple plot, and *not a single special effect*. Technically it's a "bad" film, but it's a bad film that exceeded even its creators' expectations. When you think about it, it's a miracle the thing worked.

Invasion of the Blood Farmers and *Basket Case* are both So-Bad-Its-Good films, yet each one on a different level. *The Blair Witch Project*, while technically an amateur production, went on to become one of the most popular horror films of all time, and while it wasn't the first film to use the technique, it ushered in (for better or worse) a new wave of "shaky camera" films.

What unifies these three films were the intentions of the directors. They each set out to make a good film. They each set out to make a serious horror film and received various degrees of success, even if it wasn't financial.

Not everyone who made a schlocky film after the 80s video boom did so intentionally. While a film like *Hollywood Chainsaw Hookers* (1988) seems geared to lure horror fans in with its outrageous title and cast of horror film "all stars," it's one of the few of its kind that worked. It's a genuine So-Bad-It's-Good, whether director Fred Olen Ray intended it to be or not. Other 80s offerings such as *Sledgehammer* (1983), *Cannibal Campout* (1988), and *Blood Cult* (1985), are prime examples of the genre heading in the wrong direction. How any of these films gained cult followings is anyone's guess. They're not entertaining in the slightest bit and were created by fans who should've taken a basic film making class (or in these cases, video-making class) before getting in over their heads.

There will always be someone making a film from his or her heart, and horror fans will be able to detect and appreciate it even if it doesn't live up to expectations. Likewise, there will always be those trying to make a buck by insulting the genre (and I'm not just talking about the SyFy channel films). But part of the fun of being a horror fan is to find the Hidden Gems, and to enjoy the genuine So-Bad-It's-Good films that come out ever so rarely.

For those setting out to make a bad film, please stop. There are enough of those in circulation without anyone intentionally adding to the output. But those attempting to make something "good" and/or different, please continue to go at it full steam ahead, because even if you don't achieve what you set out to do, you still might create a genuine, one day to-be-labeled *Underrated Gem.*

Or a *So-Bad-It's-Good.*

INTERVIEW WITH E.C. MCMULLEN ON THE CURRENT CONDITION OF THE HORROR MOVIE INDUSTRY

Joe: **How would you describe the synergy of art and business in the horror movie industry?**

E.C. McMullen: From donuts to art, such synergy is left to the individual or partnership/group leading that business. Looking at a historical pie slice of the synergy of art and as a business, some of the greatest, most widely respected artists who ever lived were successful during their lifetimes. This is true whether we are talking about Frida Kahlo, Pablo Picasso, The Rolling Stones, or J.K. Rowling.

I've been told by some people that artists cannot and should not be business people. I disagree. You don't diminish your art by knowing your audience.

Joe: **Who is your favorite screenwriter and why?**

McMullen: Jimmy Sangster. I know of no other screenwriter who is or was anywhere near as prolific, and as successful, as he.
As a writer, Jimmy was one of the driving forces behind the birth of Hammer Studios. This was at a time when Universal Pictures felt they had not only gone to the well too many times with their decrepit stable of famous monsters, but that they had poisoned the well. Sangster came along and creatively breathed new life into ancient tropes.

People talk of the magnetic animalism of Christopher Lee or the drop-dead sterling presence of Peter Cushing in many Hammer movies, but Sangster wrote one Hammer box office smash after the next whether Lee or Cushing were in them or (most often) not.

The only reason they were successful, and still endure long after Hammer Studios expired, is because Jimmy's work still resonates with audiences.

Joe: Are there any actors you think would make great horror characters?

McMullen: You mean besides actors like Lance Henriksen (*The Terminator, Aliens, Near Dark*), Doug Jones (*Pan's Labyrinth, Hellboy*) and Chloë Grace Moretz (*The Amityville Horror*—2005, *Let Me In*), Brad Dourif (*Child's Play, Death Machine, Alien Resurrection*), Sean Bean (*The Dark, Silent Hill*), Ron Perlman (*The Island of Dr. Moreau, Alien: Resurrection, Hellboy*), Clancy Brown (*The Bride, John Dies at the End*), Dee Wallace (*The Howling, Hansel & Gretel*), Jennifer Connelly (*Phenomena, Dark Water*), Emily Browning (*Death Ship, The Uninvited*), Tony Todd (*Candyman, Final Destination*), Sigourney Weaver (*Alien, Cabin in the Woods*), Naomi Watts (*Down, The Ring*), and Sam Neill (*Omen III: The Final Conflict, Daybreakers*), no, none that come to mind. Seriously though, I feel an actor hasn't 'Made It' until they wow everyone in a Horror movie. Whether we are talking about Jack Nicholson's scene-chewing turn in *The Shining*, Nicole Kidman's coming out in *Dead Calm*, Anthony Hopkins in *The Silence of the Lambs* (not his first Horror movie), or Brad Pitt leaving his 'Pretty Boy' image behind forever in *12 Monkeys*.

Joe: Should every independent film be made in a unique way, or should producers and directors stick with what the audience wants?

McMullen: Every independent film must be made in a unique way, because that *is* what the audience wants. Outside of sequels, nobody wants to pay good money and waste their valuable time seeing a movie that is by the numbers, watered down, or an overblown version of a movie they've already seen. That includes remakes.

Audiences hesitate to take a chance on an unknown drama, romance, or comedy. Yet they are always there for an unknown Horror movie only so long as that Horror movie appears original. Can you think of a single *Texas Chainsaw Massacre*, *Alien*, or *A Nightmare on Elm Street* rip-off that was successful? That endures?

Joe: **How would you say has the horror movie genre evolved over the last few decades?**

McMullen: It hasn't evolved, it's static. Here and there we've seen glimmers of talent from *The Ring* to *Final Destination* to *Saw* to *Paranormal Activity* to *You're Next*, but overall, independents are lazily content to make ultra-cheap copies of what Hollywood is awkwardly doing, and so flooding the market with direct to DVD 12 and 20 packs.

That's not to say some brilliant indie Horror movies haven't unjustly gone to the DtV bin. I'm thinking of movies like *Alien Raiders*, *Outpost*, and *Wer* just off the top of my head.

Joe: **Why do you think people enjoy the horror genre so much?**

McMullen: Horror movies are all of the scare with none of the threat. They're a rollercoaster to nowhere that (is supposed to) return us safely back home. For the same reason we try a new restaurant instead of the ones we know. For the same reasons we try new things in—or especially—out of the bedroom. We seek a safe thrill. A thrill makes us feel alive instead of just surviving from day to day.

The year is never over faster than when you fill your days with repetition, and the years never seem longer than when you look back on a wide variety of experiences.

That's what makes all movies work to a various degree: vicarious living. I'm talking Horror Thriller movies. now. There is a whole other animal breathing down your neck when you are reading Horror. Then you aren't safely sitting within the numbers of a crowd in the dark of a movie theater, suspending your believe in fake blood, latex, and CGI.

When you are reading a book, you are alone in the dark of your mind, and what lives there is will always be real to you.

Joe: What advice would you give someone interested in creating, acting in, directing, or writing for the movie industry?

McMullen: Do it right now. Make a Vine with your cell phone. As in anything you want to get good at, Practice! Practice! Practice!

The moment you wow everyone, opportunity will hammer at your door.

"Be so good they can't ignore you."

—Steve Martin

Just always remember who came for whom. If they came for you, you didn't go to them. So don't be eager to desperately grab the first opportunity that comes your way. There's a pathetic caterwaul that predators salivate over whenever they hear it or sense it: "Aw . . . but I just wanted to get my movie out there!"

The best way to commit hara-kiri in this business is to beg people who are coming to you.

I can't possibly tell you what to do at the James Wan or David Slade level. But at the low budget independent level? People in this business will always have a level less of respect for you than you have for yourself. And if you have no respect for yourself, people will despise you no matter how much they like what you did. This business is filled with one hit wonders. It overflows with near-miss wonders. Don't make yourself look like one.

Joe: What would you say are the wrong reasons for getting into this business?

McMullen: Thinking of it *Only* as a business of art instead of *The* business of art. Thinking that it will ever make you rich or even support you.

The Show comes first, then the Business. Putting it in reverse brings garbage Horror movies, often made by people who feel contempt for Horror movies and their audience.

Writing left Edgar Allen Poe, Emily Dickinson, and H.P. Lovecraft to name a very few, in poverty. When you trace the history of their great legacies now, you know their modern fame came entirely by chance.

In books or movies, writing will only make you rich through a combination of Luck and Nothing Else. Stephen King himself often tells the world about writers he feels are every bit as good as he or maybe better—yet they don't have his success. King tells the world about the writers he reads who scare *him*. These people are wonderful artists without a business sense or a business person protecting them. King is also surprised that hideously untalented, hack awful writers also find an audience and go on to become rich.

As we see from the past, the light of such worthless writers quickly dies out with them. They were nothing more than the celebutards of their era.

That said, they have great business people managing their careers.

Joe: **What traits should youngsters work on before getting started in this industry?**

McMullen: Never approach it as an industry. Always deal with the art first, then the business, then the industry.

Industry is a sharp cleave from the business of Show Business. Show is making your work. Business is selling your work. The Industry is all of the enormous niggling infrastructure that goes into preparing your work for distribution: the distributors, manufacturers, and marketers who get your work seen.

Leave that to the agents (if you are ever lucky enough to find a *Good* one), who act as your personal real estate agent and treat your every work as a piece of property to be bartered and leased to the highest bidder.

Never treat your own work as property. If you care about your creation, then your work is entirely the child of your mind. It's great to let your child out into the world to play, and the more people who are delighted by your child, the better. But no matter how well or poorly received your child is by others, it will always be your child.

Director Guillermo Del Toro bought the rights to Mike Mignola's *Hellboy* and went off to make his live action and animated movies. But at one point Del Toro felt he'd been living with Hellboy for so long that he should have a stake in it. So he approached Mike about publishing his own del Toro Hellboy stories, or collaborating with Mike on a story.

Mike told him in no uncertain terms, "Hellboy the movies is yours, Hellboy the comics is mine."

(Collider.com: 'Guillermo del Toro Says It's "Very Unlikely" *Hellboy 3* Will Happen; Talks Difficulty of Getting the Sequel Off the Ground.'

Joe: Are there any recent occurrences in the horror film industry that excite you? Any possible directions opening up for future talents?

McMullen: I see no horror film industry. The Industry serves all movies (we're going to have to move away from the term 'film') regardless of genre. The following will seem pedantic to some, but let's return to the basics: Art and Creation is Art and Creation.

Like farming, growing the food is entirely separate from selling it, which is entirely separate from getting it fresh to market. So it is that the mechanics of creating a movie has zero to do with the business end of selling it. The two join together in Show Business, but they remain two distinct species and both are distinct from the Industry (in our case, the tools to make your movie and the theaters and home video that show it).

It is critical to acknowledge these separate borderlands as being distinct from each other, regardless of their associations.

For Example: Many of my friends who raise the funds from investors for their movie, find themselves adrift when trying to sell the movie. It seems bizarre, doesn't it? That the same people who can sell an unknown quantity to an investor—or group of investors—cannot sell a known quantity to a distributor? Some have been making movies for over 20 years yet still dread what, appears to them, an unfathomable, intentionally byzantine process of dealing with distributors.

These people aren't clods. Many of them are bright. Yet they can't get their heads around the business end of Show Business in any way that will protect their interests.

And Yet—a professional wrestler like Fabulous Freddie Valentine, totally gets it and makes a great living off of making crap. Moreover, Freddie is wide open, basically telling people, "Hey, this is how I do it and it's a piece of cake!"

Seriously, if Fred Olen Ray can make full productions using paid crew and still make a profit on his Retromedia stuff, what's stopping everyone else?

> "There seems to be a perverse human characteristic that likes to make easy things difficult. The academic world, if anything, has actually backed away from the teaching of value investing over the last 30 years. It's likely to stay that way. Ships will sail around the world but the flat Earth Society will flourish."
>
> —Warren Buffet

Too many artists, creators, don't understand the distribution side of the business. Some, in their confusion become suspicious and demonize the very people they need to get their movie in front of audiences.

The writer who creates the original story, the director who tells the story, and the actors who bring life to their characters (to name a few of the most prominent creators who work on a Horror movie or any movie), are the artists.

To make it a business (in this example the movie business) you move to the next step which actually is business—the selling and buying/procurement of tangible and intangible goods. As any successful business person who has written a book on the subject will tell their readers (and I've read many), Business is Business.

Neither Art or Business is industry. Where Show business is a business involving the movement of money and purchases to create a show. Industry are the companies that make tangibles to provide infrastructure to make the show.

Hardware and software manufacturers like Camera and program makers are the Industry that create the tools for those business people who are involved in the movie business.

THE HORROR FILM INDUSTRY

When studio heads talks about "Our industry," they are thinking of the full encompassing expendables and tools of their company like all of the machinery and warehouses they have that are full of earth movers, forklifts, and paint that they use to create movies.

Studios large and small that gather the resources to create a movie or series are a business. Many, who have a staff of people building sets day and night, are also an industry.

But Business and Industry without Art are equally successful in the Manufacturing, Energy, Agricultural Industry or the Banking Business.

So many artists don't understand that money doesn't come from magic or good will or pure luck. Someone somewhere sacrificed everything to make that money, and now you want them or their children or whoever to give their money to you for something you want and they don't.

So an artist has to know how to share their dream in such a way that someone who never wanted it, suddenly wants it!

When Michael Palin and Terry Gilliam shared their vision of *Time Bandits* with George Harrison, he suddenly wanted to see their vision become a movie so bad, that he spent nearly all of his money to get it made.

That's how you pitch your movie! Then you get your distributors excited in the same way!

Tom Malloy (*The Alphabet Killer, The Attic*), bestselling author of *Bankroll* admits that his book will teach you how to raise millions like he did for his movies. It will *not* teach you how to market and profitably sell your movies, which is not his forte.

Some folks clearly see all of the distinctions, while others see only a nonsensical miasma, but that's okay. It's okay if, as an independent film maker, you don't grasp the whole picture. Film making is a concerted effort. The thing is, just as you would try to find the best actors, editors, sound people, and more to help you make your picture, try and find the best attorney and business managers you can to help you sell or lease your picture.

Joe: **What is the best thing a fan of the horror film industry can do for its writers, producers, actors, directors, etc?**

McMullen: The best thing a fan can do is what they are already doing and have been doing for years. Nobody has to be told to talk about something they love. That's natural. All of the chatter, the cosplay, all of the fun that brings the attention of the world and makes genre conventions the largest, most profitable conventions in the world. The fans are doing their best already. It's up to the creators to reward them.

The one thing that a true fan should never do? Don't rip off the creators by watching a pirated video. Counterfeit copies have never improved the value of anything. They destroy the value of everything they copy—which is exactly what they are supposed to do.

Any person who does this is a parasite. Period.

If a person uses the excuse, "The information wants to be free!" then that person is anthropomorphizing a non-living entity to clear their self-inflicted smear of being a parasite. Which also makes that person a stupid parasite.

There's An Exception To Every Rule:

Obviously in some countries like the rural states/provinces in Mexico, Brazil, and China (many more examples), it is almost impossible to see a movie in any other way as most of the towns have no theaters, cable, satellite or legitimate video rental. If someone hasn't established a market where I live, then they aren't losing anything by my enjoying their work.

Naturally if I create a livelihood for myself by establishing a market for someone else's creations where none existed, then I owe that person their rightful share.

Just because my work isn't translated into Japanese doesn't mean others can translate my work into Japanese, sell my work, and keep all the money (or Torrents Glory, etc.) for themselves.

This is all easy to understand even by the thieves who attempt to (so poorly) argue in knots around it.

TRICKS OF THE TRADE

SCREENWRITING

I've always been intrigued by the art of screenwriting.

Make no mistake, it's not the same as writing novels and short stories. During the time spent interviewing screenwriters, I learned quite a few things you can't be taught in a How To book, because I took the time to personally connect with each author—learn about what makes them tick.

What follows is a glimpse into not only the craft but the screenwriters themselves. You'll notice there is no set way to becoming a great screenwriter (except sitting your ass in the chair), so not everyone will share the same opinion.

Just like writing novels and short fiction, it's up to you to find what works for you.

Joe Mynhardt

TRICKS OF THE TRADE: SCREENWRITING

WHAT MADE YOU WRITE YOUR VERY FIRST SCREENPLAY, AND CAN YOU STILL RECALL WHAT IT WAS?

Jonathan Winn: My first script was written in August 2004, but the process started in 2001 when I worked oh so briefly as an actor with the director Sidney Lumet on a short-lived TV show he had. He casually mentioned, as we chatted, that I should consider writing because I sounded like a writer to him. Although he thought I was very good as an actor, the writing thing just stuck in his head. The words I used and the way I phrased them felt to him like a writer. Fast forward three years: in a moment of frustration, I sat down and started writing a script. Had no idea what I was doing. But I had a story to tell and, through trial and error, figured it out. I was also lucky enough to have friends in the business who were able to take a look, shake their heads, sigh, and then take me by the hand and show me what I was doing wrong and how to fix it, and what I was doing right and how to capitalize on that.

Ed Naha: I was bored. I was working at Columbia Records and had just published my first non-fiction book, *Horrors: From Screen to Scream.* I thought I could write a horror movie. A friend of a friend introduced me to this cigar chomping, fat producer who made low-budget movies. This was in New York in the mid-seventies and it never occurred to me that all the real producers were in Los Angeles. Duh. Anyhow, I wrote a script called "The Devil's Loose." Then, it was "It's Loose." The guy actually helped me rein my writing in (something I'm obviously not doing in this interview). He accidentally taught me stuff. I didn't know it at the time but the low-budget movies he produced were all gay porn. Needless to say, "The Devil's Loose" wasn't exactly in his wheelhouse. But I had fun and, a dozen years later, I reworked it and sold it to MGM. It was never made and, later, I turned it into a paperback original novel.

John Russo: My very first screenplay or stage play was inspired by a book I read about the Dead Sea Scrolls. It was called *Why Have You Forsaken Me?* and represented my take on the secular notions about Jesus. I was starting to break away from organized religion and was intensely interested in exploring the origins of it.

Harry Shannon: Actually, I think it was around 2002. My first small press collection *Bad Seed* had a lot of crime stories in it, and I got interested in turning three of them into a stage play. That led to writing one as a short film, so I needed the software. The first one shot and sold was *Dead and Gone*. Others have been optioned, "Pain" and "Clan" in particular, but nothing much happened. I'm still hoping someone will bite on *The Hungry* series.

Mick Garris: I've always loved horror films, and I started seriously writing horror fiction when I was twelve years old. In my early twenties, I wrote a script called *Fear Itself* that was a non-supernatural horror story. It never got bought, but it helped me get my first agent. And I used the title many years later for the *Masters of Horror* spinoff series on NBC. But that's another story, long and kind of ugly.

Jeff Strand: I was in high school, and I'd spent a couple of years trying to break into comic book writing (unsuccessfully, because at age fifteen I was writing comic scripts that read like they were written by a 15-year-old). I decided to give screenwriting a try. My first one was a comedy called *Curses*, which was about some kids who get cursed by a Gypsy. It was a frickin' mess. The curses basically just involved random bad/weird things happening to our heroes for ninety pages. I knew it was a mess at the time, although I thought it was an extremely funny mess. I suspect that if a copy still existed, I'd be less amused by it now. This was followed by eleven more feature-length screenplays, none of which are probably filmable, before I turned to novel writing instead.

Stephen Volk: Yes, I wrote it in school and it was called *Tales of the Shroud*. It was during the boom of those Amicus portmanteau-type horror films featuring 4-5 short horror films strung together with a narrative cutaway such as Dr Terror on the train or an antique dealer. My script was an unashamed imitation of those and I sent it off to Milton Subotsky at Amicus. Imagine my face when I come home from school one lunchtime and he had sent me a reply! I opened this package and it contained the script of *From Beyond The Grave*. The letter read: "This is what a screenplay looks like and here are a few pages of notes. If you feel you can address them, I think we have a chance of making this film." Of course it never happened. I phoned Milton every week for about five years but portmanteau films had gone out of fashion. But he was a lovely man, and that was an amazing day.

Stephen Johnston: My first script was a short, about thirty pages, that I wrote on spec as a teenager. It was about a monster who stole youth from children, sort of like an existential vampire, if that's not too pretentious a notion! I actually submitted it to the old *Monsters* television show. They didn't buy it, but they wrote me a very nice letter.

Patrick Lussier: I tried writing an episode of *Lies from Lotusland*, a little CBC series a million years ago (well, back in 85/86). It was not accepted as it was not in keeping with the series, but it was fun to write. Not sure why I wrote it. Like so many things, you do it because you can't not.

Denise Gossett: LOL. I have not completed one. I have started several TV shows and one feature. Writing is not something I love to do, so, basically I'm forcing myself to do it just to know what it's like. My hats off to all of you writers out there.

ARE THERE ANY RESOURCES YOU CAN RECOMMEND TO SCREENWRITERS? ONLINE SITES, WORKSHOPS, BOOKS, OR FORMATTING PROGRAMS?

Mark Steensland: Talking about creative stuff is like going to marriage counseling: everyone who had a great experience with some technique or resource or whatever wants to share it with everyone because they think they'll have the same experience. Maybe they will. Maybe they won't. But I tend to beware of any of the so-called "solution" books. You know what I'm talking about? Those books that promise to achieve results if you just follow their formula. I think the most important thing in screenwriting is format. And I'll tell you why: because producers love to find a reason to say "No" and that's the easiest one to pick on. You have to think of formatting like sheet music. If you don't do it right, the conductor can't conduct, the musicians can't play, and your music won't be performed. Sure, there are people like Ligeti who made blobs on paper and told musicians to play it. But he's Ligeti. And sure, there are people like Kubrick, who let the dialogue run side to side and centered all the stage direction. But these are exceptions, not the way you should be doing it if you want to get your work read. I like Final Draft. But that's a personal preference only. I also think that you must read screenplays to see how other writers have written. There's no better way I can think of to learn the craft than to study the experts.

Jonathan Winn: I use Final Draft to write my scripts. I suspect most writers do. It seems to be the standard and the one most producers, production companies, and studios prefer or, at the very least, accept. I've been working with it for a decade now and it has yet to fail me.

Now, when it comes to books, online sites, workshops, etc., I realize the question is geared toward the how-tos of writing a script, but, honestly, the sites I visit every day without fail are www.deadline.com and www.variety.com. For me, the business aspect of what I do fascinates me, so I do best being aware of who's doing what with who and, more importantly, what new companies are setting up shop who have a track record with the kinds of stories I write. If you can get those producers and directors when they're hungry, they're going to work that much harder to get your script to the screen. Now, when it comes to writing, I've always believed the best way to learn is by reading a lot of screenplays and writing a lot of screenplays. Dig in and get to work. Be horrible. Make a ton of mistakes. Then go back and fix 'em. Lather, rinse, repeat and then start again.

Ed Naha: I've never read a "how-to" screenplay book that has done me any good, creatively. Plus, I read them after I started working. If you buy a book, probably the best you can get from it is the structure. Also, you can buy actual screenplays on the web so you can see how the "CUT TO:'s" and "EXT.'s" and "INT.'s" fall. I've only used the Final Draft program when I finally go to script format. I write everything out in narrative form before I actually go to script, including the dialogue, descriptions, settings, etc.

There are a lot of "rules" to screenwriting that are just totally bogus. Just horseshit. I learned to write screenplays by reading plays. When I lived in New York, the stage was something I quickly became addicted to. I'd read nothing but plays for months on end (screenplay used to mean literally that; a screen play). The whole three-act structure is there just for the hell of it. For the most part, the three-act theatrical play has been obsolete for decades. Most plays are two acts. Why scripts still adhere to the three-act structure is beyond me.

I think everyone should read (possibly underline passages in) *Day of the Locust* by Nathanael West. *Barton Fink* should be required viewing. It'll give you the sense of the absurdity you'll be dealing with after you've started.

John Russo: I heartily recommend my own books because they are known as Bibles of the industry, and they make a career in movies *accessible*. They cut through the bullshit. Quentin Tarantino, Darren Bousman and many other notable filmmakers have learned from my books. Also tons of less famous filmmakers. My 18-month associate degree course at a business college in PA was one of the best and least expensive in the country, and the students benefited greatly from it and acknowledged that. But it wasn't promoted properly, so we pulled it out of there. We will probably launch some seminars and workshops soon, so watch for the announcements on Facebook and so forth.

Harry Shannon: Writer's Store.com is an amazing site, and there are a ton of others to choose from. I favor the old fashioned three or five-act structure Hollywood prefers, and Final Draft as a program. Of course, I'm getting old. I'm sure there are newer choices.

Mick Garris: I've never really gone the textbook route to screenwriting, so I've never used online sites (there was no such thing when I started) or workshops. Final Draft is the industry standard, as far as formatting goes, and everybody uses that. I'm not big on screenwriting classes or textbooks, because I think most of the people who take those classes are studio executives, who think that there are rules to writing scripts. And now, of course, there are. They look for scripts that follow those rules, which is why movies all seem the same so often.

I think the most useful book on writing of any kind, or of any creative process, whether it's writing, painting, filmmaking, acting, or anything, is Stephen King's *On Writing*. It's like sitting in a room and having a conversation with an incredibly generous, accomplished friend who's telling you how he does it. It's quite freeing and encouraging, and incredibly inspiring.

Jeff Strand: I started out writing on a regular word processor, which meant that any time I made a change that added or subtracted a line from the script, there was a potential formatting nightmare (people who started out writing scripts on a manual typewriter are probably unsympathetic to my plight). Then I downloaded a sample version of Movie Magic Screenwriter, just out of curiosity, and after writing about a page and a half I screamed, "I can't live without this! Don't make me go back to my primitive ways!" That's the only program I've used since.

Stephen Volk: The "Story" seminar by Robert McKee is the temple at which all screenwriters prostrate themselves, but he's by no means the only fount of all wisdom. There's John Yorke, John Truby, Linda Seger, and excellent books of interviews with screenwriters, which I find the most useful of all. My philosophy is, you can get help to unlock problems anywhere, but don't obsess about reading every "How to" book because your work will be formulaic and turgid and conform to fashion. They can help you avoid mistakes but they are seldom any direct use when you are trying to figure out the story in front of you. Knowing the dubious machinations behind *Casablanca* is fuck-all use, frankly—analysis of a film after the event, which any schmuck (or critic) can do as easy as pissing standing up. Analysing what is wrong with this unfinished, unformed and chaotic thing here in front of me is a different kettle of fish altogether, and that comes from a lot of watching movies and a lot of thinking about storytelling—plus knowing what is in your heart about the tale you want to tell (oh, and get Final Draft. Oh, and no software is as good as a hundred index cards, in my opinion).

Stephen Johnston: The Final Draft software is pretty much the industry standard, and sort of mandatory in a professional sense, but I'm a big proponent that people write using whatever method works best for them. In terms of anything else, nothing can teach you to craft except applying yourself to it. Of course, you can't create in a vacuum, so things like workshops can be immensely beneficial.

Jack Thomas Smith: I use Final Draft when I write screenplays. It formats the script as you go and it provides such features as scene reports, cast reports, and location breakdowns. All of this saves time and makes life easier when preparing to shoot.

I didn't go to film school so I had to teach myself the proper screenwriting technique. I read instructional books (Syd Field's instructional books are amazing) and other screenplays until I figured out the structure and standard screenplay format.

James Cullen Bressack: A great read is *Save the Cat* and Sid Field's screenplay books. Read as many screenplays and watch as many films as you can. See what you like and format around that. Never be afraid to face the blank page. There may not be enough time to do it perfect, but there's always enough time to do it again.

Patrick Lussier: Final Draft, for formatting. Read scripts. Read stories. Read. Read. Read.

Denise Gossett: Final Draft for formatting, books . . . there are so many, Syd Field is great, as for sites and workshops, ask around, if you can't find a group, start one. Inktip is great too. There are so many writers out there looking for mutual support. The ones that have that support fare much better than those who don't.

WHAT LEGAL PITFALLS SHOULD A SCREENWRITER WATCH OUT FOR WHEN SELLING THEIR SCRIPTS?

Jonathan Winn: Copyright Infringement is huge. And there's little to be done about it. That's why it's always good, when someone says, "Oh, I'd love to read your work", to offer to send the first ten pages and only the first ten pages. Legally, and any reputable producer will be terrified of this, anything more sets the studio or production company up for accusations of theft should a similar project suddenly materialize. With those first ten pages, someone can tell a lot about your strength as a writer as well as the gist of the story. And if you can't sell 'em in the first ten, get back to work.

When it comes to contracts, get a lawyer. Period. End of story. I believe any writer facing the option or sale of a script is touched in the head if they think they can navigate it on their own. It's worth the outlay of cash or a percentage of the Option or final sale price to have someone who DOES know what they're doing walk them through and offer guidance. Everything from Credit (which affects how much you get paid both upfront and with residuals) to Sequel Rights, what the Ceiling is and what the Floor is, production and box office bonuses, Separated Rights and contingent compensation, optional writing steps and Reversion of Rights. You see? There's a lot to consider that can affect not only how smooth the production process is and whether or not you're even a part of it, but your potential standing in the Union and whether or not it ends up being "your" film in the end. So, again, get a lawyer.

Still, at the end of the day, barring the inclusion of a Work for Hire Agreement, the writer is the only one who owns that script. So if a deal falls through, at least the writer walks away with a property they can still sell to someone else. So, the second thing I'd say is beef up on Copyright Law. Know your rights. At least the bare basics. Knowledge is power, especially when it comes to this business.

Ed Naha: Whatever you write, register it with the Writer's Guild. It's not expensive and you're protected from anyone purloining your story. When you're writing an original, don't pay homage to your favorite films. Or, to be more blunt, don't plagiarize. You'd be surprised at how many people think nobody will notice. I once had a guy pitch me a wrestling fantasy that sounded suspiciously like *The Wizard of Oz*. He was surprised by my lack of enthusiasm. "It sounds like The *Wizard of Oz*," I said. "So?" he replied. "It's been filmed before," I pointed out. "Yeah," he acknowledged, "but not in years!" Uh. No.

In terms of you getting ripped off, it happens. If you pitch a story and it's turned down, don't be shocked if elements of it or all of it winds up being "paid homage" to down the line. I once did a re-write on a script where I introduced an entirely new secondary plotline. The script was filmed but without my plotline. My plotline, however, did turn up in an entirely different movie done by the same director, written by the fellow who re-wrote my original re-write. I used to get nosebleeds a lot.

John Russo: Well, you just have to pay attention to all contractual matters, and if you can't comprehend the contracts or the pitfalls on your own, or even if you can, you need to have the advice of a very knowledgeable—and probably expensive—attorney. Watch out for your agents or business managers, too. Many of them will try to rip you off and will largely succeed.

Harry Shannon: Everything, but particularly how long the rights can be extended for very little money. If a so-called producer can get you to accept a low enough figure, they will sometimes just sit on the option for years in case someone else wants to buy it. And that beautiful slice of the back end? Don't get your hopes up.

Mick Garris: Well, don't adapt something you don't have the rights for and then try to sell it! But other than that, I have never had legal issues in mind when I've written a script.

Stephen Volk: Copyright, first and foremost. Don't even think of adapting something you don't own, and don't use characters who are not yours, and don't knowingly steal an idea (even though ideas can't in themselves be copyrighted). Also, never base a character on a real person, or the truth, unless you have a watertight deal with that person. Generally, don't sign a contract without advice. Get an agent—and I mean agent who knows film contracts, not a book agent. Don't give someone your story for a kiss and a promise, and don't let an option be open-ended. If you collaborate with somebody, get the agreement up front in writing, even if you are best friends:

e.g. "X cannot do anything with this project without Y's permission." Another thing to watch out for: don't be unrealistic. They won't let you direct it. You will have to make changes. They will own it and there isn't a damn thing you can do about it except make sure you don't give it away for nothing after all your hard work.

Stephen Johnston: Oh man, there's a book in itself. No, seriously, Hollywood has this reputation as a place where evil intentions are borne, and it's not entirely undeserved, but such a thing isn't exclusive to the film industry. It's like anything else in life, you have to trust your intuition, and it's a good policy not to put too much trust in people who seem to tell you nothing but what you want to hear. Always, always, always register your script with the WGA (moving forward they will become indispensable,) and of course have an attorney read anything you're considering signing your name to. The irony of representation is it can be hard to secure until you've made your bones professionally, which of course can be difficult to accomplish without representation.

James Cullen Bressack: Get a good lawyer and register with a WGA with your first draft as soon as possible.

Patrick Lussier: Get a lawyer to help navigate those pitfalls. There are many, the biggest of which is the 'writing for free' with a promise of money that will never happen, and producers who will attach themselves to a project while contributing nothing just because you mentioned it to them.

Denise Gossett: There are many, so, get a lawyer or really good agent. And talk to other writers about companies they may have worked with . . . people are willing to talk, especially if they had a bad experience with someone.

WOULD YOU RECOMMEND WRITING COLLABORATIVE SCRIPTS TO BEGINNER SCREENWRITERS?

Jonathan Winn: This is one of those Yes and No type of answers. There's a lot to be said for partnering up with someone who has more experience. Someone you have great energy with and who you can bounce ideas off of, and together, create a great script. A lot of people work this way and do so quite well.

But before you put pen to paper or fingers to keys, have a contract. A signed legal document clearly outlining the partnership, the writing credit, all that stuff. May sound a bit crass—dude, this guy's, like, my best friend! There's no way he's going to turn on me or something, you know?—but trust me: if your partnership can't survive a discussion about the possibility of drafting a contract protecting your work and your individual effort, it simply won't survive the often brutal process of writing, rewriting, shopping or selling that script.

So, use your head, protect the investment of your time and talent, and just have a document signed by both of you clearly detailing the nature of your working relationship just so everything is understood and in writing, and there's no confusion as the project moves forward. In fact, it'll be appreciated when the studio or production company is buying the property as the Chain of Title (ownership of the script) is already clearly established.

Ed Naha: Mmmmm. That depends on your relationship with the collaborator. If it's someone you're comfortable around, who you see as a mentor, and he or she accepts that role, fine. If it's someone who's not patient and is into the words "I," "me," and "mine,"—nope. I've seen newbie screenwriters pair up with good friends, too, with awful results. It's like watching two dogs in a pissing match to mark territory. I tend to work alone. When I need feedback, I show the script to a couple of friends whom I love dearly before I show it to anyone professionally. My wife is also wonderful. She knows when I'm being lazy and when I fall back on old tricks and she calls me on it.

John Russo: If that's the only way you can do it successfully, go right ahead. But you will be better off if you don't have to depend on anyone else. Working with others is the greatest jeopardy financially or in terms of making deadlines and so on. You are better off developing your own talents to the fullest.

Harry Shannon: I love to collaborate and if you can work with someone who has experience, grab it and study like hell. We learn to write by writing, so working together can be a great thing. It's also less lonesome.

Mick Garris: That's interesting; everyone's route is so completely different. I started writing on my own, and didn't do any collaborations until I had already pretty much established a career. It's really how you write best. I've enjoyed collaborating, but I think I work best alone. If you're excited about what you're writing, you just get lost in it. You get eager about finding those secret tributaries that reveal themselves to you in the process.

I know that most comedies are written in collaborations, which makes total sense. But it depends on how you work, who you work with, and how well you inspire one another.

Stephen Volk: Not really. It sounds appealing because it sounds like half the toil, but first you need to find your voice and attain a level of skill. Get a bit of experience behind you, too, because when you are writing together it's imperative to be open and honest and not crumble when an idea is criticized—you also have to be nimble enough to come up with ten solutions to a problem and not get possessive or intractable about ideas: that only comes with time.

Stephen Johnston: I had never collaborated on a script until I was "established" as a writer, so it's a little hard for me to address this. I would say, it's probably a good idea to find your individual voice as a writer, before you engage in some sort of collaborative endeavor.

James Cullen Bressack: I prefer writing collaborative scripts because it is fun to play off of someone and you are not writing in a tunnel. I usually elect to write with a partner because ultimately it makes the process more fun.

Patrick Lussier: Depends on the project and the temperament of those involved.

Denise Gossett: Sure! It can really be helpful to bounce ideas off of someone.

WHAT WOULD YOU SAY ARE THE BIGGEST PITFALLS WHEN WRITING A SCRIPT?

Jonathan Winn: Speaking as a writer who bounces between fiction and screenwriting, there are several. First is learning the format. Wrapping your head around all that white space, the general rule being the less words the better. Second would be shifting the story in your head into something that can be seen onscreen that isn't just prose. Taking the intended narrative and moving it into dialogue and, again, a visual. Third, and this is the kicker, realizing that everything you're putting on the page in the script will probably be cut, shifted, sliced, moved around or rewritten into oblivion at some point in the process. So, it has to be as perfect as possible to get in the door—a lot of blood, sweat and tears on your part, in other words—only to be totally changed (and not always by you—writers are the first to be replaced on the team) into something very different than what you first intended by the time it hits production.

Ed Naha: Planning it out so clinically that there's no room for inspiration or variation.

John Russo: I don't worry about pitfalls because I know what I'm doing. I just work hard to craft the best possible script that I can. If you master the craftsmanship and if you work hard, success may follow. I say "may" because there are no guarantees in this business.

Harry Shannon: Fighting the urge to add one thing that isn't essential. A good script should be lean and mean, and since film is collaborative that is one hell of a lot harder to pull off than people realize. A script has a million moving parts. Structure everything very carefully before you write, and try hard not to change the map until you have a tight first draft. You'll be sorry if you lose perspective, even once.

Stephen Volk: Tackling something you don't know how to pull off e.g. something that is supposed to be funny, but you aren't a comedy writer, or scary and you aren't naturally a horror writer—that is the kiss of death because we will smell you a mile off. Write the genre you love. Push the envelope by all means, but don't write a romantic comedy because it's where the big bucks is at the moment and you don't really even like those kind of films—actually: "fuck you!" if you think that's what a career in screenwriting is about. Write the film you want to see that you can't see. Do it from the heart and if you do money will follow. Yes, have career in the back of your mind but never write ONLY for money because it's hard, hard work. Sometimes you will be weeping in a hotel room, and it's not worth it if you don't love it (also, the biggest pitfall in terms of launching into writing a screenplay is having to learn brevity, which only comes with experience, especially if you come from writing novels. Less is more. Always, always. Cut, cut, trim, trim. It always gets better).

Stephen Johnston: I think hands-down the biggest pitfall is characterization. I don't care what the plot is, or how outrageous the situation you're trying to create, if your characters aren't believable, it's simply not going to work.

James Cullen Bressack: Honestly the biggest pitfall I face is things sometimes make more sense in my head than they do on the page. So finding a way to translate things from my lizard brain into something that makes sense for everyone is the most difficult pitfall.

Patrick Lussier: The daunting blank page and the failure to rewrite and rewrite and rewrite and rewrite.

Denise Gossett: Many scripts are too long. There should not be anything in your script that does not move your story along, period. Same goes for filmmaking . . . if the scene is not pertinent to the story, cut it out.

WHAT KIND OF SCHEDULE DO YOU KEEP WHEN WRITING SCRIPTS ON A DEADLINE?

Jonathan Winn: I usually write seven days a week, from morning to night. Whether it be screenwriting, fiction, TV scripts, short stories, outlines for future work, it's my job so I write everyday. To answer your question, though, I tend to usually slam out a minimum of ten pages a day. Once you set up the outline, what the scenes are and how they follow and feed each other, what the narrative is and how each scene fits into it and moves it forward, the writing of the script itself, for me, is fairly straightforward. So it doesn't take me too long. But everyone's different. I know writers who get three pages a day—or a week!—and others who do twenty. I'm good with my ten.

Ed Naha: I've never been someone who set aside time to write according to a clock. So, you pace yourself according to the deadline (of course, if you're attached to a TV series, then, the question should be "What kind of schedule do you keep to make sure you find time to sleep when writing on a never-ending deadline?"). In terms of the creative process, the best piece of advice I ever ran across came from novelist/screenwriter Mario Puzo. He had a couch in his office. If he napped in his office, he considered that working. I laughed when I read that but I've found it to be true. I do that when I hit an impasse. I'll go to sleep thinking about it. When I wake up, I usually have found a way to deal with it.

Harry Shannon: My deadlines are seldom for scripts these days. I believe people should try to set a daily time and stick to it, but the ugly truth is that I usually write in bursts once I get started. At my best, I write from five to seven or so each morning until the project is done. I have a day job like everyone else.

Mick Garris: I've actually never bumped up against a deadline. I write very quickly once I get going. I do most of my writing in the morning before lunch, and then I feel okay if I just do a couple pages in the afternoon. Most writers write a lot at night. I don't. I'm best in the morning.

When I get going, I write six to ten pages a day.

Stephen Volk: Ten pages a day, if I can. At the beginning of a script the first page may take two, three days because it's cracking the ice, and the first blank page is always daunting and incredibly important to get right. Then you warm up. I tend to divide up the treatment—I need to get to page 5 of my treatment by the weekend . . . Then when you're into it you can write maybe fifteen pages a day, on a roll because you know what you're doing. But page count is an illusion of achievement anyway when you're looking at twelve, fourteen drafts in front of you.

Stephen Johnston: My typical schedule is to get up in the morning, put the coffee on, check emails, then stare at the infernal flashing cursor for a few hours. If I'm on deadline, then I quite literally do whatever is necessary to meet it.

James Cullen Bressack: I lock myself in a room with a bottle of Jack Daniels and I'll finish the script by the time the deadline hits or the bottle is empty.

Patrick Lussier: Procrastinate less, circle it less, attack it more, keep hitting it until it drags you to the finish line.

Denise Gossett: I would say start with your deadline and work backwards on your calendar and mark every little thing that you need to have done. This way you have a set assignment for each day up to your deadline . . . It will help you to not feel so overwhelmed, too.

HOW INVOLVED DO YOU THINK A SCREENWRITER SHOULD BE ONCE PRODUCTION STARTS?

Jonathan Winn: I think the writer should be involved every day if he or she wants. But that's neither realistic nor is it how things are done right now. If it's a studio project, the writers are lucky if they get two tickets to the premiere. Most big budget Hollywood films have a lot of writers they cycle in and out, this writer focusing on the action in Act Two, this other writer working exclusively on so-and-so's dialogue in the first seven pages of Act Three, etc. and so on. So the writer they bought the script or concept from is usually the first on a long list of people who have a hand in the final product. It's rare that first writer will be a part of the production process.

TRICKS OF THE TRADE: SCREENWRITING

Indie film is different. The writer, if negotiated in the contract, can be involved on a daily basis. It just really depends on the people involved. But they can be available to rewrite a scene if it becomes obvious it can be done better. They can approve slight dialogue changes the actors want. You see? Whereas the studio shoot is kind of set in stone where every change needs to be approved by several chains of command, an indie film can be a bit looser and not as strict. Again, this is something the writer can discuss during the negotiation process.

Personally, I believe that the more the writer knows about the mechanics of making a film, what goes into the shooting of a scene, etc., the better they'll be at writing a great script. And being on-set is a great way of seeing that.

Ed Naha: I don't think a writer should be involved, in general, once the camera rolls. I think that can be a real soul killer unless you're working in small, independent features where things are less territorial. The usual trope is: "Film is a collaborative medium." Yes, it is. At a certain budgetary level, though, a writer has to hand off his work and allow the director free rein. If he's open to it, he'll bonk heads with you before production. Once production starts, however, you'll find yourself painfully out of the loop if you hang around and you're not attached as a producer. If you're not actively involved in the physical production, a film set can put you into coma.

Harry Shannon: I was fortunate to be involved at all. There is an old joke in Hollywood that one actress was so dumb she slept with the writer. Most of the time the director will take the script and you will be rarely, if ever, consulted. That's too bad, but the truth is, we often get too married to what we've written, and have a different perspective. Of course, sometimes we're dead right but no one wants to listen.

Mick Garris: That's a question that's rarely up to the writer. When I've directed from another writer's script, I like to have them involved, and present if possible. But the director has to make the final choices. Most of the movies I've written but did not direct were made without my involvement once production began.

Stephen Volk: Ideally the writer and director should be in cahoots, as one mind by the time the cameras roll, but that rarely happens. If you are lucky, in television (in the UK) the directors are generous and secure enough to work with you closely and invite you to the set, because in the pecking order the writer is quite important. In film, the writer is completely unimportant when the director takes over. The director is all that matters and it's like "Who are you again?" because all they want is that "Un film de" above the title, and if he/she wants to rewrite your script it's, "By all means! Be our guest!" The producers never side with the writer or with the script they have maybe spent five or ten years developing. Which is quite . . . character building. We have to accept it because we can't change the system, the "auteur" system that is, claiming every film is the work of a single intelligence—the director. And that is simply bullshit most of the time, as any screenwriter will tell you.

Stephen Johnston: I'm sure a lot of scribes will disagree with me on this one, but outside of production revisions, by the time photography starts, your job is effectively complete. If you want to be a director, by all means, go be a director, but that's a whole other can of worms.

James Cullen Bressack: If they aren't directing the movie, get the fuck away from set because you will have a nervous breakdown seeing how many things are being changed on the fly. The control is out of your hands and you have to accept it. Be available if they have questions of clarity, but if they don't you have given your baby up for adoption and you have to accept that.

Patrick Lussier: Depends on the director and producers and how collaborative they are.

Denise Gossett: They really aren't that involved. I know it's hard, but, at some point you have to trust and let your baby go. Now, that's not to say that there won't be some rewrites during shooting, but, writers are not as involved as you might think once production has started.

TRICKS OF THE TRADE: SCREENWRITING

HOW DIFFERENT IS WRITING FILM SCRIPTS FROM SERIES SCRIPTS?

Jonathan Winn: Totally different animals. And the differences are a bit hard to explain. Most film scripts have three Acts whereas TV sometimes has four or five, so the structuring of your narrative and where the acts break is different. Film tells a cohesive story. There's a beginning, a middle, and an end. Series are episodic, so although you're telling a beginning, middle, end-type of story in each episode, it's part of a much larger story stretched out over six or thirteen or twenty-two episodes. The story you're telling in that script has to stand on its own while still having a very important place in the narrative arc. So, a film wraps it up at The End. A series is always To Be Continued with every script ending with a bang that brings 'em back for more. That's definitely an adjustment for someone who's used to the finality of a film.

HOW STRESSFUL AND CHALLENGING IS IT TO WRITE A SERIES PILOT?

Jonathan Winn: I can only speak from personal experience, but the writing of the pilot is a cinch compared to the writing of the Pitch Doc that has to be submitted with it. What's a Pitch Doc? It's this, basically (and this is but one variation of what's expected): the series described in a sentence, and then a brief paragraph. Then a brief synopsis of not only the series, but also the first season story arc and the pilot episode. A brief description of all the characters and then a paragraph (brief, again) of the following three episodes—or first six episodes—followed by a summary of everything. I'm also finding producers wanting more in these Pitch Docs. Marketing thoughts, potential advertising tie-ins, demographic strength, how many quadrants you're hitting (a quadrant being a demographic, i.e. males 18—24), other strengths for the Network to consider. In comparison, the Pilot is easy-peasy.

DO YOU HAVE ANY ADVICE FOR SCREENWRITERS OR THOSE INTERESTED IN THE FIELD?

Jonathan Winn: For screenwriters, I always tell them to read as many scripts as they can. We're lucky because, with a little imaginative digging, most of them can be found online for free. Have a favorite movie? Read the script. In fact, during awards season, production companies release scripts to garner buzz and hopefully a nomination, so there's a ton of great stuff to read. So do it. See how those moments you enjoy onscreen started on the page. Follow the transitions between the acts. See how they smoothed 'em out. And, more importantly, see how what was on the page transitioned to the screen via the director's vision, the production design, the actors, the lighting, the editing, the sound. Doing this really does help you see that the script you're writing truly is the blueprint for everything onscreen. But it's not the be all, end all. Your words are the beginning just waiting for everyone else's talent to bring it to life.

Ed Naha: Don't go into the movie and/or television business to get rich or to get famous. The entertainment business is, for most people, a matter of feast and famine. And, usually, famine lasts the longest. And don't go into it thinking in terms of stability. Anything that can go wrong, will go wrong. At least twice. Once you've finished your script, if it's an original, hold it. Hug it. And, then, bid it farewell. It's the last time you'll see your baby intact. If the script is sold, it will be changed by everyone. I once wrote a script in ten days. It sold for a lot of money. I, then, contractually, had to destroy it for the next two years. I was getting notes from everyone. I think the janitor even took a crack at it. It was never made. A bazillion things can happen to your work. Your studio contact may leave (as did mine) and you'll be assigned a new overseer who just doesn't get it. A financial downturn may curtail the number of movies made at the company. A studio may be sold. I've written and sold over thirty scripts in my career and only a handful have actually been made. Of those, only one has been what I envisioned it to be, *Dolls*.

Another thing to remember is that very seldom will you receive accolades. If a movie is tremendously successful, it will be considered the director's film. If the movie tanks and gets reviews like an STD, it will be credited to the writer. It helps if you have an absurdist sense of humor about all of it. Thankfully, I do. I read a lot of Vonnegut and Nathanael West growing up.

TRICKS OF THE TRADE: SCREENWRITING

I think writers, in general, can be likened to Don Quixote. If you believe that what you're writing is true to yourself and can change or affect the way an audience thinks or feels, then you're willing to proudly ride into battle on its behalf. You'll get knocked down a lot but, if you're a true believer, you'll get up again. Sometimes, unlike Quixote, you'll realize that impossible dream. Then, it's time to put on the suit of armor again and pick a new windmill to joust.

Harry Shannon: Learn the rules before you break them, as usual. Read *Story* by Robert McKee, the Syd Fields books, John Troby. A class or two wouldn't hurt. Don't just dive in for the hell of it and think you'll get something great. Learn how to lay things out and think them through. You can tap dance in a story or a novel, but scripts have to be right there on the page, and mostly in dialogue or action, not description.

Stephen Volk: Be true to the kind of stories you want to tell, horror or otherwise. If you want to be Ingmar Bergman don't write a Stallone action flick—or vice versa. Our lives are short. Concentrate on the genre you want to get really, really good at. But also take yourself out of your comfort zone and try stories that stretch you. Take risks. It's only paper after all. It's only then do you find what is "you" as a writer and realize the themes that are at the core of your storytelling.

Stephen Johnston: Write. At the end of the day screenwriting is just storytelling, so you have to apply yourself to the craft. I often have people tell me they "have a great idea for a movie," but when they tell me their idea I typically discover it's a scenario in which a story might occur, but it's not a story in itself. And don't focus too much on formatting. That's ultimately the least of your worries.

James Cullen Bressack: Just do it, don't allow your fears to dictate your life. If you want something just go for it.

Patrick Lussier: Read, write, and read and rewrite and rewrite and rewrite. Your fist pass, no matter what you think, is never good enough.

Denise Gossett: Read, take a class, read other scripts, network, get involved with other writers.

Billy Hanson: The biggest thing is just to stick with it. Come out to LA, start working in the business, it doesn't matter what position at first, just get out here and start meeting people. If you want to write, start writing and keep on getting better at it. Sooner or later, you'll wind up in a position where somebody will be willing to read something and you should be ready with something you're proud of. And when that person shoots it down and says it's not good enough, then you keep at it, make it better, and submit it again the next time you have a chance.

And going back to something I said earlier, just be honest with yourself. You may come out to LA wanting to be a writer/director, only to find out that directing is not your biggest strength. You might be more of a producer than anything, so you should explore that. Don't write it off just because it's not what you said you originally wanted. I don't think a lot of people move out here to be gaffers, but there are those who excel in that position and wind up loving it and having great careers. If you're sure you want to write, then you've got to get good at it, work on it, perfect your skills and sharpen your understanding of story and character. If you're going to rub elbows with the likes of William Goldman and the greats, you've got to be able to tell stories that are fresh, effective, and original.

SCREENWRITING

THE ART OF THE PITCH

TAYLOR GRANT

DID IT on a dare.

It was one of the most terrifying experiences of my life.

I stood on stage in a packed room and tried to make a jaded audience laugh.

They didn't.

I'll get back to that in a moment . . .

At the time, I was doing a little acting here and there and had casually mentioned to a couple friends that it might be fun to try an "Open Mic" night. This was many years ago, during the standup comedy boom of the late 80s/early 90s.

I immediately regretted my comment, however, because my friends then *dared* me to give it a try at a local comedy club. They even promised to come out to support me.

To my horror, I heard myself agreeing to the challenge.

At the time, I had a little writing experience under my belt (very little), and managed to cobble together a five-minute standup routine. Once I felt I had enough material, I began to practice. I agreed to perform at a date about three weeks away, and I rehearsed that damned five-minute set until I could recite it in my sleep (hell, I probably did).

The hour prior to my big debut was excruciating. I paced backstage while other would-be comedians faced the crowd with varying degrees of success—and failure. My heart sunk when one of the comedians—an older man—was literally booed off the stage.

I was up next . . .

I came on stage to a smattering of applause (from my friends, of course). Moments later my first joke went over about as well as a fart in church. Somewhere towards the back of the room I was sure I heard a cricket chirping—or he might have been heckling me. I don't know, I don't speak cricket.

I told the second joke and winced. It was like tossing a grenade in room and holding your breath—wondering if it would go off.

And then . . . I heard it. The sweetest sound imaginable: a few chuckles emanating from somewhere in the room. It gave me the nudge I needed to leap headfirst into my routine.

I have no real memories of what happened after that. It wasn't until my friends were patting me on the back afterward that I realized the nightmare was truly over. The next day I watched a videotaped recording of the show, and was shocked to discover that I had done much better than I thought. I mean, I was no George Carlin by any stretch of the imagination; I stepped on laughter, my timing was off, and I wasn't paying any attention to the ebb and flow of audience response. But people were actually laughing—quite a bit, in fact. And not *at* me, but *with* me.

So what saved the performance, and why in the hell am I telling you all of this?

I wanted to illustrate the importance of preparation, one of the single most important factors to a successful pitch.

THE POWER OF PREPARATION

I had practiced that five-minute performance so many times, memorized it so well, that when it was game time, the words came automatically, despite my terrible anxiety.

Preparation carried the day.

It was a great lesson. And when I eventually broke into professional screenwriting, I recalled that lesson, and it made all the difference in my future pitches. Over the years, I sold, optioned and developed scripts for major Hollywood studios, such as Imagine Entertainment, Universal Studios, Lions Gate Films, etc. I wrote for several TV series and also created an animated series called *Monster Farm*, which aired on the Fox Family Channel.

There was a lot of pitching involved.

Eventually, I became what they call "good in a room." You will want to be good in a room, too.

The good news is that you are not expected to perform at the level of a professional standup comedian. But you *are* expected to present at a professional level—after all, you are a professional, right?

If you want people to actually hire you, buy your stories, you're going to have to pitch yourself and your wares occasionally. It's part of the game. *You are in the business of selling and telling stories.*

Keep in mind that pitches don't always happen in planned meetings with studio executives or production offices (sometimes called a "meet and greet"). You might have an opportunity at a cocktail party, a casual lunch meeting, or down at the local car wash while you're waiting for your car to be dried. If you live in Hollywood, you can't throw a rock without hitting someone who has ties to the film and TV industry (and that's a good thing, as opportunities to pitch your story abound).

You must be prepared to tell your story at the drop of a hat, and you have to know it like the back of your hand. That's the first step to a successful pitch. I'll get into the other steps in a moment.

Occasionally you will pitch to a captive audience. They will politely listen to your story from beginning to end without interrupting you. That's pretty damned rare. Most likely, the person listening will stop you throughout your pitch to ask questions.

The questions might be thoughtful, they might be inane, or they might be downright ludicrous—but you have to be prepared to answer whatever they throw at you . . . and jump right back in without missing a beat.

I once had a development executive suggest that I add aliens from outer space to my character-driven thriller. He thought it was a brilliant way to give the story an unexpected twist. I politely listened and somehow managed not to burst into uncontrollable laughter. After he'd finished orating his bizarre suggestion, I politely responded that "it was an interesting idea," and went right back into my story without missing a beat.

He didn't throw me off my game. That's the power of preparation.

You'll want to create a short version and a long version of your pitch. The short one can be told in, say five minutes. The long version can be twice as long, or as long as the person listening needs to understand your story.

If your pitch goes over ten minutes and they're still asking questions about characters and plot points, then you've got a live one. Use your common sense. Give them as much detail as they request. That's a sign of genuine interest and your preparation will pay off, because you won't be thrown off by specific questions about your story.

How do you prepare? Practice your pitch so many times that you don't have to think about it, so when your flow is interrupted intermittently—and believe me it will be—you'll know exactly where you are in the story and won't get flustered or lose your place.

Another important benefit of extensive preparation is the confidence you'll gain by knowing the material well. Pitching your work can be nerve-racking enough without the added stress of struggling to remember a plot point.

Here's something you don't hear much, but that can make a huge difference in your ability to pitch well. Take an acting class. Better yet, take an "improv" (short for improvisation) class. The experience of performing or presenting to a live audience—and thinking on your feet—is invaluable.

Use a camera to record yourself at home (web cam, cell phone camera, etc.). It might be painful to see yourself the first time, but you'll catch things that you wouldn't expect—and it will help you adjust your performance.

THE ELEVATOR PITCH

So now you know your story upside down and sideways. But you're going to want to open your pitch with the big idea . . . the concept. It is sometimes referred to as the elevator pitch.

An elevator pitch is an age-old term, suggesting that you should be able to tell your story to someone in the short time you're on the elevator together.

Don't take that too literally, of course. But it does highlight the importance of brevity and being able to communicate your basic story in a concise manner. You'll thank me if you're ever put on the spot, particularly in a situation you weren't expecting (again, like running into a producer at a car wash). Yes, it happened.

If you're having a hard time condensing your complex, sophisticated drama down to a few sentences, you can practice on films you're already familiar with. Remember, first and foremost you're a storyteller. *A pitch is just another way to tell your story.*

A tried-and-true method for nailing down the concept is by asking a "what if" question. Here are a few examples:

Rosemary's Baby: What if the devil had a son?

Memento: What if a man tried to solve his wife's murder while dealing with short-term memory loss?

Pretty Woman: What if a wealthy businessman fell in love with a hooker he hired for the weekend?

Castaway: What if a commercial plane crashed on a deserted island and you were the only one left alive?

Liar Liar: What if an attorney couldn't lie?

Your goal is to get your audience engaged immediately, and one of the best ways to do that is to spark their imagination with the question: "What if?"

Whatever technique you use, make sure you can distill your story into an elevator pitch.

YOUR MINDSET

We've all seen a desperate person trying to ask someone out on a date—either in real life, or in a movie or TV show. The result is always the same—they are rebuffed.

Desperation: the ultimate turnoff.

There is no need to be desperate. You have a great story. Believe in it. Be prepared to pitch it and you will gain a new level of confidence. Getting the right mindset is critical before you say the first word.

First of all, remember that the person hearing your story is hoping you won't be boring, long-winded . . . or desperate. Most people on the other side of the desk have heard countless pitches—and it's a genuine relief when the person pitching is entertaining, knowledgeable, and confident.

Be that person.

A man named Joe Girard holds the Guinness World Record for being the world's greatest salesman. While most car salespeople sell four or five cars a month—Joe averaged six or more cars . . . A DAY.

Joe said, "I have no big secrets which nobody else has, I simply sell the world's best product, that's all. *I sell Joe Girard.*" Joe knew that people buy from people they like and trust. So he focused his energy on establishing rapport.

He told them he loved them, he told them he liked them. He made sure they understood that he appreciated them.

And guess what? They did. To the tune of five or six cars a day.

One of the most successful books on sales ever written is "The Greatest Salesman in the World" by Og Mandino. In the book, Mandino writes: " . . . only the unseen power of love can open the hearts of men and until I master this art I will remain no more than a peddler in the marketplace."

Too weird for you? I get it. But I'm here to tell you that changing how you perceive the person you're pitching to will positively change the dynamic of the meeting.

No one likes to be "sold," but everyone likes to hear cool stories by likable people. Force yourself to like them first.

This is a very important point. It is something I practice in interviews, pitches—you name it. I go into the situation appreciating the person I'm pitching. I remind myself to be grateful for the opportunity to meet this person before I walk in the room.

If you are grateful to be there, the person you're pitching to will sense it. Believe me. Give it a try. What would it hurt?

Here's another Hollywood secret. One of the things you're being judged on in your pitch meeting is whether or not you're a jerk, psycho, or prima donna. Think about it. If they say "yes" to your pitch, they are also agreeing to work with you for an extended period of time. No one wants to spend two years or more working with a jerk.

You're never just selling your project—you're selling *yourself*.

YOUR PRESENTATION

Going back to the standup comedy analogy, if you've ever seen a great comedian, you'll notice the two most important criteria for a successful set:

1) Great material.

2) Great delivery.

At this point, I'm assuming you already have great material. Now, we have to work on your delivery.

Don't think about your pitch as selling someone something—think about it as telling a story that's so compelling you can't wait to share it.

Ever see a great movie or episode of a TV show and then relay that story excitedly to a friend? That's very similar to what you are doing here. Producer Robert Kosberg was often called "Hollywood's King of Pitch," and his approach was described as "telling bedtime stories to adults."

Remember, you're a storyteller. Pitching is just another way of telling your story.

I once had a lunch meeting with Bo Zenga, a Hollywood producer/screenwriter known for his masterful pitching technique, and who once sold twelve pitches in a single year. Bo told me that brevity and enthusiasm were essential to a successful pitch. He told me that your goal is to whet your buyer's appetite—give them just enough, and to be passionate above all else.

And that is the last, and in some ways, most important piece of advice I can offer: You must bring passion and enthusiasm to the pitch. Without it, you're sunk. It doesn't matter how well thought out your story is, and it doesn't matter how well prepared you are. If you're not enthusiastic about your story, you can't expect anyone else to be either.

Remember, we go to the movies and watch TV shows to *feel* something. If the story doesn't elicit emotion, we check out. Your job is to create that feeling in the room. That's your job as a storyteller. You must provide the buyer with a positive emotional experience.

Make your listener *feel* something. That's what they yearn for. That's what all humans yearn for when they hear a story.

Don't think of yourself as a salesperson, think of yourself as a storyteller. You have a great story to tell!

I wish you every success with your pitches, your projects, and your career.

PITFALLS ON THE WAY TO THE HELLPIT

JOHN SHIRLEY

WE WANT TO dig a hellpit for you. And strangely enough you want to plunge into it.

You do, anyway, if you like horror films. If it doesn't scare you, if it's not dark and deep enough for you, you're not going to like it. "Make that hellpit dark and deep enough and I'll jump in!"

Those of us who write horror, in novels, short stories and scripts, are trying, we really are, to make your hellpit hellish. Just for you.

But there are pitfalls, traps, on the way—especially when it comes to horror movies.

"The devil is in the details" is an old expression. And in terms of the logistics of realization of a horror film, the hellpit naturally contains devils, and all too many details. Complexity along the way is one of the pitfalls. Once you have your hopefully engaging premise, some grand horror concept, the general pathway to getting the film made starts with financing. There's big studio financing, which horror films don't get very often, and there's independent financing . . . and there's self-financing, a form of indie financing that is fraught with risks, because another old saying is, "Don't use your own money".

There's more than one way to get hold of someone else's money to finance your hellpit. I heard that the original *Evil Dead* film started with 8 millimeter footage made in the film maker's garage. This famous auteur then went out and demo'd his stop motion horrors for dozens of smalltime financiers. For example, he went around to dentists, who often have cash to invest, and he'd bring a little projector and show the thing, without sound, right on their white office walls! The dentists would be impressed and sign on for a few grand each, and eventually Sam Raimi had enough money to get *The Evil Dead* into a few grindhouse theaters. It did well enough that he got a more professional budget for *The Evil Dead 2*, and went on to make *Army of Darkness*, and lots of other films, raking in big bucks with *Spider-man* (he presumably gave those helpful dentists their royalties).

But some people use a handful of credit cards to make inexpensive indie horror films. Sometimes it works, as in *The Blair Witch Project*. Other times it doesn't and bankruptcy follows. The risk is pretty high. Because if you don't finish your film, or if it comes out shabby, and doesn't get any sort of distribution, not even straight-to-dvd, you're unlikely to get a second chance in the marketplace. Or with the relatives you may've gotten the credit cards from. Or your wife.

So, instead, most people try to come up with a strong concept and script, something they can pitch, and they take it to a production company for the financing, if they can get that meeting. This entails risks first of all . . . theft. One problem is, stealing an idea isn't a violation of copyright. It's just an idea. There has to be enough story, plot, characterization, setting in common, along with the concept, for the theft victim to win a lawsuit. And lawsuits cost money. I had, to my certain knowledge, one television movie concept stolen, and produced by the thieves, and one TV series concept and some of the story stolen. At the time I couldn't afford to sue and couldn't get anyone to do it on contingency. Another issue is that agencies repping writers are working for themselves more than they're working for the writer. The agency representing me, which had set up the meeting where the TV movie was swiped, did not want to provide evidence of the meeting. They had documentation, but refused to provide it. The television production company was a big one, and the agency didn't want to risk pissing it off. They were afraid of losing meetings for other clients, and thus losing money.

On another occasion I was pitching a story and concept—I'll name this one—called Crawlers. This was before I turned it into a novel (the novel is still in print). I pitched to an under-producer at a company run by a former special effects wizard now looking to produce its own pictures. This under producer said *Naw, we don't want this*. I moved on to something else. Years later I remembered

SCREENWRITING

my premise and story and wrote the novel *Crawlers*, same title and concept, which was published by Dey Rey books. This cyberpunk flavored body-snatcher horror tale was then optioned for good money by a major film investment outfit, who sent it around the studios. But the studios keep a list of projects pitched to them, going way back—and a bunch of them had turned down a whole, finished *script* called *Crawlers*, with exactly the same concept and nearly the same story. "Hey we've already turned this down, a couple years ago!" My agent and I investigated and found that the author of the *Crawlers* script was the guy who'd turned down my Crawlers pitch at that production company! He had taken the title, the premise, and much of the story and written a bad script based on that. He had simply stolen it. And he had inadvertently created an obstacle for the real *Crawlers* script. "We've already read this" was the automatic, indeed automated (almost cybernetically body-snatched) response.

We sent him a cease and desist letter but my whole project still fell apart, because of this guy's theft.

The way to avoid this kind of outcome is to write out a full script, and submit it to the Writer's Guild of America which, for a smallish fee, will register it digitally. I have learned to register everything. They'll send you a printed and (most important) dated note of registration. You then write "registered with the WGA" on the script's title page. They'll back you up if it's stolen—and you don't have to be a WGA member just to register a script. But again, if it's just a concept—you can't really protect it very well. Flesh it out!

But suppose you pitch something and it gets a *yes,* and gets produced? More pitfalls await! Those detail devils are budget directors, marketing people, producers and sub producers and sub sub producers and the director—all people who can put their stamp on your story, your idea, and totally bollix it up.

Or—just as bad—they can lose interest at a critical point.

I wrote a horror movie for a movie channel. One of the producers actually gave me some notes that improved my script. The others went along with my ideas for the most part, but the problem was . . . they lost interest. They are now-famous producers who were just establishing themselves then, and when a much bigger project was greenlighted they lost interest in seeing ours through. They failed to make sure it got full financing, failed to keep its standards up, and while it did get made and on television, the production values were half of what it was supposed to have been. The cheapest actors were the default choice, who spoke the lines in the most stilted way; the director, under budgeted, did a weak pass at shooting and editing. It was one of those three-story movies, three separate horrors in one feature, with a frame, and one of them came out pretty good, one was so-so and one ended up dopey. But all the original stories had been strong. Weak production values resulted in a cheap looking film. Not even the sound was carefully produced, so critical lines were muddily recorded.

I was merely the writer—what's the joke about the Polish actress? She married the writer.

Writers usually are low on the totem pole of cinematic power. It can vary—a hot A-list writer can get special input, maybe executive producer status, and a successful auteur like Woody Allen or Kathryn Bigelow, a writer-director, can get complete control. This can be good . . . or disastrous if you have a Heaven's Gate situation.

Stephen King can get special consideration in his contract. But most of us have to suck it up and walk gloomily away.

Famously, if you get your beloved horror novel and/or script bought by a studio of any size, the concept and the script then go through a sausage making machine. It's filtered through numerous producers, of course, each wanting a turn cranking the grinder. They have to justify their titles, their paychecks—and they hope someone will notice that they put some kind of imprint on it. "Can you make this woman a prostitute instead of a nun?" "Can this guy turn out to be Jack the Ripper instead of Dracula?"

The more producers, the more likely the film will go wrong. Each producer is a potential pitfall. There are production meetings where everyone has notes on the script—including the director—and the concept and plot gets flayed down and down and down from what it had been . . . or the concept gets other ideas awkwardly larded onto it. Hollywood projects have a notorious Frankensteinian look about them—but they're not about Frankenstein. They are, though, monsters of almost randomly sewn-on parts: a love-story sewn on where there shouldn't be one, a plot twist without any internal logic forced onto the body of the story like an arm sewn on backwards.

SCREENWRITING

Those films that go through this project without any intelligent guidance come out looking ridiculously patchwork and thrown together. One of the most obvious examples was the remake of *The Haunting*. The original Robert Wise film was a masterpiece, that should never have been remade. But if you're going to do it, do it respectfully, do it with an overall vision. The hodgepodge of jerky direction and clumsy scares that emerged in the remake of *The Haunting* is itself a shameful cautionary tale.

You're better off making an indie film, even fairly low budget. I've got nothing against low budget horror films, if they're done right. Look at *Paranormal Activity*. That movie, famously, was made not all that long ago for something like 20 thousand dollars . . . and it works well. It was a big hit, spawning a series. They were smart. They filmed *Paranormal Activity* all in one location, they got the very best actors they could financially manage, they exploited their premise fully and didn't bloat it up with too much dialogue or false personal drama.

I once had a producer friend approach me to write a low budget film based on a classic 19th century horror story. The real horror story was in the film making, as it worked out, not the film. My producer friend meant well—we'd worked on successful things before—but he had to put the financing together from various sources, many of them based in somewhat-mysterious Russian and Eastern European cash. Some of these guys were fly by night, and some of them didn't stick—so the budget got cut back. When this happened, the original, fairly solid director split—naturally he preferred a decent paycheck—and a first-time director was brought on. Sometimes a gifted first time director is a happy revelation. But this guy was strictly amateur, and the film making devolved. A couple of name actors, "name" in a B-movie sort of way, were involved, and a young actor from a TV series was set to star. But it turned out one of the name actors . . . and I won't name the film, let alone the actors . . . was failing at trying to stay sober. He got to the set in a fit of the DTs, and finally started drinking again right on the set, chugging Jack Daniels. The budget constrained the time the little production could afford to spend—so they had to go with this guy's slurred interpretation of the lines. In many cases he made up his own lines. At one point the other name B-movie actor understandably lost his temper with the drunk, and slugged him for his drunken unprofessionalism. They got in a fist fight on the set. I wish the fist fight were in the script . . .

But the real nail in the coffin, as it were, was the young TV actor supposed to have been the star of this ill-starred picture. He had a freebasing problem. The guy was huffing vaporized cocaine in his hotel room, and wouldn't come out. They finally had to force the door and practically drag him to the set. He didn't know his lines, or blurted them unintelligibly.

Eventually the film was "completed." It is a film I can't stand to watch. They'd cut the script, as they cut corners—losing almost all of the necessary special effects and the scenes that went with them. I didn't recognize my script. I wanted to take my name off it but my producer friend asked me, as a personal favor, not to, so I didn't.

The deepest pitfall here was the production not having its ducks in a row before shooting. Just to keep on track, they improvised as they went, cobbling things together . . . and that usually doesn't work. The details rise up and bite you in the ass. A film, even a cheap one, is a complex thing, and the complexity has to be worked through over time. It's like a machine with lots of working parts. If the machine is hastily constructed, it will fall apart as time and the stress on lots of moving parts take a toll.

Success in making a horror film is about smart, consistent guidance. It's about a unifying vision that can survive producers and problematic actors; it's about careful casting and careful location set up, good storytelling that isn't sacrificed to producer caprice . . . and then maybe you'll get a cinematic hellpit the audience can happily tumble into, instead of just a series of disastrous pitfalls.

AN OPEN LETTER TO AMBITIOUS AUTHORS EVERYWHERE

JONATHAN WINN

OKAY, I GET IT. No, I do. I really do. After the super-sized success of authors like JK Rowling and Stephenie Meyers, writers everywhere want to see their books become films. And who can blame them? I mean, c'mon. It looks glamorous. It looks exciting. It looks like a buckin' boatload of money, right? So why wouldn't you harbor not-so-secret dreams of franchise glory? To be the Big Name Writer with the capital W? And since you wrote the book, well, obviously it makes sense that you'll write the script. Of course. It'll be a cinch.

Or not.

Now, before I go on to somewhat apologetically massacre your red carpet buzz with a bloody buzz saw of reality, let me rein this in a bit with a simple question:

What's a script?

No, really. I'm being serious here. What's a script?

No doubt you can envision what one looks like. Maybe you've held one in your hands. Perhaps cracked it open for a quick sneaky-peek. But do you know what it really is? Because if we're going to talk about snagging that Hollywood brass ring with a stunning adaptation of your beloved book, we have to start at square one. And square one is the script.

So, what is it?

It's a blueprint. A map that guides everyone through the chaotic, messy, frustrating process of making a film. It's the touchstone that keeps everything in line. The constant in a sea of chaos. But first and foremost, a script is the necessary first spark that asks questions, demands answers, and puts everything in motion. Everything. The budget of the film. How many weeks it'll take to shoot. What locations need to be found. What sets need to be built. How those sets need to be dressed (furniture, walls, floors, etc). What wardrobe needs to be sourced or created by hand. What lighting will be needed.

The script even controls how many people are hired. Actors, director, assistant directors, casting directors, set builders, wardrobe, make-up. Office staff handling payroll and schedules and permits. Attorneys drafting contracts and negotiating insurance. Crew and grips and riggers and lighting. Caterers and drivers. Travel and the renting of hotels and apartments. Everything.

More complicated than you thought, right? Exactly. That's why I'm mentioning it. Working with a realistic sense of the planning and expense that goes into translating page to screen will help you create, from the get-go, a clean adaptation that's easy to shoot. And if you do that, you'll be ahead of the game.

To hammer this home, let me give an example of how a quick scene in a book can be a complicated headache for a filmmaker.

Picture this: 17th century village. The Main Character taking a break from a quest. Maybe it reads something like:

"He sat in the tavern sipping his brew, his eyes watching the mob seething with rage in the square, the hangman's noose moments from snapping the neck of yet another innocent soul."

Or something like that. Whatever. It's off the top of my head. Anyway, if we were to take that scene, that one quick scene that isn't all that integral to the plot, and faithfully adapt it, it would take a few weeks to schedule and rehearse and maybe a week to shoot.

Why?

Let me break it down for you.

Based solely on what's in the book, production will need a village and a gallows, both of which need to be built from the ground up. That's where the set builder and his or her crew will come in. And they'll need building materials. At a cost. And, because of the time period, the 17th century, they'll do everything under the experienced eyes of historians (again, at a cost) who will give a thumbs-up to the authenticity of everything. The tavern, the brew, the mug, the chairs, the floor. The scrawl of a menu in the background. The window he looks through. Even the eaves on the houses across the square and the size of the front doors. Everything.

And let's not forget that crowd. The one the MC spies seething in the square? A casting director who specializes in extras will be hired to find a few dozen anonymous bodies who will then have to be fitted with 17th century costumes. And if they can't be found, they need to be created by hand. At a cost.

Of course, these extras will need to be on-set. Since insurance rules and regulations sometimes prevent actors and extras from driving themselves to the set, they'll need drivers. And vans to ferry everyone from there to here and back again because, you know, it's a crowd of people.

Oh yeah! I almost forgot. The innocent soul destined to have his neck snapped in the hangman's noose? Stunt person. Yep. Different casting director. Different Actor's Union. Now that I think about it, there'll be a need for two actors, two stunt people: the guy who gets hanged and the guy who hangs him. Both hired at a day rate much higher, because of their specialized skill set, than an ordinary actor. And there's still the choreography of the hanging to work out, the endless rehearsing of the scene, planning the shots (what's called "blocking"), rehearsing the extras, exhaustively working out the safety measures the various Unions demand and then rehearsing with those in mind.

Needless to say, all of the above changes the insurance the shoot has to legally carry in order to even exist (hint: It's now more complicated and expensive.) And all of this affects the schedule, the budget, and the bottom line.

For one scene that takes three seconds of film time. One event noticed through a window while the MC sips a beer in a tavern. But you see? What was a brief mention for the author on a single page in an 80,000 word story ends up becoming a huge deal when it comes to shooting a film.

But as more and more writers actively lobby their way past Hollywood's Golden Gates, being aware of how important the script is and the work, planning and expense that goes into the smallest of moments, like this, will help the process move more smoothly from Day One as well as making it easier to cut or condense things that don't drive the plot forward.

Which brings me to actually taking a book and making it into a film script.

Of course, going through every element of doing an adaptation and explaining each and every aspect of the whole process in great detail would be both exhaustive and exhausting and would eat up more words than I frankly have the energy for. Besides, for the more dedicated, ambitious and curious among you, there are books out there. Many, many books. Good books, I'm sure, written by talented people, no doubt. Books that explain way more than I ever could here.

So I'm just going to briefly touch on a few things.

Let me begin with a handy Pro Tip: No matter how many months you spend doing everything I'm going to suggest or how amazing you believe your finished script turns out to be, someone else will be brought in to rewrite everything. I guarantee it. Someone—in fact, a lot of someones—will eventually rework every single thing.

Every single word. Every carefully plotted scene and motivational moment. Every nuanced shade. Everything on every single page is destined to be read, questioned, debated, argued over, questioned again, doubted and attacked by everyone before being handed off to be rewritten, reworked, chopped up and rearranged by someone you don't know, have never heard of, and will probably never meet.

So, seriously, after all that, why even bother? I mean, if you're going to bust your butt for, like, forever to write this damn thing only to be shown the door while some other writer just comes in and changes it all, why do it?

Good question. In fact, I can see disheartened thousands turning the page right now, choosing to keep the dream alive by ignoring this inescapable rewriting fact. And that's okay. No, really. It's a tough business. That's why I cold-clocked you with the worst of the worst first. But if you still have an interest in adapting your book into film, even after being broadsided by that little bombshell, keep reading.

You still with me? Good. You've got grit and courage. And a touch of bombastic delusion. I like that. You *need* that.

So, usually when writers hit me up for advice on "how to be" a screenwriter, the first thing I tell them is read a script. Seriously.

Have a favorite movie? Go online, hit up Google or whatever, and nine times out of ten you'll be able to find a free version of the script somewhere. So clickity-click-click-click, download that puppy, sit back, get comfortable, and read. Because that's how you're going to learn.

Sorry. Seems like boring advice, right?

But trust me on this because A) I'm not phoning it in—really, I'm not—and B) it's true. If you pay attention to the script, to what the format, the lack of words, the pace, the transitions, to what everything on the page is telling you, you'll learn almost all you need to know. But you have to *pay attention*.

Okay, working with the understanding that every page counts as one minute of screen time, i.e. a 90 page script will become a 90 minute movie, more or less, take a look at each individual scene. See how they're broken down? What's the length of each scene? How many lines of action are there? Count the lines. Go ahead, count them. Are there four lines? Five? Remember that. How many pages does a scene take? How many half-pages? Count that, too. Pay attention. There's an industry standard, a definite pattern, experienced writers follow and everyone expects, from producers to directors to actors, when they crack open a script. And it's shouting at you from every single page.

Continue reading. Take notes. How much of the story is driven by dialogue? And what kind of dialogue? Curt and quick? Or long-winded and dense? Is there both? How is it balanced? And where is it quick and where, in the story, is it long-winded? How many lines of dialogue does each character have? Yes, the lines on the page and, yes, count them. Is it three, four? Seven? Is there a pattern there as well? There is. Trust me.

Point is, if you channel your Inner Sherlock, you'll pick up a ridiculous amount. And it's stuff you need to know. Producers can tell from the quickest of glances whether or not something is worth reading. Within moments of opening to the first page, they've eyeballed the bare bone basics and decided whether or not to continue. But if you're armed with at least an armful of screenwriting knowledge, you'll come to the table as someone who's cared enough, and respected the work enough, to do their homework. And it'll be evident on Page One.

But even then, Mr. or Mrs. Producer still might not be impressed.

Yeah, it sucks. But here's the deal: Books and film are two different worlds. Even if you work like a demon to break down the How and Why of screenwriting, cracking the code and eyeballing every single pattern, and then create what you believe is a good screenplay, there's no guarantee it'll actually be a good screenplay.

Why? Because that's life. And being a writer who can knock out a great book doesn't mean you'll have the skill set to stun someone with a brilliant script. Yes, writing is writing. But even though fiction and film come from the same family, they're distant cousins who live in different countries and see each other once a decade or something, if at all.

Which brings us back to our beginning. Even if you learn the ropes, soak up the patterns, and beat the odds by slamming out an amazing script, remember everything will be rewritten. By someone else. A stranger who will flat-up toss out everything you've done.

So why do it?

Why indeed?

Besides the obvious business advantages of having a writing credit on a film—benefits of WGA membership, a nice paycheck, possible production bonuses, potentially generous residuals, the publicity feeding book sales, etc—what's so wrong with stretching your wings and trying something new? A new format, a new way of looking at a story. A new way of putting things on the page.

I've seen those who've spent years writing fiction break through writer's block after trying their hand at screenwriting. And I've seen screenwriters discover a whole new level of freedom by shaking away the stringent rules of writing scripts and sinking into the more relaxed language of books.

But not everyone will be able to travel between both worlds. Some write books. Some write film. And that's all they can do. There's nothing wrong with that. As I said earlier, brilliance with one doesn't guarantee a proficiency with the other.

But, listen, if you dig into an adaptation only to find, in frustration, that books really are your calling, take comfort in that. It's an enviable gift to be able to touch hearts and move souls with only words on a page. Whole worlds created with no bells or whistles, actors or costumes, clever lighting or CGI special effects. Nothing but words. Only words.

And, I don't know, perhaps that's how it should remain sometimes. Books remaining as just books. Simple words sitting quietly, speaking to your heart and soul, to your imagination and hopes and dreams, your fears and doubts, all from the elegant power of the page.

STEPHEN KING'S MILLION DOLLAR BABIES

AN INTERVIEW WITH BILLY HANSON

MY NAME IS Billy Hanson. I'm a writer, director, musician, and producer originally from the great state of Maine. After graduating from Old Orchard Beach High School, I was accepted into Florida State University's Film School, so I moved to Tallahassee and dove head first into the movie making process. I've been in love with movies ever since I was a baby. My father has a great video of me when I was two, completely engrossed in *The Wizard of Oz* (still one of my all time favorites), shouting the lines back at the TV right as they happened. I always nailed Dorothy's "Oh!" as her house landed after the tornado.

I graduated with a couple of successful short films and moved to L.A. where I was hired in post production on several different shows at Nickelodeon, including *Zoey 101, iCarly*, and *Victorious*. While maintaining a career in post and slowly rising through the ranks, I was constantly writing, and I was producing and directing my own projects whenever I could.

In 2009, I was able to put together a little weekend shoot for a short film called *Apology Day*, which screened at a few different festivals and was nominated for Best Comedy at the Action On Film Festival. After that I produced a few smaller projects, including an improv comedy spoof of ghost hunter shows called *Total Ghostage*. Then in 2012 I wrote, directed, and produced *Survivor Type*, which was taken around the world with over forty screenings to date.

I continue to work as a Post Production Supervisor on different television shows, most recently *Black Jesus* and *Dallas Cowboys Cheerleaders: Making The Team*, and I have a few of my own projects now in development with different companies, one of which should be released in late 2015 called *No Place To Fall*.

Joe: How did you first get involved with Stephen King's 99c babies, and how does it work?

Billy Hanson: Being from Maine, I've been a Stephen King fan forever, so I've always wanted to adapt his work. I heard about the Dollar Baby deal from an interview King did, can't remember where exactly, but I do remember wanting to jump on it immediately.

The Dollar Baby deal is an agreement set up by King himself, granting young filmmakers the rights to produce a film based on a selection of his short stories that have not yet been licensed for the screen. The only catch is that the films produced cannot be streamed online and more importantly, cannot generate any sort of revenue, so the filmmakers will be paying for these films with no hope of getting their money back. I've found however that it's not really a deterrent for hungry filmmakers, ready to tackle King's work.

Still, it's an amazingly generous deal from King, especially considering the amount of money he could be making from it, but he's always been a huge supporter of film, and so the deal has been in place since the late 70s. Hundreds of films have been produced under this deal, ranging from high school productions in the back yard to award winning festival gems. Having made one of these films myself, I can honestly say that it's a hugely rewarding experience, even if it is limited by the Dollar Baby contract.

Since making the film, I've organized two Dollar Baby Film Festivals, with another one possibly happening in late 2015. It's a great opportunity for people to catch these movies that they aren't able to find anywhere else, and it's a must for King fans who know the stories.

Joe: What made you choose *Survivor Type*?

Billy: Even though I've been a King fan for my whole life, the short story *Survivor Type* somehow slipped by me until just a few years ago. When I finally did read it, it knocked me on my ass and I was awake that whole night thinking about it. After that, I checked to see if it was on the Dollar Baby list and thankfully it was. I thought I could do the story justice and tell it with my own style, so I got to work right away on the script. I liked how it was coming out, so we went forward with the production. I honestly don't know if I would have done another Dollar Baby if *Survivor Type* hadn't been on that list.

Joe: What made you write your very first screenplay, and can you still recall what it was?

Billy: I remember it well. The first time I attempted a screenplay, I think I was maybe 13 or 14, and I wrote this strange high school time travel action story that kind of stalled out without making much sense. I'm not sure if there's a copy lying around my father's basement or not, but I think it's probably better lost to time. In it, I think someone traveled back in time to write a popular song before it could be written by the actual writer, and that devolved into lots of gunshots and car chases, and somebody's mom being murdered. Naturally.

Screenwriting has always been the best fit for me in terms of pacing and workflow, and I'm lucky enough to have known what I wanted to do since I was very young. My first attempt, as most first attempts go, was a rather embarrassing failure, but also taught me a lot about my own style, what appealed to me as a storyteller, and how to do things differently the next time around. I hope I can find a copy of that script someday.

Joe: What legal pitfalls should a screenwriter watch out for when writing or selling their scripts?

Billy: For a screenwriter, I would say don't worry about the legal side of things at all, unless a producer tells you specifically not to write something. A screenwriter is the only person on a film that has the benefit of (nearly) total freedom in what they work with, so there should be nothing, or at least very little that stands in their way of what they write. Let the clearances and the standards and practices people worry about that stuff. You write what feels right, make the script work properly before it's combed through by the legal team.

SCREENWRITING

Joe: **Would you recommend writing collaborative scripts to beginner screenwriters?**

Billy: I haven't actually written anything with another writer before, but I can say that collaboration is almost always a good thing. My writing got exponentially better when I started working closely with a writers group, and I still meet with them as often as I can after three years. Screenwriting isn't like a novel or poetry, where you can get really internal with everything and just write and write. Screenwriting is like architecture, its building and crafting and shaping and sculpting, so it requires a lot of re-writing to get everything to work perfectly to achieve the moments and the overall feel that you're shooting for. Often, the best way to get that kind of perspective is to have others weigh in and give you their thoughts. It's enlightening to have someone tell you that something isn't working the way you think it is. Then you take that information, and go back, find a way to fix it, and your script is all the better for it.

Joe: **What would you say are the biggest pitfalls when writing a script?**

Billy: It's pretty easy to fall into the trap of "making a movie" instead of "telling a story," especially if you've been hired to write something and you've got producers breathing down your neck about budgets and sex appeal and market value. The trick with great screenwriting is to manage all of those curveballs, but still be able to have a meaningful story at the heart of it.

I've screened at a ton of film festivals over the last few years, and the one thing that drives me crazy is that most of them are well-made, beautifully shot, decently-acted, but only a handful of them are well-written, fully realized stories. The same goes for Hollywood, lately. Even the buzzed about films of the last few years, aside from a precious few, are seriously lacking in terms of story.

Horror is unfortunately one of the victims of this trend, focusing on shocks and new ways to kill people, or just completely ripping off other films, rather than crafting original and captivating stories and characters. *The Babadook* is a film that people are raving about right now, and it's not because it's the scariest film, it's because it tells its own story and it tells it exceptionally well. You feel for the characters, you understand what they're up against and what they have to overcome to emerge victorious, and if they fail, the consequences are dire.

Your job as a screenwriter is to know the characters and the story better than anybody else, and your main goal should be to preserve those two things during the hellish and crippling process that is producing a film. It's easy to get wrapped up in the craziness, but as long as you can roll with the punches and keep your story intact, you're already ahead of the curve.

Joe: Are there any resources you can recommend to screenwriters? Online sites, workshops, books, or formatting programs?

Billy: *Save The Cat*, for sure. You may be thinking that you don't need to reference anything to be a screenwriter, that it comes naturally and you can't fight your instincts, and you'd be right to a point. Writing is re-writing, and it's never truer than in writing a script. With a book like *Save The Cat*, or even Sid Field's classic *Screenplay*, they don't present a set of rules you need to follow in order to cram your story into a cookie-cutter formula, but instead lay out a structure that makes you look at your characters and their problems in a different light. In fact, I found that I was already doing a lot of the things these books were suggesting, but being able to understand why certain moments felt necessary and what they did for my character arcs allowed me to hone in and strengthen everything. Realizing what each beat means in the sequence of an arc will clarify your instincts.

These books help to maximize your conflict and drama, and map out the best ways to build to a satisfying climax within the idea that you have and the world you've created. They'll also give you a few pointers on how to circumvent problems that are common and often discouraging to young screenwriters. It's reassuring to know there are ways around those, because they do happen, and if you don't see them coming, it can be deflating.

It boils down to the simple fact that in screenwriting, there are things that work and things that don't work, despite how subjective the whole thing is, and people who came before us have figured out how to make things work. I would highly recommend reading the *Save The Cat* series and *Screenplay*.

As for formatting programs, Final Draft is the standard, and it's not all that expensive, so I would say save up for that and you'll be set for years.

Joe: What kind of schedule do you keep when writing scripts on a deadline?

Billy: I've been lucky in that regard, because pretty much everything I've written—save for one film I was hired for—has been on my own schedule. That being said, I don't waste any time in moving forward. Most of my time is spent brainstorming, listening to music that might conjure up some images and ideas for scenes, that sort of thing. Then comes basic outlining and just writing little snippets of ideas for characters, and sometimes I'll even do some sketches of characters, locations, monsters (if there are any), just to get my head in the right head space for nailing down a theme.

Once I've got my hands on the core of the story, then I'll sit down and hash out a rough outline of the entire thing, beginning to end. This starts to focus in on where the conflict comes from and how the main character deals with it. That's my favorite part of the whole writing process, because it's really working my imagination and forcing me to think of the fun stuff, but it's all focused around one idea, so this is the most fertile time for useful ideas.

After letting the outline sink in for a week or so, I'll sit down and try to get through a first draft. If I've had enough time to prep, I can get through a draft in about six weeks, but it's by no means ready for people to read at that point. A first draft is always, and will always be, mostly garbage, jumbled ideas that don't work together, scenes that are forced and messy, but that doesn't mean it's bad writing. That's just the process. It's almost impossible to see the whole thing clearly before I've got a full draft in front of me, at which point I'll quickly see what works and what needs to go. That's when I dive into a re-write and start getting the pieces to do what I want them to.

All in all, I'd say I can write a solid first draft of a script in about 3 months, if I work on it every day. Life obviously interferes, especially since I produce and direct at the same time, but that's the basic brainstorming to first draft timeline I like to follow.

Joe: **What should you consider when choosing a location for your movie?**

Billy: It's pretty different for each project, and what you need from each location. But the basic things to look out for are practicality of shooting, transportation to and from, access for the art department to make changes (painting, building, set decoration . . . etc.), and simple things like where you'll pull power from, parking and bathrooms. Those are surprisingly difficult things to get sometimes, so it's something you need to really look out for, because you don't want to get a crew of thirty people out to a place only to realize that you have nowhere to go to pee all day. Believe me, it's happened, and it's not pretty. You'll end up carting people to the nearest gas station every thirty minutes.

Also, if you're shooting multiple locations in a day and one of them is an hour away, a lot of your day will be packing, unpacking, and driving. If that's not planned for, it can really put a damper on your day, as well.

After the practical requirements, you've got to find a place that's interesting to look at. Beautiful views or old decrepit buildings, anything that will draw an audience's eye is key. A lot of the great cinematography of the past is aided by beautiful locations, so when focusing on a visual style for everything, be sure to consider what you're going to have in the background of each shot. I'm a big fan of the John Carpenter style wide shots, but it's tough to pull those off without a great location to shoot in.

Joe: **What was it like working on the location of Survivor Type?**

Billy: That was a really tough spot to find. There was no way we could fake the entire film on a stage, nor did we want to try, so we had to find a place to shoot for four days. We considered a small island at one point, but the idea of hiring a boat to ferry the crew and the equipment sounded horrible, so after driving up and down the PCH in Malibu, we eventually found a big rock that juts far enough out into the water for us to shoot on three different sides and make it look like a tiny little island. We used one quick camera trick to do a full 360 degree look around, but after that it was just the three sides that sold it for us.

It was also important to me that we be able to have different spots on the rock that looked different enough to keep it visually interesting for the audience. It's a found footage film, so it would have been easy to just have him turn on the camera and have the empty ocean behind him every time, but we needed to imply that time was passing and that he was actually doing things, moving around, finding shade, fishing, trying to catch seagulls, and so on. We shot on every square inch of that tiny rock to make it feel like it was a little bigger, but at the end of the day, I think it works pretty well.

The rock was in Leo Carrillo State Park in Malibu, so there were a lot of tourists and beach visitors there. They were nice enough though, and when we told people that we were shooting they usually got out of our way quickly. It was surprisingly chilly for being on the beach during summer.The breeze was endless and when the sun went down, it got legitimately cold. Poor Gideon Emery was barefoot out on the wet rocks in very little clothing, giving his all for this great performance, and shivering the whole time.

The other thing that took us by surprise was how windy it got around sunset every day. We had sand and salt covering everything, including (somehow) the inside of all of our bags, coolers and cars. After every scene, I'd have to wipe down the camera lens and make sure there was no sand inside the gears and everything. Two years later, I still feel like I'm scraping sand out of my ears.

While it had a ton of difficulties, we were lucky to get that location. It looks great up on screen, and it's believable as an island alone in the middle of the ocean, which is really all we could have asked for.

Joe: **Do you have any advice for screenwriters or those interested in the field?**

Billy: Well there's a lot to say about screenwriting as a profession. It's a strange position, caught between the collaborative process of filmmaking, and the hyper focus needed to nail down character arcs and themes. It's full of rejections, disappointments and frustrations, but I'm one of the lucky people who stuck it out long enough to find some success with it. Here are a few pieces of advice that I would offer:

First, always be honest with yourself. You'll never be able to escape criticism in this business (nor should you try to), but one thing you can do is be 100% honest with yourself that your script is good enough to share. When I was starting out, I was so excited to get to that last FADE TO BLACK, and I just wanted to share it with friends and colleagues immediately. The drawback is that when they do read it, they'll probably just tell you it doesn't work and give you a list of notes that you already know need fixing. Then, you've got a handful of people who read something that's not actually representative of your writing talent, and ultimately, you get nothing helpful in return. Not to mention you've wasted a favor from that person and it will be that much harder to get them to read your next script.

One of the most valuable things I've learned is to take the time to go through a script a few times before anyone else reads it. Give yourself the opportunity to catch your own mistakes and solidify your ideas before others weigh in. If it's not good enough yet, if you have things you know you need to fix, don't send it out. If you have a time-sensitive opportunity, then stay up all night going through it again before sending it. I promise, you'll find things that you don't want other people reading.

I've ditched several ideas and outlines, even a couple of completed scripts, because they simply weren't that good. If something's not working for you then let it go, move onto something else, at least for a while. I know too many people in their early 30s, still tinkering with the first screenplay idea they had when they were 22. I'm guilty of this, too. At one point, I think I did ten fully revised drafts of a script that I already knew wasn't any good, and wasted about a year of valuable writing time just trying to get it to make sense. But the story itself wasn't great, and deep down I knew that from the start. Thankfully, only a few people read that one before I shelved it. I may go back to it in the future, but at the time I had other ideas that needed writing, which leads me to the next point:

You always have to be writing. So many people in L.A. will introduce themselves as writers, only to backpedal and say, "Well, I'm fleshing out a few ideas, but no scripts yet." There's a big difference between a writer, and someone who wants to be a writer, and it's very obvious to tell which category someone falls into. Do they have material? Writing well is difficult, and it's something you probably have to do while working a full-time job, but people get it done. Additionally, the more quality material you have, the better chance you have of someone noticing and being interested in you.

The dreaded scenario is when someone reads a script or sees a film and says, "Wow, this was great. What else you got?" That's happened to me before, a few times now, and I've always had something else to pitch them, or at least talk about. It gets you into rooms, it keeps people interested. They'll see not only that you can complete a project, but that you've got potential. Film festivals are the biggest opportunity for this, because you'll leave a theater and find yourself in a crowd with hundreds of other filmmakers that you may work with in the near future. So, you should always have something that you're writing.

Third, learn the production process. While most of your work will be done alone or with a couple other people in a quiet room, you're still in the movie business and should understand what will be done with your words as they go through pre-production, production and post. It will make your scripts better, cleaner and more efficient if you know the information a director will need for any given scene. Knowing how to properly lay out information on the page is a skill in itself, and if you understand the kind of decisions a director has to make in the hustle and bustle of set, you'll have a clearer understanding of just what to communicate on the page.

Lastly, and most importantly, just stick with it. It's the cliché thing that most successful people will tell you, but it's absolutely true. The people who fail are the people who quit. You also have to remember that there's not really such a thing as "making it." It's a business like any other, with lots of moving parts, so there's a place for aspiring writers, actors, directors, cinematographers, etc. You're not a failure if you're not famous in five years. If you're out here working, meeting people, creating material, contributing to the medium however you can, then you're doing alright. One day you'll look back and realize that even though you haven't gone to the Oscars and you're not best friends with movie stars, you've done some great things and been part of films you're proud of. That in itself is a rewarding experience.

Joe: **How involved do you think a screenwriter should be once production starts?**

Billy: Ideally, they'd be there through all of production to oversee any big changes and work to preserve the story. Sometimes that happens; sometimes a writer is already onto another project when filming starts. I think the latter is more often true. But as I've said a few times now, the filmmaking process is complicated and it's bound to real-world issues, so scripts have to be messed with to make a film work. While I feel like the screenwriter is the person most in charge of the story, the director is ultimately the person who will make the decisions on the day. If they need to change the script, they will, but it would be nice to think that the screenwriter is there to at least discuss it with them.

Joe: **Was it out of necessity that you stepped into a few acting roles, or is this something you always wanted to do?**

Billy: A bit of both. I started out acting a long time ago, and while it's not something I usually pursue, there have been a few occasions where friends will have a part for me, or need a favor, and I'll usually do it. It's really fun to be on the other side of things sometimes, and the different experience on set helps me when I'm directing. Also, and this is just my personality, I'm pretty much willing to humiliate myself on camera in any way my friends ask me to, so they know who to call when they've got somebody who needs to be humped to death on screen, or a guy that gets his penis bitten off by a zombie-hooker, or a super intense cop to bust up an illegal game of pogs. It's all lead to some pretty great experiences though and it's always interesting to work on something with a different set of responsibilities.

SCREENWRITING

Joe: **Except of course for a script, location and actors, what else do you need to start shooting your first film?**

Billy: Just the determination to figure it all out. Even on small productions, there are tons of moving parts, but if you manage to put together a script, camera, sound (never ignore your sound), actors, a place to shoot, and a way to edit, you can make a movie. That's why a good script is so important. I think the saying is, "You can make a bad movie from a good script, but you can never make a good movie from a bad script." If your writing is solid, people will forgive the wooden acting, or the sub-par lighting. If you have a good idea, get it done.

Be prepared to handle a wave of unforeseen problems, though. Productions are tricky to put together once you start dealing with variables like actors' schedules, make-up prep time, VFX planning, but if you have the patience to get the gear and the crew on set at the same time, you'll do alright. It's kind of like planning a party, but one with a delicate obstacle course that everyone needs to go through.

Joe: **Having won some awards with Survivor Type, how do you go about entering a finished short film into competitions and awards?**

Billy: There are a couple of websites that really help with the overwhelming task of submitting to festivals. There are thousands and thousands of them now, and it can sometimes be difficult to find the ones that aren't just collecting submission fees, but with a little bit of research, you can see which ones will be worth it. If you're looking to submit a film, you should create an account with either Withoutabox or Film Freeway. Both are free to join and will give you a comprehensive way to research festivals and provide a simplified submission process. It makes it easy to find the right fests and track all of your materials.

We had some great luck with *Survivor Type* because we had a plan of attack for when and where we would submit. We did research on what kind of films each festival had screened in the year prior, and found the ones most likely to want to share something as graphic and intense as *Survivor Type*. We tried not to submit to any festivals after their regular deadlines had passed, because by the time those late deadlines came around, the festival had already started choosing films and filling blocks of time, making our chances even slimmer than they already were.

The festival process can be just as frustrating as shooting the film, but if you do your research, find a good fit, and submit at the right time, you'll find more success and you won't throw away money on submission fees for festivals that were never going to accept your film in the first place. This is especially true for horror films. Even though they should, most non-genre festivals don't screen horror films. *Survivor Type* was screened at a handful of non-genre fests, and we had some great success there, but overall it was about 90% rejections. It's an unfortunate fact, and I would argue that one of our best screenings was at the Arizona International Film Festival, a tiny gem of a fest known for its huge selection of dramatic films, but it's something to keep in mind when submitting those $30-$75 fees.

SCREENWRITING: THE COMPROMISED ART

AARON STERNS

"Screenwriting . . . is the toughest part of the whole racket . . . the least understood and the least noticed."

Frank Capra

THE CRITICAL RESPONSE to films is often bemusing to the screenwriter.

The writer rarely gets mentioned in reviews (unless the movie's a stinker, in which case the script is often blamed—although I would guarantee the reviewer would've never read the script, or indeed even *a* script). Instead, the director is lauded as the sole visionary, and the actors up on the screen as the embodiment of the project—credited to such an extent it's as if they made up the dialogue and action on the spot.

This seems to be part of the long-established deal governing the screenwriter's place in the film world, but it doesn't mean it's not galling. Some producers see writers as a necessary evil to the process, resentful perhaps that they need someone to do the creative stuff they don't understand and upon which the whole house of cards relies. Perhaps directors are happy taking all the credit. Actors don't want the public to see through the charade and realize the massive team behind their ten foot emoting face. As Irving Thalberg once said, "The writer is the most important person in Hollywood, but we must never tell the sons-of-bitches."

Part of writing for film is the knowledge and acceptance you'll be treated like an over-willing prom date—courted, encouraged to put out, then most likely dumped once you've done the business. The best experience on a movie is when the writer is allowed to stay on board: through draft after draft to final shooting script, consulted on rewrites throughout production and allowed on set—even given a cameo if you're really lucky—and then becoming one of the voices in the editing suite and in post-production meetings (I was indeed privileged enough to stay in the loop throughout the shooting and post-production of both *Wolf Creek* and *Wolf Creek 2* thanks to the good graces of Herr director Greg McLean). It surprises me that this doesn't happen on more productions, even if just for the writer's ability to alert how alterations will affect logic and story—seeing as no-one's probably closer to the story, at least for a while than, you know, the person who wrote it. And yet that's the exception rather than the norm.

This wresting away of the story from the writer is necessary to some extent: the director has to pull the whole production together and channel the story through their vision, and the screenplay is a curious piece of creativity in that it is only ever a blueprint or guide to a finished product. Film is a collaborative medium interpreting and realizing a script into a coherent series of very expensively-staged moving images. The initial words on the page aren't—and can't be—the final vision of the film. The benefit of this for writers is that it can lead to an emotional liberation from the work (a developed skill that is handy when transposed to fiction, where most beginning writers see every word they write as golden and unchangeable). Part of learning screenwriting is accepting the script as entirely malleable. You'll encounter reams of notes, directorial interjections, dialogue changes from actors, last-minute rewrites due to budget disasters. For every (possibly apocryphal) tale of an *American Beauty* that is bought and filmed without a line of the script changed, most scripts will require a torturous reworking again and again and again. The idea at the heart of the script will be constantly attacked and challenged—so it better be strong. Yet while bad or conservative notes can lead to the work becoming unfocused or homogenous (if you listen to them, and part of the writer's job is knowing which advice is beneficial), the maelstrom of opinion can also strengthen and elevate the story. This can be difficult with the more-singular vision of fiction (which is usually shaped by a smaller group of author/agent/editor on behalf of the publisher/copy-editor). Of course, knowing when a script is finished—if it ever is—or whether the latest page-one rewrite is better or worse, is a brain-melting dilemma every screenwriter faces. But that's where it's *good* to have a director and producer who hopefully have a clear vision for the project, as well.

The shame is that the inevitable casting aside of the screenwriter leads to a suppression of their involvement with, power over, and contribution to the project. There's an old adage: Don't sleep with the screenwriter. While the joke niggles at me, it's also an important piece of advice: Be prepared for the casting aside, be thankful if you're allowed to hang around, and if you're not, at least bathe in the internal satisfaction of seeing your little idea up on the screen—even if it's not *quite* done the way you would have done it—and then move on to the next script. For no-one can stop you coming up with ideas except yourself.

An even more perplexing aspect about film reception though, is that it never seems to take into account the practical compromises which affect the script and its translation into a finished (or stagnated) film. Reviews and film criticism seem to see films as a fixed artefact created in an economic vacuum.

Perhaps this is understandable: It's human nature to judge what's before us, and the reviewer can't be privy to all the little machinations that influenced and moulded the work every step of the way up until the final moment the print hits the screen and it is set in stone. In fact, there's *no-one* involved in the film that can know every step of the process: the moments of self-censorship and structural wrangling in the writer's head through draft after draft, the editing decisions of the director in their pass of the script, the artistic or egotistical reasons an actor requests changes or adlibs on set, the film editor's ideas coming to the completed rushes with fresh eyes. Reviewers don't (or can't) take into account nervous editing following test screenings, budgetary constraints, accidents or hiccups during filming, reshoots or studio-mandated edits. They presumably also won't see the fifteen variations of the film during test screenings, so that when the final incarnation is finally locked in, it's hard for the filmmakers to remember the audience hasn't also seen all the variations, or the nice bits of character development sitting on the editing room floor.

Yet when is the reality of filmmaking or pressure of the

marketplace ever acknowledged when discussing a film? Most reviews seem to credit the filmmakers (or at least director) with full artistic control over the story, comparing the work only to others of its ilk, and either praising or criticizing it based on its decisions to go down a certain path. I personally like negative or downbeat endings in horror movies—because all our stories, if taken far enough, have a downbeat ending—and yet it's extremely hard to shepherd these through the process of film funding (I've had producers and investors 'encourage' me to shelve such endings for more audience-pleasing fare, as I'm sure many screenwriters have). I'm often reminded of the story that Andrew Kevin Walker sold the script for *Seven* only to then be requested to rewrite ten or more drafts without the 'head-in-the-box' ending. Lacking the emotional power of the first draft, the film looked headed for development hell until lead actors Brad Pitt and Morgan Freeman supposedly said they'd walk unless the story was returned to the original draft. And so one of the great endings in movie history played out on screen with the audience none the wiser. How inconsequential could *Seven* have been without the willingness to go down the dark path the movie works so hard to lay out? Yet this battle is wrought with perhaps every script (Walker is said to have distanced himself from *8MM* because the studio demanded the violence be toned down, and there were reported to be similar problems on *Sleepy Hollow*. I know the feeling).

This isn't intended as a request for reviewers—or movie watchers—to cut films slack. It should though highlight how impossible it is to demarcate sections of the filmmaking that work and those that don't, such as denigrating the quality of the writing but commending the acting—because where does one stop and the other begin? Rather than a reviewer (or the rest of us) criticizing a film for going down a certain route, or blaming a script they've/we've never seen, perhaps they/we could take into account the compromises that film has probably had to undertake along the way to even get made. And then if the film has still somehow retained its ambition and desire to challenge (which I would argue the *Dark Knight* series did, if we're talking tentpoles), it should be all the more championed. For this also isn't intended to be an excuse about how great a movie could have been, if only everything had gone right—

"you shoulda seen our ideas!"—but more to highlight how tenuous and haphazard the whole thing is, and how amazing that any films *ever* get made.

Most of the arts are what I would call limited. Sculpting for instance is necessarily limited by the laws of physics (what can and can't be wrought with stone and clay), by the technical limitations and knowledge of its practitioners, by access to the usual materials. Fiction is limited by the written word itself, language being one of humanity's main forms of expression and yet a frustrating and imprecise one (even if I'm only speaking for myself here). Music is predominately aural (though engenders a different experience when watched performed live or accompanied by video). Painting again is limited by the materials, and its two-dimensional approximation of imagery. All are limited by how they deliver their art to the public—either through the traditional establishment (theatre, television, gallery), or in more intimate, guerrilla ways. None are yet shunted straight into the brain *Matrix*-like, but have to be interpreted and completed in the receiver's mind, which is part of the endearing half-completed Roland Barthes quality of art.

Yet none of these mediums seem as *compromised* as film. Although a negative ending might feel more artistically satisfying to me, film is only partly (maybe peripherally) an artistic medium. The costs of making film as opposed to perhaps any other form of expression mean it is governed to a large extent by economic considerations—a return on the massive investment. Numerous articles have recently pointed to the notion that success in the film industry was once pursued by identifying well-written, engaging scripts, filming them with the resources at hand, and then deciding how to market and capture the audience. The 1970s and early '80s was an era of huge creativity in film, churning out socially-challenging, incredibly dark works like *Taxi Driver*, *Raging Bull*, *Apocalypse Now*, that would arguably struggle for release now. The costs of many films have become so exorbitant that a wider audience has to be pleased (upwards of $US200 million, plus half again in advertising for 'tentpole' films such as the seemingly script-free *Transformers* and *Pirates of the Caribbean*). And that means nullifying challenging themes and ideas, particularly when the international market is even more important than ever in the wake of challenges by the internet and other distractions to film's status as top of the culture tree.

Studios increasingly put all their effort into these big audience-drawing special effects bonanzas, hoping to make a safer and safer bet. A studio's entire future may rest on these films (the relative failure recently of *Transcendence* sent shockwaves through its backers). This has meant the quirky mid-tier films like the wonderful plethora of films we saw in the 1980s such as *Ghostbusters*, *Gremlins*, *The Terminator,* and *Highlander,* are disappearing. It's much harder—if not impossible—to secure funding for a $US10-20 million film than it was even ten years ago. These films used to be the bread-and-butter of assignment-based screenwriters and spec writers looking to sell new ideas.

But all is not lost.

Because the good news is that although it's difficult to get your wonderful anarchic, genre-expanding ideas through an increasingly-cautious set of studio and funding body hoops, the horror screenwriter can still make an impact, and there are still avenues. Many of the more ambitious, non-tentpole, non-overly-crowd-sycophantic ideas are finding their way into long-form television series (*True Detective*, *Breaking Bad*, *The Shield*, *Sons of Anarchy*, and of course actual horror shows finally appearing on TV like *The Walking Dead* and *Salem*). And while the majority of films coming out of studios now are the big tentpoles (mostly comic books, remakes and sequels of earlier successful tentpoles), the other type of films still being made are small micro-budgets and indies on budgets of $US1-2 million. Horror has historically been the most successful example of such films. *The Night of the Living Dead, The Evil Dead, The Texas Chainsaw Massacre*, and more recently *The Blair Witch Project* and *Paranormal Activity,* were all made on miniscule budgets but made massive returns. (*Blair Witch* was famously said to cost $US25,000 [though after studio-ordered reshoots, re-editing and a new sound mix was closer to $US500,000] and made $US250 million worldwide; and in Australia *Wolf Creek* cost US$1 million and became the highest-grossing R-rated film ever in that country, raking in about $US30 million worldwide, and even scoring the first horror sequel made in Australia). That doesn't mean every horror film can make such a return—and nor should that be your aim. All that should matter to the horror screenwriter is that these figures give them a bigger chance of getting their work up on the screen, and hopefully more following that.

For horror doesn't need to have massive budgets (and the few attempts at an A-list horror film rarely work—*The Exorcist* and *Silence of the Lambs* stand out precisely because big-budget films like *The Happening*, 1999's *The Haunting,* and *What Lies Beneath* failed so spectacularly). Horror is about the concept, the idea. The emotion of fear. It need only take place in one location (*The Evil Dead*), even one room (*Bug*). It doesn't have to play it safe, and indeed as long as the producer and director back you, smaller budgets should arguably give screenwriters more freedom to push the boundaries. Concentrate on finding a unique concept rather than rehashing old tropes. Aim for subversion rather than easy, gratuitous violence. Pare back the script of any unnecessary action or special effects. Make a statement.

With the new modes of distribution there are potentially even more ways for a film that stands out to find its audience. The theatre experience may be becoming limited for smaller budget films, but Video On Demand and the internet are opening up movies/visual narrative stories to a vast global audience. While some say the world of film is in a massive state of transition, even crisis—buffeted by competition to viewers' time and wallets, slumping ticket sales, the threat of piracy, and the narrowing of choice as mentioned above— it is still the dominant form of cultural expression, as it has been for the last hundred years. And in an increasingly-visual culture it looks set to retain that mantle for many years to come.

So even though you may be working (or aspiring to work) in a compromised art, and your role can indeed be annoyingly misconstrued and often overlooked, it just might be the best time of all to be a horror screenwriter.

NO BULLSHIT ADVICE FOR SCREENWRITERS

ERIC MILLER

THESE DAYS IT seems like everyone is writing a screenplay, or at least thinks they can. News flash: Writing a script is not easy, in spite of the seeming short length and lots of white space. Scripts look easier to write than novels, but they are not. You have to tell a story the same way a novel does in far less space and words, while adhering to a strict format and page count and relating it in a way that can be visually executed. A screenplay is very hard to get right, and most people never do. But that doesn't mean you shouldn't keep trying; most writers will get better with every script and every draft until eventually they master the craft. The ones that don't? Well, you can always be a producer.

Writing a good script is just the first step in your screenwriting career; after it is done, you have to sell it. Keep in mind that there are thousands of scripts written for every one that gets made. Maybe more. Selling a screenplay is a numbers game with odds worse than a casino. So you have to do everything you can to even those odds, to tilt the game in your favor. You can do that by presenting a terrific story, great characters, and stunning dialogue in a professional quality script. And by using the following tips, of course. Easy, right?

There are a thousand more tips and tricks than these, but space is limited here. So I'll touch on the lessons that come to mind most often when I am asked for advice. All were learned by me the hard way, so I hope they save you some time and anguish as you make your way down the path of becoming the next great horror screenwriter.

To start with, a screenplay should look like a screenplay. It should not look like a book, a magazine article, or a Twitter post.

SCREENWRITING

Proper screenplay format is essential. If your script does not follow it, your chances of being read—and produced—plummet no matter how good the material is. I know, this isn't the sexy, million dollar secret you were looking for when you started reading this article. But if you want someone to spend a couple of hours reading your script the least you can do is spend five minutes learning what proper format is. You can find it in books, on the internet, in scripts you can buy or borrow. Screenwriting programs will even automatically format your screenplay for you. I use Final Draft, as do most writers I know, but there are others. I suggest you buy one and use it. Otherwise your hard work could go unread.

Spelling and grammar count. Some readers will reject a screenplay if there are typos. Even one. Big time writers can get away with them; you have no excuse. Every computer writing program has a spell checker, and some have grammar checkers. Use them. Then have two friends check the manuscript for errors. Then you check it again. And I don't care that the script you downloaded for "Billion Dollar Grossing Sequel #4" was littered with typos and errors. That writer was most likely a well-connected, produced pro writer with a great agent. You aren't, or you wouldn't be reading this article looking for clues how to become a well-connected, produced pro writer with a great agent. So stop arguing with me and check for typos.

Screenplays should be between 90 and 120 pages long. And the closer to 90, the better. Only established writers get to turn in 150 page monstrosities. You should be lean, mean, and to the point. On a side note, no matter how long your script is, you will be told by pretty much everyone who reads it to "cut ten pages" or some similar length. It's an annoying Hollywood thing, but usually right; most scripts (even mine) could stand to have ten pages cut out. So grit your teeth, take the advice, and look for the extra fat that is surely lurking in your pages. And if you can't find any, just do what I do: Cut the two or three extra scenes you put in for the sole purpose of cutting them out later to "cut ten pages" and make the producer happy. And if you tell anyone my secret, I'll have to kill you.

Do not put large blocks of prose in your script. The more words there are on the page, the less likely the reader will read it. Use just enough words to explain what they should see, and no more. I try to never have a paragraph be longer than three sentences, but this is not a hard rule. Sometimes it is helpful to break up a page of description with dialogue even if none is called for. Like this:

ERIC MILLER
See how this inane dialogue makes
the page more visually appealing?

Having a character yell "hey" or something similar can make the script easier on the eyes. Just don't go overboard with tricks—try to write simple, clean text to start with.

Read your dialogue out loud. Or better, have some family, friends, or actors read it to you. The reason is simple: The way you write dialogue is most likely not how people talk. Take the example above. In the real world, I would never say something as grandiose as "visually appealing." I'd say, "makes it look better." Some writers have a gift for writing good dialogue, most of us do not have that innate talent. So until you master the craft, just talk it out. Say the dialogue out loud and use words your characters would use.

Try not to cut into conversations with extra stage directions. Basically, if people are talking, let them talk, unless a stage direction or action comment is critical. This helps the reader—and the writer— get into the flow of the dialogue and makes the characters come alive.

Use the same character names consistently through the script. In other words, if the character is named "Bob Smith," use either "Bob" or "Smith." Do not bounce back and forth. And try to avoid using character names that sound or look alike. This can confuse the reader. And a confused reader is a bad thing.

Do not number your scenes. The production staff will do that.

Limit the use of "Cut To" and "Fade To" and similar transitions. Most of the time a new scene heading is all you need.

Do not use "Continuous" or any other similar word in your scene headings to denote the time of day, when the action is carried over from the previous scene. Use "Day" or "Night" or similar times. Yeah, yeah, every other script in Hollywood has "Continuous" in it. And guess what? Production people hate the word. Because when a breakdown is done the scenes get ripped away from each other and there's no way of knowing when the previous scene took place. So your cute little "Continuous" is really just "Confusing Us." Just tell us the freaking time the scene takes place, already.

When writing a horror script, keep in mind that all of the people reading it might not be hard-core fans of the genre. So large amounts of detailed gore might turn them off. The difference between "Bob's head hits the wall and leaves a dark stain" and "Bob's head hits the wall with a sharp crack and his brains splatter everywhere, drenching the room with fountains of bright red blood, slimy guts and yellow-green vomit" might not seem like much to *you*—but it might be to the executive who reads it. Focus on writing a story with some gore, not a dissection manual. Find a happy medium on the page, and let the FX guys figure the nastier bits on set. Unless you *know* James Wan or Eli Roth or a similar gore-lover is going to personally read the script—then let the face-ripping begin. In glorious detail.

Be wary about writing for free (or deferred payment) on a project you don't own the rights to, such as when a producer or director asks you to write a script based on his idea or property. Sometimes it is worth the shot, especially if the producer is a reputable person with extensive industry credits. When you are starting out, it sometimes helps to get a foot in the door with an unpaid assignment. I have done it (one too many times, unfortunately) and while none of those projects got made, they did lead to further paid work. Just be careful, and remember that the time you are spending writing the producer's project for free could be time spent writing your own.

Real agents and managers do not charge you for representation. They take a percentage of your earnings. If someone tries to charge you up front, run. It is a scam.

Have an entertainment attorney review your contract before you sign it (you *did* get a contract, didn't you?). Notice I specifically said "an entertainment attorney." Your uncle the divorce lawyer is not right for this. There are lots of low-cost lawyers in Hollywood, and some will even work on contingency, but whatever you pay, it will be worth it in the end.

Write the script *you* want to write. This is the one lesson I wish I had followed more over the years. You know the story you want to tell, so tell it. I don't care if your agent or writing partner or some producer wants you to do something else. If they are paying you, fine. Write what they pay you for. But your free time is *yours*—so write the script *you* want to write. Years from now you will thank me for telling you this.

And remember, writers *write*. Posers sit at Starbucks pretending they are writing so people will ask what they are working on and they can make new friends and/or feel important. "A screenplay" is generally regarded as way sexier than "an email to my Mother," which is what the majority of people at Starbucks are really writing. Real writers are at home typing away at the next great American screenplay. Or a monster movie for the Syfy Channel. Either way, writing is not a social game. It is serious business. Get serious about it. Write every day. Set schedules. Don't go to bed or watch TV or do anything else until you have done your pages for the day. Don't talk about it or dream about it—do it. Writers *write*.

After you follow all these and other rules, and write the most perfect screenplay that was ever written and made angels weep for joy and then manage to sell it, you will get story notes from the producer for the rewrite, a dreaded process that will blow up your beloved script and turn it from a horror masterpiece into a musical comedy. Ok, notes usually aren't *that* bad, but they can be brutal when you are in love with your screenplay. But no matter how much you hate them, notes are part of the movie-making process. So you *will* follow them, or you will be fired and some hack (I'm available, call me) will be brought in to do the rewrite. You will probably be fired anyway, even if you manage to incorporate all the notes, but that's a story for another time. Welcome to Hollywood.

ME AND THE SERIAL KILLERS

STEPHEN JOHNSTON

FOR ME IT started when I was a kid and I stayed up late, unbeknownst to my parents, and watched *Abbot and Costello Meet Frankenstein* on the late night creature feature. I was transfixed. Previously I had known monsters as creatures from the stories my parents told me when they tucked me into bed at night. Now I saw them made flesh. Some time later I learned the scariest monsters are in fact human.

When I first heard the name Ed Gein it was in the context of movies like *Psycho* and *Texas Chainsaw Massacre* and *Silence of the Lambs*. He existed as a real life boogeyman, the horrific inspiration behind books and movies, but he himself remained obscured in the shadows. Like some sort of murderous Wizard of Oz, he had never stepped out from behind the curtain.

I decided to look behind the curtain. What I discovered was Gein had been defining psychopathic behavior before it was fully understood or defined as a pathology by the world at large. Talk about a trailblazer, he was the Chuck Berry of homicidal behavior, and his back-up singers were the lost souls of the graves he desecrated. My thought was, instead of creating a fictionalized account inspired by his actions, why not tell his story as is actually happened, in all its horror, a monster movie made scary for being all too real . . .

OPEN ON A BLACK SCREEN.

The WIND HOWLS. The disembodied VOICES OF CHILDREN can be heard laughing and giggling as they recite a silly rhyme in unison . . .

> *CHILDREN (v.o.)*
> *There was an old man named Ed*
> *Who wouldn't take a woman to bed*
> *When he wanted to diddle,*
> *He cut out the middle,*
> *And hung the rest in his shed.*

That was the opening of my script. As it unfolded, I focused on telling the story of a monster who was still very much a man. I didn't flinch from the horror, nor did I shy from the humanity. Provocative storytelling comes down to balancing the two, the darkness and the light, especially when working within the horror genre. Screenwriting (or any storytelling) inevitably involves a protagonist and antagonist. This goes back to Grimm's Fairy Tales and Westerns with John Wayne wearing a white hat. There's always a good guy and a bad guy (even if sometimes the bad guy comes in the form of an obstacle, or in my case the main character's own unraveling psyche). I strove to write a movie that would be a balancing act between the two conceits, with a main character who was both protagonist and antagonist at the same time. A man made monster. I was treading upon some of the same ambivalence inspired by Frankenstein's Monster; the creature's actions were horrific, but the monster was humanized. I was doing the opposite: making the human monstrous.

ANGLE ON ED

Ed sits at the end of the bar, nursing a half-empty bottle of beer. The moment he realizes Gus and Leonard are laughing at him, he averts his eyes, embarrassed at having been caught eavesdropping.

> *LEONARD*
> *Yeah. How 'bout it, Ed? Wanna share some*
> *of your vast knowledge of the female gender*
> *with those of us less informed?*

That was an early scene in which I'm trying to illustrate Ed as a sympathetic character, a sort of village idiot tolerated by townspeople, but condescended to at the same time and never really made to feel part of the community. He was bullied, not just by his overbearing mother, but his environment, as well. This wasn't meant to mitigate the horror he perpetrated, but to provide a context in which it happened, grounding the story in reality and thus making the horror of it real in the process.

With my script thus grounded in reality, I decided to introduce a subplot of the unreal, to serve as a sort of metaphor for Gein's fracturing psyche: his mother as not just an overbearing oedipal influence, but a ghostly presence made literal.

MOVING OUT

Revealing more and more of Ed, his sleeping form, the covers at the foot of the bed, the refuse surrounding the room, as the SOUND OF THE ROCKING CHAIR GROWS LOUDER . . .

ANGLE ON AUGUSTA GEIN

Sitting at the foot of Ed's bed, rocking slowly in a high-backed wooden rocking-chair, is his Mother. The putrid, rotting flesh that was once her face masks her perpetual frown . . .

My intention was twofold; I wanted to show Ed as a character psychologically troubled by the incessant misogynistic preaching of his mother, but also present him as literally haunted by her. Part of the purpose was narrative metaphor, but at the end of the day I just wanted to scare the pants off people.

When I finished the script I called it *In the Light of the Moon*, after a Slayer song they had recorded about Ed and his exploits, and I even entertained fantasies about making the movie with a similarly heavy soundtrack. Then I mothballed the whole idea and made the pilgrimage to Hollywood, and my goal of getting the movie made was overshadowed by my need to get a job, pay rent, and feed myself.

Then came the fateful day when a conversation about me took

place, and I wasn't even present. A friend of mine met with film distributor/producer Hamish McAlpine. Hamish had on his desk a bust of Ed Gein, and upon seeing it my buddy Mark said, "Hey, my friend has a script about that guy." Initially skeptical that somebody would have taken the time to write about such a subject, Hamish said he'd like to read it. The rest, as they say, is all history.

We were in production within six months, with Steve Railsback as Ed and Carrie Snodgrass as his mother. When completed the movie would win Best Picture at the prestigious Sitges Film Festival in Spain, and I was awarded Best Screenplay at the Fantafestival in Italy. During the year of its release on video, it would earn a spot in the top twenty-five highest grossing releases, the only title on the list that wasn't a studio release.

There's an adage in Hollywood (as in the rest of the world) that says follow the money. Adhering to this philosophy, we promptly decided to make a sequel. Of course, within the realm of this new serial killer biopic genre we'd stumbled upon creating, the very concept of sequel was turned on its head. We couldn't very well make a movie about Ed Gein in prison, so the decision was made to expand on the concept, and follow up our first movie with a companion piece of sorts, documenting a different sort of human monster.

Ted Bundy as a character was completely dissimilar to Ed Gein. Gein was *pre-modern*, before a general understanding of his sort of pathology even existed, while Bundy was a *modern* reality, whose horrific actions would make the term serial killer part of the popular lexicon. Ed was socially crippled and a momma's boy, whereas Ted was erudite, and devious. If Gein was The Beatles, Bundy was the Rolling Stones. Bundy was evil made charming.

ANGLE ON TED

Several feet behind Maher, Ted gathers up the load of books he's just dropped, favoring the cast on his arm.

Maher walks back and smiles at him . . .

SCREENWRITING

> MAHER
> *Only time I ever see anybody carrying that many books,*
> *they're studying to be a doctor.*

This was the sort of gambit Bundy used to draw victims into his spider-web, so I figured I'd write the script accordingly, like a sociopath with a sunny smile at first blush, and a razor sharp knife revealed just beneath the surface. In short, I set out to write a romantic comedy turned upside down.

She looks to the floor at her feet, then feels beneath her seat. Shocked, she finds a metal hatchet . . .

> LIZ
> *. . . Ted?*

> TED
> *I don't know where your keys are, Liz.*

> LIZ
> *Why d.250 you have this?*

Irritated, Ted walks back and looks in the car. He's obviously surprised to see her holding the hatchet, but he puts the best spin on it . . .

> TED
> *It's for chopping wood. Why does anybody have a hatchet?*

Bundy was a monster, but as a personality type he was different than Gein, and thus telling his story required a different approach. If the adage is life imitates art, and vice versa , the script about Bundy required a lighter touch. The material would be just as dark, but Bundy was charming where Gein was aloof, Bundy was warm where Gein was cold. To the degree there's humor in *Ed Gein*, it's incidental. In *Ted Bundy* I decided to make it more overt. Humor, when black, cuts with the same razor's edge as horror. A large part of this construct is when the horror came it would sound with the finality of a dead joke . . .

Inside this place, Janice Ott returns to consciousness, blinking at the blood that's run into her eyes. She's bound and gagged, her wrists hand-cuffed to a rusting engine.

As abject terror overcomes her, she screams into the gag in her mouth and struggles against the hand-cuffs. Neither effort accomplishes anything.

Then a CAR PARKS OUTSIDE, and she looks up hopefully.

The door to the shed is pushed open, and Ted enters, pulling a barely conscious Naslund behind him. He pushes Naslund to the floor and turns his attention to Ott . . .

TED
Hello, princess. Miss me?

This causes Ott to scream into her gag some more.

TED
Exercise in futility, my dear. Only people who can hear you are me and her. She can't do anything, and I invited you to this party.

Somewhere along the way, while writing this sort of diseased romantic comedy involving a homicidal Svengali, I came to realize I would have to rely on the director, producers and, in particular, the actor who would play Ted, to interpret the material accordingly. When attempting to blend the blackly comedic with the horrific, if you miss the mark you risk ending up with a finished product that's satisfying on neither count. This brings up an issue that seems rarely considered by aspiring screenwriters: You have to remember the screenplay must stand on its own, but also serve as a blueprint for the movie. You might very well write the most structurally sound screenplay ever written, that is a blueprint for a movie nobody wants to see, or more importantly, produce. You're not writing a book, where the only words that matter are your own. As a composition a screenplay may work on its own, but if a movie isn't made from it, then it's just an exercise. Hollywood is replete with stories about "great screenplays" that are "unproducible." That's like a chef who never gets past writing recipes.

Anyway, end of digression. In the case of *Bundy* I was fortunate; Matthew Bright came onboard as director, and his approach tonally was ideal. Michael Reilly Burke was cast as the eponymous character, and he brought to the role the perfect mixture of charm and menace, humor and horror. The resulting movie rather admirably maintained a balance between charm and revulsion, not unlike Ted Bundy himself did in real life.

Now that we had successfully completed two serial killer bio-pics, each serving as informal chapters charting the evolution of the modern American serial killer, the decision was made to turn the "franchise" into a trilogy and make a final companion piece, this one documenting the arrival of the *post-modern* era. Ladies and gentlemen, I give you the *Hillside Strangler*.

The series sex murders initially attributed to a single "Hillside Strangler" were, in fact, the gruesome work of two people, a pair of cousins whose failure as singular human beings was only superseded by the horror they wrought as a sadomasochistic team of serial killers. If Ed Gein was The Beatles and Ted Bundy was the Rolling Stones, then Ken Bianchi & Angelo Buono were the Sex Pistols.

The challenge in writing this particular script lay in how thoroughly detestable the two protagonists were. The successful creation of a character, even one based in reality, is realized by finding their ambivalence as human beings. Bianchi and Buono had no such ambivalence; separately, and especially as a duo, they were devoid of anything most people would regard as redeeming human qualities. These were the kind of guys who possessed the charm of something you find at the bottom of a septic tank.

So the challenge confronting me was how to write a compelling script about two guys who were undeserving of any attention beyond clinical case study. Obviously the plot was already laid out before me, but how was I to approach their story in a way that was interesting beyond the luridness? This was a genuine challenge. As I've said, storytelling in general, and screenwriting specifically, isn't simply a matter of relating moments in chronological detail, it's about describing a journey. Confronted with protagonists who were corrupt from the get-go, it was hard to create an overreaching character-arch for them to follow. Then I realized that *was* the soul of the story; their arch was that they had none. My protagonists were two failures as human beings who would never know recognition beyond that accomplished by their horrific actions. This was evil as banality.

Ken and Angelo sit on the couch with EMILY and SARAH, two girls who look barely old enough to drive, watching a PORNO VIDEO on television, passing a JOINT . . .

> ANGELO
> (at television)
> . . . that chick's takin' it up the ass!

Emily and Sarah giggle as if this were the height of humor. Standing, Angelo takes Emily's hand and pulls her toward the bedroom . . .

> ANGELO
> Come on, honey. I wanna get somethin' straight between us.

He swats her on the fanny and she trots obediently to the bedroom. Then Angelo turns back to Ken and Sarah . . .

> ANGELO
> You two gonna be able to keep each other entertained?

> KEN
> We'll see what comes up.

SCREENWRITING

ANGELO
Yeah. Okay. But fuckin' get your ass outta bed and find a fuckin' job tomorrow.

I had cracked the nut and realized the best approach to the script was to tell the story of these two despicable dudes in a straight forward and naturalistic fashion, like a documentarian without authorial embellishment. I had written *Ed Gein* according to a structure that mimicked his fractured psyche, and *Ted Bundy* I told in a blackly comedic fashion that was in keeping with his personality. *Hillside Strangler* I approached with the unflinching perspective of studying bacteria under a microscope. Writing the rest of the script followed accordingly.

If my attention to *Hillside Strangler* seems brief, it's because as a script it didn't require a lot from me. Once I figured out my approach to telling the story, I had little to add as a screenwriter, beyond the obvious. I'm proud of the finished product, and C. Thomas Howell and Nicholas Turturro did great work, but it's not one I feel I have an "authorial stamp" on.

At the end of the day, screenwriting is an instrumental part of making a movie, but make no mistake, it's still very much a discipline of writing. Storytelling (notice I keep using the term) is what it's all about, and a large part of the challenge isn't simply telling the story, it's ascertaining the best way the story should be told. Structure is a key part of the craft, but if you don't tell a story, and create characters who follow a satisfying arch, nobody's going to want to read your script, let along make it into a movie. In the case of the three scripts I've spoken about, I may have been relating real life events, but I allowed the subject in each case to dictate how I approached telling the story. This applies whether writing a script about imaginary monsters, or the all too real ones.

PLACEBO INTERVIEW AND SCREENPLAY

AARON DRIES

GUESS 'ROUND here you could consider me amongst the newer kids on the block. Right now, I'm an author and short filmmaker, but who knows what the future holds? I'm a fly-by-the-seat-of-your-pants kind of guy. There's plenty more room on that block for me to explore. When I'm not writing or behind the camera, I paint, illustrate, and work as a video editor. I'm a full time *hungerer*. I proudly stand in the shadows here with everyone else, writers and filmmakers whose appetites, I imagine, are as strong as my own. The moment you stop being hungry for more, you start to fail. I really believe that.

My novels include *House of Sighs* (about a lonely bus driver who kidnaps her passengers and takes them home to meet the family who drove her to insanity), *The Fallen Boys* (about a father's journey to find out why his young son committed suicide, discovering a secret Internet bullying network, and a hell-bent serial killer along the way), and the recently published *A Place For Sinners* (about a woman's nightmarish trip to a Thai island where she and other backpackers must fight for their lives as the remote location spills its secrets, and reveals hidden inhabitants both human and very . . . otherwise).

I've written and directed a number of short films, but the one that opened the most doors for me, the one that truly shaped my career, was *Placebo*. I owe everything to that film. It was made for no money, with no-name actors, with borrowed equipment, but a hell of a lot of love, dedication, and determination. It payed off. Big-time. We're all nothing without the big bang that brought us to where we stand now.

Placebo was that for me.

SCREENWRITING

Joe: **What made you write your very first screenplay, and can you still recall what it was?**

Aaron: My first completed feature-length screenplay was for *House of Sighs*. I never actively shopped it around. There just wasn't time. I was in my early 20s, backpacking abroad, and I stumbled into a bookstore and found a copy of Rue Morgue Magazine. In it was an advertisement for the *Dochester/ChiZine/Rue Morgue Fresh Blood Writing Contest for Unpublished Authors*. The first prize: a publishing contract. But it was three months until the deadline. Could I write a novel in such a short time span? I took the screenplay for *House of Sighs* and adapted it into a novel, whilst still backpacking. I used borrowed laptops, wrote in long-hand, banged away in grimy hostels. Somehow, I got it done. And after a year's worth of Survivor-esque elimination rounds, I actually went on to win first prize. That's how my first novel, *House of Sighs*, actually came to be. And the rest, as they say, is history. But the seeds of the screenplay for *House of Sighs* started many years earlier.

Joe: **What were those seeds? Where did it start?**

Aaron: They started with an award-winning short film I made at University called *Placebo*, the original screenplay for which is published here for the first time. The spirit (and some of the content) of *House of Sighs* began with that eleven minute short. *Placebo* was about . . . denial. How about that for keeping things spoiler free? It played in festivals worldwide, got me connections in the industry, got me a job. They still show the film at my university, which is a real honor. The short *really* worked. It was surreal; people were moved by it; and it evoked screams.

Joe: **Where did you get the idea for *Placebo*?**

Aaron: A true incident. I was a teenage pizza delivery boy. There was a woman on my route who always ordered for herself and her three children every week. I never saw the father. I remember her as being beautiful; and those kids were gorgeous, too. One day, however, the orders stopped coming in. She never called our store again. It turned out she shot her three children and then turned the gun on herself.

This rocked me to my core.

What would make a seemingly sane woman commit such an awful crime? What happened behind the door I had stood at so many times over? That house looked like any other. Actually, looking back, it reminds me of the one I grew up in. It had the same eye-like windows built into the façade.

I dreamt about that family. The only way I could sweat them from my system was through writing. That writing turned into *Placebo*.

I still remember that woman's order. Two Supreme Pizzas, one Vegetarian. No sloppy meat pizzas for her kids. It was as though she cared about their health. Or maybe it was just some kind of awful joke I didn't know I was a part of.

Interestingly enough, just last year, I went to visit my grandfather's grave. I hadn't been in a long time, and I remember feeling guilty about that. As I laid down my flowers I noticed the gravestones next to his. That woman and her children were buried right there.

Neighbors. Knowing this chilled me.

Joe: **So what's next for you? Any future goals you're working on? Writing advice?**

Aaron: Survive. Survival is everything to me. In order to do that I've got to keep on creating. Like a shark, it's imperative I push on. I'm working on a trilogy of horror novels right now, and there are more short stories and novellas on the horizon. I'm always writing spec scripts, illustrating, and developing future films.

All I want to do is move people, create an emotional reaction that they won't forget. And I don't know, or necessarily care, through which medium I achieve that—be it books, movies, or art. I'm a determined son of a bitch. I have no other choice. A shark has got to keep on moving.

As for advice, I'm going to K.I.S.S. Keep it simple, stupid, as my dad used to tell me.

So here we go.

SCREENWRITING

Firstly, show some restraint. When it comes to your first feature screenplay, don't write a two-hour epic. Less is more. Aim for that magic 90 pages mark on the understanding that one page equals one minute of film, even if it doesn't. Remember: you get the viewer's first 90 minutes for free, but every second that comes after must be *earned*.

Secondly, learn how to write. You'd be insanely surprised by how many people can't. Grammar, spelling, and structure is important. Close to every amateur script I read is poorly composed. The mechanics of storytelling are too often forgotten because of a writer's enthusiasm over his concept.

Thirdly, if there isn't a hook on the first page, you're just another Joe Nobody being sent back into the crowd with your hat in your hand. That doesn't need to be a plot hook, by the way. It can be a character, a situation, the development of a mystery, a revelation, a snappy line, a striking image. Just get their attention. And fast.

Fourthly, write what you know. It's an old but good adage. So you're a dish-pig at a pizza restaurant? Hey, that's okay. That's where I started out, too. But you're a dish-pig who wants to write a science fiction epic. Awesome! Try writing your script from the perspective of the mess hall kitchen-hand on the primary Star Fleet as opposed to the captain. I'd read *that* story. The only way you'll rise above the stinking piss and masturbatory spermatozoa of the writerly world is to reveal something of yourself in your work. Your fetishes, mistakes, obsessions, flaws, and passions, all of your *shit*—it'll float above the rest. Anyone can write a screenplay, but only *you* can write *yours*.

And lastly, you've got that script into the hands of someone who loves your project and the light has turned green. You also want to direct. That's awesome. So do I. Let's keep it humble, okay? There's enough ego in the world already. Don't forget that this is your first endeavor into the cinematic landscape.

It's not *A Film by Aaron Dries*.

It's: *Written and Directed by Aaron Dries*.

Like time, like pretty much anything worth a damn in this weird world, certain credits must be earned. And that goes for me, too. Always.

PLACEBO

BY

AARON DRIES

COPYRIGHT 2005

PLACEBO BY AARON DRIES

EXT. DRIVEWAY—DAY

There is BIRDSONG, the rustle of LEAVES, and crunching GRAVEL as ELIJAH (23) draws close. He's dazed and confused, a state that clouds the otherwise keen intensity of his handsome face. He's covered in BLOOD SPLASHES, and holds a silver HARMONICA.

He doesn't know what he's doing, but we watch—equally unsure yet compelled—as he breathes a single note of MUSIC into the instrument.

Whatever confusion had been holding Elijah captive vanishes. His eyes grow alert, and after a beat, widen with disbelief.

TITLE CARD: PLACEBO

INT. ELIJAH'S BEDROOM—DAY

It's EARLIER THAT MORNING and Elijah is in BED. Morning LIGHT spills into the drab room. Elijah's CELL PHONE BEEPS; it's on the windowsill next to a framed PHOTOGRAPH of his girlfriend, SANDY (22). She's a good-old-fashioned knockout, with her long brown hair, those huge and empathetic eyes. Elijah grabs the phone. It's a TEXT.

At that moment, the door to his room opens and we see the inquisitive, bright faces of Elijah's soon-to-be-beautiful SISTER (13) and his cute-as-a-button BROTHER (9), who wears a red and white SANTA'S HAT.

HORROR 201: THE SILVER SCREAM

                    SISTER
        Oh, he's already awake.

The two kids cross the room and jump on Elijah's
bed.

                    SISTER
        Wake up, sleepy-head. It's almost
        eleven!

                    ELIJAH
        Okay, okay. I'm awake.

                    BROTHER
        Hurry up. I want my lunch!

                    ELIJAH
        Oh, do you? What day is it, again?

                    SISTER
        It's Christmas, you der-brain.

                    ELIJAH (PLAYFUL
        Oh, is it? What does *that* mean?

                    SISTER
        It means we get presents.

Brother glances at the cell in Elijah's hand.

                    BROTHER
        Oh, a message! Is that from your
        ghuurl-friend?

                    SISTER
        Is that a message from Sandy?

150

PLACEBO BY AARON DRIES

                    BROTHER
        A message from lover-girl!

                ELIJAH (SMILING)
        Hey you two. Don't be immature.

Sister gives him a friendly slap. Elijah feigns
hurt.

                    SISTER
        You deserved it.

        BROTHER (PRETENDING TO READ MESSAGE)
            'Dear Elijah. I *love* you. I want
            to *sex* you. I wanna have your *babies*.'

                    ELIJAH
        Yeah, you're all so clever. Off now.
        Gotta get up. Christmas is coming.

                SISTER (LAUGHING)
        Christmas *is* here, you goober.

It's all fun and games. But as the two younger kids
leave—Brother stopping to poke his tongue out before
closing the door—all of the warmth in that room
freezes over. Elijah stills. Alone. He finally READS
the message. Brother was right. It is from Sandy

MESSAGE READS: **Hi Elijah. Merry X.Mas. Hope ur
doing ok. So is ur dad coming? You'll be fine.
Ur tough. Just ask yourself what u can do to make
this better. xSandy**

INT. BATHROOM—DAY

151

WATER BEADS off Elijah's dread-infused face. He steams melancholy in the calm of the shower stall, the glass FOGGING OVER.

EXT. HOUSE—DAY

The HOUSE itself is a run-of-the-mill, nondescript assembly of weatherboards and unfinished RENOVATIONS. The kind of place you glance at without thinking twice. It could be *any* house, *anywhere*.

MOTHER (39) stands in the DOORWAY to the BACKYARD where Brother and Sister are playing tag. Mother is dressed in her FESTIVE REDS AND GREENS, with a WHITE OVEN GOWN on top. She watches her kids with a look that suggests, *yes, despite everything, we made it*. Mother is well versed in the domestic charade that has become her life.

INT. BATHROOM—DAY

Elijah TOWELS himself dry and stands before the MIRROR, concentrating. Fakes a smile. He's prepping himself for another performance, another day of denying how he feels. He holds an IMAGINARY PRESENT as though it were a skull, and this a lazy rendition of Shakespeare in the Shower.

> ELIJAH (TO IMAGINARY PRESENT)
> Oh, thank you. I love it.
> It's just what I wanted—fuck!

PLACEBO BY AARON DRIES

EXT. HOUSE—DAY

Mother waves her kids in.

                    MOTHER
          Come on! In for lunch!

Brother and Sister come a-runnin'. They pass
CHRISTMAS CUT-OUTS of two ANGELS, one MALE and
one FEMALE, propped up on the lawn.

INT. HOUSE / HALLWAY—DAY

The kids RUN down the hallway.

                    ELIJAH (V.O.)
          Yeah, these things happen. It's
          okay. Fuck! . . . I LOVE my present.
          It's just what I wanted.

Mother closes the door. Her smile fades as she
leans against the frame. Time to face the music.
We're beginning to understand that the adults in
this family have perhaps hurt the kids, and
Elijah has taken it the worst. All this and more
is right there in Mother's haunted expression.

                    ELIJAH (V.O)
          I hate you most . . .

INT. BATHROOM—DAY

Elijah averts the reflection. He can't stand
looking at himself.

> ELIJAH
> Stop talking to yourself.

> MOTHER (O.S)
> Elijah, lunch is ready!

> ELIJAH (WITH RESIGNATION)
> Just ask yourself, what can you do
> to make this better?

INT. DINING ROOM—DAY

The dining room is decked in full CHRISTMAS REGALIA—TINSEL, a big BANNER. There's a hot ROAST on the TABLE, plus DRINKS, and PARTY FOOD. It would seem this year's Christmas theme is 'over-compensating!'

Mother leans over the roast, KNIFE poised. Brother and Sister are sitting there. Brother plays with one of his new toys: a JAR OF MULTICOLORED MARBLES. He FLICKS one across the table and Sister snatches it up. She's envious—not that she wants the marbles, just what her brother has. Teasing is the foundation of their relationship.

> MOTHER (WITH A TINGE OF IMPATIENCE)
> Elijah, I said lunch is ready!

INT. BATHROOM—DAY

Elijah runs a comb through his hair.

                    ELIJAH
          Okay. Time to smile. Back straight.
          Here we go.

INT. DINING ROOM—DAY

Elijah enters. He's dressed in A PLAIN WHITE T-
SHIRT. He stops in the doorway, affronted by the
garish decorations.

Mother is in the process of pouring her two
youngest kids a drink. She makes eye contact
with Elijah. Stops. It's a brief but very real
stalemate. Elijah notices that there is no place
set for his father.

Mother rounds the table and approaches her
eldest son, pulls him into a hug. Elijah fights
it at first, but caves in. He loves her, there's
no denying that, regardless of the decisions she
has made in the past.

Brother and Sister exchange an awkward glance.
Their mother might think they're too young to
know what's going on, but they know.

Kids always do.

                    MOTHER (TO ELIJAH)
          You okay?

                    ELIJAH
          Yeah. All's cool.

> MOTHER
>
> Good boy. You can sit at the head
> of the table if you like.

INT. CAR—DAY

We're inside a MOVING CAR. FATHER'S hands (39)
clench the wheel. CHRISTMAS CAROLS play through
veils of RADIO STATIC.

INT. DINING ROOM—DAY

Lunch is underway. Elijah has taken his seat at
the head of the table. Cutlery CLINKS,
interrupting long stretches of silence. Until—

> BROTHER
> Mom, can we open our presents?
> Ple-eeasse?

> MOTHER
> After lunch we'll all sit down
> together.

EXT. COUNTRYSIDE—DAY

The car weaves its way through the LANDSCAPE,
past skeletal TREES.

INT. DINING ROOM—DAY

The silence has grown thick. Elijah swallows a
lump of food and takes the initiative.

ELIJAH (TO BROTHER)
Like the food? Chicken's nice, don't
you reckon?

Brother looks at Elijah, tired of this
particular game, over being under-estimated.

BROTHER
You didn't cook it. *Ma* did.

Mother, her sad eyes unblinking, takes a bite.
The FORK SCRATCHES against her clenching teeth.

EXT. COUNTRYSIDE—DAY

The car continues its journey.

INT. DINING ROOM—DAY

Mother can't quite handle this festive guilt
trip, which admittedly came from her own doing.
But she won't say sorry—that would be tantamount
to admitting she'd done wrong. So she drags a
smile onto her face instead and addresses her
two youngest children.

MOTHER
Hey. Joke time! There were two birds
sitting
On a perch. And one said to the other:
do you smell fish?

No laughter from the nosebleed section. Zero charm. Brother focuses on the jar of marbles next to him. A desperate giggle from Mother.

> ELIJAH (CUTTING TO THE BONE)
> Is Dad coming?

Mother sighs.

EXT. BACKYARD—DAY

We can see the car from the backyard. A SHEET blows on the LINE.

INT. DINING ROOM—DAY

Brother cocks his Santa's hat.

> BROTHER (TO ELIJAH)
> Is Sandy coming? Is she? Is she?

> ELIJAH
> Yes. Later on.

EXT. DRIVEWAY- DAY

The car pulls up in the DRIVEWAY. CRUNCHING gravel under the wheels.
INT. DINING ROOM—DAY

Sister has had enough of the silence.

> SISTER
> Mom, can I put on one of my CDs?

Mother shrugs. Sister stands.

> SISTER
> Fine. I'm putting one on. And I'll
> be taking *these*! Ha-ha!

Sister SNATCHES up the jar of marbles. She
giggles.

> BROTHER
> Hey, they're mine—

We HEAR THE SOUND OF THE FRONT DOOR OPENING. It
ECHOES down the hall and into the dining room.

Sister stops in her tracks.

> SISTER
> Dad's here!

Sister runs toward the hallway, excited.

Mother is too shocked to react. All of this hard
work . . . for nothing.

> BROTHER (TO MOTHER)
> You fibber. *You* said he wasn't coming.
> Does he have any presents?

INT. HALLWAY—DAY

Sister bounds up the hall. Her Father is by the
door in SILHOUETTE.

                    SISTER
          Dad—

A FLASH OF LIGHT. An enormously loud GUNSHOT
BANG. The jar EXPLODES against the floor.
Marbles SCATTER.

CUT TO:

EXT. HOUSE—DAY

We see the face of the female ANGEL Christmas
cut-out. That eternal smile. Those dead eyes.

INT. DINING ROOM—DAY

The gunshot makes everyone in the dining room
JUMP in their chairs. Brother covers his ears.
He doesn't hear the approaching footsteps. He
glances up in time to see—

A SECOND gunshot opens Brother's face, thrashing
him to the FLOOR.

CUT TO:

EXT. HOUSE—DAY

We see the face of the male ANGEL Christmas cut-
out. Those ruby cheeks. Those dead eyes.

INT. DINING ROOM—DAY

A beat of silence, and then Mother's SCREAM

builds. It's a feral, guttural sound. She stands and throws her arms out in front of Elijah, attempting to shield him.

A THIRD gunshot rings out. Her chest flowers. She lands face down on her so carefully decorated spread.

All is silent. We can hear the sound of a DRIPPING TAP.

Elijah, panting heavily yet still as stone, remains in his seat. His eyes are on Father, whose face we never see. The moment is STRETCHED TO ITS ABSOLUTE LIMIT. Father's SHADOW falls over Elijah's FACE. The GUN is pointed at Elijah's head.

Elijah doesn't do anything. He stares. Unthinking. Waiting. The dripping tap, the gushing blood, his pulse . . . it all fades away.

We see the FLARE OF GUNFIRE. The shadow FALLS.

Elijah is still alive. But now his face is SPLATTERED with his FATHER'S BLOOD. Elijah doesn't follow his father's suicidal tumble to the ground, instead continuing to stare into the space left behind.
INT. HALLWAY—DAY

The wind picks up and SLAMS the front door shut.

CUT TO BLACK.

FADE IN ON:

HORROR 201: THE SILVER SCREAM

INT. DINING ROOM—A DREAMY TIMELESS HOUR

We're back on Elijah in the same room. And yet everything is different. This place doesn't hold the same awkward, frigid atmosphere as before. There is NO bloodshed here, either. It's warm and homely. A FANTASY.

Elijah's face IS NOT COVERED IN BLOOD.

He looks at the empty space where his father was, though only for a moment. CAROLS play within the room; the lyrics are drawn out and slow.

Elijah's Mother, Sister, and Brother are at their seats around him. They are angelic, beautiful. Alive. Like happy faces on an old Christmas card.

Mother takes Elijah's HAND. Her touch is genuine, as are her tears of joy. She stands. Elijah rises, and follows her. They leave the room.

INT. CORRIDOR TO LIVING ROOM—A DREAMY TIMELESS HOUR
Mother doesn't so much walk as glide. Her happiness is its own kind of poetry. Carols continue. She passes us by. Elijah close behind.

He continues down the corridor toward the—

INT. LIVING ROOM / HALLWAY—DAY

—living room. We're back in REALITY. We see the fully decked-out CHRISTMAS TREE in the corner. There are PRESENTS in red wrapping.

Elijah is ALONE. His face and white shirt are covered in splashes of blood. There are no carols.

We hear the sound of distant LAUGHTER, and then the pitter-patter of FEET. Elijah turns around and—

CUT TO:

INT. THE LIVING ROOM / HALLWAY—A DREAMY TIMELESS HOUR

—Brother and Sister run into the fantasy room. Elijah's shirt and face are no longer covered in blood. His mother is sitting on the carpet next to him. She gestures for Elijah to join her by the tree.

The carols play, still drawn out. Everyone is full of Christmas morning optimism. And maybe even forgiveness.
Having eaten, they're sitting together by the tree, just as planned.

> BROTHER
> Where are my presents?

> SISTER
> Why don't we let Elijah go first?

Elijah is a little shocked by Sister's patience. He looks to his mother, as if to ask 'Are we really doing this?'

Mother's reply: a smile that says 'I love you'.

Elijah takes a breath. For the first time today he actually seems relaxed. He picks up a PRESENT and hands it to his mother. This gesture speaks volumes: this isn't about me anymore, and it probably never was.

Mother is humbled. Overwhelmed and proud, she leans forward to give her eldest son a KISS.

Only it's NOT his mother leaning forward anymore. She's changed.

It's Sandy, his girlfriend, the total knockout from the photograph beside Elijah's bed. Her hair tumbles over her shoulders as she leans in to KISS him on the lips. They hold this special moment together.

Sandy WHISPERS in Elijah's ear. A secret we're not privileged to.

And then the lights in the room FLICKER.

Mother, inexplicably, is now by the OPEN FRONT DOOR. Brother and Sister leap up and dreamily walk from the room like puppets on strings. The door eases shut, leaving Sandy and Elijah alone.

Sandy looks at her boyfriend, her face half in shadow. She's beautiful; it's hard not to love her.

A soft, AMBER-GLOW radiates from Sandy. It dims as she picks a PRESENT from the pile and hands it to Elijah. She nods, approvingly.

Elijah opens the present. The red wrapping falls away. It's a silver HARMONICA.

                    ELIJAH
          I love it. It's just what I wanted.

Sandy is happy that he's happy.

Elijah brings the harmonica TO HIS LIPS and starts to PLAY. He doesn't so much make music as *breathe* it into the instrument. Each chord is comforting, like the hum of a respirator keeping a dying man alive.

CUT TO:

EXT. BACKYARD—A DREAMY TIMELESS HOUR

Outside, Brother and Sister are playing tag. Mother watches from where she's resting against the broken FENCE POST near the back door. The O.S. harmonica DRONES on.

The sky is heavy with CLOUDS. LIGHTNING flashes in the distance. The GRASS around them blackens, curls, and dies beneath their feet.

BIRDS fall from the sky in soft, tumbling pinwheels. All unnoticed.

HORROR 201: THE SILVER SCREAM

INT. LIVING ROOM / HALLWAY—DAY

A glimpse into reality: Elijah sits alone in front of the Christmas tree, covered in blood. But he doesn't know this. He continues to breathe into the harmonica. He's opened the present himself, obviously.

We can see his sister's akimbo legs in the hallway, resting in a dark pool of gore.

CUT TO:

INT. DINING ROOM—DAY

We see the CARNAGE in the dining room. His dead mother. His dead brother. All that tinsel. The harmonica continues. In and out.

INT. LIVING ROOM / HALLWAY—A DREAMY TIMELESS HOUR

Sandy is breathing in tune to the harmonica. LIGHT dances around her.
CUT TO:

EXT. BACKYARD—A DREAMY TIMELESS HOUR

The harmonica breathes on.

Those birds fall around the three members of the family. They continue to play. We can tell from Mother's posture -- that stance, her dutifulness—what kind of woman she once was: observant, conscientious. Protective.

Mother becomes distracted. She views her husband approaching OVER THE HILL. Father's hands are BEHIND HIS BACK.

Brother and Sister stop playing. Sister spots her father. Just as she did before in the dining room, she excitedly runs to greet him.

INT. LIVING ROOM / HALLWAY—A DREAMY TIMELESS HOUR

Elijah continues to breathe into the harmonica. Sandy reaches up to take it off him.

EXT. BACKYARD—A DREAMY TIMELESS HOUR

The harmonica continues.

Sister runs across the field towards Father. Her feet kick up dead grass. FLOWERS SHRIVEL as she passes by.

She's almost within her father's reach—and for one terrible moment we think he's going to pull his hands out from behind his back and reveal that gun—but he doesn't. Not this time. There's mercy in this empty fantasy. He embraces his daughter. She's at home in his arms, and closes her eyes.

INT. LIVING ROOM / HALLWAY—A DREAMY TIMELESS HOUR

Sandy TAKES the harmonica from Elijah. And yet that disembodied drone CONTINUES to breathe on. Once it was comforting; now it's eerie. It snaps the earnestness of Sandy's visit, revealing it as something artificial. Contrived.

A LOW RUMBLE fills the living room. Elijah grows frightened, a tidal awareness lashing his senses. It dawns on him: *This isn't real* . . .

He watches as Sandy's face goes SLACK. Her eyes ROLL back in her head. Her HAIR falls out. Those elegant FINGERS twitch as though descending into rigor mortis.

An invisible force grabs her and DRAGS HER BACKWARDS INTO SHADOW. Her scream fades, taking the sound of the breathing harmonica with it.

CUT TO:

INT. LIVING ROOM / HALLWAY—DAY

Blood-splattered Elijah is in the empty living room near the tree. His PANTS are around his thighs. He's hardly conscious at all, trapped in some awful space between awake and asleep. His hand is clenched around his flaccid PENIS. He jerks off. Desperate. It's completely non-sexual.

The ultimate fantasy.

Elijah's eyes bolt open. He looks down at himself, realizing what he's doing. Ashamed, he pulls his pants up. The harmonica is still in one hand.

Elijah stands, dizzy. Panic sets in. He runs into the corridor leading to the dining room and SLIPS in a PUDDLE OF BLOOD. His head THUMPS against the floor. He grimaces, rolls over, and sees Sister's CORPSE.

Gagging, Elijah scuttles to his feet, leaving a trail of splotched gore in his wake. He escapes into the—

INT. DINING ROOM—DAY

—dining room, where we can hear the DRIP of a tap.

Elijah registers the carnage in the dining room for the first time. The hole where his brother's face should be. His mother's body over the table. The wound in his father's throat from where he shot himself.
And Elijah also sees something else: his own warped and manic REFLECTION in the contours of a STAINLESS STEEL JUG on the dining table. The bloodied face of survival.

The TAP DRIPS for the last time.

CUT TO BLACK.

FADE IN ON:

HORROR 201: THE SILVER SCREAM

EXT. DRIVEWAY—DAY

Elijah, covered in blood, walks down the driveway. He looks lost. The harmonica is in his hand. BIRDS cheep. The WIND blows.

He stops near the end of the driveway. Something compels him to bring the harmonica back up to his mouth, as though in a desperate attempt to rekindling the fantasy. The cool metal feels nice against his lips as he BREATHES into the instrument. A single note. Without gratification. The world remains the same. Dead is dead.

At this moment, A CAR screeches to a stop at the end of the drive. The door flings open and a woman's elegant HAND emerges. It's Sandy. She takes a few steps and stops. Eyes widen with shock.

Elijah glances up. The musical note dies. A tear carves a line through his bloodied mask. He breaks, the reality of what has happened finally hitting him.

The harmonica DROPS.

Elijah tumbles to the ground, curls into a FETAL position. He SCREAMS. Like his mother before him, the sound is guttural, an agonizing thing to hear.

And poor Sandy—her hands shaking, eyes still impossibly wide—does not know what to do. So she simply stands there, the wind ruffling her bangs. There is no reconciliation. No hope.

BIRDS begin to fall from the sky.

INTERVIEWS (PART 1)

JEFFREY REDDICK

MY NAME IS Jeffrey Reddick. (I feel so high school writing that.) I'm a horror geek. Screenwriter. Actor. Director. Producer.

Joe: **You are the perfect example of never giving up when it comes to getting into this business, even from a young age. Would you care to share your story?**

Jeffrey Reddick: I grew up in a small town in Eastern Kentucky. When I was 14, I saw the original *A Nightmare on Elm Street*. The movie scared me more than anything I'd seen before. It was so original; the character of Nancy was the coolest heroine I'd seen and the movie just blew me away. I went home and wrote a treatment for a prequel and mailed it to Robert Shaye (the head of New Line Cinema.) I got a standard rejection letter, because the treatment was unsolicited. So, I sent Bob a surly response. I explained that I had watched three New Line movies and spent $5 on his stuff, so the least he could do was read my treatment. Thankfully, he read the treatment and wrote me back. Bob said I had a fertile imagination, but told me I needed to work on story structure. For me, this was all the encouragement I needed. I didn't know anything about the business, but I started reading scripts sent to me by Joy Mann, Robert's assistant. I stayed in touch with Joy for years. When I was a sophomore in college, I went to New York for a summer acting program and got an internship at New Line. I ended up working there for over a decade and they produced *Final Destination*. I had the blessing of working at the company during its creative peak. Sadly, we lost Joy Mann, a wonderful woman, who I owe my career to, along with Bob Shaye.

On a professional level, I owe a great debt to *Nightmare*. I was devastated by the loss of Wes Craven. He was such a profoundly kind, intelligent and creative man. A true master, not just in the horror genre, but in film in general.

Joe: Can you describe the moment you realized *Final Destination* was going to be a hit.

Jeffrey: I personally always believed the movie was going to be a hit. Just based on the concept, I felt it was something we hadn't seen before. It was a slasher film where Death was the killer. It was tough to sell the studio on not having a personification of Death, but they finally took a chance and it paid off. The movie opened at #3 at the box office. But unlike most genre films, it didn't drop the next week. In fact, the box office increased over the next several weeks. It was a true word-of-mouth hit.

Joe: Are there any resources you can recommend to screenwriters? Online sites, workshops, books, or formatting programs?

Jeffrey: I think Final Draft is a good screenwriting program. It makes formatting scripts easy. The only downside is they upgrade it every few years and then eventually you need to buy the newer version for customer support. I never took a screenwriting class. I read Syd Fields. And *Screenwriters on Screenwriting* by Joel Engel.

But the best advice I can give writers is read scripts online in the genre that you want to write. I think books and classes can give you the basic structure. But reading great scripts was the biggest teaching tool for me. http://www.simplyscripts.com is a great resource. So is http://www.script-o-rama.com.

Joe: What made you write your very first screenplay, and can you still recall what it was?

Jeffrey: My first full script was called "Across The Lines." I'm a huge Tracy Chapman fan and that song spoke to me. I grew up poor. Bi-racial in an area that was very racist at the time. Gay. And a member of the Bahai Faith . . . which in a very conservative Christian area, was frowned upon. So, like most newbie writers, my script was very autobiographical. It was about a bi-racial kid, who befriends a gay kid and deals with the drama they face as prom approaches. I was actually voted on prom court in high school and a lot of parents called the school because they didn't want their daughters to have to walk with me. Times have changed. But this was back in 1986, so it wasn't back in the 60s. Anyway, the script was earnest, but my writing skills were non-existent. So it turned out pretty sappy.

Joe: What legal pitfalls should a screenwriter watch out for when selling their scripts?

Jeffrey: If you copyright your script and keep an email trail of every place you send it, you should be okay. One of the misconceptions about writing is that you make a million bucks and tons of money if the film is a hit. The truth is, until you've sold a script or two and get in to the Writer's Guild, people can pay you whatever they want for your script. And sadly, screenwriting is the only art form where you actually sell the copyright to your work. If you're a painter, you own your painting and people pay to get copies. The same if you're a songwriter. But with scripts you actually sell the ownership of your script. So, a lot of people don't realize that. You'll get residuals from DVD sales and TV broadcasts, etc. But you won't see any back end participation. Studios have a way of accounting so that movies never see an actual profit. It's nothing illegal. It's just a loose system of accounting. So, I always say, just make the best deal possible. But realize that once you sell your script, it's no longer yours. Now, if you get really lucky and have a string of huge hits, you can get higher quotes for your script and demand more control. But that takes a lot of time and work.

Joe: Would you recommend writing collaborative scripts to beginner screenwriters?

Jeffrey: I think every writer has to find out what method works for them. Personally, I like to write solo. Finding a writing partner is hard. You need to find someone you click with and who can help you elevate your game. I have written with partners before. But I usually do a draft and then hand it off to them. As I've gotten older I realize that I don't have the time to tell all the stories I want to, so I've started bringing on writers on some projects to write with me. But personally, I enjoy writing on my own. However, several of my friends love having a partner. It gives them structure and someone to be accountable to.

Joe: **What would you say are the biggest pitfalls when writing a script?**

Jeffrey: Procrastination. I fall victim to this, too. But I'll start on a script. Write ten pages. Then rework those ten pages. Then write five more. Then rewrote the first fifteen. I know a lot of writers who do that. Then, about half-way through the script, you're sick of it. Or, you come up with another great idea and start working on that. I think it's very important to get that first draft finished. Most of writing is re-writing. It's a cliché, but one that happens to be true.

Another big pitfall is not being able to take constructive criticism. Now, everyone has an opinion. So it's important to find a few trusted people to read your script. These should be people who will read the script on its own merits and not try to change it to the script they would have written. But I know a lot of writers who will ask me to read a script. And when I start to give them notes, they argue with every one of them. Not that all my notes are perfect. But if you write a draft of a script and don't think it needs any work, then you'll shoot yourself in the foot. You only grow by taking in constructive criticism and working on areas that you need to work on.

Joe: **What kind of schedule do you keep when writing scripts on a deadline?**

Jeffrey: Crazy hours and lots of Redbull. I'm usually juggling a few things at once. So, I roll out of bed and start writing. And I just write until I get tired. Then I'll take a break, or write a little on something else. But I've rarely had the luxury of having one project, where I could put off all of my other work. But, ideally, if you're working on one project at a time, you try to set it up like a job. Find a place to go write for eight hours a day and try to have a life. If you're in the

Writer's Guild, they give you twelve weeks to write a script. They figure that's enough time for the writer to work full time on the script and still have a life.

Joe: Do you have any advice for screenwriters or those interested in the field?

Jeffrey: 1) Be sure this is what you want to do, because it is a long road. 2) Be patient with yourself and open to growing and learning. 3) Go out and live life. You can't write about life if you stay holed up in your apartment behind a computer all day. 4) Pick a genre you love writing and stick with it. We always want to show how versatile we are. But there are so many writers in Hollywood that the industry is almost forced to put you in a box. So if you sell a comedy script, everyone is going to want to read your next comedy script. 5) While you don't want to stifle your creativity, don't write a script that's going to cost $100 million to make. Only James Cameron and a few others can do that. 6) I always suggest writing something that shows your skills and if you can connect with strong filmmakers, try to shoot something. A strong short can open doors for you. 7) If this is something you are passionate about doing, don't give up. There are no overnight success stories. It was ten years after I graduated high school that I sold *Final Destination.* So be ready to put in the time. The rewards are worth it.

Joe: How involved do you think a screenwriter should be once production starts?

Jeffrey: I personally think they should be involved throughout production. But that's not the reality. Unless the writer is directing, or financing, the film—the writer's involvement is totally up to the production company. Most production companies keep the writer out of the picture. They buy your script and invite you to the premiere. However, some directors are cool with keeping the writer involved in the pre-production stage. And a rare few will keep the writer involved during shooting. But that's rare. Once a film starts production, it's considered the director's movie. So, unless the director trusts the writer . . . they don't want them on set. The fear of the director is a writer will be on set and be like, "That's not how I wrote that scene."

Joe: **What do you look for in a screenwriter or screenplay?**

Jeffrey Reddick: As a producer, I look for scripts with characters and a concept that really grabs me. I've recently gotten more in to producing, but even when I just read scripts for contests, the story and characters were the most important thing to me. I look for stuff that are unique, but also will appeal to an audience.

Joe: **What goes into setting up a budget for an independent film?**

Jeffrey Reddick: Every budget is different. You start with what you think the film will cost. But then, as you start bringing the pieces together, the budget often changes. It can get smaller if you're not able to attach name talent. But if you can get enough of an investment to attach a star, the budget can get bigger. It really depends on the investors you have access to.

Joe: **So you're movie is finally made, now what?**

Jeffrey Reddick: There are several options. A lot of people will opt to hire a sales company to go out and try to sell the film at various film markets. This can be good, but the sales companies take a huge chunk of the profit. If you have access to distributors directly, you can often reach out to them. Or even rent a theatre and set up a distributor screening. The reality now is a lot of films, even with name stars, will often go direct to video. While it may sting the ego . . . you're more likely to make a profit with a direct to video title, because there aren't all the marketing costs associated with a feature film. And theaters also take a large cut of the profit at the box office.

Joe: **If you could remake any movie, which one would it be and why?**

Jeffrey Reddick: I would love to remake *One Dark Night*. I love the movie . . . but feel the set up, and themes, could be explored more fully. It's about a psychic vampire in a mausoleum . . . and some sorority girls locked in for the night. I'd love to take a crack at that one.

Joe: How has the horror movie genre evolved since you started out (content, theme, CGI)?

Jeffrey Reddick: I think it's always evolving. We went from adult horror in the 70s, to teen slasher films in the 80s, to supernatural horror films, to torture porn to found footage. I think the old fashioned way of telling stories will be making a comeback. More a focus on story and characters. At least I hope.

Joe: Do you think today's CGI capabilities improve or impede on the quality of horror movies?

Jeffrey Reddick: If done in small doses and correctly, CGI can help a project. The issue now is that with everything being in high-definitio, a lot of CGI just looks fake.

Joe: Which horror scene haunts you the most?

Jeffrey Reddick: The scene from *Salem's Lot* when Danny Glick, a kid who was turned into a vampire, appears at the window of his best friend Mark Petrie and scratches on the glass, begging Mark to let him in. But I think the most awesome death I've ever seen is the death of Tina from the original *A Nightmare on Elm Street*. That scene has yet to be topped in my opinion.

Joe: What's your favorite book/author, and why?

Jeffrey Reddick: I'm torn. I've always loved Stephen King and Clive Barker. I admire how Stephen King is able to make you feel like you're visiting a real small town in America, populated with realistic and relatable characters. And then he'd unleash hell on it. Clive Barker was like a shot adrenaline to the genre. He introduced fantastic worlds and bizarre ideas . . . yet managed to make them relatable.

Joe: **Which movie inspired you the most in your early career?**

Jeffrey Reddick: *A Nightmare on Elm Street.*

Joe: **Which other careers did you almost join?**

Jeffrey Reddick: Acting was my original passion. I still have the acting bug.

Joe: **Any advice for newbies, or perhaps a recap of how you got where you are now?**

Jeffrey Reddick: I always tell people to be patient, persistent, open to rolling with the punches. Stay focused. Always strive to grow. Don't let partying or drugs derail you. And treat everyone well.

WES CRAVEN

Joe Mynhardt: **I can still recall a very young me hiding behind an oversized pillow as Freddy Krueger walked towards me. As the writer and director for *A Nightmare on Elm Street*, which elements of the Freddy Krueger character were written by you, and which parts came from Robert Englund's take on this iconic character?**

Wes Craven: I'm pretty sure that all the basic things about Freddy were in the script, but what Robert brought to the table was enormous enthusiasm for the role, a fearlessness that had no hesitation at playing a character that was deeply evil and a predator of children, a fantastic vocal instrument, and endless inventiveness in manner and movement, right down to his use of the glove—how he gestured with it, how he draped it over things, how he brought it to his face. Freddy was written as an evil old man, but beyond that, Robert inhabited Freddy with a stunning interpretation of that, and send chills up and down the spines of a whole generation. In fact, maybe two or three generations.

Joe: **When I start watching your movies, I always wonder if you'll do another appearance. But only after I lose myself in the story do you pop up. Tell us a bit more about your acting experiences.**

Wes: I think I'm a lousy actor. For one thing, I can't remember lines, and I think I look weird, especially now. I secretly thought I'd make a great actor, until I tried it. Then I saw the wisdom of my staying behind the camera except for a very few exceptions.

Joe: **I'm certain all the writers out there would love to know who your favorite author is. Or perhaps a specific book that inspired you.**

Wes: Endless authors. I was a kid who always had a book in my hand, especially since I wasn't allowed to see movies for idiotic religious reasons. The names won't ring many bells to today's generation. Hemingway, Thomas Mann, Dostoevsky, Brecht, Terry Southern, Beckett, Roald Dahl's "Kiss Kiss" short stories, Mailer, Poe, Dickens, Kerouac, Kesey, King, you get the idea. In many, many ways that deep history of reading helped and matured me, and I needed it. It didn't help me at all with knowing the techniques and concepts of film, though, and when I started making movies, I was starting from absolute scratch. So, I just invented my own version of what a movie should be. It seems to have worked.

Joe: **Definitely. Can you recall the funniest story that ever happened on set or during the development of a movie?**

Wes: No. My sets are full of laughter and funny things, actually. There's something about dealing with gore and death and all those forbidden topics that lightens things. We're like little kids making mud pies, in a way. Doing what would horrify mom and having a hell of a good time doing it. At least until the killing starts. Then things get very, very quiet.

Joe: **And what was the scariest moment you've ever experienced on set?**

Wes: The scariest things are the real things. Making movies is a fairly dangerous thing. Lots of heavy equipment, things hanging overhead that just might fall down on you, like a 50 lb light, for instance, not to mention Grips hanging off rafters or up 80 feet in the air on condors packed with lights in the middle of the night. Then there's stunts . . . I have all of those things go bad in the middle of shooting. Those are the truly scary things.

INTERVIEWS

Joe: **Another great movie that inspired me personally was** *Swamp Thing*, **which you also wrote and directed. Is there anything specific for you that stood out from that experience? The location must've been a nightmare, but you really managed to use it effectively in the story.**

Wes: I'd never been to that part of the country, and I found it fascinating. The swamps were full of things that wanted to bite you, from alligators to stinging black caterpillars that fell out of the trees and down the neck of your shirt, to water moccasins. The grips all carried side arms, I kid you not.

Joe: **Some of my other favorite movies include** *People under the Stairs, Scream, The Last House on the Left*, **and** *The Hills Have Eyes*. **You've been creating great films for over 40 years now, as well as equally amazing memories for yourself and your fans. So what are the biggest highlights of your writing and directing career?**

Wes: There sure is something terrific about directing something you've also written. So *Last House, Hills, Swamp Thing, Nightmare, My Soul to Take* all have special places in my heart. But every once in a while you get your hands on a terrific script that someone else has written, and that is a very, very good feeling as well, and you don't have to stay up all night while shooting to do re-writes. So, thanks to Carl Ellsworth and Kevin Williamson and many others for their terrific work on scripts I've directed and done very well with.

Joe: **I'm sure I'm not the only one who'd love to know, but are there any future projects can we look forward to?**

Wes: Yes.

LEE KARR

I GREW UP in Savannah, Georgia but always considered myself a "Pittsburgher" at heart. In 2004 I made that official when I finally made the move to "The 'Burgh" at the age of 32. Whether it's because of the Pittsburgh Steelers, the Pittsburgh Pirates, George Romero, or Tom Savini, Pittsburgh has always been a special place to me.

After high school I thought a career in the U.S. Air Force was my future, but migraine headaches snuffed that dream out. For years afterwards management jobs, mostly with movie theaters, would occupy my time.

My interest in writing came about through an experience on the set of George Romero's *Land of the Dead* in 2004. I was able to be a zombie extra in the film thanks to Greg Nicotero. I wanted to put my memories down on paper before time took them away from me. Greg suggested that I send my journal of that experience to homepageofthedead.com, a website devoted to the films of George Romero, to start getting some positive buzz about *Land of the Dead* going online. That decision would start this new hobby of mine.

From there I would do set reports for *Diary of the Dead* and *Survival of the Dead*, along with interviews with Greg Nicotero, John Amplas, John Harrison, and the master himself, George Romero.

I also covered AMC television's hit series *The Walking Dead*, interviewing Gale Anne Hurd, Jeffery DeMunn, and Scott Wilson. And I wrote a retrospective on the making of Romero's classic *Dawn of the Dead*. Some of those pieces would actually be published in *Horrorhound* and *Famous Monsters* magazines, which gave me a tremendous sense of pride.

Since then, seeing a book that I worked for over four years on become published has been one of the biggest thrills of my life. I mean, I'm just a regular, everyday person. How did I manage to sell a book to a publisher? Well, I did. And I did because I loved the subject matter and devoted myself to seeing it through. I hope that other fans out there will take something from that and accomplish their own dreams. Don't ever think you can't because I'm proof that you can!

Joe: What made you compile a book about *Day of the Dead*?

Lee Karr: I've been a fan of *Day of the Dead* since the age of 13, when I saw Tom Savini plugging it on *Late Night with David Letterman*, nearly 30 years ago. It was the film that introduced me to the work of both George Romero and Tom Savini. I saw it at the theater on Halloween night in 1985 and I've been fascinated by it ever since. For years I'd always hoped that someone would write a truly comprehensive book about its filming, but no one ever did. After waiting so long I finally decided to do it myself! And with the help of many of the cast and crew I set off on that journey.

Joe: What made the movie so special?

Lee: For me it was a case of being in the right place at the right time. Before that fateful evening when I saw Tom Savini on television plugging the film I was not a fan of horror. I was petrified of anything with blood and gore in it to be honest with you. But watching Savini demonstrate how the effects were done fascinated me and took away that fear.

Afterwards I bought the current issue of *Fangoria* at the time, which had *Day of the Dead* on the cover. I read it countless times, which only continued to strengthen my interest in the film. When I finally was able to see it a couple of months later it delivered completely, not letting me down in any way. It had horror. It had gore. It had intelligent dialogue. It had a great story. And it flew by . . . I didn't want the film to end!

So as I said it was simply a case of me being in the right place at the right time.

Joe: **The nice thing about putting a book like that together (just like this one) is the experiences you have with all the people you meet. So what are some of the best stories you heard or experienced during your project?**

Lee: The "best" stories weren't positive ones, unfortunately. I was shocked to hear of the disdain that co-producer David Ball had for George Romero. He was brutally honest in our interview and several controversial quotes from him were removed from the manuscript by the publisher.

Also, the strained relationship between Romero and director of photography Michael Gornick was surprising to learn as well. Those two had worked closely together for over 10 years, and finding out that their friendship had deteriorated at the end was really sad to hear.

But there were other stories that were really fun to discover too, so I don't want to paint too gloomy of a picture. The young group of makeup effects artists that worked under Tom Savini, guys who would go on to incredible film careers, provided me with lots of funny stories about working for Savini.

I learned a great deal about the film's creation while researching the book and provided myself with quite an education by the time I had finished.

Joe: **What lesson do you think screenwriters, directors and producers should take from the original *Day of the Dead*?**

Lee: Well, the obvious answer would be that film making is just as much of a business as it is an art form. And that can be unfortunate a lot of times. *Day of the Dead* was a compromised work; a situation where George Romero was forced to scale back his original vision into something smaller and more "intimate" to fit the budget parameters allowed. Unless you're a powerful player in Hollywood, which there are very few of these days, you will have to compromise to get your work to the screen. And that can be a painful process. Trust me, I know this firsthand. I had to compromise with my publisher about my book. It was tough to see things removed before publication, but I had to accept it or the book might not have ever seen the light of day. It's one thing to hear other people say such things, but when you are faced with that reality it's very hard. So understanding ahead of time that sacrifice and compromise WILL be a part of your project will be doing yourself a big favor.

Joe: **Just like any movie, I'm sure there were a lot of problems and turmoil. Who needs to take charge and keep things smooth? Who needs to keep relationships in check?**

Lee: I've never made a film before, but in my humble opinion I think it's the director. The director is the captain of the ship, the head football coach. Everyone is looking to that person to lead them in the right direction and you have to be strong and ready to answer any and every question that comes your way. You have to project an image of being in control, even if inside maybe you feel unsure that you are. Perception is reality. Now, there are countless stories of directors being usurped by producers and at times even actors. Sometimes there is nothing they can do about that, it's out of their control for whatever reason. And I would imagine that is a terrible experience and it takes a true professional to handle it gracefully. Honestly, I'm not sure if I could or not. But most of the time it's the director who should be in control.

Joe: **How much work went into *The Making of Day of the Dead*?**

Lee: Putting my book together took a lot of work! But the funny thing is it never felt that way because I love the subject matter so much. It was a labor of love.

The most important thing, the most "labor intensive" aspect to the book, was the interviews. I had to conduct all of the interviews myself and then later, because I could not afford to hire a transcriptionist, I had to transcribe all of the interviews myself. And trust me that *is* a tedious and time consuming process! When people talk they use words such as "uh" and "like" and "you know" quite a bit. We're all pretty much guilty of that. Aren't we? Well, you have to edit those things out most of the time so that they don't sound silly. Also, when people talk they'll start a sentence and then abruptly stop and start talking about something else because our minds just work that way. So transcribing that can be awkward. And the worst thing about transcribing is that at times the interviewee will say something inaudible. That happened many times and I had to listen to it over and over trying to figure what they had said. At times I just had to forgo those quotes because I wasn't sure what they had said!

Also, I was very fortunate while researching the book to have close connections to the production due to friendships I have with some of the cast and crew. Greg Nicotero, who wrote the book's foreword, provided me with stacks of files and memos he had kept from the production. Christian Stavrakis, younger brother of Taso Stavrakis, helped me as well with a lot of important paperwork that his brother kept from the filming. Several other cast and crew helped me piece together the film's call sheets as well. And others generously contributed photos to help bring the book to life graphically. It goes without saying, but I'll say it anyway, that without those people the book simply would not have happened. I relied on the kindness and generosity of many people.

Joe: For authors interested in doing a similar project about their favorite films, where would you say they should begin, and which obstacles should they expect?

Lee: In my opinion the first thing you MUST have is a passion and love for the subject you're writing about. Otherwise it's going to show in the writing. When you love what you're writing about it literally flows out of you.

Don't skimp on the research angle. You need to really know what you're talking about. The obvious first step would be securing interviews with cast and crew. Sometimes you have to be part private detective to track these people down! Ask people you talk with if they kept any paperwork from the film such as call sheets or production memos, that sort of thing. Collect as much information as you can. You'll also want to ask if they have any behind the scenes photos from the filming that they could contribute to the book. Rare photos are a must!

One obstacle you'll probably encounter is that some people won't talk with you. I encountered that with several people for my book. In that case, even if they're extremely important to the film, there is nothing you can do. Your only hope is being persistent. Keep trying, be very polite about it, but keep leaving those messages for them. Maybe you'll get lucky and they'll come around? That happened to me once during the writing of my book. I had pursued one crew member for well over a year and had gotten to the point of giving up. Then one day out of the blue this person called me back and said "Do you still want to do that interview?" Success! Persistence pays off.

ED NAHA

FOR ME, WHATEVER success I've had in writing had to do with the fact that I was dumb enough to try things that I had no logical right to attempt. I've never had a grand plan. I think being a teenager during the 60s counter-culture helped me fashion a "Let's see what happens if I do this?" attitude. I always drew the line at tonguing plug sockets, though.

Joe: **So what's the story leading up to the creation of *Fangoria* magazine?**

Ed: *Fangoria* was an idea concocted by the publishers of *Starlog*. I was working at *Starlog* (writing both under my own name and at least a half-dozen pseudonyms to make it look like we had a bigger staff) and co-editing *Future Life* when the publishers decided to launch a one-shot horror magazine.

We used to get a lot, a LOT, of unsolicited articles at *Starlog,* and many of them weren't suitable for the magazine in that they were more monster-oriented. We had a massive article submitted on Godzilla and the publishers thought they'd test the waters with monsters. So, I rewrote the article and we cobbled together a few other pieces to flesh out the magazine. It was sort of a guilty pleasure for all of us. I grew up reading *Famous Monsters of Filmland* (my bible) as well as *Castle of Frankenstein* and, later on, *Monster World, Modern Monsters* and *Cinefantastique*. I consumed horror movies when I was growing up. We still had kiddie matinees on Saturdays where you could see two fright flicks for 35 cents. This, by the way, is still my idea of Heaven.

So, we were off to the races. I used one of my pseudonyms, Joe Bonham, to edit the magazine. I know that a lot of histories of the magazine say that this was a shared pseudonym but it wasn't. I used

INTERVIEWS

Joe (the main character from the novel *Johnny Got His Gun*) a lot in *Starlog* as well as Lem Pitkin (*A Cool Million*), William Pratt (Boris Karloff's real name) and Charles Bogle (a W.C. Fields pseudonym) during those years.

The magazine was originally called Fantastica, which always sounded to me like a name for great pasta. Anyhow, an existing magazine, *Fantastic Films*, wasn't crazy over the name and sued. So, Fantastica bit the dust-ica. A second name, Phantasmagoria, was floated with the buoyancy of cement overshoes. Finally, Fangoria was chosen. The first issue came out and did only so-so. But the publishers were encouraged enough to do a second and, then, a third issue. Bob Martin, the king of contemporary horror, was brought in as editor and, after a few issues; he shaped *Fango* as THE magazine dealing with all things scary.

Joe: You have written and worked on some of my favorite films growing up, and I see you even worked on Bruce Springsteen's *Born to Run* album during your stint at Columbia Records. I think we all need to know . . . what is the secret behind your many talents, Ed?

Ed: I think my scattershot history shows that I have a unique talent for not being able to hold a job very long.

I started writing about rock music when I was still in college. That writing, in turn, led to an interview at Columbia Record for a position that could only be described as sub-strata. I wound up getting promoted a lot—I've always believed that this occurred because so many more talented people quit—and wound up becoming East Coast Manager of Publicity. I worked with newbie acts like Springsteen, Aerosmith and Pavlov's Dog as well as more established acts like Dave Mason, Delaney & Bonnie and Chicago. I moved to A&R after a couple of years where I coordinated Springsteen's *Born to Run* album as well as producing Gene Roddenberry's *Inside Star Trek* LP. I quit after a couple of years because I was becoming an asshole. I answered an ad in the New York Times and wound up at *Starlog*.

Joe: **What made you move from rock music and film journalism to writing scores of novels and screenplays, and being a producer? Was it a natural series of events or did you have the big picture in mind from the start?**

Ed: I think the only big plan I've had in life was paying the rent. Eventually, that led to the really big plan of paying the mortgage. Oh, the glamor!

The nicest thing about my alleged career is that I've always been knocking around, and if you knew me, you could probably find me. Not too many people know, for instance, that I was the film columnist for *The New York Post* for eight years. That was going on while I was writing novels, novelizations and screenplays. I've never been really good at tooting my own horn—probably because I insisted it be a tuba.

I wrote my first novel, *The Paradise Plot*, a science-fiction mystery back in 1979. I was still at *Starlog*. I quit *Starlog* in 1980, when the book was published and accidentally got the column at the *Post*. All the while I was doing other things like writing about film and music for *Crawdaddy*, *Heavy Metal* and *Playboy*. I even did pieces for *Architectural Digest* and *Science Digest* (the common denominator? They paid). I moved out to L.A. in '82, after writing *The Films of Roger Corman: Brilliance on a Budget*. I walked into Roger's office one day and said: "I think I should write a screenplay." He said something along the lines of "Okay." So, I started writing screenplays for low-budget movies while I was doing all the other stuff. It was during this period I learned the important phrase: "Don't worry. We'll fix it in editing." (which, by the way, is closely akin to another classic: "The check's in the mail.").

THE LIFE AND THE DEAD OF KING GEORGE

FILMMAKER GEORGE A. ROMERO ON POLITICS, FILM, AND THE FUTURE

INTERVIEWED BY JASON V BROCK

Jason V Brock: **Greetings, Mr. Romero, thanks for chatting with me.**

George A. Romero: My pleasure.

Brock: **Excellent. I'd like to begin by discussing some things that don't get much play in most film-related interviews, such as your feelings and thoughts on events happening in the US political scene. I ask because your films usually have an undercurrent of sociopolitical focus—dealing with racism, voyeurism, sexism, that kind of thing. So what *do* you feel right now about the current sociopolitical situation in the United States?**

Romero: I think it's frightening! It's scarier than my movies, I'll tell you that.

Brock: **Yes, I'm inclined to agree; now we have angry ideas about stepping on people's heads at Ron Paul conventions! So, you know, it's pretty insane! You have to forgive me— I'm a liberal.**

Romero: Oh hey, come on!

Brock: **Liberal is like a dirty word now; it's been morphed into "progressive." I mean, what the hell does that mean? I don't even know what a progressive is! I'm a liberal like John Kennedy—I want the greater good, and all that, for everyone. It's not all about the bottom line for everything. Money is just a means to an end, you know?**

Romero: Yeah, I know. Just a way to get things done.

Brock: **So what bothers you the most about the current political climate?**

Romero: Well, I think that people are just reacting. It's a deep— it's a knee-jerk reaction . . . it's the old "throw the bums out syndrome." There hasn't been enough time for anything to really develop. I'm hoping that, some of this, some of these radical conservative ideas will all blow over.

Brock: **I agree with you. I think Barack's done a pretty good job, actually. He's had some formidable obstacles to overcome, the resistance and so on, but you know, what can you do? You can't win everybody over . . .**

Romero: Right, I mean there's no telling. I do think he's a bit timid.

Brock: **I agree with that. Has been, at least.**

Romero: You know, if he would just open his mouth once in a while and just . . . pop off once in a while! I think then he might do a lot better.

Brock: **I understand what you mean. I think the whole world would be better off if he did that, to be honest!**

Romero: Yeah. [laughs]

Brock: **So getting to your work. I have a question I've been curious about: I read in a couple of places that *Night of the Living Dead* was influenced by Matheson's novel *I Am Legend*. Is that true?**

Romero: Oh, yeah, completely. I mean, I basically was inspired by that book. I guess that's a loose way of saying that I ripped it off! [laughs] But definitely that was the inspiration. I wrote a short story that explored my take on those ideas. I knew I couldn't use vampires because Matheson had, so I thought that I'd invent a new sort of monster . . . I never called them "zombies." I never thought of them as zombies because to me, zombies were, you know, those guys in the Caribbean: the voodoo zombies; my guys were the *neighbors*. People you knew, people you cared about. Essentially the rules had somehow changed and they weren't staying dead. So I thought I'd come up with something new, but everybody then writing about *Night of the Living Dead* called them zombies and you know, that's the way it is. So now they're "zombies," even though I don't think that they should necessarily be *called* zombies, because zombies are not dead. My guys are dead, certainly!

Brock: **It's interesting that you bring that up because that was one of my other questions. Actually, two of those things were! One: That short story that you wrote—has it ever been printed?**

Romero: Nope.

Brock: **No? I'm surprised . . .**

Romero: No, it hasn't. I mean it was a short story that I wrote and never actually tried to get published. We turned one part of it into the first film [*NOLD*] . . . a friend of mine and I, Jack Russo, wrote the script together.

Brock: **I know you've written other short fiction. Do you write novels proper?**

Romero: I am in the process right now of writing a novel, but I've never had anything published. You know, I'm still working, I'm still making movies, so it's hard to find the time to sit down and concentrate on writing a book. So I fiddle at it whenever I have a couple of weeks, but I've never really had the time to pursue it with any energy.

Brock: **That's too bad because I've admired your cinematic writing . . .**

Romero: Well, thank you, but it's . . . I guess . . . you know, you have to make a choice.

Brock: **Right.**

Romero: And, to me, movies are too much fun! I mean I grew up wanting to make movies all my life and lucky enough to still be able to make them, so you know, I'll always choose that until the day comes when nobody wants me to make a movie again. Then maybe I'll be able to sit down and concentrate seriously on a book.

Brock: **Interesting. You mentioned you were careful not to use or overuse the word zombie, which I've always noticed about your oeuvre. What I think is interesting about that is you always have a "human side" to the dead people in the films, even making major characters out of them, such as Bub in *Day of the Dead*. Where does that fit with your personal belief about spirituality regarding the mythos of zombies? Are you trying to bring that personal aspect in there? That they're still human in a way?**

Romero: I don't think that it has anything to do with, in my mind anyway, spirituality. It is purely that I sympathize with these . . . "creatures." I mean they're *us*; they're us after we're dead. And I think that some people have made too much of a connection between, you know, an afterlife, or some sort of spiritual connection with the phenomenon as I describe it. And I just . . . I don't think of it that way. To me it's a natural disaster. I feel sorry for these guys, like I feel sorry for animals in the wild that have to cope with things, and maybe aren't prepared to; I'm not trying to, you know, send any sort of message about afterlife or anything like that.

Brock: **Fascinating.**

Romero: My stories are essentially about people; they're about the humans and how they react stupidly to situations, or mishandle situations. And the "zombies" are a disaster. It could be anything, it could be a hurricane, it could be a tsunami. It's just a huge sort of game-changing thing that's going on out there and people refuse to accept it. They keep on with their own agendas and they keep trying to think of life as it always was. And I think unfortunately that's what happens to us in the real world. I mean, we want everything to be the way it always was. We want a job, we think that we deserve a certain amount of money, you know, and that's the way we want things to be. We get angry if it's *not* that way. And we don't recognize that there are huge things happening, huge changes in the world that might affect life as we know it, and that we have to pull together and try to work things out—just the way we always have, except we don't seem to be doing it anymore. We have to try to pull together and defeat our obstacles. I mean, if we want a good life, we have to build it for ourselves, not just assume that it's in some way owed to us.

Brock: **That's well put, and I agree. So how do you feel about the violence in the films themselves? Do you feel that it's just necessary to underscore the point that we are still just humans trying to do the best we can against what's going on out there in the cosmos?**

Romero: Well, that's the way *I* view it. I know that a lot of people don't! A lot of people feel that the violence in my films is gratuitous, but I have to say that my films to some extent are comic books; I mean, the violence is sort of like the same sort of violence that's in a cartoon. Coyote and the Road Runner—it's *that* kind of violence. I know that a lot of people *don't* like it, but that's my prerogative as a filmmaker.

Brock: **Right.**

Romero: So, you know, you either like it or you don't. And if you don't, don't bother to go see it.

Brock: **I agree. I don't think it's gratuitous; I think it's very necessary the way you've put it together.** *Especially* **in a film like** *Dawn of the Dead,* **which pushed a lot of boundaries. And I think, well, even** *Night of the Living Dead,* **they all did it in their own ways, but** *Dawn of the Dead* **in particular resonates with me, I don't know why. I put it right up there with some of the grand American cinema of the 1970s, you know:** *Taxi Driver, Network,* **things like that.**

Romero: Wow! [laughs]

Brock: **I personally think** *Dawn* **is one of the best films ever made in American cinema.**

Romero: Wow! Wow! That's a great vote of confidence and I thank you.

Brock: **[laughs] No need to thank me! But . . . because it also has that European flair, you know, courtesy probably of the environment that you wrote it in . . . I think I read you wrote it in Rome with Dario Argento, correct?**

Romero: Yeah.

Brock: **Also, the outstanding music from Goblin added to the entire ambiance. I think it has a European sensibility but an American anxiety, if that makes sense.**

Romero: Well, that's a great way of putting it, I think . . . It does, at least the *American* version does.

Brock: **Yes.**

Romero: I think that Dario's cut—there was a cut that he did—is a bit more, I don't know . . . it was a hammer to the head. I mean, he cut all the *humor* out of it. [pauses] He and I are great friends and we've talked about this together often. I just think he cut too much of the humor out of it, and I think that maybe what you're talking about in the American side of it is the humor. I mean, that ability to laugh at things that are senseless.

Brock: **Well, I think it's an absurdist situation.**

Romero: Yeah.

Brock: **The characters find themselves in this strange predicament. I think that the humor is definitely needed to add emotional ballast to the intense . . . *trauma* of the circumstances.**

Romero: Well, I'm glad to hear you say that; and it *is* absurdist. I mean, you know, it's not *meant* to be taken literally. I don't know . . . A lot of people now are writing about, "Well, the eventual zombie apocalypse, and what if it happens?" And I'm here to tell you that it *ain't* gonna happen, so forget about it! I mean, don't take it so seriously, it's ridiculous.

Brock: **I think it feeds into that *fin de siècle* kind of zeitgeist that people have lately; you know, about the looming apocalypse, that type of thing. The whole absurdist idea is interesting to consider; I like Ionesco and Beckett, playwrights like that, and writers such as J. G. Ballard and William S. Burroughs; there was lot of farcicality going on in that stuff. They don't mean it to be taken seriously.**

Romero: No, exactly: That's the point. You have to exaggerate and be a bit ridiculous in order to make your point stand out sometimes.

Brock: **Right. Incidentally, I appreciate your candor about all this.**

Romero: Sure.

Brock: **So I want to ask you about a few general things. As I said, I think that the American version of *Dawn*, your version, is the better of the two major cuts of the film, although I enjoy them both in different ways—**

Romero: I do, too. I do, too. I enjoy the other version and I understand the . . . sort of visceral *dynamic* that it has. But it . . . I don't know, it's just not *my* film, you know? It's not exactly my vision. I prefer not to take things so earnestly; I would rather lighten it up a little bit.

Brock: **So did you actually film the ending for *Dawn of the Dead*? Where Fran committed suicide?**

Romero: Well, we didn't need to film much of it because . . . The short answer is yes! [laughs] We did film the shot of Peter with the gun to his head and that was going to be the last shot. We were going to cut on the sound of a gunshot. So we shot that, but then we shot more, where we decided *not* to do it. So yes, we shot that, too. And we shot the scene of Fran coming out of the helicopter and standing up high . . . theoretically to stick her head into the helicopter blades. And again, all we did was cut it short. So in that sense we did shoot both of those scenes, but during the shooting of the film it's funny, man; I mean, when we were making the film I said, I had this like little elf—or goblin—on my shoulder saying, "You know, this *is* the sequel to *Night of the Living Dead*, even though it's ten years later." And I wasn't thinking of it entirely that way. So there was some goblin saying to me, "But it *is* a sequel, and so it has to be just as tragic . . . everybody has to die, *ba-boom*," all of that. And it was during the making of the film that I said "wait a minute, it's still dark." In other words, if it's a contagion and the world is still in trouble, that's still a dark ending . . . However, if I like these couple of people, I can save them, particularly if we don't know what's going to happen and the future looks bleak; I can certainly save them for the moment. So some of it came to me during the making of the film; of course, that's the way I decided to do it in the end.

Brock: **Fascinating. I like the disjointed kind of super-narrative you have, with the original three films, in particular—all the films, actually, in that they aren't linked by *character*, they are linked by *circumstance*. I think that's a novel postmodern idea—that you can take a set of understanding and comprehension on the part of the audience and extend that into a universe.**

Romero: Well, that's funny. I think that happened accidentally because the second film came so long after the first film. I think that general audiences didn't remember or care about or want to be bothered with the first film, and I think that happened almost accidentally. In other words, I was saying, OK, this is the same phenomenon but we're going to pick it up a little later and we will, you know . . . just a little bit of back story, enough for you to understand what's going on even if you haven't seen or know about the first film. And so, OK, that worked. Then, the third time, I said, "Well, do the same damn thing." I'll take it a little further and do enough backstory in it that you're not lost if you're a newcomer. I really think that was accidental, but then it became a shtick. I said, "Wow! This is cool." And then, when I made *Land of the Dead*, which was, like, *way* later, I did the same thing again; it seemed to work so . . . And then, it was only with *Diary* . . . because I had the concept for *Diary* involved . . . I wanted to do something about film in the journalism and emerging media, and I said, "Well, this can work here." My idea was to have students as they're out shooting a student film the first night that the zombies began to walk. I said, "OK, I have to go back to the first night." And so that drove me.

It's exciting the observations that you make, because I'm most proud of that—that you can actually make a *series* of films. It's not completely unique, granted. I mean, James Bond has been in movies since the '50s, right? And he doesn't get older. They have to use different actors but it's the same James Bond. So it's not a completely unique thing. But I really liked the idea that you could tell a story over the years without referring to the same characters, or even to the same *decade:* the cars are different, everything has advanced and yet, somehow . . . it has a narrative progression.

Brock: **Yes; I would call it a "prismatic narrative," because it's like a prism—it takes a whole idea and explodes it. That's really a thought-provoking, realistic approach.**

Romero: Thanks, I try to keep things interesting!

Brock: **That makes me think a little bit of *Martin*. Now that's a pretty serious film as far as the way you treated the folklore of the vampire. How do you feel that holds up in retrospect? Do you feel that it succeeds?**

Romero: [pauses] I do. *Martin* is my favorite film of mine. I do think that I was successful; I think probably for the first time a filmmaker was trying to translate something from the written page into film. And I like it. It's the most serious film I've made, and a lot of people say it's the most personal film I've made; I'm not sure I agree with that. I think maybe a film called *Knightriders,* which I think might actually be more of a personal statement of mine.

Brock: **That's a very good film.**

Romero: I'm glad you like it. *Martin*, to me is, just . . . I felt that I was successful as a screenwriter and a filmmaker and it remains my *favorite* film. And we made it with a bunch of young people that were, I mean, cast and crew numbered, you know, twelve or fourteen people on most days! Everybody was really collaborative, and did a terrific job in it. John Amplas was wonderful.

Brock: **Yeah, he's very good, and Tom Savini. Wasn't that one of the first times you got to really work with him on screen? I read he was to be involved with *Night of the Living Dead* before he had to go to Vietnam. Is that true?**

Romero: No, it's not true. He was going to be involved in an earlier film that we were going to make which had nothing to do with *Night of the Living Dead;* he was a young guy who I liked as an actor. I met him when we were trying to cast another little film, sort of a coming-of-age, teenage movie. So I went around to high schools and looked at high school plays that people were putting on. And I saw Tom and I thought he was *terrific*. He was in one of these high school plays and I wanted him to play the role in this film that we were going to do. Well, it all blew away; we never got the money to make the film. I lost track of Tom. When he came back [from Vietnam], it was right when we were getting ready to shoot *Martin*. He re-introduced himself, and he had done a couple of small films. That was when we really first got to work together was *Martin*; not only did he do the effects, but he was an actor in it.

Brock: **Yes, he was. He's underrated. He was very good.**

Romero: He's really good. I think that's what he would like to be in life, so yeah, I think he'd like to drop the rest of it. Since he has that school now in Pennsylvania, the production and makeup effects school, he's sort of tied to that. But he's done a lot of acting and he's a really good actor.

Brock: **He is; he's a nice guy, too. I only met him once, but he was very nice to me. I've e-mailed him a couple of times.**

Romero: He's a great guy. I mean he's just the kind of guy you need to have around. I don't say this about a lot of people, but he's inspirational. I mean he just keeps the ball rolling and he's terrific; just a bundle of energy, and *very* talented.

Brock: **One more thing I wanted to comment on about *Dawn of the Dead* is that it's a fantastically edited film, referring specifically to your version. I think for most people, editing is the invisible art—**

Romero: It is.

Brock: **How do you feel about the tendency now toward remaking a lot of these films? You know, like *Dawn of the Dead*? How do you feel about that? I mean, is that a good trend, do you think?**

Romero: [pauses] You know what? It's hard to have an opinion about it because I don't always think it's wrong, I just think that it's often done for the wrong *reasons*. Like they remade a film of mine called *The Crazies* . . .

Brock: **Yes.**

Romero: . . . and they had *no* eye at all for the politics in that film. Somebody said, "Well, here's an old movie we can acquire inexpensively and remake it." Basically all they wanted to do was, I think, turn the crazy people into zombies and make another, sort of, *28 Days Later* out of it! I think Breck Eisner did a good job with that film, I just think it was misguided.

There are times when I think that you could do it and possibly be successful. I'm not sure what that is. There's an old film of mine called *Season of the Witch*, that I would love to remake because I just don't think I did a good enough job with it, and I didn't have enough money and I'd love to remake that. I actually . . . there was this thing going around a while ago that I was going to remake *Deep Red*, called *Dario Argento's Deep Red*, which . . . That turned out to be a misunderstanding because it was Dario's brother Claudio doing this. He called me and said, "Would you like to remake *Deep Red*? I happen to think you can remake it and take some of the opera out of it and make it a sort of straight Hitchcock-type thriller." So I said, sure, I'd be interested in talking about it. But at the time I thought Dario was involved: he wasn't. The moment that I found out Dario was not involved, I said, "No, forget about it."

Brock: **Wow.**

Romero: And I've been talking to some people who want to remake *Children Shouldn't Play with Dead Things*. I'm interested in that, too, but I don't know if it's ever going to happen. I mean, I've had this weird career! I say no to a lot of things. If I'm intrigued by something right off the bat I'll say OK and investigate it and try to find out whether it's real and whether there's any sort of creative process that I can have some degree of control over. I mean, that's always the stuff that bothers me. I don't take "jobs," if you know what I mean. I don't want to just sort of "take a job." Like "Here's the gig—come make this movie." I've never done it, and I don't think I ever will. I hope I won't; at this point in my life I probably wouldn't.

So, on the one hand, I don't think you can *automatically* say that remakes are terrible. Most of them are, but I think it's usually because the *motive* to remake them is terrible. Nobody seriously approaches the idea for a remake in terms of trying to "improve it," or because we can "do it better now because we have computer effects," or whatever. That's *never* the approach. It's usually just, "Here's a great old title like *Halloween*. We can make a lot of money on this again." And that's usually what it's about—making a *lot* of dough. That's disturbing, but I don't think you can therefore automatically say that remakes are bad as a result.

Brock: I concur with that to a degree; I suppose it's all in the intention, as you're saying. I admit I'm still a bit conflicted over the "remake-itis" and "sequel-itis" afflicting Hollywood, though! [laughs] So, after *Martin*, what are your favorite films that you've done that didn't quite meet your personal goals? You mentioned a couple; what I mean is, what do you think *you* could have done better? What are you most disappointed by?

Romero: Well, with regard to my biggest personal disappointments, there are two films—*There's Always Vanilla*, which had a million titles, and *Season of the Witch*; they were the two films that we made right after *Night of the Living Dead*. We didn't have enough money; we were sort of spunky filmmakers trying to do the best we could with limited resources, and we should probably *not* have attempted films that were . . . [pauses] I don't want to say *heavy*, but that were so serious. I don't know how to phrase it exactly . . .

Brock: Ambitious? Kind of ambitious in their scope?

Romero: Yes. Yes, good word. And so those two are the most disappointing. And behind my favorite film *Martin* comes *Knightriders*, and then a little film that I made called *Bruiser*, which

I just really love and nobody ever saw. Those are my favorites, and they're not among the zombie films! Among the zombie films, I think *Day of the Dead* is probably . . . it remains my favorite. I don't know if it's the *best*, but it remains my favorite.

Brock: *Day of the Dead* is fantastic. Now I have to say I saw *Day of the Dead* when it came out—*in the theater!* It was me and one other black guy in the entire auditorium, and that's too bad. It got, I don't know . . . just not enough people saw it. I thought it was great; Joe Pilato was excellent. All the acting was quite good.

Romero: It's very arch; the performances are really sort of broadly stroked and all that, but that's what it was meant to be. It's meant to be a comic book, so you have to sort of forgive it for that. But you know what happened to that film, all of a sudden, I mean, there was a guy that wrote the most *scathing* review of that film that I've ever read; the most scathing review of *any* of my films that I've ever read. And he wound up three years later doing jacket notes for it on the DVD release and apologizing for the review!

I find that my stuff I don't know, I don't want to make the *same* movie over and over. The fans want the same movie over again, it seems—I don't know, it's this TV mentality. People tune in to *CSI: Miami* every week, to see *exactly* the same show! I'm always trying to do something different; some of the fans out there want it to be the same as the last one. When they first see one of my films like, *Survival of the Dead*, they don't get it. But then I meet fans at conventions and they say, "We thought it was great!" It's going to take a while, but I predict that eventually *Survival of the Dead* is going to be one of the favorites among the fans. It takes a while for my stuff to catch up; I don't know *when*, I don't know *why*, and I don't exactly know *what* that's about except that I know that if I have an idea to do something and do it a little differently, that's what I do and I'm not sure that sits well with a lot of the fans.

Brock: I think that kind of phenomenon happened to Carpenter with *The Thing*.

Romero: Oh yeah.

Brock: **You know, that movie bombed, sadly, but it's really one of his best films, I think. Or perhaps his best *realized* film.**

Romero: I think it is, completely. But you know, it wasn't *entirely* the fault of the fans in that case. It was a Universal film; they didn't like it *in the least*. They didn't support it and thought it was terrible. That's actually how I met John; after I saw *The Thing* in the theater. So I wrote him a letter, and I'd read a couple of really *terrible* reviews. I wrote to John through his agent and I said, "John, you know, keep going, man, because it's just really great." And it's how John and I got to meet and, you know, we're still friends. I didn't see his last film, *The Ward*, but I'm just pulling for the guy.

Brock: **Interesting. Along the Carpenter lines, I wanted to ask you something about one other film. How did you feel about *Return of the Living Dead*, and that treatment by Dan O'Bannon?**

Romero: Hated it.

Brock: **What was it you didn't . . .**

Romero: You want me to put it simply?

Brock: **[startled] Yeah—don't hold back! What was it that you didn't care for?**

Romero: Oh man! [laughs] I mean, I just thought it was . . . I thought it was ridiculous! Too comedic. You know, my zombies don't *talk*: they *can't*. They're too *weak* to dig their way up out of graves. And I have a whole different reason for using these creatures. Anyway, I hated that usage. And this is not to say that I don't like anybody spoofing the genre, because I love *Shaun of the Dead*. I mean, I thought *Shaun* was really almost *too* referential. So that wasn't my complaint. I just thought *Return* was capitalizing on the trend at the time. They bought the title from my partner, Jack Russo, who had written a novel called *Return of the Living Dead*. They bought it promising to involve him; they promised that they were going to do his script. In the end, all they wanted was to buy the title, and that's all they did, and I thought they thrashed it.

Brock: OK! [pauses] That's too bad. Do you still work with Russo?

Romero: Oh, we see each other all the time. We haven't worked together for years, but we see each other a lot. There's a project on the table that we're talking about doing together. But . . . Listen, Jack is one of my oldest and best friends, but that's not why I'm saying this about *Return*.

Brock: I understand; you're certainly entitled to how you feel, and that's perfectly fine. Regarding this venture with Russo though, do you think that'll ever get off the ground?

Romero: I don't know. I don't know, man. It depends on . . . you know, all of a sudden, zombies are *hot*. [laughs]

Brock: Right . . . right.

Romero: We were just together, and we'd say, "Hey, maybe we should make a buck out of this somehow!" But, you know, again, I'm just being honest about it. I can't tell you whether anything's going to happen. I don't know. It all depends, unfortunately, because you're only as good as your last movie and how successful that was. And I've been really lucky with *Diary of the Dead* and now *Survival*. It looks like it's going to wind up making a lot of bucks on video. I don't feel "left out in the cold." But, of course, they're not *huge*, like *Zombieland*, or whatever. And, you know, every once in a while you say, "Wait a minute, how come everyone else is getting rich on this and we're not?"

Brock: I completely understand. Did you like *Zombieland*?

Romero: I thought it was . . . [pauses] I thought there was some really great dialogue in it. I can't say that I *liked* it. Again, I have a peculiar take on this stuff. I mean, in my mind zombies are—or, *my* zombies—are something horrific that has happened to the world. And, as I said, *my* stories are more about humans and their reactions to this phenomenon. And so I have a completely different view from these other guys. I have a lot of fun dreaming up ways to kill zombies. And I can do things that are more clever now that I can use computer graphics. I have really a lot of fun with that! But that's not the point of my films. Seems to me that was the point of that film.

Brock: **I'll be honest with you, since you were honest with me—I hated *Zombieland*. Ugh! [laughter from both] That was a *dreadful* movie. I mean, I like Woody Harrelson; I think he's a good actor. But I was like, "This is just not working for me." I don't know . . . And it was such a big hit, too! That's what shocked me—**

Romero: Well, you know what? That's the amazing thing. It's the *only* zombie film that has really blown the roof off, as far as box office. It's the only one. Which is why I say that it's been video games much more than films that have made these zombies so popular. I mean, I think it's why there are these zombie conventions and stuff. I think it's video games more than movies; that's actually a little disturbing to me, because zombies have become anything you want them to be anymore. That's not *my* zombies, you know. My guys will still be slugging along, moving slow as death until . . . until I'm done, anyway! [laughs] Then, maybe I will come back and make one final film!

Brock: **Do you feel you have accomplished everything you set out to when you were younger? I mean, your career has taken some unexpected turns, a lot of them for the good, but is this what you . . . maybe not what you thought was *going* to happen, but are you pleased and do you feel that your career is right where you wanted it to be?**

Romero: It's a difficult question that you're asking here, man!

Brock: **[laughs]**

Romero: I mean . . . I can't answer that with subtlety. Pleased? I am *extremely* pleased. I've been blessed. I've had a hell of a lot of luck. I've had terrific things happen to me. I'm seventy-odd years old, I'm still making movies, and I'm still making money and, you know, how can you be displeased with that?

Now, the other side of that coin is that when you come up wanting to make movies, you don't say to yourself, "I want to make horror movies." You say to yourself, "I want to make *movies*." And I know that I have movies in me that I will *never* get hired to make, that I would love to make. And of course, there's a certain disappointment that comes with that. So, I can't tell you that I'm . . . You know, people will say, "What is this guy complaining about?" It's like Stephen King wrote a couple of novels about the disappointment of a successful novelist, and everybody got all over his ass saying, "What the hell . . . What the hell does Steve King have to complain about?" And so I'm sure that people will say the same thing about me, and I'm not complaining. Like I said right up front, I've had a *wonderful* life, and I'm still doing it. Of course, there are things that I would like to do that I haven't been able to do, and I think partly because of being sort of locked in this niche, I probably will never be able to do them.

So maybe when I've finally put down the camera and tried to seriously write a novel or two . . . You know, maybe some of that stuff can come out. The point is that I have a lot of hope that it's still possible and I guess maybe that's the whole secret of longevity or whatever. You know, it's like John Huston was directing his last film in a wheelchair with a breathing mechanism. I'll probably do the same damn thing!

LYNNE HANSEN

'M A WORKING creative. I'm a filmmaker, screenwriter, novelist, graphic designer, and non-fiction writer. Basically, if it involves making a living from the creative output of my heart and soul and blood and sweat and tears—and I love it—I'm there.

The first short I wrote, a horror comedy called *He's Not Looking So Great*, was produced and directed by Gregory Kurczynski in New Orleans in 2013. It was nominated for Best Comedy Short at the Buffalo Dreams Fantastic Film Festival. The second short horror comedy I wrote, *Chomp*, was also my directorial debut. It is currently making the film festival circuit, playing at festivals from Scotland to California. The film was nominated for Best Comedy Short at the Buffalo Dreams Fantastic Film Festival, where I won their Filmmaker to Watch Award. *Chomp* won both Best Short and Best of Fest at the GeekFest Film Festival.

I've also got two nonfiction projects in the works. *How Not to Make a Movie in 30 Days* is a combination memoir and how-to-avoid-my-dumb-mistakes guide. The second is *Filmmaking is for Girls*, a practical guide about filmmaking for middle school and high school kids with advice from women filmmakers from all over the globe. I want to give young girls the tools they need to get their stories told.

I'm currently writing scripts for another short horror comedy as well as the script for my first feature-length film. News on my future projects can be found at WithoutWarningMedia.com, and updates on *Chomp* are at ChompMovie.com.

Joe: **What goes into keeping a movie set organized?**

Lynne Hansen: Lots of prep work in advance, and then lots of flexibility the day of. If you try to stick perfectly to what you had planned, you'll miss many opportunities.

Joe: **What's the worst thing you can do when making a movie?**

Lynne: Second-guess yourself, or maybe doubt your vision. If you're a good director, you're going to surround yourself with people who are more talented than you are in their various areas of expertise. You've got to know when to heed their advice, and when to stick to your guns.

On a more technical side, I'd have to add recording and mixing bad sound. People will forgive a lot in terms of the picture if the sound keeps them in the moment. It's one of the toughest jobs on a film, and it's something a lot of filmmakers take for granted.

Joe: **As a producer, what do you look for in a screenwriter or screenplay?**

Lynne: To date, I've written my own screenplays, so my number one goal is to write something that would entertain me—something I'd enjoy watching in a theater. You can't please everyone. When you write to please yourself, your true voice shines through. As a director, though, I'm also quite aware of budget constraints and resource limitations when I write. If I plan on directing a screenplay I write, it better not involve a gazillion characters or exotic locations that I can't afford. I write scripts that support the indie filmmaking low-budget, DIY ethic, but that also provide opportunities for larger budgets should the opportunity present itself.

Joe: **So how close to your original screenplay do you normally stay?**

Lynne: Since I wrote and directed *Chomp*, you'd think that the film I made stayed pretty close to the script I wrote. In many ways, that's true, but *Chomp* went through nine major revisions, including two during production and one in post. Some of the changes were the product of workshopping with the actors during rehearsals. Others were opportunities that came on the day. The last major revision was actually inspired by the fantastic music created for *Chomp*. Filmmaking is a collaborative endeavor. Filmmakers should never be slaves to the script. Now slaves to the story—that's a different thing.

Joe: Any advice on setting up a budget for an independent film?

Lynne: Figuring out how much you have in the bank. Nobody knows you can actually finish a film—a good film—until you do it, so financing is up to you. I've been a fulltime creative for over ten years, so that really influenced how I spent my money. Although I couldn't afford pro rates, I paid everyone involved. Lots of indie filmmakers will try to crew up and cast by telling people they're doing it "for the exposure." I think that's an insult. People don't go to the dentist and say, "Well, if you do this root canal for me for free, it'll be really good for your business." Get real. Be respectful of your talent and they will exceed all your expectations. Feed them well, too. Good stuff, not just peanut butter and jelly sandwiches. A sated crew is a happier and more productive crew. And make sure you budget for film festival submissions and travel to at least some of the festivals you get into. Marketing your film will cost a lot more than you think it will.

Joe: I'm sure you've studied quite a few film makers. Which ones stand out the most?

Lynne: John Hughes for his emotionally engaging characters and fantastic integration of music into the story. Edgar Wright for his brilliant mixture of humor and horror and self-awareness of the pop-culture tsunami we live in. Ridley Scott for being able to make the most mundane worlds exotic and gorgeous. And although he's a TV guy and not a filmmaker, I'd have to add Vince Gilligan of *Breaking Bad* fame. He knows how to get to the emotional core of a story using very unusual shots that are blow-you-away stunning and yet never take you out of the moment.

Joe: **What's your take on today's CGI and the quality of horror movies?**

Lynne: I think CGI has its place, but in indie horror it's often overused and poorly executed. If you're going to use CGI, you'd better have a good reason for not going practical. In *Chomp* we had one small bit of CGI for a very good reason. We had a little zombie girl who needed to have zombified eyes. We weren't about to put contacts in a four-year-old's eyes, so CGI was the best solution. And I often get folks coming up to me after screenings asking where I found contacts like that for a pre-schooler. That's when you know your CGI is effective.

Joe: **Which movie inspired you the most in your early career?**

Lynne: I'm still in my early career! I'd have to say *Teenage Bikini Vampire Weekend*, written and directed by Devi Snively. It's an over-the-top comedy about a girl who falls in love with a boy whose family doesn't approve—mostly because he's a slacker surfer and she's, well, a vampire. It's a micro-budget affair, but it's wonderfully effective. I learned that you can get away with a lot if you have sympathetic characters and clever writing.

Joe: **Any new projects you're working on?**

Lynne: I've written a script for another short that I'd like to film this summer—another horror comedy. And I'm working on my first feature-length script. Over the next year, I hope to interview lots of women filmmakers for my *Filmmaking is for Girls* book, find a home for it, and travel around to schools encouraging young filmmakers to tell their stories.

WILLIAM F. NOLAN—THE LIVING LEGEND

WILLIAM F. NOLAN writes mostly in the science fiction, fantasy, and horror genres. Though best known for coauthoring the acclaimed dystopian science fiction novel *Logan's Run* with George Clayton Johnson, Nolan is the author of more than 2000 pieces (fiction, nonfiction, articles, and books), and has edited twenty-six anthologies in his fifty-plus year career.

Of his numerous awards, there are a few of which he is most proud: being voted a Living Legend in Dark Fantasy by the International Horror Guild in 2002; twice winning the Edgar Allan Poe Award from the Mystery Writers of America; being awarded the honorary title of Author Emeritus by the Science Fiction and Fantasy Writers of America, Inc. in 2006; receiving the Lifetime Achievement Award from the Horror Writers Association in 2010; and as recipient of the 2013 World Fantasy Convention Award along with Brian W. Aldiss. Nolan won another Bram Stoker Award—for Superior Achievement in Nonfiction—in May 2014 for his book about Ray Bradbury, called *Nolan on Bradbury: Sixty Years of Writing about the Master of Science Fiction*.

A vegetarian, Nolan resides in Vancouver, WA.

Joe: Can you recall the steps leading up to your *Logan's Run* novel being turned into a television series?

William F. Nolan: I wrote a film outline, *Logan's World*, for MGM shortly after they produced the first film—and they liked it, were going to do it as a follow-up to *Logan's Run* when they got a huge offer from TV to do a series. They said yes, and I turned my outline into a sequel novel.

217

Joe: **How difficult was it for you to write the pilot episode of the *Logan's Run* series?**

William: Very difficult—as they had no idea what to do with the series. It was doomed from the start. I co-wrote the pilot, but they changed it all around and the result was a disaster. That's when I left the series.

Joe: **Any legal scenarios a screenwriter should watch out for?**

William: Make sure an outside lawyer goes over the contract.

Joe: **Can you still recall your very first screenplay?**

William: It was one called *The Day the Gorf Took Over*, and I wrote it from a short story of mine, "Gorf!" Had a lot of fun with it, but the screenplay never sold.

Joe: **Do you set out to write a novel or a screenplay from the start, or do you just write a story and see where it leads you?**

William: Each story takes its own length from the original idea. When I get ideas I *know* if they are for a short story or a novel. No writer in his right mind writes original screenplays! You have to do them on assignment—as I did with Dan Curtis's *Burnt Offerings* with Bette Davis.

Joe: **Do you have any books you can recommend to screenwriters?**

William: There are many good books on all forms of writing. In all modesty, I think my own *Let's Get Creative!* is a good starting point. Get it via Amazon—or elsewhere.

Joe: **You've written a few collaborative scripts. Would you recommend this to beginning screenwriters?**

William: If the writer you collaborate with has *your* kind of mindset it works fine. If not, don't try it!

Joe: What would you say is the biggest challenge when writing a script?

William: Trying to fit a much larger story into a 120-page screenplay can be daunting!

Joe: And your biggest career or personal accomplishment?

William: *Logan's Run.*

Joe: Being the inspiration man that you are, do you have any advice for screenwriters or those interested in the field?

William: Stay away from "spec" scripts!

Joe: You have met and worked with some of the most inspirational folks in the industry. Would you care to recall some of the best and most informative moments you shared with them?

William: Too many! I was a close pal to Ray Bradbury for over 60 years, but we never wrote anything together. Director Dan Curtis was a dear friend of mine, and we worked on several things—*The Norliss Tapes, Trilogy of Terror I* and *II*. Also, Richard Matheson was another close friend and we did *Trilogy* and other things; of course there's *Logan's Run* with George Clayton Johnson . . . Even Ray Harryhausen on an unrealized project. Charles Beaumont, of course—we were best friends for over ten years. Also Clive Barker and Peter Straub on things that never materialized. Understand that only one out of ten projects ever reach production stage in Hollywood!

Joe: So what's next for you, Mr. Nolan? Any projects in the works?

William: I'm *always* working. Hell, I made it to 86, so why stop now? Right now it's a 900-page bio on Dashiell Hammett (*The Maltese Falcon*) for Knopf. I am constantly invited into anthologies. In 2016 Centipede Press is going to publish an omnibus of my best short stories (I've done over 200) for their Masters of the Weird Tale series. Jason V Brock and I are working on another book in the Logan series called *Logan Falls*, too.

RICHARD GRAY

INTERVIEWED BY E.C. MCMULLEN JR.

AUSTRALIAN WRITER, DIRECTOR, and Producer of Independent cinema, Richard Gray began his career making documentaries and dramas. For Writing and Directing inspiration, Richard draws upon a diverse pool including The Coen Brothers, Paul Thomas Anderson, Quentin Tarantino, Wes Anderson, Michael Mann, and David Fincher.

Since his 2012 Horror Thriller, *Mine Games*, Richard ventured into darker territory with *The Look-Alike* and the upcoming *Sugar Mountain* starring Cary Elwes (*Saw*) and Jason Momoa (*Game of Thrones*).

I spoke to Richard, during his somewhat less than copious free time, about how he works with the tools of his trade.

E.C. McMullen Jr.: **A director is a teller of stories, usually someone else's tale. Yet you often write or co-author your screenplays. What do you look for in a writer or story?**

Richard: I love to collaborate, and there's nothing more important than the script, so I just look for writers that are open to work closely and want to be on set with me. I'm lucky that's usually my wife! But in the case of *Mine Games*, the writers had a fantastic concept and it was really just about making it work in a different setting, and adjusting it to suit the cast.

E.C.: **From budget to run-time and so many other constraints, the original screenplay always changes from script to final edit. Looking back over your arc of work,**

how close to the original screenplay do you feel you normally stay?

Richard: I'd like to say fairly close. We often find new elements we'd like in the edit, and head off for minor re-shoots, or a particular story arc no longer works due to pace or a change in what we thought was important versus what a test audience now tells us. But that said, the majority of changes to the screenplay come in pre-production and when we first cast actors. Their opinions are the most crucial.

E.C.: Who is your favorite screenwriter?

Richard: Tough question! Over the years and depending what I'm working on I'd give you very different answers, so perhaps I can just say that when I was coming up through the ranks it was always Writer / Directors that inspired me, so I'd have to go for: The Coen Brothers, Paul Thomas Anderson, Quentin Tarantino, Wes Anderson. They were huge inspiration at crucial times of my life.

E.C.: Are there any actors who have not worked in Horror, that you think would make great horror characters?

Richard: Oh certainly, I was just thinking about how much I'd like to see Clive Owen in a horror—and apologies if he already has! [1] His performance in *Children Of Men* was just so special. There are dozens actually that I've thought about. If the script is right, I don't believe anyone would rule themselves out of this genre.

E.C.: Now you have your script. As a Do-It-Yourself Independent film maker, what goes into setting up a budget for your film?

Richard: The script is the most important piece. You can print yourself as many glossy packs as you want, but in the end it's just the script, the script leads to actors—the better the script the better the actor, and so on. Script, cast, shake that can for money!

1/ Clive Owens was in the big budget, nearly, almost, could-have-been-good Horror Thriller, *Intruders* (2011).

INTERVIEWS

E.C.: **Your movie is finally made. What are the next three most crucial steps and why?**

Richard: Seeking trusted opinions of what you've got. Testing it. knowing your audience. And then, if you haven't yet got distribution, it's the hunt for the perfect Sales Agent or Producer's Rep to sell your film.

    This process shouldn't be rushed, nor should entering festivals. You need professionals who care about you and your movie to guide you, as this phase is littered with the worst kind of people in our industry. You have to know who and who not to talk to / work with.

E.C.: **Should every independent film be made in a unique way, or should producers and directors stick with what the audience wants?**

Richard: The story is the story. What ever best tells and best suits the story you are trying to tell. The story should dictate all.

E.C.: **Werner Herzog tells newbie film-makers to do whatever it takes to make their movie. What line will you not cross to make yours?**

Richard: I agree with him. But the line we must never cross is Safety. Safety of our crew and cast trumps all.

E.C.: **Quentin Tarantino has said that when he steals, he steals from the best. Who are your best?**

Richard: I wouldn't know how to define best. But I know someone like Paul Thomas Anderson made me so excited about making movies at just the right time in my life. As did the Coens. Films like *Boogie Nights, Magnolia, Fargo, The Big Lebowski*—absolute, absolute gems that I watched and watched and watched and dreamed.

DAN CURTIS

THRIVING IN THE DARK SHADOWS

INTERVIEWED BY MICHAEL MCCARTY

D *ARK SHADOWS,* **CREATED** by producer/director Dan Curtis, is a pop culture phenomenon. The series ran for a half-hour each weekday from June 27, 1966 to April 2, 1971. The success led to two feature films, *House of Dark Shadows* and *Night of Dark Shadows*. The gothic soap opera has a cult following reaching Beatlemania proportions and a fan-base stretching over four decades.

Other movies directed by Curtis include *Burnt Offerings* (which was co-written with William F. Nolan, also in this book). He made several TV movies: *The Night Stalker* and *The Night Strangler* (both written by Richard Matheson, who is also in the book) led to *Kolchak: The Night Stalker* series. Curtis and his company Dan Curtis Productions designed such classics for the tube such as *The Strange Case of Dr. Jekyll and Mr. Hyde, Dracula* and *Frankenstein*.

Curtis directed such TV movies as *The Norliss Tapes* (also written by Nolan), *Scream of the Wolf, Trilogy of Terror,* and *Dead of Night*. At that time, he was dubbed "Television's King of Horror." In the 1980s, he made the mainstream made-for-television movies *The Winds of War* and *War and Remembrance*, based on the books by Herman Wouk.

Dark Shadows has been resurrected on DVD, and Tim Burton directed a *Dark Shadows* movie starring Johnny Depp, as Barnabas Collins, and Michelle Pfeiffer in 2012.

Dan Curtis passed away on March 27, 2006, at the age of 78.

INTERVIEWS

Michael McCarty: Why do you think *Dark Shadows* has had such a devoted following for over 40 years?

Dan Curtis: If I knew the answer to that I'd be a genius. Obviously it has some kind of deep seated appeal that reaches down into the bowels and the hearts of the viewers. It's not just a horror story—it's a romance story that crosses centuries as well. It's a reincarnation story of lost love. It can be very scary at times, with a lot of imaginative twists and interesting characters.

It has a universal appeal, because it appealed to people of all ages and continues to appeal. It wasn't just a question of whether it would appeal to kids in the late '60s. It seems to appeal to all who watch it.

Michael: Of the 1,225 episodes of *Dark Shadows*, what were your favorite story lines?

Dan: My favorite story is when Victoria Winters (Alexandra Moltke) goes into the past and we find out how Barnabas Collins (Jonathan Frid) became a vampire, the whole Angelique (Lara Parker) story and the cursing him and all that whole business.

Michael: You introduced Barnabas Collins in episode 210. Was the vampire going to be just a short-term character?

Dan: I had turned the show supernatural and I was going to see how far I could go with it in terms of how much the audience was going to buy it. I put on a vampire, which I consider the scariest of all supernatural creatures; that's how it happened.

When Barnabas Collins turned into such a huge hit, I couldn't kill him off, which I had originally intended to do. I had to find a way to keep him alive.

Michael: Why did you kill Barnabas Collins off in the end of the *House of Dark Shadows* movie?

Dan: That is what I always wanted to do with that story, but I couldn't on the television series. So I did it in the movie.

If one looks very closely, right around the time of the credits, you see a bat fly up toward the camera, which would have given us the opportunity to come back and do a sequel. It's a little hidden fact that probably nobody knows. (Laughs)

Michael: **What are your thoughts on *Kolchak: The Night Stalker* series?**

Dan: I had nothing to do with the series. I made the first two pictures. I made the original which was the big hit, *The Night Stalker*. Then I made *The Night Strangler*. I didn't want to do the series. I had nothing to do with the series, the Monster-of-the-Week formula of what happened to Kolchak after the first two movies.

Michael: **Over the years there have been a lot of comparisons made between *The X-Files* and *Kolchak: The Night Stalker*. What are your views on this?**

Dan: I could never understand that. I don't know what the similarity is.

Michael: **We never do discover what happens to Norliss by the end of *The Norliss Tapes*. What do you think happened to Norliss?**

Dan: (Laughs) That was supposed to be a pilot for a series. I just left everyone up in the air. When they didn't pick it up as a series, I laughed my ass off.
What do I think happened to him? I have no idea. (Laughs)

Michael: **_Trilogy of Terror_ is famous for the last story, about the Zuni Fetish doll that chases Karen Black with a knife. Was the Zuni doll done with puppets or stop-motion photography?**

Dan: We had ourselves a hand puppet and another puppet that had a rod stuck up its ass and was held up above the floor. The floor of the set was held up by risers. We cut lines into the floor that were covered by the carpet and we had some idiot underneath running with this thing that moved its (the puppet's) arms up and down, and its legs. It was pathetic. (Laughs) It was the worst looking thing I had ever seen.

This was done in desperation. It was the last day of shooting and everyone went home. I kept the puppeteer there. I said to him, "I'm going to get a bunch of close-ups of this thing against a black (backdrop) and you stick your hand in that puppet and just have it open its mouth—keep it moving within and without of the frame."

So I basically made it all work in the cutting room. I sped those shots up, by skip framing them; I flopped them over to make them go from left to right and right to left. The knife would jump from one hand to another—but nobody had ever noticed that. It was against black—I would cut to it anytime I wanted.

I shot the whole thing in four days.

Michael: **Why did you get out of the horror field in the late 1970s?**

Dan: I was just getting so tired of doing it. It is a very difficult thing to do, to do a horror film properly and make it good. Far more difficult than a normal drama.

I love scary stuff, so it was fun. I was just hungering for the time to do real stories, dealing with real people, where every line isn't suspect, where you didn't have to constantly squeak the door.

That is why horror films stink. Because people don't know what the hell they are doing, they think it's a horror film and they can do anything. They can't. They do a horror film, they have to be really careful. You have to use logic. Just because there is a ghost or a monster involved, it can't become totally illogical and if you do that, and they always do—you lose the audience completely, all realism and believability are gone. They never know how to end these things.

I used to say, "Anybody can write a horror story if you didn't have to end it."

I just ran out, I couldn't come up with another great scary idea. I couldn't find any existing material. I just wanted to forget it and put horror behind me.

Michael: **Last words?**

Dan: *Dark Shadows* will live forever.

HARRY SHANNON

MY NAME IS Harry Shannon. I started in the entertainment business as a singer and actor in commercials, but signed a songwriting deal with ATV Publishing in 1974, and thus ended up working mostly in the music and film businesses as an executive. I didn't start writing novels until I was 50. I've been Music Supervisor on a number of films, including Basic Instinct and the original Universal Soldier. I wrote the screenplay and title song for *Dead and Gone*, which was released by Lionsgate.

Joe: **Exactly how important is the right music for a movie's success?**

Harry: In my opinion it can make or break a movie. A great score can lift a mediocre film to entertaining, and a terrible score can actually hamstring a hit. Scoring is an art form, and I hope it survives cultural changes. We've lost some great ones over the last several years, from Jerry Goldsmith to Elmer Bernstein.

Joe: **What goes into being a music supervisor for a film project?**

Harry: In my day it was mostly working as a liaison between the composer and the director. We sometimes found a title song, and even created the source cues as required. I'd negotiate the soundtrack record deal, and all the licensing as well. These days a lot of people stuff songs into a movie without much regard for the underscore, and I think that is a shame.

Joe: Personally, I realized how much I enjoyed the writing process when I tried to write a few songs. Was it the same for you, or is writing music just another way for you to express yourself?

Harry: I've always loved writing songs, though I don't as much these days. It was one of my first real passions. My daughter is into it as an artist and songwriter, and I've had a lot of fun watching her, teaching her things about the craft.

Joe: How is putting a story into song different than writing fiction?

Harry: I guess it's similar to doing a screenplay instead of a novel. The action and characterization has to be shown, not told, and compressed to the smallest possible size—then set to a melody or visa-versa in a manner that feels seamless.

Joe: How should producers/directors go about choosing the right music for their project?

Harry: Listen to the composer of the underscore. Let that person loose creatively before jamming songs into tight windows. Some of the great ones will prefer not to put a cue in a specific scene simply because the acting or photography works beautifully and the music could actually weaken the moment. After all the music cues have been decided upon, then consider songs as well, but not before. Sadly, it doesn't always work that way. In a few cases, commercial needs prevail and songs are chosen to be inserted before the movie is even shown to the composer.

Joe: What are the biggest pitfalls to watch out for while composing music for a film, as well as during the actual writing process?

Harry: A natural human tendency is to accent what is already there. Sometimes going the other way works brilliantly. This bit is overdone now, but the way Barber's heartbreakingly sad piece

INTERVIEWS

Adagio for Strings first played against the violence in Platoon was spectacular. Elmer Bernstein did a light, ironic score for *Ramblin' Rose* and made a sad movie feel warm and delightful.

L.L. SOARES

'M A NOVELIST, short story writer, film critic and editor. My debut novel, *Life Rage*, won the Bram Stoker Award for "Superior Achievement in a First Novel" for 2012. My other books include the novels *Rock 'N' Roll*, and *Hard*, the short story collection *In Sickness* (with my wife and fellow author Laura Cooney), and the novellas *Green Tsunami* (also with Laura) and *Breaking Eggs* (with Kurt Newton).

I'm also the co-author of the Stoker-nominated, horror movie review column *Cinema Knife Fight*, with Michael Arruda, which we've been writing (more or less) weekly for over 10 years now. The column has a whole site built around it these days at *cinemaknifefight.com*. I'm also the editor/publisher at the site, and we have a staff of writers who turn out entertaining reviews.

Aside from literary influences, movies have had a tremendous effect on me as a writer. When I write, I am very visual, seeing a story cinematically in my head as I put it down on paper. The first movie I ever saw as a child that had a lasting impression on me was the 1931 *Frankenstein* starring Boris Karloff and Colin Clive. That was the first time I can remember being exposed to a horror film, and I knew immediately that this was something that would become a lifelong passion of mine. The horror genre, in all its mediums, was just something I wanted to be a part of from an early age.

To keep up on my endeavors, I'm at the usual places (Facebook, Twitter) as well as my official website at *www.llsoares.com*.

Joe: How should a person go about critically evaluating a movie?

L.L. Soares: I guess on some level, everyone who goes to see a movie is a critic. We all have certain criteria we use to determine for ourselves what a good movie is, and what a bad one is. The sometimes difficult part is to determine the exact reasons *why* a movie succeeds or fails to capture one's imagination. When I was younger, I wanted to go to film school, but I didn't, so I guess on some level I'm a frustrated filmmaker who never got the chance to make movies for myself. For me, like a lot of people, my film school involved sitting down and actually watching as many movies as possible. In movie theaters, on television, on video, basically wherever I could find them.

This started from an early age. When I was a kid, I watched whatever I could on television—the 1970s were a helluva great time to be a horror movie fan, especially—since there were "Creature Feature" programs on every weekend, where horror hosts exposed us to lots of movies. That's how I first saw the Universal horror films of the 1930s and 40s, the Hammer films of the 1960s and 70s, and everything else from 1950s giant insect movies to Godzilla movies to movies by directors like Roger Corman and William Castle. I didn't have a lot of friends growing up, and I was addicted to horror movies, so I watched as many as I could. I also read the horror movie magazines of the time, especially *Famous Monsters of Filmland* and *Castle of Frankenstein*, to learn as much as I could about what I was watching.

When videotape arrived, along with mom and pop video stores in the 1980s, I suddenly had a lot of movies at my disposal that I never could have seen before. Back then, either you saw something in the theater, or maybe it came on TV (likely cable) at some point, and that was it. Which meant there were always tons of movies you would hear about that you were never able to actually *see*. VHS eliminated this problem. The assumption being that now you could see any movie you wanted, and that opened up a whole new world to me. I remember renting three and four videos a week, which is how I finally saw the movies of people like Herschell Gordon Lewis, Russ Meyer, Mario Bava, Argento, Fulci, and a whole lot more. And around this time I was reading magazines like *Psychotronic Video*, *Film Threat*, and *Fangoria*.

But I didn't limit it just to horror; I tried to see as many great movies outside the genre as possible, too. It's just that a big part of what I sought out was horror movies. But it's good to expose yourself to everything you can.

It also doesn't hurt that I'm a writer—that aspect always has me thinking about how I would change a script when I'm watching something that doesn't work. *How would I rewrite this to make it better?* And that helps a lot, as well.

So, as you can see, I pretty much ate, drank and breathed movies (and books and music). All of this, combined, is what I draw from when I see a movie. I would just say see as many movies as you possibly can, and it'll become pretty obvious what works, what doesn't, and why.

Joe: After reviewing movies for years, and being an avid fan, what are the biggest tips you'd like to give upcoming producers, editors and actors in the horror genre?

Soares: Well, I know what I want as a movie-goer. I'd like a lot less remakes and sequels and the like. More movies that are original, that expose us to something new, instead of tired old tropes of the genre. Of *any* genre. In the horror field, there are so many great authors whose work has never been adapted for film, so many untapped resources, that would be a breath of fresh air in the movie world.

But Hollywood isn't going to listen to me. As far as they're concerned, I'm not the target audience. The target audience is teenagers and people in their 20s who spend the most money going to movies, especially horror movies. A lot of these people haven't seen the original films the remakes are based on, and—especially, if the original film was in black and white—probably would **never** bother to check them out. So all this is new to them. And they keep spending money to see them, so the industry is pretty content to keep things business as usual. As far as they're concerned, if it's not broke, why fix it?

Historically, horror movies tend to do very well their opening week, and then the numbers dwindle after that. So they make most of the money all in one weekend. A lot of these movies are pretty critic-proof. On a Friday night, kids are going to see a horror movie if it opens, and they're not going to bother reading a review. So by the time word of mouth gets around that a particular movie isn't that good, it's already made most of the money it's going to make. Also, a lot of times horror movies are not screened for critics before they're released, so reviews of horror movies matter even less in that regard. They're also notoriously cheap to make. For a horror film, you don't necessarily need a big star to bring people in. Just the fact that it's a horror movie is often good enough.

But for a horror movie to have a lasting impression, to have *legs*, to stick around more than just that one week, they've got to be better than the norm. They've got to be more ambitious and smarter. And one way to do that is to look at the best horror fiction that's out there and adapt something new that people haven't seen before.

Another thing I just can't stand is horror films that are rated PG-13. This is done so that they can cash in on the widest audience possible, but I can name on one hand PG-13 horror films that have been any good. In some ways, horror is a genre that thrives on extremes, visually and in subject matter, and I'm sorry, but if a horror film is rated PG-13, chances are incredibly high it is not going to be scary. You can't take it as far as it often *needs* to go if you have a barrier like that blocking the way. Horror needs the freedom to shock, to scare, to repulse. And it's always going to seem sanitized and safe if it's saddled with a PG-13 rating.

Joe: **Which type of horror movies have been done to death?**

Soares: Just look at the newspaper any given week, whenever horror movies are released, and you'll see the same kinds of things. Ghost stories, possession, hauntings, movies that use shaky camerawork (shaky cams). Oh, and of course zombies. Which is not to say any of these things are bad. They just continue to be done, over and over, in the same exact way. No one ever does anything different. How many zombie stories have you seen that have the same exact plot? It's an apocalypse and most people are zombies, and the humans left alive struggle to survive. And it's done the same way over and over again—sometimes the zombies move fast, sometimes they slow down—but that's about it when it comes to creativity. I've always been a huge fan of George A. Romero, and he's the guy who started the whole zombie thing, and in a movie like the original *Dawn of the Dead* (1978), he used zombies to make statements about consumerism and our culture, and there was always this layer of social commentary in his work. But those who came after him—for the most part—have completely jettisoned any ambitions to say something with their work. They just keep the basic monster elements and rehash them over and over.

I always say a great writer can take any subject matter and make it fresh and interesting again. The thing is, most people writing Hollywood horror movies don't seem interested in good writing or being original. They just want to grab the cash while they can.

I also see an awful lot of movies bring in occult elements when they run out of ideas, and they have no real understanding of what they're doing. There is absolutely no interest in accuracy or authenticity. No attention to details. When in doubt, bring in some guy who can read incantations from a forbidden book and make the demon go away. It's just tiresome.

Joe: How can writers interested in reviewing movies get on board, as well as get recognition?

Soares: I'm not sure if I'm the best person to ask that of. I pretty much just carved out my own niche. I'd been reviewing movies wherever I could, blogs, anything, and then Michael Arruda, who was doing the same thing, agreed to team up with me, and we tried to do something completely different with *Cinema Knife Fight*, by adding humor and having different characters pop up, and trying to make the review as entertaining as the movie itself. We deliberately set out to do something completely different, and I'm happy for any success or recognition we've gotten over the years.

But as far as getting a regular gig reviewing movies, I'm not really sure. In our case, we saw a gap and we filled it. But I think it's generally pretty hard to make a name for yourself as a movie critic, especially if you specialize in a genre like horror.

Then again, right now, aside from the rare magazines, there are so many horror sites and blogs that it's easy to find *somewhere* to write reviews. A lot of them don't pay, so don't expect to make a living at it.

Just see as many movies (of all kinds) that you can, read about movies and the filmmakers behind them. And basically just be as honest as you can in your review.

INTERVIEWS

Joe: **Any thoughts on how the horror movie genre has evolved over the last few decades?**

Soares: When I was a kid in the 1970s, I saw a lot of movies on television, and they were older films, and they relied much more on things like atmosphere and lighting, and nobody seems concerned about that anymore. But atmosphere is a huge thing if it's done right—it can add a lot of unspoken eeriness to a movie. Then the 1970s erupted with the whole gore scene—which I think is unfairly maligned. Sure, there were movies that relied on gore more than a good story, but there have been movies that told a good story and used gore as a tool. And that's all it is, really. A tool that you can bring out if you need to. But too many people started to think gore and atmosphere were the same thing, and they're not.

Now, there's too much reliance on CGI. It's the gore of the new millennium. And a big, blockbuster movie is more concerned with how it can dazzle us with CGI visuals than with a satisfying storyline. When I see movies that use CGI for blood spurting—they can't even use fake blood anymore!—that just bums me out.

Also, there used to be more reliance on things like makeup and costume design. Someone like Rick Baker could completely amaze you with what he did with masks and costumes. Now, they'll just create a creature that's all CGI, and, frankly, it often looks a lot more fake than a mask would. Great makeup effects are a dying art, and they work on a level CGI doesn't—a more visceral level. Something you can reach out and touch instead of playing on a green screen afterwards.

And then you have lower budget Hollywood films that use CGI, but don't have the budget to do it well, and their creatures just come out awful. When an old-fashioned makeup effects monster would do the job so much better.

So there's the over-reliance on CGI. And the way they use the same story over and over. And the lack of real creativity. Creativity is not encouraged in today's horror films—they're much more interested in the familiar, in making a movie that's just like the last big hit. People like the familiar—it's like comfort food—but, most of the time, it's creatively sterile.

But whether it's gore or CGI or whatever, the most important aspect of any good horror movie is its script. *The story*. And most Hollywood screenwriters seem to have forgotten how to tell a good story, especially in the horror genre.

Joe: **What do you think the horror movie fans want to see? What should we look out for in the future?**

Soares: I think the majority of horror fans—the ones who buy movie tickets—just want more of the same, and that's what they're going to get. As long as they go to see bad horror movies, more bad ones will continue to get made, where CGI and shaky cams are used to replace good stories, where lame concepts like the *Twilight* Series are popular (which, let's face it, is not horror at all, but romance using horror tropes. There's not one thing about the *Twilight* films that is scary or horrific).

There's also a trend lately to make everything into superheroes. In something like *Dracula Untold*, we're given a Vlad Tepes who is basically a good guy who makes a really bad choice in order to get amazing powers (super strength, control over bats) to defeat his enemies. Or the vampires in the *Twilight* movies, who can run really fast and are super strong. They just can't come out in the daytime or they'll sparkle, which I guess hurts or something. But, see, not everything has to be retooled to be a superhero. And horror characters definitely don't need to join the Avengers. **They need to be scary!**

Every once in a while someone will do something interesting and different (for some reason, a lot of these filmmakers seem to be outside the U.S.) and you'll get a jolt. But you'll have to seek it out. I know a lot of people claim to hate the *Human Centipede* movies for example, but at least they were something different, and completely bizarre enough to stand out from the crowd and get an audience interested. At least those movies try to be something new, and they definitely get people talking.

TOM HOLLAND

INTERVIEWED BY ADRIAN ROE

HAVING GROWN UP watching horror movies of the '80s, it is a passion that has remained with me to this day. In 2013 I decided to do something about it, and wrote *First Scream to the Last*—the definitive guide to '80s horror. Within the book I covered all pivotal and influential movies of this era, and was fortunate enough to have the support and input of many film directors involved in these movies. One such director was Tom Holland, who had written and directed *Fright Night* and *Child's Play*, arguably two of the biggest horror films of the decade. Tom's contribution toward the horror genre is without question, with both *Fright Night* and *Child's Play* becoming huge commercial success stories, as well as iconic genre pieces of the time. The influences of these movies can still be seen today, with a recent re-make of *Fright Night* proving popular with a new generation of fans. As for *Child's Play*, this became a successful franchise, with Tom's original idea and movie spawning five sequels to date. I had the pleasure of interviewing Tom regarding these movies for my book, and to follow is a small extract from that conversation. The full interview is available in *First Scream to the Last*—www.firstscreamtothelast.com."

Adrian: **Where did the inspiration come from to write *Fright Night*?**

Tom: I was writing *Cloak and Dagger*, which was based on *The Window*, Cornell Woolrich's adolescent version of *Rear Window*, and thought how funny it would be if a horror movie fan became convinced his next door neighbor was a vampire.

I didn't have a story until I thought of Peter Vincent.

Adrian: **Were there any obstacles that needed to be overcome, in order to realize the vision you had for *Fright Night*?**

Tom: Yeah. My lack of experience. LOL. I had a great team around me. Shell Schrager, who was head of production at Columbia at the time, surrounded me with superb craftsmen.

Best among them were Richard Edlund, who had just finished *Ghostbusters*, and John DeCuir, Sr. and Jr. I was working with people who have done huge movies on my 1st small production.

I was dumb lucky.

Adrian: **Did the film go to plan, or were there any changes that had to be made along the way that you had to deal with?**

Tom: The studio pressured me to cut some of the end sequence in the fight with Jerry Dandridge, but it didn't hurt. We were a small throw-away at the studio. All eyes were on *Perfect*, the big hot talent studio production. I had total control and no interference. 1st movie. Never happened again. Ah, well, so it goes.

In this business, you never know.

Adrian: **Did you have any idea whilst filming that it would be the success that is was?**

Tom: None. I just wanted to survive the experience. After you're well into production, it just became a matter of physical survival. You physically sag in the middle and then begin to gain energy as you approach the end.

Shooting is an endurance contest, you against your body (and sometimes sanity).

Adrian: **Why do you think the film has become so enduring and regarded as a classic within the genre?**

Tom: It has a heart. You care about the people. Hard to find today. It also has humor and warmth. Also not easy to come by.

I cared about the people when I was writing it. I am/was Charlie Brewster. It's my love letter to horror movie fans, of which I was one, back in the day of Hammer and AIP.

Adrian: **Where did the inspiration come from to write** *Child's Play*?

Tom: There was an original screenplay that was like an episode of Twilight Zone. The question was how to make it work for a wide release.

What I liked was it keyed into the universal fear we have all had when we were small children of our play things. What if my doll did come alive? What if my Raggedy Andy did try to strangle me? Is that damn stuffed bear looking at me in the dark?

I finally solved it when I created Charles Lee Ray. When I finally had a bad guy, a serial murderer, inside the doll, I had a story people could identify with.

Adrian: **What was the most difficult scene to direct/film and why?**

Tom: All of them with the doll. There was no CGI, hadn't been invented yet, all had to be done in the lens. Had a crew of puppeteers working to make Chucky come alive. Had to use everything from forced perspective, to a little person, the fabulous Ed Gale, to using Alex Vincent's 3 year old little sister (when the doll runs behind Dinah Manoff, the baby sitter).

Adrian: **What is your fondest memory regarding the whole** *Child's Play* **experience?**

Tom: When I first previewed it and the audience laughed and yelled, and I knew it was a success. They loved Chucky, 'cause he was such a profane evil little shit.

Adrian: **Why do you think the film has become so enduring and regarded as a classic within the genre?**

Tom: It works, and, once again, you cared about Mom and her little boy. Also, Brad Douriff was fab.

You're only involved if you care about the people in the story. There is very little as strong as Mom trying to save her son, even if it's from an evil doll.

Adrian: **Brad Dourif's voice has become instantly recognizable as Chucky's voice—was he always a favorite for the role?**

Tom: No, I tried to electronically treat it to match the quality of the dolls of that period and it didn't work. I had Jessica Walters in to voice the doll, but a woman's voice wasn't right either.

Ended up right back where I started, with Brad, who, of course, was perfect.

Adrian: **Where did the design for the Chucky doll come from?**

Tom: I went out and got a "My Buddy" doll (the original name for the doll, and the reason I couldn't use it) and a Raggedy Andy, and told Kevin Yaeger to combine the two, the size and body from My Buddy, and the coloring and freckles from Raggedy Andy.

Then I told him to give me a range of expressions from dolls, benign to the meanest SOB doll anybody had ever seen. Obviously he succeeded. I think there were at least a dozen different doll heads with a different expression, which we changed, depending on the scene.

TRICKS OF THE TRADE
NOVELIZATIONS

Novelizations—the best way for authors to enjoy one of their favorite franchises. But with strict guidelines and deadlines, it might not be for everyone.

I took some time to sit down with professional novelization and tie-in authors, and this is certainly an ideal option for authors who can work on tight deadlines, and those looking to bring in more money with their skills.

Joe Mynhardt

TRICKS OF THE TRADE: NOVELIZATIONS

HOW DID YOU FIRST GET INVOLVED IN THE HORROR MOVIE AND NOVELIZATION INDUSTRY?

Graham Masterton: As the editor of the UK edition of *Penthouse* magazine I was approached to write a series of "how-to" sex manuals. I had some very good friends and contacts in the sex business, including Xaviera Hollander, the so-called "Happy Hooker"; the Dutch dominatrix Monique von Cleef; Jenny Fabian, who wrote *Groupie;* and Tuppy Owens, the sex therapist who wrote *The Sex Maniac's Diary.* My first sex book *How To Drive Your Man Wild In Bed* sold over 2 million copies and is still in print after 40 years (it was the first non-medical sex book to be published in Poland after the fall of Communism). In all, I have written 27 sex books.

After the publication of the third or fourth sex book, however, my US publishers realized that the bottom had fallen out of the sex book market, so to speak. I still had a contract with them for the next book, however, so I sent them a supernatural thriller which I had written in the five days which I had spare between sex books. It was based on my wife Wiescka's pregnancy with our first son, combined with an idea which I remembered from reading The Buffalo Bill Annual when I was a boy—about manitous, the Native American spirits which possessed trees, rocks, wind, water and animals. It also told how shamans or wonder workers could commit suicide only to be reborn in the future, in the body of a modern woman. My editor liked the book although he asked me to rewrite the ending. Originally, the reincarnated wonder worker Misquamacus was laid low by the sexually transmitted disease which the woman he used as his host had caught from her boyfriend, who had returned from Viet Nam infected with "Saigon Rose." In the amended version, it was the spirits that live in today's computers that defeated the ancient Native American spirits.

The Manitou was an immediate success, and was picked up by the young Hollywood director Bill Girdler. He made a movie out of it, starring Tony Curtis, Susan Strasberg, Stella Stevens, Michael Ansara and Burgess Meredith. Of course I immediately followed it up with a second supernatural thriller *The Djinn*, using the Arabian Nights story of Ali-Baba to suggest that the Forty Thieves were evil spirits contained in jars which had been acquired by a modern-day American with malicious intent. Then came *The Revenge of the Manitou, The Wells of Hell,* and so on. I took a couple of years' break from writing horror after that and wrote some historical sagas like *Rich, Railroad,* and *Lady of Fortune,* which were all bestsellers (and, again, are still available as eBooks these days), but returned to horror with *Tengu,* which postulated that a vengeful Japanese was using ancient spirits to get his own back for Hiroshima and Nagasaki.

Armand Rosamilia: Thanks to Hobbes End Publishing and especially Vincent Hobbes, who liked my work. They also liked the fact I was a full-time author and I wrote a fast and clean first draft. They asked me to do what turned into *Miami Spy Games: Russian Zombie Gun.* That was a couple-three years ago. Since then I've written over a dozen adaptations for various movie projects.

Ed Naha: A: The novelization period was fun and, again, it just popped up. I had written *The Making of Dune* in '84 and had stayed friends with the merchandizing folks at Universal (ohhhh. The stories I could tell about the making of *The Making of Dune*). The Universal folks knew a woman—whose name escapes me—who agented out of her house. She was a chain-smoking, gravely voice saint, long gone now. Tough talking, no b.s. She represented Robocop. She hired me to novelize it after we blabbed for a couple of hours. I got hold of the script, met with the producers and screenwriter, and wrote it.

The tricky thing about novelizations, back then, was the fact that the manuscript had to be finished before the final cut of the movie was done. The book had to be released at the same time as the film and old-fashioned publishing took some time. So, many times, you'd be working from a script that changed dramatically during the film's production. In *Robocop,* for instance, there was a through-line concerning the wife and a moon colony that was totally excised from the script. Some of it is in the book, though. The ending of the novel features that.

There are times when your brain just freezes over. *Ghostbusters II* was filming when I wrote the book and they hadn't decided on an ending. They had three possible endings. I incorporated parts of all three.

Dead Bang, a police/action flick with Don Johnson, had a great, great script in terms of the character. I loved dealing with that. The third act of the film was rough, though, in that it was a chase. It's really, really hard to write page after page of people running.

I was at the first cut of the movie with all those involved in a screening room. Nearly all the great character stuff was cut out of the film, but the chase went on forever. After the lights came up, I was introduced to all the folks involved with the film. There was one fellow who seemed to be in shock. I was introduced, "And this is our screenwriter."

I didn't know it then, but I'd wear the identical expression many, many times in years to come.

I don't know what the guidelines are now but, back then, you pretty much had to adhere to the script as much as possible and include all the dialogue. You could elaborate and add quite a bit of background narrative showing how the characters thought but you couldn't just pull stuff out of your butt. In the middle of *Ghostbusters II*, for instance, you couldn't just insert a massive alien attack. Although, thinking about it now, it wouldn't have hurt.

Jonathan Maberry: I was sitting at home watching a monster movie when I got a call totally out of the blue by the vice-president in charge of licensing at Universal. She'd seen a thread I'd started on Facebook talking about werewolf movies and was on the prowl for an author to write the novelization of the Benecio Del Toro/Anthony Hopkins remake of *The Wolfman*. Funny thing was, she opened that conversation by asking me if I'd ever seen the original. Hilarious. I landed the gig and the novel went on to become my first NY Times bestseller and it won the Scribe Award for best Novelization. Good thing I answered the phone.

Later I was approached by Max Brooks to write a novella for a GI Joe anthology he was doing for IDW. How could I say no? Later I created the *V-Wars* shared world and invited other writers to write stories set in that world. *V-Wars* is now a series of anthologies, a comic book, a board game (coming out in December) and is in development for TV. And the CEO of IDW asked me to edit a series of X-Files anthologies. I also did a novel based on the role-playing game *Deadlands*, and my book, *Ghostwalkers* debuts in September.

I'm fortunate in that I'm now regularly approached about these projects. I wish I could take more of them than I do, but my other novel schedule won't allow it.

Tim Waggoner: I'd already published a number of non-horror tie-ins, and I'd been talking with some of the editors at Games Workshop in the UK about the possibility of doing a Warhammer novel for them. They got the license from New Line Cinema to produce original novels based on *A Nightmare on Elm Street, Friday the Thirteenth, Jason X*, and *Final Destination*. When I discovered this, I pitched novel ideas for all of these properties, and I ended up getting a contract to do a novel based on *A Nightmare on Elm Street*. I was going to get to write a *Final Destination* novel, too, but Games Workshop decided to discontinue their New Line books before I could. Since then, I've written horror tie-in fiction (novels and short stories) for *Supernatural, Grimm, X-Files*, and *V-Wars*.

IS THERE A SPECIFIC WAY YOU APPROACH ALL THESE PROJECTS?

Graham Masterton: I was trained as a newspaper reporter and a magazine editor, so I recognize a potential story when I see one. My tried-and-tested technique is usually to take a legendary or mythical evil and bring it to life in the modern age to see how some ordinary everyday people would cope with it.

Armand Rosamilia: They all seem to be unique. Sometimes I write based off of a screenplay. Sometimes watching the dailies. Other stories have been written just by talking to the producer and him telling me the basic ideas and then having to flesh it out myself.

Ed Naha: Not really. Anything I don't write from scratch, including punching up scripts and articles, I just take a few steps back and think: "Now, how do I solve this problem?" It's almost like a school assignment. Someone tells you to write a term paper on The Crusades using specific reference books. The challenge there is:

TRICKS OF THE TRADE: NOVELIZATIONS

"How do I get all the information across in a way that hasn't been done before?" It's just puzzle solving, really.

Jonathan Maberry: For *The Wolfman*, since I did not get to see the movie until after the book was in stores, I approached it like a novel. After reading David Self's lovely script, I did extensive research and then sat down to write a Gothic horror novel. It's a disservice to your readers to just wrap paragraphs around lines in a script and call that a novel. The best media tie-in writers in the business (Keith DeCandido, Greg Cox, Nancy Holder, Christopher Golden, James A. Moore, Max Allan Collins, etc.) go full-tilt in writing true novels. To do a media tie-in book that you're proud of means finding the story you'd fall in love with, the one you'd go out and buy, and then writing the hell out it.

Tim Waggoner: First, I try to come up with an interesting idea that hasn't been done before with the property or an interesting angle on it. I also try to think of a character arc so that by the end of the book or short story, the character is changed by the events that have taken place. This can be difficult since if the character belongs to the IP holder—such as Sam and Dean Winchester—then I have to find a smaller character arc, one that will end with the characters growing, but not changing so much as to make them too different by the end of the story. The general rule with tie-writing is that you can play with the toys, but you can't break them. They must be the same when you put them back on the shelf. I try to capture the stylistic feel of the property, as well. In *Supernatural* there are dark moments that alternate with humorous moments, and sometimes they are combined into darkly humorous moments. Certain types of stories won't fit in the world of *Supernatural*, such as science fiction or straight suspense/mystery, so those are out. I try to capture the characters, their relationships to one another, and their voices as best I can. I often go back to the original material—books, TV shows, movies—and binge on them to immerse myself in their worlds before I start writing. Once I write, I stay away from that material and concentrate on writing my book. I think of all my novels as mine, regardless of whether they're original or tie-ins, and I approach tie-ins with the same care and respect as I do my original creations. Thinking of a tie-in as mine keeps me from worrying how the IP holders and fans might react to my work, otherwise I'd be too self-conscious about pleasing everyone, and I'd never get a word written!

WHO NORMALLY APPROACHES YOU AND HOW MUCH CREATIVE FREEDOM DO THEY GRANT YOU?

Graham Masterton: I am approached by my publishers (or I approach them, if an idea occurs to me). I have two main publishers in the UK and US—Severn House for my horror fiction and Head of Zeus for my crime fiction. I also work very closely with three publishers in Poland, who are all my friends as well as my publishers. Like *How To Drive Your Man Wild In Bed, The Manitou* was the first Western horror novel published in Poland after Communism fell, and so it made a considerable impact there. My late wife Wiescka was Polish and was my agent at the time, so we made very strong and close connections there. I visit Poland at least three times every year for promotion and to see my friends.

I am given complete creative freedom, but I have very exacting editors and line-editors, and so I have to make sure that everything I write is completely watertight.

Armand Rosamilia: My contact will call me up cold and tell me they are ready for the next book. They are usually 40,000 words and I get 21 days to write it. They'll sit on it a few weeks before sending back their notes on what needs to be changed. Sometimes it is minor (word choice or no profanity depending on the movie) but sometimes they've since removed a character or plotline from the movie and I need to change the book. They allow me to get inside the character's heads and add back-story and flesh out the plots, and (if I do say so myself), the book is always richer than the movie.

Ed Naha: I don't think my literary agents ever brought me a novelization. They always resulted from bumping into people or shooting the breeze with someone who'd say, "Hey, I know someone who's looking to get this done . . . " I was very, very lucky to move out to L.A. when there was still low-budget film work being done.

Everyone did everything. There was a network of folks who weren't high up on the food chain but always had a friend who knew a friend who had a friend. We were all just so excited to be part of whatever the hell it was we were doing that we spread our good fortune around.

Jonathan Maberry: The approach can come from any direction. I've been asked by editors, producers, licensing people, game developers, comic book companies . . . it really varies. The trick is to have a strong social media presence. Writers need to be easy to find. And it's also important to establish a tone to your personal brand so that you get a reputation as someone who is willing to try new things and, when doing so will go full-tilt on it. You also have to know the world –even if it means binge-watching, binge-reading, etc., and one critical thing that comes with this is respecting the fan-base who love that world.

As for creative freedom, this varies license to license. With *The Wolfman* they pretty much left me alone. With *X-Files* the people at FOX were very involved with making sure it fit their product line. In the actual storytelling it would be a mistake to accept a project where your creative freedom is severely limited. I won't take that kind of gig.

Tim Waggoner: I've done tie-ins based on movies, TV series, video games, and role-playing games. I've yet to do a novelization of a film, but I'd love to one day. Writers can go about getting tie-in gigs a couple different ways, but before they even attempt to do so, they need to publish their own novels first, preferably through traditional publishers. Tie-in publishers and IP holders need to know that not only can you successfully produce a professional-level manuscript, but that you can also work collaboratively with others. After all, the IP holder has the final say on how a property is handled, meaning that you will have to collaborate with them and that ultimately they're the Boss with a capital B. Indie authors may not have experience working in the organizational hierarchy of traditional publishing. Assuming you have a track record as a novelist, tie-in editors may come looking for you, or you might approach them in person at a conference or via email. Once you've been writing tie-ins for a while, editors are more likely to seek you out for future projects. Networking with tie-in writers can help. You can ask them who their editor was for a certain project then query that editor to see if he or she has any openings for new writers.

In terms of contacts, the editor at the publishing house is your first and generally only contact. The editor is in contact with the IP holder's representative, but usually you don't work directly with them, although the editor does pass along their notes on ideas, outlines, and manuscripts to you. That's been my experience, at least.

In general, as long as you follow the "play with the toys; don't break the toys" philosophy, there's a lot you can do in tie-in fiction, especially if you can create your own main characters or, if you have to use established main characters, you create your own supporting characters. That said, you need to use your common sense. You can't have established characters behaving in a way they normally wouldn't, and you can't do anything too "fannish," like shipping characters that don't have an established romantic relationship in the original property. I try to think of myself as a staff writer for a show or studio writer for a film when I do a tie-in and write a story that the IP holder would approve for broadcast or filming.

WHAT IS THE ONE MOVIE FRANCHISE YOU'D LOVE TO WRITE NOVELS FOR AND WHY? WHICH OF YOUR BOOKS WOULD MAKE A GREAT FRANCHISE?

Graham Masterton: I would love to have my own movie franchise, especially for my *Night Warriors* novels, which are horror fantasies based on ordinary people becoming well-armed warriors in other people's dreams and nightmares. I have several friends in the movie business in Hollywood, but it is far from easy getting a novel made into a movie, especially a horror novel which requires expensive CGI. At least 10 of my novels have been optioned over the years by serious Hollywood production companies, including Paramount, Universal, Gold Circle, Phoenix Pictures and Libertine Films. Almost all of them have got to script stage and had talent and directors attached, but failed to find sufficient finance and/or distribution. Jonathan Mostow (*U-571*) optioned *Trauma*, about a crime-scene cleaner, Fred Caruso, who was one of the producers of *The Godfather*, among many other pictures, has written a brilliant script for *Demon's Door,* my novel about a Korean demon who possesses a class of LA college students, but we are still looking for investment.

I have written two novelizations of movies—*Phobia*, which starred Paul Michael Glaser, and *Inserts*, which starred Richard Dreyfus.

Armand Rosamilia: I'd keep the *Expendables* franchise going. There are so many other action stars you can incorporate, and so many in-jokes you can add to it. It might not be the first thing you think of when talking about movie franchises, but it is mindless fun.

Ed Naha: Well, since most of the franchises today are ancillary rights deals for comic books, novels or toys, there's slim pickins out there. It's not like I'm going to write: *Legos: The Uprising*. It's going to sound weird but I think *The Expendables* (if you can consider that a franchise) would lend itself to one kick ass series of books. There are so many characters that are just broad-stroked in the film. You could do some serious writing expanding upon them. I'd also like to be joined at the hip to Luc Besson. His movies are just so over-the-top and fun. It would be trippy to tackle them.

Jonathan Maberry: I've got my sights set on projects in the worlds of *Star Wars*, *Aliens* and *Firefly*. We'll see how that plays out.

Tim Waggoner: *Halloween* or *Friday the Thirteenth*, maybe. I think it would be creatively challenging to work with the slasher formula and try to bring something interesting and original to it.

WHAT IS THE ONE THING YOU SHOULD NEVER DO WHEN WRITING A NOVELIZATION?

Armand Rosamilia: Begin before you get the parameters of what they are looking for. You aren't rewriting the wheel (or reinventing, whatever), so make sure you have all the info upfront. It saves a lot of time. Trust me.

Ed Naha: Think it's your own.

Jonathan Maberry: There are some real bear-traps you can step into when writing any media tie-in book (or short story). Each, though, has an implied solution if you think about it. Don't disrespect the fans. Big one. Don't try to write one of these stories if you don't know the subject matter. People do this all the time and it shows. Don't mail it in. Even if you've been paid up front and it's a done deal, approach the work with your whole heart and use every tool in your creative toolbox. Your name is on it, when means it stands as an example of you as a writer. Also, get to know the other media tie-in writers. They're a nice crowd and they're incredibly supportive.

Tim Waggoner: Have contempt for the IP. You don't have to be the biggest fan of a property to write tie-fiction based on it, but if you can't respect the property for what it is—even if you're doing the project primarily for money and not love of the property—then you shouldn't write the book.

HOW HECTIC ARE THE DEADLINES, AND WHAT KIND OF ARRANGEMENTS ARE THERE ABOUT YOU MAKING FACTS ABOUT THE MOVIE PUBLIC?

Graham Masterton: I was approached to write both *Phobia* and *Inserts* about a week before a finished manuscript was needed. I was sent the scripts of both movies and it was arranged for me to have a private screening of both of them on Monday morning. By Friday I had completed them. They are a piece of cake, really, because all the plotting and dialogue is already written for you, and all I did was add some back stories to the beginning and end, and try to covey what the characters were thinking inside their heads, which of course a movie cannot do.

TRICKS OF THE TRADE: NOVELIZATIONS

Armand Rosamilia: I sign a non-disclosure agreement for each book. I've written over a dozen books but only a few are currently out, and not all of them under my name. So I can't talk about most of them until they get released, if they ever see the light of day.

Ed Naha: In terms of deadlines, whenever you do work for someone who gives you a check, you're given a deadline. Either you make the deadline or they break your legs. Or at least spread the word on how lazy you are. Legs will heal. Reputations take longer.

As for spilling the beans about movie plotlines, when I was writing and dinosaurs ruled the earth, nobody thought about contacting the dork doing the novelizations. With me, it was a little different, because I also wrote about movies.

As a moviegoer, I've never appreciated people revealing too much about a movie before its released. I'm one of those cranks who still wants to experience the movie as it's happening before me. I still won't read news articles, detailed reviews or spoiler-saturated sneaks before I see a movie.

Jonathan Maberry: Deadlines for media tie-in books can be a little frightening at first. When I took the gig to write a novel based on *The Wolfman* I was given a due-date of seven weeks. Yikes. It was my fourth novel, and I'd taken nearly a year with each of the last three. I had to cowboy up and refine my work ethic while still bringing my creative A-game. The effect was that I became extremely focused, which then helped with the rest of my career. After that I never took longer than three months to write a novel.

All media tie-in work comes with some kind of non-disclosure agreement. If you're adapting a movie, then you are not allowed to share any plot details. Which makes sense . . . though the books themselves are usually published a few weeks before the movie hits theaters. Crazy. If you're writing a novel tied to a TV series, or one that is 'in the world of' a movie or show but is an original work, you have fewer restrictions about sharing. While writing *Ghostwalkers*, my novel inspired by the *Deadlands* role-playing game, I teased the public with a few details because this was an original novel.

Tim Waggoner: I usually get three months of writing time once an outline is finally approved by the IP holder, but it's not uncommon to get less time than that. I've known writers who've only had a couple weeks to deliver a finished novel. The approval process can take a long time. First the editor has to approve your initial pitch, then the IP holder has to approve it. You'll do some revising of your pitch before you finally get the go-ahead to write an outline. The editor and IP holder then have to approve the outline, and you'll probably need to revise it several times before they're both satisfied. Only then can you start writing Chapter One. The approval process could take months, and you may be left with relatively little time to actually compose the novel. So if you want to be a tie-in writer, it helps if you can write fast! Whatever you do, don't be tempted to start writing the novel before you get the final go-ahead. When I wrote a *Nightmare on Elm Street* tie-in several years, New Line Cinema took a long time to respond to the outline. The editor told me to start writing, confident that New Line would approve the story. I'd written sixty pages when New Line finally got back to us and told us that the storyline wouldn't do and that I had to start all over. I learned my lesson, and since then I won't write a single word of the actual novel until it's officially approved.

Tim Waggoner: I've already discussed deadlines earlier. I've rarely had to sign non-disclosure agreements for any of the tie-in projects I've done, but it's not uncommon. I've been given episode scripts for an entire season of a show before the episodes have aired so I'd know where the season was headed and could plan my novel accordingly. I wasn't told not to disseminate the scripts, but of course it's a given that you keep any advance knowledge to yourself. It's part of being a professional. If you do reveal something you shouldn't, you'll be less likely to get offers for future tie-in projects because editors and IP holders won't trust you—and why should they?

FOR SOMEONE INTERESTED IN DOING NOVELIZATIONS, WHICH BOOKS ARE THE BEST RESOURCES OR CASE STUDIES (INCLUDING YOUR OWN WORK, OF COURSE)?

Ed Naha: I haven't a clue on that one. For writing, in general, it's always good to know the basics. Spelling is nice. So is proper grammar. Karen Elizabeth Gordon has two painless books that should be read by all: *The Well-Tempered Sentence* and *The Transitive Vampire—A Handbook of Grammar for the Innocent, the Eager and the Doomed*. They're both fun reads as well. And, in order to write, you have to read. Read. Read. Read. It doesn't have to be French Existentialism. Read fiction that interests you.

It's pretty amazing, to me at least, how many people can't spell or construct a sentence. Something has short-circuited the art of cognitive learning. Today's society actually encourages people to be stupid. Why take time to learn anything or explore a topic when you can push a "like" button or just agree with pre-chewed soundbites? It's only a matter of time before we forget how to use our thumbs—which will really screw up our texting, u bet.

Jonathan Maberry: The *Aliens* novelization by Alan Dean Foster is a great place to start if you want to see how this kind of thing should be done right. And check out the winners of the annual *Scribe* Awards. They're the awards given by the International Association of Media Tie-in Writers. The list of nominees and winners provide an excellent door into the best of this kind of writing. Start there.

Tim Waggoner: The International Association of Media Tie-In Writers is a wonderful resource. Their website address is www.iamtw.org, and you can find a lot of advice on writing tie-ins there. The organization has also published a useful book on tie-ins called *Tied-In: The Business, History, and Craft of Media Tie-In Writing*. It includes articles by such professionals as Max Allan Collins, Greg Cox, Jeff Mariotte, Elizabeth Massie, Donald Bain, Nancy Holder, William C. Dietz, and more. Donald Bain's book *Murder, HE Wrote* is another great resource.

ANY ADVICE FOR SOMEONE TRYING TO GET THEIR FOOT IN THE DOOR?

Graham Masterton: Get yourself a good agent.

Armand Rosamilia: Know that writing for a movie company is completely different from writing for a publisher. The deadlines are crazy and they change on a dime, depending on too many factors for a writer to comprehend. Just roll with it. You might get three books in a row but then nothing for six months. Then, right in the middle of dinner, the phone rings . . .

Ed Naha: I'm pretty much clueless about the current process. I would imagine that things are much more corporate and less loosey-goosey now. Plus, the entire film/TV industry is so diffuse in terms of fandom. Everyone is a writer/actor/director/YouTube generator. I'd try to become part of a network of professional or semi-pro folks that are within, even if it's only tangentially, the gravitational pull of actual production companies and publishing houses. The problematic aspect of the contemporary scene is that, although we're all connected via social networking and instantaneous feedback, most of it doesn't translate to actual creativity or, if it does, a creative work that makes its way to the marketplace. F'rinstance, nearly everyone feels that they have a great novel within them. They don't. Today, however, you can spew out a novel, self-publish it and bask in the glow of your Facebook friends. This is closely akin to having your parents like a painting you did. You're not destined for an art gallery unless you actually take the time to hone your craft. A lot of folks today feel that, if they think it, it's great. In general, the secret to writing is writing. Just write. Write to both express yourself but, just as importantly, to entertain and inform. Start contributing to local publications or web sites. You can't take shortcuts.

Jonathan Maberry: Professionalism is key. That includes accepting the requirements of the license. And it also includes not being a prima donna. No one wants to work with a problem child. Everyone wants to work with the fun kid in the playground.

That said, it's also important to become part of the world of the licenses you really love. Join the Twitter and Facebook groups. Speak up. Have fun, be positive. Never talk anything down. Be a part of the community but always deport yourself as a professional. That sends a great message.

TRICKS OF THE TRADE: NOVELIZATIONS

Tim Waggoner: Write and publish your own novels first. Go the traditional publishing route to show you can work with a corporate hierarchy. Read as many tie-ins as you can to get a feel for how an IP is translated into novel form. Network with tie-in writers at conferences, on Facebook and Twitter, and read their blogs. Learn as much as you can about the business. Find out which publishers are doing which tie-ins and try to find out who the editors for those series are. If you want to write some fan fiction to practice, that's okay, but professional editors don't consider fan fiction a credential for writing officially licensed tie-ins.

ANY LEGAL ADVICE YOU THINK AUTHORS NEED TO KNOW BEFORE SIGNING A NOVELIZATION CONTRACT?

Tim Waggoner: It's work for hire, so you own nothing. The novel belongs to the IP holder, and they can use it in any way they see fit, including taking anything you created and using it in a TV series, etc. You will get no additional compensation for that. You will probably get royalties, though, assuming the book earns out. After all these years, I still get royalties from the books I did for Wizards of the Coast. It may not be a princely sum, but the checks are always welcome.

HOW STRESSFUL WAS YOUR VERY FIRST NOVELIZATION OR TIE-IN?

Tim Waggoner: My first tie-in novel was for Wizards of the Coast's new *Dragonlance* YA series. I contacted one of the editors about writing for them, and they wanted to get the new series going, but no one had done any work on it yet. So I developed characters and the basic storyline for the series, and I wrote the first and fourth books in the series. There was less stress because I could develop the characters instead of working with already established characters, and I was familiar enough with the *Dragonlance* setting so I wasn't stressed with working in that world. Helping to launch a new series—especially one that I knew *Dragonlance* co-creator Margaret Weis would help oversee—was more daunting.

VENOMOUS LITTLE MAN PRODUCTIONS—A CASE STUDY

A STATEMENT OF truth: making movies is not glamorous. It's hard work, takes time and resources and has as many lows as it has highs.

But we love it. Fact.

What is also a fact is that we made our first film, *Ascension*, as total novices. It has since gone on to be shown on screens worldwide and has won several awards. Somehow, some way, we did something right.

This chapter is our attempt to show how we went about doing it. This is our story, freezing fields and all.

Dave Jeffery & James Hart
Venomous Little Man Productions (UK)

LET S MAKE A MOVIE!

GETTING THE IDEA

James Hart: It sounds cliché, but I've always loved film, and the thought of making one was a dream that I never thought I would be able to fulfill. Film was the first media I ever had any affinity with and, as I've got older, that affinity grew stronger. After attending years of Horror Film Festivals and finding it increasingly frustrating to find the gems amongst the rough, I felt it was time to stop moaning and make something I'd prefer to watch.

I'd had ideas for short films in my head for nearly two years, but they were never fully conceived. I would sometimes find a start and an end point, but that middle third was always elusive. A brief chat with Dave at work changed that. I think he sensed my passion for the media, and much to my surprise he offered to let me try and make a film based on one of his soon to be published stories.

Handy Hint: If you're passionate about making a film, then start making a film! If you have little ideas, get them written down, talk to people you trust about those ideas, start to develop and nurture them. If they don't grow into anything you think is special then put them in a safe place and come back to them. Nothing gets made until you make it.

DECIDING ON THE STORY

James: The original short story, "Ascension," was engaging and haunting. It was one of those rare reads that transports you, makes you feel like you're walking next to the characters, but the thought of putting it on film was almost as terrifying as the narrative.

My friendship with Dave was in its infancy, making the thought of suggesting any changes to the story a worrying concept, but he quickly reassured me that he wasn't 'precious' about those sort of things and we soon started to discuss and modify the script. The story worked perfectly on paper, but we had concerns about how certain elements would translate to screen, namely the opening scene and the finale.

We also had to get clarity on filming the story as it was due to be published in ALT-ZOMBIE. A few emails with Peter Mark May (CEO at Hersham Horror Books) later and within two days he'd sent me a first draft of the script.

Handy Hint: Allocate time to get intimate with your story. Reread it, discuss it with your team and family, explain it to them as you see it in your mind . . . then do it again, until you feel like it's a part of you. If you're directing you need to have a clear vision for the project, there can be flexibility in that vision but you need to know the stop off points.

SCRIPTING *ASCENSION*

Dave Jeffery: Ascension was the first script I had ever written. I guess that, because I was so familiar with the story, I thought it would be relatively easy to adapt. Wrong. And then some. One of the chief differences between writing a script and writing a story is that the descriptive narrative, which puts the scene into the reader's head, becomes redundant due to cinema being a visual medium. Conversely, the ability to give background to the characters so that the reader can connect with their 'story' is also removed. Instead it is through dialogue and behaviour that the audience gets to understand how a character functions and why they do what it is they do.

We also decided to expand the ending of my original short story, which concluded on a visceral note, to a final scene that is highly emotive. James and I are fans of the kind of horror films that have an emotional impact. It's our experience that these are the kind of films that people carry with them. It had always been our dream to have members of the audience saying, 'I watched your film and it has stayed with me.' This has happened over the past few years and it makes us immensely proud.

I'm not ashamed to say that defining my first efforts as 'a script' is somewhat misleading. It had no formatting as such, just a bunch of dialogue and loose descriptions of the scenes. I had not become familiar or had any awareness of scriptwriting software such as Final Draft. It's different now of course, but I do look back on the first script and it makes me smile. If we were to use the *one minute per page* scriptwriting rule, *Ascension* shouldn't have lasted longer than ten minutes. In the end it became 32 minutes. We call it a 'not so short, short.' I watch the film today and recognise that I would write it very differently. But would I change its essence? No sir. Not a chance.

THINKING SMALL

James: 'How do you make a horror movie?' It was a question I asked myself a few times an hour every day for about five months of pre-production. Not that I ever used the term 'pre-production' because that would infer that I knew what it actually was at that time. So, having no idea what we were doing meant one thing to us: *start small*. The original plan involved myself and Dave doing just about everything from filming to acting. Considering neither of us knew anything about either of those aspects, it's a good thing that's not how things worked out. Within those first few weeks I went into every high street camera shop I could find to look at hand held camcorders that were around the £200 mark. The aim was to get this filmed, any way we could.

Handy Hint: Deal with the issues/problems/hurdles that you can manage first! Build! If you don't know what you're doing that's fine, learn as you go but try and approach obstacles in a logical way—do the stuff that you know how to do first.

PLOTS AND BEER MATS

Dave: Planning meetings were held at The Hopwood Inn, a pub in Worcestershire. There was a sense of irony in that most of what we knew about film making could probably have been written on the back of the proverbial beer mat, so there were plenty of those to hand. During these meetings we would discuss how to move forward with the production. By this point James and I had established the script and this had been storyboarded, so it was about breaking these down into their nuances and, what's more, establish the means by which it could all be co-ordinated. Fortunately we had access to a wonderfully organised person in Christina (Schulte—production manager). Basically the preparations, including co-ordinating props and amenities such as port-a-loos and vehicles, came down to her.

THE IDEA GROWS

James: Social media had a massive impact on the evolution of our ideas. We created a Facebook page for *Ascension* and very quickly people started to show interest and offer encouragement. Friends began to offer their help, then friends of friends, and before we knew it, people we didn't know, people with useable skills, started to approach us. Our aspirations began to grow. People began to connect us with other people and we then had the makings of a crew: a make-up artist, a camera man, even a sound man with industry experience offered to work with us. It was at this time we decided to rethink our approach and adapt our vision to make full use of the talent available to us. I started to dream of using an airplane for the opening shot.

Handy Hint: Talk to people about what you want to do. You may be surprised what that guy at work knows about making films. Don't tell people everything, but show people your passion and see what can happen organically to your movie when other people get involved. Making a movie can be like driving a car or walking to the shop, you have a destination but you may have to deviate along the way. Keep the journey flexible and you are more likely to make it.

GETTING VENOMOUS: CREATING A PRODUCTION COMPANY

James: One of the first people we approached to be involved was Richard O'Connor (producer and editor). I knew him via an athletics club and he'd worked in theatre and TV, and has a head for the technical things in this world. Richard jumped at the chance to be involved and shared our enthusiasm for making a movie. The three of us attended a Zombie Walk event in Birmingham with the intention of cheekily getting some footage of zombies, but it served better to highlight the importance of quality make up/prosthetics if we wanted our creatures to be believable and frightening. Quality over quantity was an overriding ethic we tried to embrace after that day. A few hours in a local pub to get lunch and discuss the way forward turned into a discussion about how we would protect the rights of what we would make. Creating a company seemed like an ideal resolution. Names were bandied around, but nothing really stuck until I jokingly suggested naming it after something I'd once sarcastically called Dave. Myself and Richard are over 6ft, Dave isn't.

Handy Hint: It is always recommended that your films are released through a registered production company. This provides investors with a transparent funding stream. Register your company prior to attempting to use any crowd funding platform as these aspects are integral to accessing such platforms. Registration is low cost, but make sure that you do your research on the statutory implications of setting up a company.

FINDING THE FUNDS

James: Money is tight for everyone from a working class background. That's not a plea for sympathy—it's a simple fact. I don't know anyone that has money to fund a project for a group of guys that had never made a film before, so the only way to get this made was to fund it ourselves. We were incredibly lucky that so many people involved didn't want money; they wanted to make a film, too. They worked for free. But for plenty of the people involved, particularly the actors, this was how they made a living and they needed to be paid. We were still lucky, though. No one was greedy and all the professionals believed in the project, so they worked for base rates and expenses. If they hadn't, two nurses and an engineer could never have found the money to make a film with so many talented actors and crew involved!

Handy Hint: Don't expect people to give you their hard earned cash, and don't insult talented people by asking them to work for free or for a credit. Get creative with how you make the movie, spend time actually making bits of gear that you want. Don't wait around for cash to fall into your hand to buy that expensive dolly, make it with what you have lying around. You really don't need much money to make a movie. You do need time, effort and commitment, though. There are many examples of do-it-yourself film making on platforms such as YouTube. Information ranges from building basic rigs such as dolly tracks, and getting creative with simple visual effects.

PRE-PRODUCTION

CASTING THE NET

Dave: As we've mentioned, our first thought was to get hold of a small camera and use a guerrilla approach to telling the story. This meant that we would shoot and act in it. As the script writing process finished and we had a story that was no longer just visceral but charged with emotion, it became pretty clear pretty quickly that this piece had become something that needed a different perspective. I think we felt during the writing and storyboarding process that the film had to be made to the best of our ability, and anything less than this kind of investment would be doing the story an injustice. It was at this point we stopped talking about a hand held video recorder and less than amateur actors.

I had recently watched a British horror flick called *Inbred* and was taken with the performance by one of its stars, Derek Melling. I suggested to James that we have a go at securing him in the cast. I found him on Facebook and he accepted my friend request. I struck up a conversation with him and over the next week we were talking about *Ascension*. I asked if he would like to see the script and he thankfully said yes. His response to it was amazing and after a SKYPE chat he was on board as its star. He recommended Mark Rathbone who came on board almost immediately, as we'd seen him in *Inbred* and knew he could play the role of Eddie with ease. From that point we gained confidence and accrued professional actors via Fizzog Theatre Company (UK) and Laurence Saunders came on board after Jacky Fellows (who plays Annie) suggested we approach him. Laurence's feedback on the script was highly receptive and we cast him as Tom without hesitation. Sam Knight (who plays Carl) came on board at the suggestion of our camera man who had worked with him on another short project.

Once we'd assembled the cast and crew, the project took on a solid feel. That was when we started to get scared!

Handy Hint: Always invest in good actors. Even if your budget is meager, make sure there is enough to pay actors a fee. Many actors may well choose to waive fees if they believe in the project and script. However, this should never be taken for granted and funding for actors should be integral to the initial budget.

Handy Hint: If you are using freelance crew, make sure that the agreed deal in terms of payment (or waiver of payment) and final credit is written down and signed by all parties. This makes sure that everyone is clear once the film is in the can (and potentially heading to Cannes) what to expect in terms of return.

FINDING LOCATIONS

James: I was nearly arrested! Living in the Midlands (UK) has its benefits; it has an incredibly varied landscape and lots of open space which seemed perfect for a tiny budget film. Knowing the area worked for us, but it still involved a degree of driving around, paying far too much attention to the surroundings and not the road! We knocked on a few doors, asking for permission. On the occasions where no one answered those doors, enthusiasm got the better of me. I accidentally came across a location that took my breath away. As an old land fill site, complete with open expanses, existing portacabins and giant, heavy plant machinery, it had everything we wanted to create a post-apocalyptic landscape in one place. It looked bleak but had a real 'survivors camp' type feel to it. It also had a big locked gate. There was no bell and no one around to ask for permission, but it did have a large hole in the fence. I had a look around the site, calling out for an owner, and avoiding the large ferocious chained up guard dog. I took pictures on my phone and it felt like I'd struck gold. When I left I put a note on the gate with my phone number asking for the owner to give me a call.

That night I got a call. The owner laughed at how he'd watched me on CCTV with one hand on the phone ready to call the Police. Again, we got lucky. He said we could use his site for nothing more than a credit on the film. I was starting to think this film was meant to be made.

Handy Hint: I'd never advise anyone to go onto someone else's property; it's risky and potentially very stupid. I was lucky to meet people that bought into what I was doing, but luck can be like the wind—so don't rely on it. Be polite, courteous and respectful to land owners and always get every type of permission that is needed.

STORY BOARDING

James: On occasion, having no experience or reference point can be a good thing. The story boarding process proved to be invaluable in not only helping me plan shots, but also to develop the story. It was a process that ran through pre-production in its entirety, starting off with stick men and lots of directional arrows and notes. Slowly, as my ability to draw improved, it became much more detailed and involved more artistic expression. The entire opening sequence of the film, including the aerial footage, was developed through the story boarding and, as a director, it become my most useful and reliable tool. I also experimented with stop motion. Using paper cut outs of the actors and vehicles, I was able to plan the entire 'standoff' scene from the film. My notebook and sketches are never far from hand on set. Not only does it serve as a great *aide memoire*, but it's also a great visual tool for directing actors and Directors of Photography.

Handy Hint: A notebook is cheap, quick, easy and incredibly valuable. Helps plan, describe, direct and is a great memory aid when you've been on set for 12 hours. Also, it isn't dependent on a power outlet!

THE NEWSREELS

James: *Ascension* opens with a montage of newsreel clips to set up the backstory for the audience. It could be suggested that using a montage is a lazy way of telling a story but, given the restrictions we were faced with, it was a perfect and cost effective vehicle for telling a larger story. The newsreels were initially created as a means of viral advertising—an attempt to gain more interest—but also to learn something about making a film. For me they were invaluable. They were short and simplistic pieces to camera that gave me an opportunity to direct people and manage the logistics of a film crew. Made almost entirely in one day, over four locations across Birmingham and Worcestershire, it was probably the most fun I had over the whole making of *Ascension*, as they were nowhere near as pressured as the actual shoot.

With hindsight, the newsreels didn't really work in isolation, but I'd not change that as we learned so much from them, that I can confidently say the main shoot would have failed without them. Their visual and narrative benefit as individual pieces could be questioned, but as the opening montage, they work beautifully, and that's a huge testament to the skill and creativity of our visual effects editor, Carl Braid. With minimal direction, Carl made the reels feel real, look like found footage or a memory, and linked them to the opening scene. This is just one of the examples of the team approach behind our film making.

Handy Hint: Practice as much as possible before you shout 'action' for the first time.

THE PRACTICE SHOOTS

James: Another incredibly important factor in making the main shoot work was planning each scene as mapped out in the story boards in real time and shooting footage. Social media again played an important part in making these practice shoots work. Through our page we asked for anyone local to come and read lines for us while we experimented with shots and scene setting. We also found a few actors that we have worked with since. Maybe not perfect, but practice certainly makes for reducing errors and making friends!

THE SHOOT

WINTER WONDERLAND

Dave: If you were to ask any member of the cast and crew what they remember about filming *Ascension*, I'd stake my house that they would say how cold it was. For most of the shoot (two and a half days) the temperature didn't get above freezing point, and when we were shooting in an open field in the small village of Studley, the highest point in the Worcestershire countryside in fact, the wind showed absolutely no mercy.

Christina and her production team did what they could to keep cast and crew in some modicum of comfort. We had stoves and water and the tea and coffee flowed like hot rain. A gazebo was built to offer some protection from the elements, but by the end of the first day it had taken flight in a rogue gust of wind, which had half of the production staff chasing after it so it didn't get into shot! But for all of the adverse conditions on that hillside, not one person complained. Not cast nor crew. Everyone was there to make this happen, and what we lacked in warm weather was made up for in the high spirits pervading the shoot. It was a privilege to work with such professional people, and what is on screen became testament to this ethic. It has been said that the bleak Worcestershire countryside is as much a character as the humans. On that day it was the only member of the cast with an ego.

James: No amount of practice could have prepared us for the weather we woke up to that morning. Nearly a foot of snow had fallen in places. Now, compared to some parts of the world, I know that may not sound like much, but when a scene depends on you getting two vehicles into the middle of a farmer's field that's up a steep hill, it's far from ideal.

I don't mind admitting that I was terrified at this point. I was already scared of the task ahead of us, but now it looked like I may have to make the call to stop the shoot.

To get the main vehicle onto the field (and that was the 4x4 Land Rover), we had just about everyone that was able pushing and pulling that prop. People were getting covered in mud. It nearly rolled over into a ditch, and all the time I was close to running away to hide in a hole.

It took two hours to get the Land Rover into position; the filming schedule was already incredibly tight as we could only afford the actors for two days. With time running out, the decision was made to abandon the van we planned to include in the scene and continue on with the shoot. All the planned shots were thrown out of the window, the script needed amending, and Dave was miles away from the set. I was entering full panic mode.

The next few hours are a blur for me. I changed the shooting schedule but wasn't really in the moment. My mind was skipping ahead trying to work out how we could fit everything in.

It's funny looking back at those first few hours now, but at the time I wanted to be anywhere else but on that freezing cold field. All that snow really added to the production value, though!

Handy Hint: Did you practise? The first shoot—actually every shoot—is stressful! It's fun but it's stressful. Try not to let the fun disappear and don't take yourself too seriously. Getting angry or aggressive will not help you make your movie. Work with people to overcome problems, listen to the people around you, and don't be ashamed to ask for help. It has been our experience that those who have worked in the industry love to share their expertise.

HARD DAY'S NIGHT: SHOOTING THE SCHEDULE

James: The planned two days of shooting were just that: *two whole days*. I'm not sure we had completely expressed this to everyone involved, but thankfully everyone was beyond professional and they stuck with us. Day one started at 07:00 on set and I arrived home at 02:30 the next morning, with day two beginning at 08:00 that same morning. My sister had stayed over at my house to help out on set and for moral support. She turned into a private nurse when I arrived home and curled up on the kitchen floor with stomach cramps. At 02:30 in the morning I realized I had not eaten all day, save for a cookie on set, and I'd also not had a chance to go to the toilet, either. I wasn't a pretty sight! The second day of filming wrapped at 04:00, but I'd found time to eat, and coupled with adrenaline, I was feeling much more positive than I had that morning.

All the lost time on day one had a huge impact on the filming schedule. Daylight started to fade and, despite Gary Rogers working tirelessly behind the camera, we were way behind schedule. The second half of the schedule—filming at the compound—went like clockwork. The actors fought through fatigue and delivered some of the film's best lines, often in one take, and we started to claw back some of the lost time.

All the pre-production planning, things like food and a 'green room,' really had a positive effect on the shoot. Remember the ferocious guard dog we mentioned? Well she turned out to be not so ferocious. She was named 'Nelly' by cast and crew, and ended up sharing the green room with them and becoming the film's mascot. Another lesson learned: a happy, well fed cast and crew will put up with a lot.

On day two we had to go back to the dreaded freezing cold hill. On day one it was covered in snow, but by day two it had rained overnight and now most of the snow had gone. Panic, again. Getting the Land Rover to its spot was another challenge, but the biggest problem now involved continuity issues. Everything that second day was filmed low to high with as little of the background in shot or focus as possible. The 'stand-off' scene in the middle of the film bears no resemblance to what I'd planned based on all the changes we had to make. Everything that could go wrong did for that scene; one of the actresses even lost her gun, meaning that for half the time on screen she is just holding her arms out in the air! The magic of cinema, eh?

Handy Hint: Be prepared to think on your feet. With all the best planning in place, things can and invariably will go wrong on set. This even happens on films with huge budgets. Think creatively how to resolve these things by having a good support team around you; the assistant director, the cinematographer, the writer are useful if you need to make changes to a shot or a section of script based on a presenting, unforeseen issue. If having a team about you is not possible then have contingency plans in place for things like inclement weather or prop failures. Pre-production is more than just a script and storyboarding the director's vision!

IS IT A BIRD?

James: During pre-production, via the storyboarding process, the idea of introducing the principal characters and the world they inhabit through the eyes of a bird of prey considered a viable option. I'd envisioned this as a metaphor for the characters' journey through the story, but the weather had other plans. We had discussed various methods of achieving the aerial footage before agreeing on an RC Plane and fitting it with a GoPro camera. In truth, the shot was indulgent in that it wasn't needed, but Dave and Richard agreed that it could add a degree of quality to the film. On paper the plane was to fly over the 4x4 while it was driving across the field, circling to show the zombie, and again fly over the Land Rover and cut to the main characters in the cab. The snow had put a stop to the pass over the car and, not to be out done, the high wind put the plane into a tree! We lost the plane and the GoPro, and at that time thought the footage was lost, too. Later we found out that we'd got some useable test footage. My brother, Mark, had built the plane and drove just over a hundred miles in the snow to watch it crash into the only tree for three square miles!

YOU COULDN'T MAKE IT UP: VISUAL MAKE UP FX

Dave: Visual make up FX were provided by Justin Becker and his assistant Ben North. The original FX team let us down last minute, and at one point we were in panic mode as the shoot was only four weeks away. On occasions you do get this lack of commitment in the low budget film sector, but we were lucky to learn from it and these days make sure we get what's been promised in writing! I guess it was meant to be as Justin and Ben's efforts on screen have always been touted as one of the strengths of *Ascension*. We were always concerned about the make-up FX as, just like poor acting, these elements can pull the audience out of the drama and affect the entire production. What they were able to achieve with such a tight budget was amazing and testament to their skill and knowledge of their craft.

The zombie extras were provided by Silent Studios, a horror promotion company based in the UK. These guys were stalwart in their commitment to bringing the undead to the screen, with many of them lying in snow for up to thirty minutes at a time as Justin applied the gore effects.

FAMILY COMES FIRST

James: For anyone who has a dream to make a low budget film, I cannot stress enough the importance of keeping the set a happy and creative place. We did this by investing in a family ethic from the outset. We made sure that the actors and crew were all aware that this project was reliant on everyone, and in order to achieve it we needed people to pull together. This certainly came to the fore when the weather made for a very long and difficult shoot. So it wasn't unusual to have actors carrying camera cases, producers dismantling equipment and driving a documentary film-maker around Worcestershire, writers making cast and crew cups of tea. That was the norm during the shoot: family coming first, from the actors to those wonderful souls who prepped and cooked the food, no one was any better than anyone else. Everyone had a common purpose and we stuck to it.

We always talked about VLM not as a company but as a family

of creatives with a common goal. This ethic remains today. Anyone who works with us is always lauded and their work shared with whoever wishes to see. That is the promise we make and we never renege on it.

POST-PRODUCTION

EDITING

Dave: *Ascension* was edited by Richard over a period of four months. The editing is another aspect of the film that those who see it enjoy. Given that this was Richard's first outing as an editor, there was an element of trial and error involved. As a small company with limited fiscal means there was no way we could afford a full editing suite, nor massive online data storage so we could centralise footage in order for James to agree or ask for amendments to the cut. This meant driving all over Worcestershire for multiple viewings until agreement was reached on the final cut.

Another issue was that, because of the impact of time constraints on the shoot, the amount of shots per scene were limited, giving Richard only a few choices as he edited things together. This learning point was important for us and we now shoot as much footage as we can in order to give more choice. Though, as Rich says, you can sometimes have too much choice. As you can tell, he's a hard to please kinda fella, but what he does is amazing.

Handy Hint: Don't be afraid to be creative in order to remedy mistakes during filming. Usually indie film makers don't have the budgets or capacity to recall actors to reshoot a continuity error or blown out scene. We have discovered that creative editing can fix most issues.

VISUAL FX

Dave: Visual FX was completed using After Effects. This was used mainly in the freezer scene at the end of the film. It was unbelievable that, despite being below zero outside, inside what was meant to be the freezer it was warm! So Carl had to put Jacky's frozen breath on the air and crystalize the walls and floor. Again, a smoke machine hired for this scene failed to materialise so we had to improvise in post-production. The dream sequence is perhaps the most striking VFX shot. It reminds us in many ways of Jackson's *Lord of the Rings* shot where Frodo puts on the ring at Weathertop and is sought out by the witch king. But for considerably less money! Carl demonstrates a level of patience that makes us suspect he's not human. We've never been brave enough to ask him to prove it, of course.

Handy Hint: Don't compromise on quality. Whilst it is understandable, short film makers are forever doing this in their haste to get their film out and shown on the many media platforms available. This means cutting corners on the project in post-production rather than taking the time to make sure the final cut is as good as it can be. The odds are stacked against indie film makers as it is; don't let poor quality add your film to the pile.

SOUND

Dave: Richard also used sound recorded at the time of the shoot by sound man Jeremy Stephens. Again with no access to professional sound equipment, Richard had to use the best sound clips available as there was no scope to use over-dubbing. The main issue was the low rumble of the wind on the clips recorded at the hillside. Rather than have inconsistency, Richard placed the steady rumble of wind low into the mix so that it gave out a kind of growl throughout the hill top scene that added to the tension. Again, we learned that investment in our own sound equipment would be needed for future projects and made sure this happened as soon as we were able.

Handy Hint: Gather together a small group of trustworthy people to peer review your last cut of the film. Use their comments to guide the final cut. Some comments may be things you have already identified. Others may be a revelation. Never be too proud to make changes based on the view of others. Sure, keep to your fundamental vision but recognise on occasion objectivity can be lost during the creative process, and this is easily brought back on track with an alternative perspective.

SETTING THE MOVIE FREE!

THE PREMIER

Dave: The premier was held at The Electric Cinema in Birmingham on July 1st 2013. It was an opportunity to give thanks to all those who had stood on that freezing cold set for three days. In many ways it felt as though this was drawing a line under the project, and on reflection this mind set once more proved how naïve we were in terms of the film making process. Watching the film on the big screen for the first time, even with its imperfections, was an incredible feeling. This was bolstered by the fact we were surrounded by our families and those who had now become part of the VLM extended family. James and I didn't watch the film; instead we watched the audience, and when we saw that people were crying at the end we knew we'd made something that was affectively special.

This was reaffirmed when festival submission acceptances came in during the summer of 2013. During that time we were invited to the Bram Stoker International Film Festival (England), Feratum Festival of Fantastic Film (Mexico) and SCARdiff (Wales). We were at SCARdiff when Mark Rathbone called to inform us James had won the Best Director award at the Bram Stoker festival. Everyone was kind of stunned by the award as it implied we might actually know what we were doing after all!

Ascension went on to be shown at thirteen festivals throughout the 2013-2014 period in places ranging from Southend-on-Sea in England to Latvia. In the winter of 2014 Ascension received its second award for Best Film at the Worcestershire Film Festival. This was pretty much confirmation to us that the first award was no fluke, and we've now accepted that the passion we ploughed into the project had connected with both an audience and critics. *Ascension* is now going stateside with an invite to the Tri-Cities Fantastic Film Festival circuit in the summer of 2015.

Handy Hint: Be very selective about your choice of festival submission. Research the best ones and those that are value for money. Become familiar with the submission platforms online and be prepared to invest significant time and resource into the submission process.

CONCLUSION

Dave: I guess we have to talk about what's next for VLM, as there are many things in the pipeline. In some ways having a successful first project is as daunting as if it had failed. There is level of expectation on us in terms of follow up projects, not least from what we place on ourselves in terms of pushing the boundaries of low budget film making.

We have submitted *The Junction*—a five minute experimental piece—to several festivals worldwide. The project was an opportunity to test new equipment and VFX software. We are very pleased with the results and are hopeful that it is picked up by the festival circuit. There is also *Bad Medicine*, a portmanteau feature in the vein of *Creepshow* and *Asylum*. At this time we have Barbie Wilde (*Hellraiser II: Hellbound*) on board and we are looking for investment in order to shoot in 2016. In the interim, VLM have written another short film (*Derelict*), which should be shooting by the time people are reading this, and a web series (*Hangman*) which will feature many people we have already been honoured to work with over the past two years.

I guess all that remains is to thank the many people who have supported our endeavours. To name them all would be impossible, so we shall leave it to the cliché: *You know who you are!*

Final Handy Hint: Never lose sight of your goal. Even when all is seemingly against your production, never forget why you are standing in that field in the freezing snow, or shooting on that car lot in the blazing heat. Everyone is there to create something magical, to tell a story in a medium that captivates. A collection of likeminded souls with only one aim: to make a movie.

So, with all that said, what are you waiting for?

DJ/JH—VLM Productions

TRICKS OF THE TRADE
PRODUCING & DIRECTING

If you're like me, you have the insatiable desire to create. For me, it's about the stories, books, fictional worlds, and the careers of talented authors. For the folks below, it's about visual art.

It's certainly a popular form of storytelling, a form many of us love, especially in the horror genre. Who doesn't remember the first time they watched *Child's Play* or *A Nightmare on Elm Street*. *Final Destination* was my 'go to movie' when I had to entertain a girl or two—thanks Jeffrey Reddick.

What follows are a few gems I picked up (as an author and fan) while chatting with various filmmakers, producers, directors, and editors working in the film industry today. Who knows, perhaps one day we'll both give it a try.

Again, not all of them share the same viewpoints on certain things, especially about the direction horror movies are moving in, or the use of CGI. But I think we can all agree that everyone has their own preferences when it comes to these things.

Joe Mynhardt

WHAT DO YOU LOOK FOR IN A SCREENWRITER OR SCREENPLAY?

Mark Steensland: I have always either written my own material or closely supervised the writing of the screenplay, so this question applies to me differently, I think. I don't think there's any one thing that I look for. It's more about how the whole thing is working. I read screenplays professionally in Hollywood and it really is amazing how hard it is to find something unique.

Billy Hanson: In a screenplay, I hope to see a writer's understanding of the story they're telling, a fully-realized vision built from the underlying theme. And in a writer, I hope to see someone that's willing to work toward finding all of that, if they haven't already. I get frustrated if I'm reading something and it becomes clear that the writer has no idea what they're actually saying with their story. It's easy to write, but it's never easy to tell a meaningful story. That being said, it's often that the true meaning of a story doesn't show itself until a few drafts in, so as long as the writer is working toward that, it makes me happy.

I helped a friend with his script a couple of years ago, and he turned in this jumbled mess of a first draft. I wasn't sure how he'd pull anything coherent out of what he had, but after a round table discussion with other writers, he had found his theme, his statement, and the reason that he was telling his story. He came back a couple of months later with a draft that was infinitely better. Everything had just clicked into place. He had found the center on which to hang every action in the script, and it was, and still is, one of my favorite unproduced screenplays. I know it was passed around to some big-wigs at the studios, so I'm hoping it will eventually get sold.

Edward Lee: Since I am my own screenwriter, I essentially look for whatever intrigues me visually. I'm trying to shoot vignettes of the most objectionable scenes from my books, scenes that would likely NEVER be considered filmable by anyone else. The effects work and production quality are amateur-level, but I don't care. My view is that production quality doesn't matter if the content is creative, different, and unique.

John Russo: I just want to see good craftsmanship and a story that's fresh and works and is marketable.

Mick Garris: Freshness, originality, readability, surprises, engaging characters, and over anything else, entertainment. A voice, something that captivates me, originality, but also a sense of reality and believability, no matter how outrageous the situations. An eagerness to work together and truly collaborate, and absence of ego. Personal compatibility, if we're going to work together. You don't want to spend weeks working with someone you can't stand to be around. Someone with an imagination and joyous work ethic.

Patrick Lussier: A collaborator. Someone who can be a partner through the process who can navigate their characters through the practical challenges of making a film, understanding that changes may need to be made to make the film affordable, shootable, etc.

Jason V. Brock: Personally, I prefer realistic treatments of characters and subject matter. Satire and comedy with respect to horror must be quite deft and not topical or they get stale. For example, I found *Zombieland* and *Shaun of the Dead* boring, whereas I felt that *An American Werewolf in London* and *The Return of the Living Dead* were both excellent and hold up to repeated viewings. My favorite TV and screen writers tend to be individuals with an approach closer to novelists; in other words, they develop the backstory and characters in a mindful way, rather than just building to a cheap pay-off. They treat characters as real individuals rather than as talking props. Given the ephemeral and collaborative nature of film and television, it is rare to see a screenplay or teleplay with the writer's vision intact, though it has happened in a few exceptional instances. I am actually an advocate of the auteur theory of filmmaking, and generally respect the wishes of directors over the intentions of screenwriters.

HOW CLOSE TO THE ORIGINAL SCREENPLAY DO YOU NORMALLY STAY?

Mark Steensland: I tried to stay as close as possible when adapting things. I remember after I made *Dead@17*, which was based on Josh Howard's comic book, and he watched the film and he really liked it. And he told me that he was really amazed by one shot where I show the axe flying through the air spinning. He said, "I wish I'd thought of that." And then he went back and re-read his own comic book and saw that he did. That's where I had gotten the idea and that's why I had put it in there. My feeling is that if you love something enough to adapt it, you ought to stick as close to it as possible.

Edward Lee: If I were directing a flick based on someone else's work, I'd say that it all depends on the project. Take Lovecraft for example. Most HPL movies aren't terribly faithful to the original story, and people bitch about that. But then you have to consider the viewing audience which is quite different from a reading audience. Most of Lovecraft's work COULDN'T be filmed faithfully because the flick would cost more than Avatar and would be un-narratable. Finding the way to keep the essential ingredients in place while revising things for the palatability of the viewer (as well as the money people!), that's the key. Some good examples, I think, are *Die Monster Die*, a cool version of "Colour out of Space," and "Haunted Palace," a Poe title but actually a marketable use of "Innsmouth" and "Charles Dexter Ward."

John Russo: When I'm directing, I'm constantly changing and improving the scenes based on what I may see on the actual location or in rehearsals with inventive actors.

Mick Garris: That depends. I have shot a white script a couple of times (meaning no color-coded draft changes), but there are always production issues or adjustment to an actor's personality or various reasons for changes. It is rare that one shoots a script that has not been tinkered with or (hopefully) improved.

Jack Thomas Smith: I normally stay pretty close to the original screenplay. So far, I've written both feature films that I've directed, *Disorder* and *Infliction*, and I've had the luxury of final cut on both projects. When I wrote those screenplays, I knew I would ultimately direct them so I detailed the action sequences and character actions more so than most screenwriters. My screenplays are a very detailed blueprint, but I make adjustments along the way based on discussions with the cast and the production team. I see my films as a team effort from start to finish with the screenplays providing the foundations.

Patrick Lussier: It depends. You want to stay close to the intent but sometimes budget and production limitations demand changes. Trick is to make those changes align with the intent of the script.

Jason V. Brock: Since I am a director and a writer and tend to work with my own material, I feel that I stick as closely as possible to my initial vision, at least in the pre-production and early production stages. I do enjoy collaboration however, and have a background in theater and improv, both as a musician and a performer, so I am flexible in the moment, especially with an eye toward experimentation that might create dramatic tension or memorable contexts from a performer or interviewee's input. Later, I try to be open-minded to observational points-of-view that make the work stronger, whether that's the producer, or, in post-production, the editor's take on how a scene should play in the overall framework of the narrative.

WHAT GOES INTO SETTING UP A BUDGET FOR AN INDEPENDENT FILM?

Mark Steensland: As little as possible, in my case. Most of my films have been made for under $1,000. My first feature film, which was not a horror film, was made for $10K. My second feature (a documentary about Philip K. Dick) was made for $7500. In many cases, I spent more money on film festival entry fees than on the film itself.

Billy Hanson: Well, for this, I'll have to go back to a piece of the advice I gave earlier. Be honest with yourself. You probably don't need a crane for a 3 minute short in a diner. You DO have to have a sound guy and you should pay people when you can. These things sound a little trivial, but making a budget is a piece of the puzzle that transitions a project from the script phase to production, so you need to really have someone who understands where to put your money.

If it's an indie film, you won't have a lot, so you'll have to use every bit of cash carefully. I've never done a budget by myself. Even though I'm knowledgeable about production and I might even be able to do one myself, I always have one or two people to go through everything with me, just to make sure I've covered everything. Since every project has its own variables and issues, it's a delicate process. If something is messed up in the budget, you may find yourself scrambling for money down the line, and that's never a good spot to be in.

It's a simple breakdown of cast, crew, equipment, locations, props, stunts, post production, and final delivery. Knowing the end game for a project will help lay out the full plan, beginning to end, and from that you should be able to see where you need adjustments. And you should be creative with budgets, like using one location for multiple sets. That kind of thinking goes a long way in the early stages. Just make sure that everyone signs off before submitting it. I've seen bad things happen when people are left out of that loop.

Edward Lee: With me? Whatever disposable income I happen to have in my wallet any given weekend! I don't want to make movies the "regular" way; in other words, with a production budget, a shooting schedule, a crew, licensed locations, top-end equipment, etc. None of that! I'm the crew, my bank account is the budget, my locations are either my house, friends' houses, or any place in public where I can get away with shooting when no one is looking. To me, THIS is fun, the "regular" way is dull and a pain in the ass. I believe that my experience as a novelist is all I need to make entertaining movies. It's about nothing more than that: entertainment. In fiction, you conceive of images in your head and try to effectively translate them with words. In an Edward Lee movie, I conceive of images in my head and try to effectively translate them with videography. My movies may well look like crap, but they will be provocative, singular, and entertaining (And did I say brilliant?).

John Russo: To answer this would require a major section of a book, and you will find that in my movie making books.

Mick Garris: Something I'm not very good at. Really, *Riding the Bullet* and *Masters of Horror* are the two things I've done independently, but I'm not a guy who is good at—or who *wants* to be good at—raising money. I wouldn't know how. BULLET took forever to get it off the ground. We thought it would sell to a studio, but none of them wanted it. They wanted either a pure horror story or a coming of age type movie. I thought it could be both, and thoughtful, and character-oriented, and heartfelt. The studios didn't want that.

We found financing because of King's name, but the movie was not a financial success. On the other hand, when we pitched MASTERS OF HORROR to three companies, all of them wanted to do it, but one of them said, "How much and when can we start?", and that's who we went with.

James Cullen Bressack: Normally that's the job of the line producer, and as a director I'm usually their biggest headache, but we usually find a way to work around the budget to make the film great. Pretty much whatever your budget is for the movie is what you have to make it for. You find as many ways to get it done as possible and pull many favors if it's low budget, so make sure you build a good network.

Patrick Lussier: Breaking down the script creatively with an eye towards the 'what can be done for the money available.' Often it's reverse engineered from X dollars. If we have this much money, what can we do with it given the script that we have.

Jason V. Brock: Most of the concerns are divided into "above-the-line" (fixed costs, especially vital players such as the producer[s], director, writer[s], and performers) and "below-the-line" considerations (other crewmembers and considerations that are subject to changes in the project's conception). A lot of that is boring to detail, but an often-overlooked aspect of it is to realize that not all people are motivated by money alone: Frequently people are enthusiastic to feel part of something larger than themselves, or to relate a great/important story or idea. Folks are surprisingly willing to do more than anyone would ever have a right to expect—behind-the-scenes or in front of the camera—if they understand that they're part of something special. It must feel like a "mission" in some sense, and inspire a sense of *esprit de corp*. This is vital for indie film production, I feel.

SO YOU RE MOVIE IS FINALLY MADE, NOW WHAT?

Mark Steensland: Find an audience. Not your friends. Get into film festivals. Watch your film with those audiences. This is what truly separates the amateur from the professional. When you watch your movie with an audience over and over and you finally understand what works and what doesn't and why. This experience completely changed my approach to directing because suddenly I knew what I needed to do in order to produce a particular effect on an audience.

Billy Hanson: For indie films, the first step is usually festivals, but the real goal is getting the film seen. Ideally, you can screen a film at a festival, promote it as much as you can, and make sure it gets in front of people who are shopping for films. Even the small films get bought, so as long as your stuff is out there, it's possible. It's easy to sort of let a film sit on a shelf, especially after putting years and years of work into making it, but it's important to remember that the work isn't done yet. You have to keep on plugging away, talking about it, sending it out, getting it up on screens, however you can. Then, if someone is interested, you might find yourself in a position to sell the film for distribution.

Edward Lee: I distribute it myself, or on Amazon. Simple. Digital technology has changed the entire face of book publishing; it has also changed the entire face of film making. If it's good, it will sell. It doesn't matter if you can't get Lion's Gate to be your distributor.

Mick Garris: Good luck! So many issues to deal with, especially in these days of marketing by social media. Is your film getting a theatrical release? VOD? Disc? Your movie is your baby, and you have to be ready, willing, and able to do anything you can for its care and feeding. Festivals are a bigger deal than they ever were before, especially in the horror genre. A film that makes a splash at a festival has a great chance of international notoriety, and often brings financing to your next endeavor, if not an offer for the next one.

James Cullen Bressack: Promote the shit out of it, and look for a distributor or sales agent.

Patrick Lussier: Hope you get distribution and people see it.

Lynne Hansen: Film festivals. Lots of them. I was so lucky to have so many talented people involved in *Chomp* that I'm morally obligated to get it shown as many places as possible. At the moment in time that I'm writing this, I've submitted *Chomp* to over fifty film festivals. My goal is to submit to over one hundred. We've still got a ton of festivals left to hear back from, but we've been accepted to over twenty festivals worldwide and currently have a 91% acceptance rate, which is bizarrely outstanding for any film, much less a film from a first-time director.

Jason V. Brock: My friend William F. Nolan, who has written classic TV and film scripts in addition to novels and short stories, has a saying that I agree with: "If you're handing out diamonds on a street corner but no one knows about it, then what's the point?" It's so true. The next step after a film—any project, really—has been completed is to raise awareness and promote it, dare I say it, relentlessly. It used to be that people read books and looked forward to going to the movies; now we are pummeled nearly-senseless by a continual onslaught of user-generated content, as well as TV, movies, videogames, and other things, such as live performance. This glut of options in something as non-essential as "entertainment" makes gaining visibility over the static difficult . . . At the same time, there are greater options for promotion, not only traditionally with print, ads, and so on, but online, such as Twitter, Facebook, YouTube, and the Internet more generally. The key is to inform and attract an audience without alienating them with a continual barrage of "look at this!" advertising. People are cautious consumers now; they want a good return on their investment. I can't blame them.

WHAT MAKES YOUR MOVIES UNIQUE?

Jeffrey Reddick: I think every filmmaker brings their unique life experiences to the films they make. I tend to like supernatural stories that have some kind of social subtext. Whether it's predestination in *Final Destination* or bullying in *Tamara*.

Billy Hanson: I like to think that my films are all classic storytelling models that are both wildly fantastic and deeply personal. It's kind of hard for me to pinpoint what exactly makes my stuff different and unique, because for me, an idea will catch and it will kind of grow on its own. Because of that process, I've done a wide range of stories, from romantic comedies to graphic horror, supernatural thrillers to music-based dramas. Truth be told, I'd have to have someone else tell me the similarities in all of them, because each story is truly its own entity.

Edward Lee: Same thing that makes my books unique: me! No, I'm no George Lucas or Michael Bay, but, hell, did those guys ever have a headless pregnant woman doing a strip tease? I must've missed that in Transformers. I don't recall any trans-vaginal eviscerations or coitus with torsos in Star Wars.

John Russo: My unique take on life and the vital themes I choose to explore. Movies can only be unique if they have a new slant on something that is *important*.

Mick Garris: That's for someone else to say, not me.

James Cullen Bressack: At a base level, I've really never made a horror movie. I've just made movies about ordinary people that are put into an extra ordinary environment.

Lynne Hansen: Atypical characters. Too many times, indie horror films are filled with vapid, big-busted women who got cast because they were happy to take their tops off and get bloody. My lead actress Susan O'Gara was in her sixties when we filmed *Chomp*. My lead actor Kyle Porter's character was meant to be a reversal of that stereotype.

In *He's Not Looking So Great*, the first short I wrote, I created the movie around a plus-sized heroine who never takes off a shred of clothing. I think there are a lot of stories out there to be told that don't involve women with perfect figures and men with bleached white teeth and six-pack abs.

SINCE EVERY MOVIE HAS THEM, HOW DO YOU DEAL WITH THE HATERS?

Billy Hanson: Well, it's important to find the line between critics and haters, but if you do decide that someone can be classified as a hater, they're easy enough to just brush off and ignore. I think the simple fact that there are always haters no matter what, make it a little easier and just delete a comment or pretend you didn't hear something. I can't think of a time where anyone has said anything nasty that's actually gotten under my skin. Criticism though, that's torn me to pieces.

Edward Lee: They're part of the turf. If a ball player can't hack the hecklers in the stands, he needs to get off the ball field. In writing, there are people who love my books, and people who hate them. I've been lambasted by Publisher's Weekly and also praised by them, for instance. A good review means the same thing as a bad review: nothing. Just write! If your books suck, people won't buy them and publishers won't publish them, in which case you find another job. Same thing in movies.

John Russo: I kill them off and then write about them, but fictionalized so I won't get caught.

James Cullen Bressack: I don't pay them any mind. I make my movies for me, some people love them, others don't, but I don't pander to negativity. Someone who believes their reviews, both negative or positive, becomes contempt with mediocrity.

Lynne Hansen: Comedy is very subjective. You won't ever be able to find even one joke that every person laughs at. If one crowd is more receptive than another, it's okay. I chalk it up to individual differences and move on. As long as I still love the movie, and my cast and crew are still proud to have been a part of it, I'm fine. I can't worry about the nay-sayers.

WHICH FILM MAKERS HAVE YOU STUDIED THE MOST AND WHY?

Jeffrey Reddick: I love Wes Craven, John Carpenter, Dario Argento, Peter Jackson, and Alfred Hitchcock. They all have very distinct styles, which I enjoy. They can tell stories with great visual flair.

Edward Lee: The filmmakers who are obsessed with the vitality of the image: Kubrick, Bergman, Lynch, Cronenberg, Hitchcock, and, though I hate to sing praises for a criminal, Polanski. I think Polanski is the best filmmaker alive. Watch Repulsion, watch Ninth Gate, etc. It's about far more than weird camera angles and intellectual abstraction. It's about the perfect distillation of the image.

John Russo: Francis Ford Coppola, Martin Scorcese and Quentin Tarantino because their work is so exciting, involving and masterful in so many ways.

Mick Garris: Everybody. You learn almost as much from a bad movie as you do from a good one. Seeing what *doesn't* work is as important as seeing how something is achieved successfully. I also try to keep up with everything going on. I love movies, not just what movies used to be. I go to festivals all around the world at least a couple times a year, and I've discovered amazing films, unique voices in Spain and South Korea, in Australia, the UK, and even in the US. There really aren't specific directors I study.

James Cullen Bressack: Takashi Miike, Park Chan Wook, Quentin Tarantino, Eli Roth, and Robert Rodriguez. Dynamic, versatile filmmakers who are truly auteurs and have their own unique stamp on every film they do. To study is to learn.

Patrick Lussier: I'm a big fan of John Frankenheimer and Steven Spielberg. I grew up with their films and have studied their work extensively. *JAWS* is a near perfect film and changed how movies were made forever after. The original *Manchurian Candidate* is a masterpiece of storytelling and editing. But there is no better filmmaker than James Cameron. Technically, he's a true renaissance artist, breaking new ground visually with every project.

WHAT ARE YOUR FAVORITE DIRECTING TECHNIQUES THAT VIEWERS MIGHT NOTICE WHEN WATCHING YOUR MOVIES?

Jeffrey Reddick: I'm a big fan of old-style shooting. I like fluid camera movements and natural lighting. I'm not big on shaky-cam or hyper-editing. I personally think these techniques distract from story.

Edward Lee: I doubt that viewers will recognize my techniques, but I'm fairly certain they'll recognize my content. I'm simply re-assimilating either entire scenes or exclusive images from my novels, the scenes and images that no one else on earth would attempt to translate into film. Now, certainly this is all big talk from a guy who has yet to release a movie, and of course I realize I could fail. But I just don't think I will!

Mick Garris: Well, you don't really want the audience to notice your filmmaking if you want them involved in the story. The trick is to use techniques that heighten their involvement, rather than pull them out and make them say, "Wow, isn't that cool!"

I could talk about the use of wide and long lenses, camera movement, experiential filmmaking techniques, but mostly it's about creating a propulsive and believable world with characters you can share the experience with, to take you to surprising places.

Sound design is crucial, as is the film's color palette. Music. Film is an immersive, emotional experience at its best, and there are so many tools available to the modern filmmaker to enhance that experience.

I would like to think that the characters are rich, the visuals are mobile and immersive, and the story believable but surprising.

James Cullen Bressack: I like to fuck shit up and use a ton of blood.

Lynne Hansen: I think you see my directing style most in the acting. I love rehearsing with my actors, workshopping sections of the script, and really helping my actors stay in the moment. If I can do that, the characters really bring the story to life, and to me, filmmaking is all about story.

SHOULD EVERY INDEPENDENT FILM BE MADE IN A UNIQUE WAY, OR SHOULD PRODUCERS AND DIRECTORS STICK WITH WHAT THE AUDIENCE WANTS?

Jeffrey Reddick: Investors like to play things safe. I think there's a way to find that fine line between being unique and true to your artistic vision and being commercial. We're all human beings with the same dreams, goals and fears. So if you create characters that are realistic, they'll hopefully connect with an audience.

Edward Lee: Well, ultimately producers and directors must do both. You have to find that common ground, that aesthetic median strip between viewer accessibility and creative diversity. Same thing in novels. If you write a haunted house novel, you MUST adhere to some aspects of formula and familiarity, but then you MUST do new things with the remaining moving parts of the story.

John Russo: If you're talking about gadgetry, I'm not a fan of it. But if you tell the story and construct the scenes in it from the proper point of view concerning the characters, the message, and how to best get them across, then the audience will buy it.

Mick Garris: I think the filmmaker *is* the audience. Trying to predict what an audience is looking for, as far as I'm concerned, is sheer folly. However, filmmaking is an art form that requires a healthy amount of financial investment, usually out of the pockets of others. You want to tell a story that will engage an audience. You can assume that you are an audience member, I think, if you are telling a story that is something you'd be interested in. Again, filmmaking and storytelling are all about communication, which by its very definition requires an audience, whether one-on-one or to a crowd.

If you truly don't give a shit about what the audience thinks, then why should they give a shit—or ten bucks or two hours of their time—about what you have to show them? Everybody wants to be original, but you don't create the wheel each time out. The best thing a filmmaker can have is an original voice . . . unless that voice is crying out in the wilderness without anyone there to hear it.

James Cullen Bressack: Depends on the type of film you are making. Sometimes be as unique as possible, and sometimes why reinvent the wheel. I like to think of my films as a hodgepodge of everything I've ever seen. There are no such things as new ideas, just new takes on great ideas.

Lynne Hansen: I make movies because I like to entertain people. I think that's what people want. And sure, they can be entertained by traditional fare, but a good writer and director can create a story that is unique and still entertains. And if you do unique in service to the story, not just unique for uniqueness' sake, people will actually be more entertained.

HOW, IN YOUR OPINION, SHOULD A START-UP FILM COMPANY GO ABOUT PROMOTING AND DISTRIBUTING THEIR FILMS?

Edward Lee: Don't have a clue! My situation is completely different from just about anyone else in the film business. My promotion and distribution for my movies will be my name as a novelist. I'm counting on a crossover; I'm hoping that my book fans will buy my movies because I made them, which I think they will. Ah, but if I'm wrong? I've just flushed about 50 grand down the toilet!

John Russo: Wow! Another questions that requires a dissertation!

Mick Garris: I wish I could tell you. That's a part of the business that I have chosen not to pursue. I don't think I'd be good at it.

HOW IMPORTANT IS TIMING WHEN RELEASING A MOVIE?

John Russo: Sometimes timing is everything. You have to use your own judgment when and if you are the person calling the shots, but most of the time you aren't.

INTERVIEWS (PART 2)

RAY BRADBURY: *LIVE FOREVER!*

INTERVIEW BY JASON V. BROCK

R **AY BRADBURY, AMERICAN** novelist, short story writer, essayist, playwright, screenwriter and poet, was born August 22, 1920 in Waukegan, Illinois. He graduated from a Los Angeles high school in 1938. Although his formal education ended there, he became a "student of life," selling newspapers on L.A. street corners from 1938 to 1942, spending his nights in the public library and his days at the typewriter. He became a full-time writer in 1943, and contributed numerous short stories to periodicals before publishing a collection of them, *Dark Carnival*, in 1947.

His reputation as a writer of courage and vision was established with the publication of *The Martian Chronicles* in 1950, which describes the first attempts of Earth people to conquer and colonize Mars, and the unintended consequences. Next came *The Illustrated Man* and then, in 1953, *Fahrenheit 451*, which many consider to be Bradbury's masterpiece, a scathing indictment of censorship set in a future world where the written word is forbidden. In an attempt to salvage their history and culture, a group of rebels memorize entire works of literature and philosophy as their books are burned by the totalitarian state. Other works include *The October Country, Dandelion Wine, A Medicine for Melancholy, Something Wicked This Way Comes, I Sing the Body Electric!, Quicker Than the Eye,* and *Driving Blind*. In all, Bradbury has published more than thirty books, close to 600 short stories, and numerous poems, essays, and plays. His short stories have appeared in more than 1,000 school curriculum "recommended reading" anthologies."

Jason V Brock: **How did you and Forrest J Ackerman meet?**

Ray Bradbury: Back in 1938/1939, I used to go to a bookstore, a magazine shop in Hollywood. I saw a notice there about a science fiction group meeting down at Clifton's Cafeteria every Thursday night. So I left my name, and Forrest Ackerman and his friends contacted me and asked me to come to a meeting. And I was introduced to all these weird people, including Forrest Ackerman, who was just as weird as all the rest of them. And I was weird, too. So I joined the group. Immediately Forrest Ackerman decided I should be given a job, and I became his assistant to help put out a magazine called *Imagination*. I ran the mimeograph, and Forry let me write articles—terrible articles—and he let me illustrate the magazine on occasion—terrible illustrations—but he gave me things to do. I was still in high school, and I didn't really know where I was going to go, but the influence of Forrest Ackerman was incredible. I had a job writing stories by day and I sold newspapers every afternoon.

I met all of these famous authors with Forry; I continued to write for the next few years and go to meetings at the Clifton Cafeteria and go to Forry's house and meet people there like Robert Heinlein and Isaac Asimov. So you see at the very start of my life—you might say— while I was still in high school, he was a prime mover in my life. And he did that sort of thing for dozens of young people in the last seventy years. A lot of us owe our lives to Forrest J Ackerman.

Ray Harryhausen came to his house sometime in 1938, looking for pictures of King Kong, and Forry invited me over and I met Ray Harryhausen. I found out he loved dinosaurs, and I loved dinosaurs, too, and we all loved dinosaurs together. We became fast friends and Ray and I dreamt of one day doing a film together; I would write the screenplay and Ray would animate it with his dinosaurs and, by God, it finally happened. And he was also Best Man at my wedding 15 years later. So, because of Forrest Ackerman, it changed two lives here: Ray Harryhausen and myself. He was that sort of person.

Brock: **Did you ever collaborate with Forry?**

Bradbury: No, we never collaborated on anything. I helped to put out his magazine, but there was never any collaboration, no.

Brock: **And how about these people he introduced you to, or let you meet. Did any of them mentor you or help you?**

Bradbury: The main thing about Forry's life is that his home was the meeting place for all of the crazies. And we're all crazy. We love 'the wrong things.' Our society thinks we're nuts for caring about space travel, for caring about dinosaurs. And because I fell in love with dinosaurs, and because Ray Harryhausen loved them, and because Forry Ackerman loved them, I wrote a short story called "The Foghorn." Which, when it was read by John Huston, got me the job of writing the screenplay of *Moby Dick*. Which is all about a prehistoric monster, isn't it?

Brock: **Sure, the White Whale.**

Bradbury: What if I hadn't fallen in love with dinosaurs? What if I hadn't met Forry Ackerman who said, "It's okay to love them! It's okay!"

Brock: **Where do you think that came from in his character? That love of all things unusual. From his family, or do you think it was just part of his personality?**

Bradbury: Well, we all have the mystery of personality. It cannot be investigated. There is no answer. How come Ray Harryhausen decided to grow up, yet always remain a child? And Forrest Ackerman made the same decision. It's a mystery that cannot be answered.

Brock: **One of the reasons I wanted to do this documentary about Forry was I felt there was something missing about his story. People didn't really investigate Forry that much. They knew him, they would come to him and knew he was an expert on movies and science fiction, and they would ask him all kind of things, but never about him. And I think he has a great story to tell.**

Bradbury: Many years ago Henry Kuttner was one of my friends

HORROR 201: THE SILVER SCREAM

and one of my mentors. He was one of the leading science fiction writers in the United States, but he didn't get along with Forry. He said to me once, "Forry's a child." I said, "Leave him alone! You're not going to make him grow up, you're not going to make me grow up. I understand very well. I tolerate him, I love him and I never question him. There he is. Accept him for what he is. Relax, Henry!"

Brock: **That's excellent!**

Bradbury: I just finished being interviewed by a scientist for a scientific magazine back East. They tend to be so negative: "What can you name good about society? How can you be so optimistic?" Well, I've talked about libraries. Jesus Christ! Our country's full of them, and it's your fault if you don't go to the library. Don't blame your country! Don't blame your society! It's your job.

Brock: **I agree. It's your job to educate yourself about everything in the big, wide world.**

Bradbury: That's right, that's damn right!

Brock: **Like you, Ray, I didn't complete college, because I think in a way college forces your brain into these little categories.**

Bradbury: You're right! If you get a man who's teaching writing and he loves the 'wrong' people, then he's going to steer you wrong, isn't he?

Brock: **That's right!**

Bradbury: If he says you have to write like all *New Yorker* writers, and you say, "Well come on; no, no, no." So, I stayed away from the fancy stuff and I read the pulp magazines and I grew up with H.G. Wells, Jules Verne and Buck Rogers. And it's done nothing but good for me.

Brock: **Another thing I agree with you about is that the educational system is getting softer and softer. Children used to learn a whole lot from their teachers: now they don't show them the things they need—the fundamentals— so they're not learning what they should be. Back to work: I thought EC Comics did a very good job adapting your stuff.**

Bradbury: Oh yeah, they did indeed.

Brock: **On the TV side, I don't think *The Twilight Zone* succeeded as well on "I Sing the Body Electric." I'm a big fan of Rod Serling, and I like his writing, but I think that your work is very lyrical, very poetic and it's beautiful. Rod Serling's is also good, but he's a bit different—he's very talky, you know? Talk, talk, talk: dialogue heavy. I just wish they had done more with your work then.**

Bradbury: Well, we split because [Serling] didn't keep his promise to me. When I gave him the script—"I Sing the Body Electric"—he promised not to touch it. And when it went on the air, they cut the motive of the Grandma out of the script. So the night I looked at the show, there was no reasoning to it; they cut out her philosophy. 'How could a robot help you be better?' They cut that out. And I called Rod the next day and I said, "This is it, you promised." So, I waited for twenty years to have my own series [*The Ray Bradbury Theater*] because I didn't want to be treated that way.

Brock: **That was a wonderful show by the way.**

Bradbury: Well, God bless you! I did 64 scripts and they were never touched by anyone. But I waited all of those years, because I saw how Alfred Hitchcock was treated by Universal—I did nine scripts for *Alfred Hitchcock Presents*.

Brock: **I love *Alfred Hitchcock Presents*. It's a great show.**

Bradbury: Yes, yes. And now they're all out so you'll be able to see my nine things with Hitchcock.

Brock: **Didn't Robert Bloch also work on that show?**

Bradbury: Robert Bloch and John Collier and Roald Dahl. A lot of good ones.

Brock: **Roald Dahl is a wonderful writer!**

Bradbury: Yes, but back to Serling. You see, Rod's problem was [struggles with phrasing reply] . . . He was a short man. So, I have a feeling—and this is amateur psychiatry here—that because of his short stature he wanted to control things more, and that's why we never got along. Because I didn't want to be controlled.

Brock: **Also around that era was the group of writers like yourself—Richard Matheson, Charles Beaumont—some of whom worked with Rod Serling and were in your circle, as well. It was sad about Charles Beaumont and how he died so young. That was a weird thing. How did you and Chuck first meet?**

Bradbury: I met Chuck Beaumont a long time ago in the spring of 1946. My fiancée, Maggie McClure, worked as a salesperson in a bookstore in downtown L.A. I used to show up there and take her to lunch. One day this sixteen year old boy showed up there, and it was Charles Beaumont. We got to talking and he liked *Prince Valiant* as much as I did and he liked *Terry and the Pirates* and Buck Rogers and Hannes Bok . . . Three or four years went by and I got a job working in Universal Studios. I was going to be there for three or four weeks working on a film, which became known as *It Came from Outer Space*. While I was there I discovered that Chuck Beaumont was on the lot. He was working in the music department. He told me he was on the verge of changing his life. I said, "What are you going to do?" He said, "I want to be a writer. I don't want to do anymore artwork."

Brock: **So you guys bonded over comic pages. What about comic books?**

Bradbury: I had no interest in comic books at the time—he may have. Later on EC Comics began to do good work—mainly because they were adapting my stories—and there was quality in the stories which then went into the illustrations.

Brock: **What do you think caused Chuck's writing to take off? How did that happen?**

Bradbury: He followed my advice. I'm sorry to say that, but it's true. I give all the credit to him. I said, "It's very simple. You want to be a writer? During the next year write one story a week for 52 weeks. At the end of a year, you'll have sold more stories and you'll be on your way." So I set him a goal of writing every single day of his life, and every single week, and every single month. So I can't really take credit for it except I goaded him into it. I nagged him and then he did it all by himself. And by God, within two years he was selling to *Playboy* magazine and places like that.

Brock: **You also sold to *Playboy* at that point, right?**

Bradbury: Yes.

Brock: **So it was Ray Russell who was the Editor-In-Chief over there?**

Bradbury: Ray Russell was one of the editors, yes.

Brock: **Now do you remember when Chuck started falling into what became known as "The Group"—with Bill Nolan, John Tomerlin—those guys. Did his work start getting stronger as a result of interacting with them as well as you?**

Bradbury: I don't know anything about his relationship with those people. Occasionally, we got together with people like Bill Nolan and

George Clayton Johnson, but the other people that came into his life . . . I never really knew them.

Brock: **So you didn't really know Rich Matheson yet?**

Bradbury: I encouraged Richard Matheson. He sent me a short story in a magazine in 1950, and I wrote him a fan letter. I said, "If you continue writing like this your life is ensured." I'm very proud of that letter and I was able to read that letter later in celebration of Richard Matheson. So it was kind of natural that he would then meet Charles Beaumont. When Rod Serling came along, I introduced both of them to Rod Serling.

Brock: **So even though you and Rod had a bit of a disagreement over *The Twilight Zone*, to his credit he took your advice about Chuck and Rich Matheson.**

Bradbury: Oh, absolutely, yes.

Brock: **What do you think of Chuck's work now compared to back then? Do you think his work holds up well?**

Bradbury: The sad thing is that he didn't live ten more years, because his novels [*The Intruder; Run from the Hunter* (with John Tomerlin)] and all of his short stories showed his fantastic talent. He would have been remembered in the same category as John Collier. Collier, to me, is one of the greatest writers in the field. And Chuck was right up there. So, the terrible thing is he needed a couple more years to write a few more novels and a couple hundred more short stories. But that doesn't mean anything. The important thing is the quality of what he did is fantastic.

Brock: **His only solo novel was *The Intruder*. What did you think of it at the time and what do you think of it now?**

Bradbury: Well, I thought *The Intruder* was a very fine novel, but I was especially pleased with the film [directed by Roger Corman] they made of it with William Shatner. A very young, handsome man;

he did a beautiful job. And Bill Nolan was in it and George Clayton Johnson [as well as Frank M. Robinson and OCee Ritch]. Playing themselves you might say—evil monsters [laughs]. Charles Beaumont played a role, too. So it was a fantastic, wonderful experience for all of us.

Brock: **Did you visit the set?**

Bradbury: No, it was done back East.

Brock: **It's a great movie. I spoke to Roger Corman about it and I think it's a great source of pride for him. Bill Nolan gave us information that happened behind the scenes. They were all great in it, and Chuck was excellent in it, too.**

Bradbury: Oh, indeed he was.

Brock: **Do you recall the period when Chuck was starting to get sick? What do you remember about that?**

Bradbury: I sensed that something was wrong, but he didn't tell us. All of a sudden we had an old man on our hands. Terrible thing. It's a tragic and shocking event in all of our lives. I think it's one of the worst periods in my life where I lost a friend, because it shouldn't have happened that way. It was a very weird, strange, unpredictable sickness.

Brock: **Kind of like *The Twilight Zone*.**

Bradbury: That's right.

Brock: **Did you think that he was maybe drinking, because some people thought that because of the symptoms. But then he started aging, correct?**

Bradbury: People thought that his drinking had to do with it, but they were mistaken, and I was mistaken, too.

Brock: **I see. Did he physically deteriorate? His face? His look?**

Bradbury: No, by the time that happened he was removed from all of us and only Rich Matheson and John Tomerlin as I recall went to visit him and discovered this old man.

Brock: **I talked to Forry about Chuck, and he said Chuck was his "own Ray Bradbury."**

Bradbury: [Bradbury laughs heartily]

Brock: **He said, "I felt I had this wonderful talent."—I'm paraphrasing here. Right when Chuck was starting to take off, to get to the big slicks like *Esquire* and this type of thing, he came to a parting of the ways with Forry. He went, I think with your management company, right? The Don Congdon Agency? [Ed.: Congdon's agency also represented, among others, John Tomerlin, and still represents Bradbury, Earl Hamner, Richard Matheson, and the estate of Charles Beaumont]**

Bradbury: With my agent, yes.

Brock: **How did that happen? Was it time for him to move on?**

Bradbury: I told him "Forry Ackerman's a very important person in my life, and he enthused me when I was in high school. But Forry doesn't have the knowledge for the marketplace that Don Congdon has. Don was formerly with Simon & Schuster and he is a super-agent." I felt at the time Chuck needed to move up to someone who really knew literature and selling in magazines and books. I'm sure Forry may have been hurt by this, but I think it was an important thing to do, and it worked.

Brock: **Did it impact you and Forry? I can't imagine as you've been friends for so long, but did he ever mention it to you?**

Bradbury: No, we never discussed it.

Brock: Do you have any other comments to make about Chuck and what happened to him? Why is he important?

Bradbury: The way to sum him up is: In the mythological history of the characters in Egyptian myths, they have a saying that when you die and you go and meet the God of the Dead, he's going to ask you some questions. Depending on how you answer you'll either get into Heaven or Hell. So the question is: "In your life, when you lived, did you have *enthusiasm*?" And the answer with Chuck Beaumont is: he had enthusiasm. So the reason why he is known today is his enthusiasm bubbles over into his work. He is the nearest thing to being my literary son. Every time I look at those stories, I see his joy in life and his enthusiasm for writing and living. That's why he is of great value to us.

Brock: So do you think he is one of the most important writers for modern literature in general?

Bradbury: He belongs up there with Robert Heinlein, because Heinlein taught all of us, taught me how to write human stories, not technological stories. Not stories that were dry and mechanical, but stories about human desires and human wishes. So, if my stories work it's because Robert Heinlein taught me and he taught Charles Beaumont, too.

Brock: Very interesting. Do you think Chuck has taught anyone currently writing? Do you see that enthusiasm in anybody more recently?

Bradbury: He never had honorary children like I have. I've had a lot of honorary children. I've taken certain writers under my wing. I met a young teenager in San Diego forty years ago, and I encouraged him with his painting and drawing. Later he decided to become a writer, and he now has become an established writer in the field, and he has more awards than I do, and his name is Greg Bear. So, Chuck never had any young writers that he took under his wing and encouraged. He had his friends who were around him and shared his ideas, but there were no 'bastard' children!

Brock: **I think you're right because he unfortunately didn't live long enough to inherit that mantle. But his shadow over his friends—George Clayton Johnson, John Tomerlin, Charles E. Fritch, Bill Nolan, Rich Matheson, Harlan Ellison—is very large. They really do love him with all of their heart, and miss him a lot. He sounded like a great guy.**

Bradbury: Oh absolutely! Otherwise I would have nothing to do with him. I pick my friends by the joy they give life and the joy they give me.

Brock: **That's a good philosophy.**

Bradbury: Bill Nolan came to me at the same time, when I was living down in Venice [CA], and he came down and he hadn't begun to write yet. When I was in Ireland writing *Moby Dick*, Bill Nolan decided to become a full-time writer. By the time I came home in 1954, Bill Nolan was on his way and I encouraged him.

Brock: **So he's one of your 'sons.'**

Bradbury: He's one of my sons, yes.

Brock: **He's a great writer like yourself.**

Bradbury: Oh, he's wonderful. A terrific guy.

Brock: **George Clayton Johnson is another one.**

Bradbury: Well, George Clayton Johnson: every time I see him I kick his butt! He's a brilliant short story writer and he should be doing more. I believe in George Clayton Johnson more than he believes in himself! I saw him again at San Diego Comic-Con and the first thing I said is, "Are you writing?" When you see George again, you tell him I'm watching him and he's in danger of having his butt kicked if he doesn't write more!

Brock: **I'll tell him [laughs]! While we're talking about Nolan and Johnson, what did you think of *Logan's Run*, the book?**

Bradbury: It's a fine book and it deserves more attention. It's a shame the new version [of the movie] hasn't been made. The old version was okay, but not good enough really. So I'm hoping the new film will get made soon.

Brock: **So is Bill and so is George!**

Bradbury: [laughs]

Brock: **Any final thoughts?**

Bradbury: The final thought is: I'm a little put out with God for taking Chuck away. I'm very put out with God and he better behave or I'll kick his butt, too!

PATRICK LUSSIER

PATRICK LUSSIER IS a genre writer, editor and director, who has mastered the art and craft of directing live action 3D. Most recently, he co-wrote *Terminator: Genisys* with Laeta Kalogridis for Skydance Productions and Paramount Pictures, released in 2015. He has collaborated on several projects with Ms. Kalogridis, dating back to 1999 when Laeta was hired to rewrite Scream 3 which Lussier was film editing. His previous motion picture credits include directing both *Drive Angry 3D* and *My Bloody Valentine: 3D*, released by Summit Entertainment and Lionsgate, respectively (MBV3D, made for 16 million, made over 50 million domestic on 1003 screens over just 3 weekends, and over 50 million foreign in it's initial release. It is currently the 11th highest grossing slasher film of all time). Lussier directed and edited *White Noise: The Light* (aka *White Noise 2*), and directed and co-wrote the vampire trilogy *Wes Craven Presents Dracula 2000* notable for Gerard Butler's feature debut in a starring role, *Dracula II: Ascension and Dracula III: Legacy*. He made his directorial debut with the horror fantasy *The Prophecy 3: The Ascent*, the Prophecy series' final installment with Christopher Walken as the Archangel Gabriel.

Lussier edited the lion's share of Wes Craven's movies through the 1990s and early 2000s, including *Wes Craven's New Nightmare, Vampire in Brooklyn, Music of the Heart*, the original Scream trilogy, *Cursed* and *Red Eye*. Additional editorial credits include Gonzalo Lopez-Gallego's *Apollo 18*, Guillermo del Toro's *Mimic*, Steve Miner's *Halloween: H20* and the comedies *My Boss's Daughter* and *D3: The Mighty Ducks*, directed by David Zucker and Rob Lieberman respectively. Prior to a career in features, Lussier edited MacGyver for three seasons and the *Doctor Who: TV Movie* in 1996. Lussier has also worked as a visual consultant on *Darkness Falls, 54, Brothers Grimm, Exorcist: The Beginning/Dominion, The*

Return and *Whisper*, and as a music consultant on *Reindeer Games* and *Equilibrium*.

Joe: Where does your passion for horror movies come from?

Patrick Lussier: A combination of things. My sister, who was older, would often go see movies and tell me about them the next day in detail. I remember her telling me about *The Exorcist* and *The Other* and *The Omen*, all movies I wasn't allowed to see. I would sit in her room rapt and fascinated and scared as she relayed the horror! She was also an avid reader, and I remember when she discovered Stephen King and first read *The Shining* then *Salem's Lot*. I just read comic books so my folks encouraged me to read actual books. I read *Salem's Lot* first and became utterly enthralled with that story. Since then, haven't turned back.

Joe: How did you get involved with editing movies?

Patrick: I started in post-production after college, working as an apprentice editor on *The Hitchhiker*, and old HBO show that was basically 'yuppies run amok.' It was right when editing was transitioning from traditional film to electronic. I learned different electronic systems, Montage 1 and 2 and Ediflex. That gave me an edge at the time and I was lucky enough to start editing before I turned 25 on *MacGyver*. After *MacGyver* left Vancouver, where I lived, Wes Craven brought *Nightmare Cafe* to town to shoot its six episodes. I cut Wes' episode, "Aliens Ate My Lunch," and we hit it off. He asked if I would edit his next feature film which was *Wes Craven's New Nightmare* two years later. I was incredibly lucky to work with Wes for so many great years.

Joe: What goes into editing a movie? And how long does it normally take you?

Patrick: It varies on the film. Usually, it's working the dailies as they come in and crafting first each scene individually then working with the director to build those scenes into the film, trimming out the repetitions, finding the characters' journey through the story given the film that was shot, etc. How long it takes depends on a lot of things. Wes and I got it down very quickly. We could finish a director's cut in half or third of the time allotted (which is 10 weeks). Other films can be more involved and take longer.

Joe: **What is the toughest challenge in editing a movie?**

Patrick: Seeing it fresh, seeing it without the foreknowledge of what was there previously. Put yourself in the audience's eyes. They know nothing about how hard it was to shoot or what the geography of the location was—none of that matters to them; it's just the story and the characters and the impact each has on the other.

Joe: **How do balance your career with family life?**

Patrick: Not always easy, but gets easier the older you get. You realize what's important, or at least I did. I work closer to home more these days to be near my son. That's more important than any of the other stuff.

Joe: **Which movie are you most proud of, and why?**

Patrick: That is an incredibly tricky answer. I'm proud of most of them for different reasons. *Scream* was an amazing experience as it was politically very challenging. We found the movie very quickly but there were doubters during the process. *My Bloody Valentine*, as a director, is one of my favorites, even though it certainly has its flaws. I like the hero's journey in that— and yes, I consider Tom Hanniger (Jensen Ackles) the hero. During the writing, several characters embodied that role (Axel, Harry himself, and Tom), but when Todd and I landed on Tom and why it was Tom, it felt right in every way. All that aside, editing-wise, I loved cutting the *Doctor Who* TV movie, and *Wes Craven's New Nightmare* is probably my favorite. *New Nightmare* was the first feature I ever cut. It was a wonderful and surreal mind-fuck of a story with such deep emotion and heart.

INTERVIEWS

Joe: Who should have the most say about the final product? The producer, director, or editor? And why?

Patrick: All depends on who has the best intentions for the good of the film and who will protect its release.

Joe: What are some of the biggest pitfalls in editing a movie?

Patrick: Biggest challenge is when the film was shot to be something different than the script or the producers had wanted. When there's a lack of unified vision—that makes the whole process an uphill shit-fight.

Joe: You've written quite a few screenplays, as well. Where does your love for vampires come from?

Patrick: *Salem's Lot.*

Joe: Do you prefer editing or writing?

Patrick: I like both editing and writing but I'll say writing is, for me, the harder of the two. Editing, you have footage, you can see intent and find the movie. Writing . . . the page always starts blank and it's up to you to fill it.

Joe: What equipment or program should a young filmmaker or editor invest in?

Patrick: I have never bought my own editing gear because the tech advances too quickly. Watch movies, study them. Study how they're crafted and put together. Read stories, learn all you can about storytelling. That'll serve you more than hardware.

Joe: Looking back at some of the classic movies you've worked on. Did you have any idea at that time that these movies were special?

Patrick: Each movie was something we were just trying to make the best it could be at the time. You never know if they'll find an audience and catch the public eye. But you know that you've done the best service to the film you could and that's what's important. That you can control. Whether a film becomes a classic or not is up to everyone else.

Joe: Without naming them, of course, have you ever edited a movie you didn't personally like? Is it best to hand it over to someone else or just do the best with what you've got?

Patrick: Yes. And sometimes.

Joe: How do you distance yourself from bad reviews for movies you directed?

Patrick: Ha! Don't read them, which is impossible; you read them anyway. Time, time distances from everything and makes you stop flailing yourself less.

Joe: Are there specific editing or filmmaking techniques youngsters need to learn from a mentor, or does everything come from experience and a unique perspective?

Patrick: Best advice I ever got was from Michael Robison, the first editor I assisted for back on *The Hitchhiker* and *21 Jump Street* (the series, not the movie): "Cut with your gut, not your head." Mike Elliot, another editor I worked with on *MacGyver* augmented that advice saying something like, you have to feel each emotion the character experiences as you cut, the sadness, the mystery, the excitement. If you're not on the edge of your seat, no one else will be either.

KEITH AREM

INTERVIEWED BY E.C. MCMULLEN

KEITH AREM STARTED off in the music industry as writer/producer for the industrial band Biohazard PCB, which later became Contagion on Capitol Records. He soon started scoring music for motion pictures and video games for Virgin Interactive, and Electronic Arts. For over half a decade, Keith built their recording studios, handled sound design, music, voice-over, cinematics, and commercial work.

In 2000, Keith launched PCB Productions as a service-based company for predominantly interactive games including *Ghost Recon, Rainbow Six*, and *Call of Duty* (most recent 11 games), about 600 games in the last 20 years.

In about the last six years, Keith began creating original graphic novels, including *Ascend* (Image Comics), *Infex, Dead Speed*, and the upcoming Frost Road (optioned for a motion picture).

Keith recently put the lock on his first director effort, *The Phoenix Incident*, which is slated for a U.S. theatrical release in February, 2016.

E.C. McMullen: **Do you see yourself as making Science Fiction Horror or Supernatural Horror?**

Keith: I write in a variety of different subject genres, but everything needs to be based in reality. I like to take mythology that an audience can relate to, and present a "What If?"

The premise for *The Phoenix Incident* starts with the largest UFO sighting in the United States and launches from there. What If the military concealed what really happened? In Ascend, What If

Angels aren't as innocent as we think they are? In INFEX, What If someone took the cure for cancer and used it to weaponized people? I love taking a real world science and posing a new question with it.

I take science fiction and write it as if it was science fact, but I want to stay grounded in reality. There are some fantastic authors I enjoy who write complete fantasy, but for me as a writer, I gravitate toward real worlds.

As a creator, another facet that inspires me is the way people find my stories. It's not necessarily through traditional marketing either—For example, you might be in a restaurant, someone comes up to you and says they're being held hostage and you need to make a call in their behalf to help them. That begins a rabbit hole into a story that's actually happening in the real world, in real time.

It also can become part of a promotional event that leads into a movie launch. If a story engages people in the real world, they become emotionally invested in your universe, as opposed to just watching a commercial on television.

ECM: **You're writing more than the movie—**

Keith:**—Or video game.**

ECM: **You're writing an interactive promotion that gets people—the audience—physically involved in your story.**

Keith: Exactly. I think that there's a new wave of storytellers that leave traditional media for the screen and prefer to involve the audience in a more visceral way. Such as ARGs (Alternate Reality Games), using Social and Viral marketing in interesting ways that break traditional boundaries.

As a traditional storyteller, those may seem like marketing tactics or something a sales or marketing team executes, but in my opinion, it's something a good story teller can do best. Because a good story is a good story. If you can get someone emotionally invested in your world, you can have a person live in your world for months.

Look around us here at Comic Con. All of these people, these cosplayers, dressing as their favorite characters, playing and living for this brief moment in time within a story or character. They love these stories so much that they want to exist in them.

So now as creators, we have a bigger responsibility to our audience, and they are ready for it. As a director, I don't want only give you a small 90 minute chunk then say, "Thank you, please come back for the sequel." The Internet now empowers filmmakers, gives us tools that allow the audience to play in our stories, and live in our stories. When the audience leaves the theater, they go home, get on the Internet or the game, and not just relive the experience they just had, but plug into more of the story. The audience can enrich and expand the story. Our stories can now be so much bigger than the 90 minute experiences we've known for the last 75 years. I want you to enjoy my story for days, or weeks, as long as you want. And now, our stories are no longer limited to the page or the screen.

ECM: So this is where you're coming from, what you want, but after all of this, now you decided to make a movie. And despite all your past history, this is a new experience for you. Despite all of this you are now beginning with a movie.

Keith: Absolutely. It's inspiring to understand and respect what great filmmakers can achieve. After working on so many games and other properties, I was inspired by the amount of creativity directors have dedicate to compete in today's marketplace. The film industry is changing drastically. I've been in the digital side for so long, that creating a film that was a huge step in a direction I never experienced before.

I was so used to update elements online. Patch things, change as the audience changes. But films are a fixed format, it's hard to change course. It's like a massive ship sailing versus a speedboat that can turn on a dime.

Many people have asked, "Everyone's moving toward video games and interactive elements, why would you want to go into film?"

My answer is that I want to bring my experience to the film world. I think traditional films have been struggling to be relevant in a digital age of viral Marketing and Social media, and I want my film to demonstrate the transmedia opportunities my other properties have shown.

That has been a huge learning experience.

ECM: So you've been in this business for a long time, but you've been orbiting around other people's properties. You are still in every sense, an independent motion picture film maker. Now that it's your time making your motion picture, what was your biggest surprise after all this time, that you just didn't see coming?

Keith: Definitely the biggest surprise was the way the films are purchased and distributed. Projects are sometimes judged based on the budget of the film, as opposed to the content of the film. Buyers are often looking at who's in the film or what the budget is. The story is sometimes secondary.

ECM: In Jeff Ulin's book, *The Business of Media Distribution*, he says that distributors will ask that very question. "What's the budget of your movie?" Jeff Ulin says the budget of the movie is never the value of the movie.

I take that to mean: accountants are never salespeople for good reason. If someone is bean counting the budget of your movie and not the value of your movie then they don't know how to sell your movie. So forget that one and go to the next person representing that territory and deal with them.

Keith: Unfortunately, keeping the budget secret is sometimes difficult to keep to yourself.

ECM: Bad movies have made a fortune in theaters then flop in the home video market. Then you have people like Mike Judge who has made movies for 20th Century Fox, that Fox didn't know how to sell, and his movies get word of mouth and became runaway hits in the home video

INTERVIEWS

market. Suits at Fox wind up holding their heads crying over how much money they left on the table.

Keith: The thing is understanding your market and how your audience fits in. The audience is relevant to the creator / director as much as they are to the marketing department, who are normally at arm's length from the production side. I think there is often a disconnect between these sides.

ECM: **Yeah.**

Keith: If you have a marketing team that says, "We know how to sell the hell out of this, just let us do our job.", that's fantastic and they often do a great job. But I think you're starting to see filmmakers today who have a much broader story they want to tell and they have to be involved in the marketing. And if the director is excluded from that step, or they don't share their creativity with the ancillary projects (like the video game, graphic novel or TV show), then their creativity disappears and someone else reinterprets their story. That's why you often have movies where the first one does fantastic and the sequel bombs.

My intention as a director isn't for control reasons or ego reasons, but to create a 360 degree vision of my world. In my mind, I've already fleshed out that world, the characters, their stories. I've lived in it, know it, at least to the point where I know the potential of it. I'm a different type of storyteller. I see some many incredible emerging platforms like VR, AR, Apps, and mobile, and I want to use all of them to tell my stories.

ECM: **Cross platform. You were talking about that earlier with your graphic novel, *Infex*. Parts are for the graphic novel, some are for the iPad, and others a series—a different experience on each one.**

Keith: Exactly. Each platform tells a different part of the story in a different way. For example, on the iPad, I can have the reader choose their path or explore at their own pace . In an interactive experience the players don't just play a game, they become characters in the story, their characters influence the direction of the story, and world wide players can interact with other people within a world that encircles the overall story.

ECM: Not merely team players running around shooting and blowing everything up, but an actual unfolding, involving story.

Keith: Exactly. Everyone is constantly looking for the next thing to keep themselves busy. We need something to keep our minds occupied. I want something that will not only entertain me, but challenge me. I want to actively progress the story at my leisure and actually affect the story. Wouldn't it be cool if I could actually affect the world as a fan . . . change the story because the creator read my comments and said, "Wow. There's a character that the audience loves. I want to build on this character."

As a creator I want to know that the audience is either positively or negatively responding to what I'm creating. Maybe they are gravitating toward an unexpected character or not relating to a storyline, and I need to know if I have to engage them differently.

ECM: Creators never know when they are going to unexpectedly create their Boba Fett.

Keith: I think that's exactly what's happening with independent filmmakers. Creators like myself are learning from their audience. But it's a fine line you cannot cross. To keep what's unique about your story, keep your edge, you can't ever lose your singular vision. You have to remind yourself, "I may make this change for the fans, but it's still my character." I may reach a point where I say, "I know they like this character, but I have to do what's best for the story."

ECM: Because the audience is attracted to your vision. If you let the audience control the vision then it's no longer the vision they were attracted to. It becomes a story by committee and then it all evaporates.

Keith: Right. You want to find that vision that's prominent, and couple it with the influence of your audience. That's where the magic happens.

ECM: **So you've made your first feature film. What was the single most difficult part of making your film? And I mean any part from pre-production, to production, post production or sales in distribution. What made you say, "Man! This is a wall I have to knock down or go through."**

Keith: Distribution without question. Absolutely.

Making the movie was a joy. Spectacular experience! Shooting the first day on set, I couldn't believe I wasn't doing this twenty years ago. I walked on set and no one had any idea it was my first film. We had a great time. The crew would stay late and go out together after our shoots.

The moment we were done and started packaging the film, it was a completely different world. None of my previous experience mattered. I'm not a control freak, but until I realized how the industry worked, it was completely out of my control.

ECM: **As difficult as distribution was, do you feel you've learned from it, or has it left such a bad taste in your mouth that you want to go in a different direction?**

Keith: It's actually inspired me to take our film on a different path. I realized there's a huge opportunity to take what I've done in the interactive space and apply it to my film and the entire film industry—for sales, distribution, marketing, as well as piracy. Technology is quickly coming to the aid of distribution. As a film maker I intend to do many more films and television shows, and I want to actively learn how films are evolving and take them to new audiences. When I see the problems, it inspires me to turn those negatives into positives.

MICK GARRIS

BORN IN SANTA Monica, California, on December 4, 1951, Mick Garris grew up with his mother in the San Fernando Valley neighborhood of Van Nuys from age 12, following his parents' divorce. Garris was making his own 8mm home movies around that time, and when he got older be became a freelance critic for a number of film and music celebrities.

In 1977 Garris was hired as a receptionist in George Lucas' newly formed company Star Wars Corporation where, through industry contacts, he created and served as the on-screen host for a Los Angeles cable access interview program show called "Fastasy Film Festival," which aired on L.A.'s legendary Z-Channel. Guests included filmmakers like John Landis, Joe Dante, John Carpenter and Steven Spielberg and actors like William Shatner and Christopher Lee.

In 1980 Garris worked as a press agent for the newly merged Pickwick-Maslansky-Koeninsberg agency. He also began making a name for himself with photographing and directing "making-of . . . " features for such films as *Scanners* (1981), *The Howling* (1981), *Halloween II* (1981), *The Thing* (1982) and *Videodrome* (1983). In 1982 Garris was hired by MCA/Universal to write the script for Coming Soon (1982), which was a collection of horror movie trailers featuring Jamie Lee Curtis as the hostess and directed by John Landis. While struggling to find more work, Garris was hired by Steven Spielberg to be one of the writers and story editors for Spielberg's sci-fi anthology series *Amazing Stories* (1985).

In 1992 Garris directed an original screenplay by Stephen King, *Sleepwalkers* (1992). The following year Garris received story and screenplay credit for the comic horror film *Hocus Pocus* (1993), and the year after that he took the reins at the request of Stephen King for the six-hour mini-series *The Stand* (1994) based on King's bestselling horror novel. The mini-series, which had a grueling 20-month shooting schedule, was one of the most-watched shows of 1994. Garris and King again teamed up for a three-part made-for-TV rewriting of King's novel, *The Shining* (1997).

In 2005 Garris was able to assemble a group of his fellow horror film directors in the anthology horror series *Masters of Horror* (2005), which he created and executive-produced. Garris' own contribution, "Chocolate", was based on his own short story, written 20 years earlier.

Joe: **I've watched many of your online interviews and discussions, and of course enjoyed all your movies, and I'm amazed at your knowledge and insight into the horror genre. Was this something you intentionally developed through life? Did you study the genre or does it all come down to passion and what you're interested in?**

Mick Garris: It was always a love of mine. My interest in books and film and television reaches far beyond the horror genre, but it has always been at the top of the list. In my youth, I was in a band, and I wrote about music, and did lots of interviews and the like, because when you love something, when it becomes a passion, you seek out as much of the knowledge as you can. Curiosity has always been a keystone of my popular culture interests.

If I read a book I love, I want to read all of that author's works. Same with a musician, an actor, or a filmmaker. It's not really "studying the genre" so much as devouring what you love with an insatiable hunger. And literature and cinema of the *outré* was always at the top of the list for me.

Joe: **What was it about Stephen King's novels that made you want to adapt them for films?**

Mick: I think King and I have very similar backgrounds growing up, and we were drawn to similar things. He was raised by his mother; my parents split at an early age. We were brought up in relatively meager circumstances, and we were not the popular kids in school. I think being the outsider is something common to people who love and create horror.

With King, it's his distinct and human voice. The world his work occupies is familiar, genuine, filled with people who have thoughts and feelings and circumstances we can all relate to. I love his voice, and we seem to be pretty simpatico in that regard.

Joe: **Where did the idea for *Masters of Horror* originate?**

Mick: Well, the actual origination of the idea began percolating when I was working on *Amazing Stories*. I loved anthologies, even though the television networks have always kind of hated them in the last 30 years. Even back then, *Amazing Stories* was not a real success.

But in practical terms, I guess it really began with a series of dinners I organized about ten years ago. A lot of us who make genre films are friends, and we'll run into each other at film festivals or events or conventions. For years, when we'd run into each other, someone would always say, "We ought to put together a dinner or something." Directors don't work with directors, as a rule, and it sounded like a great idea.

But I realized over the course of time that no one was going to do it if I didn't. So I actually made a bunch of calls and took about a week to organize our first dinner. It wasn't to network or anything official like that, it was just to get a group of people who do the same kind of thing for a living to get together socially. We've been doing these dinners ever since, very occasionally, and from the beginning, we all would talk about what it would be like to have control over our own futures, creatively and otherwise. I came up with doing one-hour movies as a series, and it took a while to get commitments from a bunch of the filmmakers, and once we started having meetings with companies, it sold right away.

Joe: **It must've been quite the undertaking to direct Stephen King's *The Stand*. Was he involved a lot during the filming, or did he completely trust your judgment?**

Mick: Well, both, really. Yes, it was the hardest job I've ever had, but an incredible journey in every way you can imagine. King was around for over half of the shoot, but he was a resource, not a guide. In all the times we've worked together, I've never had him tell me how he thought a scene should be shot, or how a performance should be attenuated or anything like that. Once he has faith in you, he trusts you. Or at least he has with me.

Part of it, I think, is that he can separate the books from the movies. Each has to stand on its own merits, and they are very different media, even though both are storytelling. So yeah, he's the one who hired me for *The Stand*, and things went very well during the shoot. He liked what we were getting, and gave me all the rope.

Most importantly, he helped me stretch the television envelope. Network TV was much more conservative back then, and because he was the 800 pound gorilla, we got away with stuff that we wouldn't have without him fighting on our behalf.

Joe: **What was it like to be behind the scenes on Indiana and the Temple of Doom?**

Mick: I wish I knew! I was never on the set for the movie. Frank Marshall, who produced the film, also directed the documentary on the making of it. Because Steven had enjoyed his interview we did on my old Z Channel show, *Fantasy Film Festival*, he had Frank ask me to do the interview with Steven for the documentary. That's as close as I got to the movie, other than buying a ticket.

That was before I was hired to write for *Amazing Stories*.

Joe: **How was it working with Pierce Brosnan?**

Mick Garris: Well, Pierce Brosnan might be the biggest actor I've worked with at the time we worked together. With an actor of that caliber, you know when to talk about the role and when to get out of the way. Pierce was amazing to work with on *Bag of Bones*; he'd never really done anything in the genre (*Lawnmower Man* doesn't count), and approached the material with a lot of respect. We had our conversations before the shoot began, but he rarely needed much adjustment when it came to shooting. He knew that character inside and out.

One of the most difficult elements was that, in the miniseries, Pierce's character loses his wife early in the story. Pierce had actually lost his wife years ago, and it was a tender issue I didn't want (or need) to discuss with him. He had tremendous insight into the part, and I think it's one of his best performances.

Joe: Since you've taken on the part of actor on more than one occasion, do you get most of your character's traits from the screenplay or do you mostly bring in your own ideas?

Mick Garris: Depends on the writing. A good script is going to inspire you. And a good casting director brings in good, original ideas. And a good actor is going to bring a lot to the table. Good ideas come from wherever you find them.

Joe: What is the biggest pitfall actors have to look out for?

Mick Garris: Another tough question. Maybe mostly acting itself. I'm most impressed when I see an actor inhabit the role, *be* it rather than *act* it.

Joe: Any hazards screenwriters need to watch out for when writing a script?

Mick Garris: Getting started. Thinking too much. I'm at my best when my hands are writing, not my brain. What I mean by that is that when I labor too much, it's because it's not working. My intuition is a better storyteller than the laboring part of me. When I try too hard, it seems to kill brain cells.

Also, when you keep going back to fix the things that you've already done, you keep from working through from beginning to end. Just go through it, then do your rewriting. Actually getting from beginning to end is the real accomplishment; then going back and sprucing it up is relatively easy, at least for me.

That said, I want my first drafts to read like final drafts, shooting scripts, and it's the way I work.

A huge pitfall is to overwrite, to describe in detail each element and screen direction. Nothing is more tedious to me than reading an action script where the writer takes paragraphs to describe the action on the screen.

I'd recommend never making a paragraph longer than five lines. Make the script readable, entertaining to read, and not just a blueprint. You want the reader eager to turn the page.

Joe: Do you have any advice for the screenwriters out there?

Mick Garris: Everyone works differently; everyone has a different route to their careers. Listen to people who know what they're talking about, learn to know when a criticism is right, but stick to your guns if you know it's wrong. But you have to be open-minded enough to *know* when they're right, and that's kind of a big deal.

Inspiration is always my guide. I didn't become a screenwriter because I thought it would make me rich; I did it because I love writing and I love movies. I write fiction and prose as well as screenplays, and the point of all of them is to be absorbing and surprising and entertaining. Grammar counts, by the way. If I read a script filled with misspellings and "their" instead of "there" and "it's" instead of "its" and the like, it's going to take one hell of a good story to keep me reading. And that rarely happens.

Write the script that stands out from all the rest; be original. These guys read piles of scripts every day, and even if what you write isn't "commercial", it might get you a meeting that could get you an assignment. Most of my spec scripts haven't been sold, but I don't regret writing a single one of them.

What's the worst it could be? A few weeks of your life? To create something you're proud of? Well, why not?

JOHN RUSSO

THE DEAD COME TO LIFE

Joe: **You've also acted in a few of your movies, creating quite a few memorable moments. Describe your best on camera moment, and your fondest backstage memory.**

John Russo: As far as on-camera moments, the thing that stands out the most for my fans is when I played the Tire Iron Zombie in *NOLD*. By now thousands of fans also know that I did the molotov cocktail stunt without the benefit of an asbestos suit—I was set on fire with real gasoline, and I volunteered to do it because I felt that we'd look stupid if none of the ghouls got set on fire after we had made the point that, in the words of the sheriff, "they're just dead flesh, they go up pretty easy."

Joe: **Looking back at the original *Night of the Living Dead*, it seems like George A. Romero threw you into the deep end quite a few times. Would you say it brought out the best in you, and in the movie?**

John Russo: George didn't throw me anywhere, I did everything because I wanted to. I was extremely dedicated to making the best movie we could make, and so was everyone else on our staff and crew, including the actors.

Joe: **What steps should a young film-maker or screenwriter take to ensure the title of their movie is protected by copyright?**

INTERVIEWS

John Russo: There is no copyright protection for a title. That's why the MPAA Title Registration department was formed, so that signatories, mostly the major studios, would promise not to use each other's registered titles.

Joe: **How did you start out being a writer?**

John Russo: I began writing a mystery novel when I was about to graduate from high school, hoping that if I could become a published author I'd never have to work for somebody else. I never wanted a mundane 9-5 job. Still don't. But when I first started I didn't have all the skills necessary to complete a novel and get it published. I developed those skills as time went on.

Joe: **How did you first get involved with films?**

John Russo: With Rudy Ricci, my friend from grade school on, plus some other friends I had in high school. We messed around trying to film "rumble scenes" and so on with Rudy's 8mm camera, but our efforts never amounted to much. Then Rudy and I met Russ Streiner and George Romero when we were 18 years old and George came to Pittsburgh to attend Carnegie-Mellon as a fine arts major. He was already bitten by the movie bug and we contracted the disease. Russ at the time was acting in stage plays at the Pittsburgh Playhouse; he at first wanted to be an actor, but he quickly got bitten by the movie bug, as well.

Joe: **Would you say it is now easier or more difficult to start making your own movies?**

John Russo: It's much easier because of low-cost, high-quality digital production. You can make a feature film on a few hundred bucks sometimes, as with *Paranormal Activity.*

Joe: **This question pops up a lot, but do you think a screenwriter should be involved once production starts?**

John Russo: Usually you need to let the director take over and don't get in his hair unless he asks for your ideas.

Joe: **If you could go back and tell your younger self something (when you just started making films), what would you say?**

John Russo: Don't trust anybody when it comes to money. That includes not just distributors but sometimes your own so-called best friends.

Joe: **What's it like working with Tom Savini?**

John Russo: Tom has an infectious enthusiasm for everything he does in the biz. He elevates the mood of all the people around him.

Joe: **How do you manage your time with deadlines looming?**

John Russo: I just work hard and keep going and I keep the script and the ideas constantly in my mind while I'm awake—and probably subconsciously while I'm sleeping. I live and breathe every single project I'm working on.

Joe: **Any advice for young screenwriters?**

John Russo: Study hard and read, read, read—and keep creating and learning from your own efforts.

DENISE GOSSETT

Joe: **All great things of course start with an idea and the first small step. Can you still remember how Shriekfest came about?**

Denise Gossett: Yes, I am an actress and I had starred in a horror film, and when I realized there weren't any festivals dedicated to horror, I came up with the idea!

Joe: **How much work goes into organizing a horror related event?**

Denise: Tons! It started out as a 'work really hard for four months' job and now it is 'work really hard all year long!'

Joe: **What are the biggest pitfalls to watch out for when organizing an event such as Shriekfest?**

Denise: Budget, organization (I have a calendar that lists every single thing that needs to be done each month; if you let one ball drop all the rest will drop, too), and don't forget kindness to others.

Joe: **If someone wanted to set up a small horror related event (film premiere, perhaps), what kind of checklist would you offer them?**

Denise: Well, find a great venue, you want the sound and picture to be wonderful, make a budget and be very careful about going over it, invite as many people as you can, and always treat everyone with kindness.

Joe: **What advice would you give filmmakers when it comes to submitting their films to film festivals?**

Denise: Be professional about everything you do, research fests, read reviews, is your film right for the festival, how do other filmmakers feel about the festival . . . .this says a lot, pay attention to them.

Joe: **What's the funniest and most horrible things you've seen or experienced as a festival director?**

Denise: Funniest would be some of the outlandish things people send me . . . I had someone send me a g-string with the name of their film on it. J A horrible thing would be a threat I received because someone's film didn't make the cut, this email basically said how we will meet someday and how this person looks forward to that and it wasn't in a good way.

Joe: **Tell us a bit about your biggest acting role to date.**

Denise: I was in "Get the Gringo" with Mel Gibson and I just shot "I Saw the Light" with Tom Hiddleston!

Joe: **How was it working with them?**

Denise: Working with Mel Gibson was amazing . . . so professional, so giving as an actor, very funny. We had a blast. I really felt like he was looking out for me. Working with Tom Hiddleston was like sitting down with an old friend and chatting . . . lovely, lovely man.

Joe: **As an actor, what do you look for in a screenplay?**

Denise: Great, strong story, well thought out characters, strong dialogue, not too long, not too short.

Joe: **Do you get most of your character's traits from the screenplay or do you mostly bring in your own ideas?**

Denise: An actor should get most of the traits right from the script. If you analyze a script properly, you can find out so much information from your character, the descriptions, and other characters. And then, you add your own nuances.

Joe: **What is the biggest pitfall actors have to look out for?**

Denise: Being needy, desperate, flaky. I see a lot of it and it's gotten old. If you can't be a professional, find another career.

Joe: **Describe your best on camera moment**.

Denise: Working with Mel Gibson . . . and the explosions, getting drenched by the sprinklers!

Joe: **And your fondest backstage memory?**

Denise: Chatting with Dennis Hopper about golfing and life in general.

JACK THOMAS SMITH

JACK THOMAS SMITH made his feature film-directing debut with the psychological thriller *Disorder*. He was also the writer and producer of that film. *Disorder* was released on DVD by Universal/Vivendi and New Light Entertainment. It was later released on Pay-Per-View and Video-On-Demand by Warner Brothers. Overseas, it screened at the Cannes Film Festival and the Raindance Film Festival in London. Curb Entertainment represented *Disorder* for foreign sales and secured distribution deals around the world.

Born in 1969 in Philadelphia, Pennsylvania, Smith lived there until he was eight when his family relocated to a quiet island community in Michigan, which would later serve as the inspiration for his upcoming film *In the Dark*. He began to write at a very young age after reading the Stephen King novels *Salem's Lot* and *The Shining*. By the time he was eleven, he had written a 300-page novel and a number of short stories.

Smith's family moved to Sparta, New Jersey when he was a teenager. It was there in that middle-class town that he discovered the films of George A. Romero, Stanley Kubrick, Brian DePalma, and John Carpenter. Inspired to make movies, he wrote and directed a handful of short films that were shot on Super 8mm and starred his brother and friends in all of the roles.

As a young adult, Smith produced films for noted horror directors Ted Bohus and John Russo, co-creator of *Night of the Living Dead*. From that point on, it was only a matter of time for his growth as a filmmaker to expand.

Smith's current project he calls *Infliction* is a dark and disturbing assembled footage film that documents two brothers' 2011 murder spree in NC and the horrific truth behind their actions. *Infliction* opened in select theaters across the country in 2014 and is now available on DVD, VOD, and Digital HD in the U.S. and Canada by Virgil Films & Entertainment.

Smith's production company, Fox Trail Productions, Inc., is currently developing the action/horror film *In the Dark*.

Joe: You've been known for taking 'found footage' to the next level. Care to comment?

Jack Thomas Smith: *Infliction* documents a murder spree committed by two brothers in North Carolina in 2011 . . . and the horrific truth behind their actions. It's more of a psychodrama than a horror. But it does have horror elements to it. It's very character driven and story driven. *Infliction* deals with a subject matter that unfortunately affects way too many people. As the film plays out, you'll find yourself asking who are the true criminals and who are the true victims?

The filming style of *Infliction* falls into the "found footage" category. But I refer to *Infliction* as an assembled footage film rather than found footage. Found footage implies just that . . . Someone found the actual footage that was left behind by the victims as with *The Blair Witch Project*. Assembled footage means that the movie is more of a documentary that was shot for a specific reason and the footage has been assembled for storytelling purposes. I shot *Infliction* as assembled footage because the story dictated that style. The cameras serve a purpose. As *Infliction* unfolds, you'll find that there's a reason why the brothers are documenting their actions.

Joe: Can you still recall your very first screenplay?

Jack Thomas Smith: The first feature-length screenplay I wrote was the action/horror *In The Dark*. I wrote it twenty years ago and have been very close a number of times to securing financing. Unfortunately in the film business, you meet with investors and think you have a deal, then for whatever reason it falls through. Over the years, I've rewritten it and rewritten it inbetween the four features I produced and the two I directed (*Disorder* & *Infliction*). I'm hoping to finally shoot *In The Dark* in 2016. It's the one film I'm determined to make or will die trying.

Joe: **Where would you say should newbie film-makers start?**

Jack Thomas Smith: I would definitely recommend going to business school. It takes money to make a film and you need to know how to structure a deal. Once your screenplay is complete, you need to put together a budget, which ultimately dictates the amount of money you need to raise. The next step in the process is to create a business plan and PowerPoint, which details the cast and crew attachments, risks, projections, and tax incentives for investing. It's also important to know the process involved with forming an LLC for each project, the monetization of state tax credits, and the steps involved with foreign and domestic distribution. The bottom line is that your investor(s) want to make a profit, and if they do, chances are they will reinvest. It's called the "film business" for a reason.

Joe: **What specifically do you look for in a screenplay or screenwriter?**

Jack Thomas Smith: I'm a big fan of screenplays that deal with the psychological aspects of its characters. For example, my favorite TV show of all-time is *The Sopranos*. On the surface, it was a mob show. But Tony and his crew were clearly sociopaths and hit all of the markers with their lack of conscience and manipulative behavior. Human beings are imperfect creatures and the characters in screenplays should reflect that. When a character is complex, good or bad, it makes you connect. And with a strong connection to the characters, every other aspect of the screenplay becomes stronger. In my opinion, the anti-hero always makes the best protagonist because they are fundamentally good, but have internal struggles of their own.

Joe: **Which horror movies most inspired your focus when filming?**

Jack Thomas Smith: When I shot my first film, *Disorder*, I watched *Memento*, *Frailty*, *Angel Heart*, and *Jacob's Ladder* to keep my brain in the psychological thriller mindset.

INTERVIEWS

When I shot *Infliction*, I watched *Cloverfield* and *Quarantine* to keep myself in the "found footage" world.

It helps to watch films that are similar in genre. Not to copy the films, but to help put your mind where it needs to be.

Joe: **How much work goes into setting up an independent film budget?**

Jack Thomas Smith: It's a tough process to put together a budget for an independent film simply because of the lack of funds. With bigger budget films, you have the luxury of having more people on set, providing their services to each department. Money can solve a lot of production problems. With smaller films, the director and/or producer generally wear numerous hats and have to multi-task. You want to make sure that as much of your limited budget goes on the screen as humanly possible. You don't want to cut costs on effects or rehearsal time with the cast. And sound design is very important for independent films, as well. A common mistake by independent filmmakers is to cut corners on performances, effects, and sound design. These are tell-tale signs that a film is low-budget. If you plan to direct and/or produce an independent film, plan on handling numerous departments in order to put the bulk of your money onscreen. The audience only cares about the end product and what they see. Production value, or at least its perception, is everything.

Joe: **And once the movie's made?**

Jack Thomas Smith: Once you finish your film, the next step is distribution. Ideally, you want to secure a Producer's Rep, who can negotiate and secure U.S. distribution. The importance of a distributor as opposed to self-distribution is the fact that a reputable distributor will have the pipelines set up with the theaters and major retailers. And distributors will have access to print and advertising money as well. If you're unable to secure distribution, then self-distribution is an option, but the online retailers are limited and the marketing of the film is solely up to the filmmaker.

Foreign sales are another important part of distribution. You want to find a REPUTABLE foreign sales agent, who will submit the film to foreign distributors and generate international sales. Be wary of sales agents who ask for money up front. Most foreign sales agents will take a percentage of the sales and will promote it to potential buyers at the major sales markets.

The first feature I directed, the psychological thriller *Disorder*, was released in the U.S. on DVD through Universal/Vivendi and on VOD & PPV by Warner Brothers. Curb Entertainment represented it for foreign sales and secured distribution deals around the world.

My new feature *Infliction* opened in select theaters in the U.S. in the spring of 2014. It was then released on DVD, VOD, and Digital HD in the U.S. and Canada by Virgil Films & Entertainment, which is the same company that distributed *Supersize Me*.

Infliction is now being represented for international distribution by the foreign sales agency Cardinal XD and will be available at all of the major film markets around the world, including the Toronto Film Festival; the American Film Market in Santa Monica, CA; Sundance; the Berlin Film Festival; and Cannes.

Joe: Which are your favorite techniques when shooting a film?

Jack Thomas Smith: It really depends on the film. With *Disorder*, I storyboarded the entire movie . . . even the cutaways. The entire film is told from the perspective of the main character, who is a paranoid schizophrenic. So I couldn't cut to other characters on the other side of town or to other scenes that didn't include him. It wouldn't work with the story. The main character lives in a house in the woods, isolated. I shot with a lot of close-ups and tighter shots to convey his isolation, not only in life, but also in his own mind.

With *Infliction*, I wrote detailed shot lists for the entire film. Being that this is a "found footage" film (or "assembled footage" as I like to call it), it was important for the Director of Photography and the actor handling the onscreen camera to be perfectly in sync. Both the actor and DP needed to know exactly when and how to move the camera. You'll lose the audience if the onscreen camera is out of sync with the shooting camera.

Also, being that *Infliction* was shot to look like real footage, I could only show the audience what the onscreen cameras were

INTERVIEWS

seeing. It wasn't shot like a traditional film with establishing shots, cutaways, and crosscutting. It was shot to look like a documentary.

Joe: **Any advice you'd like to impart on newbies?**

Jack Thomas Smith: My advice for newbies is to work hard and network with other people as much as you can. You never know who will give you your break. The way I got into the film business is kind of crazy . . . When I was a teenager, I worked at a video store in Sparta, NJ. A customer by the name of Lee Estrada would come in and rent horror movies all the time. Needless to say, Lee and I would talk about horror films and we became friends. At that time, I had just started working on my first horror screenplay and I told Lee that. He gave me Ted Bohus's information and told me to reach out to him when I was done writing it. Ted is an indie filmmaker, who has directed a number of horror films. As soon as I finished writing my script, I contacted Ted and sent it to him. He read it, liked it, and suggested we work on a screenplay together. He felt the budget for the screenplay I wrote would be too large to shoot as an indie. So Ted and I co-wrote the sci-fi horror film *The Regenerated Man*, and raised the financing to shoot. Ted directed it and I worked with the crew so I could learn. When we completed the film, we were able to secure distribution with Arrow Entertainment and doubled our investment.

After that, I met John Russo at a horror convention in NYC. John wrote and produced the original *Night Of The Living Dead*, which is one of my favorite films. So it was cool to meet him. And I was able to raise the financing for a film he wrote called *Santa Claws*, which was about a guy dressed in a Santa Claus costume going around killing people. I learned a lot on this project as well and we secured distribution with EI Independent.

After working with Ted and John, I took what I had learned from them and applied it to my film *Disorder*, which I wrote, produced and directed. *Disorder* was later released on DVD by Universal/Vivendi and PPV & VOD by Warner Brothers.

DAVID HENSON GREATHOUSE

DAVID HENSON GREATHOUSE is a make-up effects artist, actor, director, writer, cameraman, and editor. Highly regarded by his peers for his work creating special make-up effects for over 50 movies such as *The Usual Suspects*, *Late Phases*, *Tales from the Crypt*, *All Cheerleader Die*, *John Dies in the End*, *The Rage*, *Freaked*, *Mighty Morphin' Power Rangers*, *Necronomicon*, and *Buried Alive*.

Greathouse developed his skills as a kid in Cleveland Ohio, where he shot movies with his friends, built a FX portfolio of prosthetics, and performed and managed multiple haunted attractions throughout the country.

In 1991, David relocated to Los Angeles to work as an artist in the movie industry. He has since contributed special make-up effects for many feature films and television shows.

He returned to Cleveland every October to shoot his debut film, *Legion of Terror*. A feature length documentary on a dedicated and demented ensemble of haunted house actors. The film explores the distinctive personalities, the complexities of a seasonal haunted attraction and the rise and fall of a very weird family over a thirteen year period.

In 2001 Greathouse became involved with the heavy metal band, Mushroomhead. He would design and create the band's signature masked appearance and tour the world with them as a roadie and documentarian.

Greathouse directed the band's music video for "12 Hundred," earning them the MTV's Headbangers Ball 2007 Video of the Year.

Since 2001 Greathouse is now part of Robert Kurtzman's Creature Corps in Crestline, Ohio with a dozen other relocated Hollywood film artists and technicians working toward ushering in their own brand of imagination.

In 2013 *House* was seen as a make-up artist contestant on Syfy's *Faceoff* Season 4.

INTERVIEWS

Joe: **How did you first get involved with movie makeup and special effects?**

David: I have been working with make-up and creating monsters since I was 9 years old. I was obsessed with horror as early as four. I grew up on late night horror hosts, comics, and *Famous Monsters* magazine. I was also very fortunate to have an aunt that owned a costume novelty store. So I had owned many of the classic Don Posts masks and a complete make-up kit at a very young age. From there grew Super 8 movies and haunted house productions executed in my basement.

Joe: **Are there specific formulas or guidelines for preparing a character/actor, or do you try to reinvent the wheel every now and then?**

David: I don't follow a specific guideline or technique. I determine what works best for the time and budget allowed. Sometimes it is not what you wished for, but what you have to make a reality. You always want to do your best work.

Joe: **How much artistic freedom should an artist have? Or does it all depend on the producers and directors?**

David: Film characters have much input from the writers, directors, producers and the actor. You have to respect that. If it is a one of a kind character that you want to create, it might be best to make it a personal creation and let it live on your terms.

Joe: **How do you know you've found just the right balance to make a monster or character scary, yet not over the top?**

David: The right balance is the quest. Designs are key. Sketches and sculptures of the design help the director and crew understand what we are making. Sometimes the right creature comes out onto the screen. One that we may never forget.

JOHN CARPENTER

HALLOWEEN AND BEYOND

INTERVIEWED BY MICHAEL MCCARTY AND MARK MCLAUGHLIN

JOHN CARPENTER HAS been thrilling and enthralling moviegoers for years with hits like *Starman, John Carpenter's Vampires, John Carpenter's Ghosts of Mars* and many more. But certainly his greatest fame came from his 1978 film *Halloween,* which has spawned numerous sequels and countless imitators.

Though most of Carpenter's heroes are men of action, he doesn't ignore the strength and valor of women. Laurie Strode, as portrayed by Jamie Lee Curtis in *Halloween,* proved to be the only one brave and resourceful enough to subdue the relentless silent killer, Michael Myers.

Carpenter was born in Carthage, New York, and raised in Bowling Green, Kentucky. He enjoyed westerns as a child, which may explain the stalwart outlook of most of his heroes, as well as the high-action energy he brings to his work. He attended Western Kentucky University and later enrolled in the University of Southern California's School of Cinema. As a student, he completed the 1970 short subject *The Resurrection of Bronco Billy,* which won an Academy Award. He went on to direct *Dark Star, Assault on Precinct 13* and then *Halloween,* which earned over $75 million worldwide on a budget of $300,000.

Following *Halloween,* he scored big with the suspense and horror hits *The* Fog, *Prince of Darkness, Christine, The Thing, In the Mouth of Madness* and *Village of the Damned.* He ventured into

INTERVIEWS

other genres, including the science fiction flicks with *Memoirs of an Invisible Man, Ghosts of Mars, They Live, Escape from New York* and *Starman.*

For TV, Carpenter directed the thriller *Someone's Watching Me,* the mini-series *Elvis* and the Showtime horror trilogy *John Carpenter Presents Body Bags.* As a screenwriter, Carpenter's credits include *Eyes of Laura Mars, Halloween II, The Philadelphia Experiment, Black Moon Rising, Meltdown* and the TV western, *El Diablo.*

John Carpenter's recent work includes the movie *The Ward,* a thriller centered on an institutionalized young woman who becomes terrorized by a ghost. He also directed two episodes of *Masters of Horror* with "Pro-Life" and "Cigarette Burns." His movies *Halloween, The Fog* and *Assault on Precinct 13* were remade by others.

Michael McCarty: What did executive producer Irwin Yablans give you to start *The Babysitter Murders* [later known as *Halloween*] creatively and how did you and Debra Hill develop that into the script?

John Carpenter: Irwin Yablans said, "I want a movie about babysitter murders, about a stalker, a killer going after babysitters." He thought that all teenagers could relate to that, because they all babysat at some point. So I said, "Okay fine."

Debra and I outlined an idea and I went off and directed the TV movie *Somebody's Watching Me.* She wrote the first part of the script, and after I finished the TV movie, I came back and finished it. One day Yablans called me on the telephone and said, "Why not set the film on Halloween night and we'll call it *Halloween.*" It had never been used as a title before.

Michael: Michael Myers—*The Shape*—is the ultimate bogeyman: unstoppable, without reason or humanity. How did you and Debra go about creating Michael?

John: The ultimate bogeyman? The ultimate unkillable thing? If one goes back and looks at *Westworld,* that picture involved a robot gunfighter that keeps coming back again and again. I copied a bit of that idea and added it to a horror film on Halloween night with teenagers. To make Michael Myers frightening, I had him walk like a man, not a monster.

Michael: **Was Michael Myers' character history, as conveyed in the later films, part of your original Myers mythos?**

John: Michael Myers' connection to [Laurie] was all made up in the later films because my business partners wanted to make sequels. I can't stop them from making sequels. For *Halloween II* I contributed a screenplay, but I didn't want to direct it.

Michael: **Most of Michael Myers' victims were sexually active, while the one who eludes him, Laurie [Jamie Lee Curtis], is virginal. Were you trying to make some kind of statement about sex being deadly?**

John: For over 30 years, people have brought up this so-called "sexual statement" issue. It has been suggested that I was making some kind of moral statement. Believe me, I'm not. In *Halloween*, I viewed the characters as simply normal teenagers. Laurie was shy and somewhat repressed. And Michael Myers, the killer, is definitely repressed. They have certain similarities.

Michael: ***Halloween* sparked a glut of horror movies based on serial killers attacking on holidays, for example *Friday the 13th*, *My Bloody Valentine*, *Valentine's Day*, *Mother's Day*, etc. They say imitation is the sincerest form of flattery . . . were you flattered?**

John: I was flattered, but I took it not as much about me as money. One could make money and get a career going with a low-budget horror film about killers attacking on holidays. It is always flattering to have somebody copy you.

Michael: **You shot some scenes for the TV broadcast of**

Halloween **to help pad the running time, using the cast and crew from** *Halloween II.* **Why?**

John: NBC purchased the right to show *Halloween* on network television. The minimum length requirement was 93 minutes, if I remember correctly. *Halloween* only lasted 88 or 89 minutes. So we had to pad it to get to the length NBC required. I just added a lot of foolish crap—nothing particularly good.

Michael: **You produced and scored** *Halloween 3: Season of the Witch.* **That movie broke away from Michael's story. Was the intent at that point to release a stand-alone movie in October?**

John: I wanted to get away from what I thought was the dead end of the original *Halloween* story. It's basically the same idea over and over again. Nothing really changes. *Halloween 3* was an attempt for something new. I was wrong. The audience didn't want to see a change. They wanted the Shape. So the Shape is what they got.

Michael: **What was your level of creative input with the other** *Halloween* **sequels?**

John: After 3, I didn't have any creative input. I just collected checks.

Michael: **Aliens and monsters hidden among us—that's the theme behind your movies** *Village of the Damned, The Thing* **and** *Ghosts of Mars.* **The main sense of horror in these films seems to come from paranoia: no one can be trusted. Do you see that as a dominant source of fear in today's world?**

John: Evil hiding among us is an ancient theme. Demonic possession has been with us for centuries. With the emergence of science fiction, this evil sometimes takes the form of malevolent aliens.

Michael: **You've written, directed, scored the music, edited and produced several of your movies. How do you juggle so many responsibilities?**

John: With great difficulty.

Michael: **What are your thoughts on the horror and science fiction genres?**

John: I've always had a fondness for horror and science fiction.

Michael: **You worked extensively with the late Donald Pleasence. Do you have any stories about your years of working with him?**

John: Donald Pleasence was a dear friend for many years. I admired him as an actor and loved working with him. He was one of the funniest men I've known.

Michael: **Satan and the Anti-God, as depicted in *Prince of Darkness*, appear to be science fictional as well as supernatural. For example, the Anti-God is trapped in a mirror dimension, and the liquid life-form in the ancient canister acts like a contagious virus. Do you feel the supernatural might be, in fact, another form of science?**

John: This is a difficult question. I personally don't believe in the supernatural. On the movie screen, the supernatural certainly can exist, but in real life, no. But most people on the planet have a deep hunger for supernatural meaning. One can't just ignore it. I combine science and the supernatural to tell a story, nothing more.

Michael: ***Ghosts of Mars* also combines the supernatural and science fiction: ghosts of long-dead aliens possess modern Earthlings. Do you believe in life after death, as either a supernatural or scientific phenomenon?**

John: I don't believe in life after death.

INTERVIEWS

Michael: *Escape from New York* and *Escape from L.A.* are set in a distant police-state society. Do you feel the United States is headed in that direction?

John: I don't feel the U.S. will resemble the world that I portrayed in the *Escape* movies. Certain aspects of it, yes—but I doubt to the extent of the fictional country that Snake Plissken found himself in.

Michael: **You played a coroner in *Body Bags*. Do you have any acting roles lined up in the future?**

John: If anyone asks me, I'll do it.

Michael: **What scares John Carpenter?**

John: That is another question that I've been asked for the last 30 years. I have the same answer every time. What scares me is what scares you. We're all afraid of the same things. That's why horror is such a powerful genre. All you have to do is ask yourself what frightens you and you'll know what frightens me.

JAMES CULLEN BRESSACK

Joe: **What first guided you towards horror?**

James Cullen Bressack: I've been a fan of horror my entire life, but what really made me gravitate towards horror was the fact that I realized horror was really dark fairy tales for adults. Seeing the mystical creatures was always so interesting to me, and the films really serve as a fantasy fulfillment. The darkest thoughts in our minds can be experienced cathartically through a horror movie. It was for sure obsessing over the VHS cover art for *Hellraiser* that really helped my love for horror. Pinhead looked so fuckin' cool. I would look at that cover every day and draw pictures of it at the age of four. I begged my parents to watch it until they finally begrudgingly let me, and I've been in love ever since. I used to think watching horror was a sign of being tough. That and watching the TV show *Are You Afraid of the Dark?*

Joe: **How did you get into filmmaking?**

Bressack: I guess it was just a natural transition really. I had been around the business my entire life, both parents being showbiz vets, and I happened to develop a love for film. I wanted to be a storyteller of sorts and so as soon as I had access to a camera I picked one up and started making short films, of which I made MANY. I actually made short films sometimes as school projects instead of actually doing the assignment. We were supposed to do a written report about the solar system. I made a short film parody of *Mission Impossible* where the villain stole the moon. Needless to say, my teachers hated me, but I always had a one-track mind.

INTERVIEWS

Joe: The film industry is tiring at best. How do you stay motivated and energized?

Bressack: I just keep my head down and keep working. I don't like having down time, I prefer to work and stay as busy and involved in as many projects as possible. There is nothing in the world I would rather do.

Joe: What's the best way to make people more aware of your movies?

Bressack: I'm very active on twitter and have a large following. Follow me @jamescullenb. I use my twitter to promote my films as well as good relations with all the websites, magazines, press and blogs. I make sure to send our press releases to them any time there is any news on upcoming projects. I also offer free screeners to anyone in the reviewing press. I never say no to an interview or podcast. It is important to promote your work as much as possible; it is a full time job in itself.

Joe: What was your very first screenplay like?

Bressack: The very first screenplay I wrote was a zombie stoner comedy called *Dawn of the Disabled*, and I mostly wrote it because my father is a writer and I always enjoyed writing stories. I also wanted to prove to myself and others that I could write a cohesive story. I always said I wanted to make a movie, so naturally I wrote a screenplay in the sixth grade. It was awful and it actually stands as the only script I ever wrote that was never optioned or made, but it's all history from there. As I said before, never be afraid of the blank page.

Joe: When it comes to other screenplays or screenwriters, what do you look for?

Bressack: A good story with meaty parts. I really feel the best stories are movies about people. A strong character arc makes a strong film. Also, original ideas. High concept minimal location.

Joe: **And how close to the original screenplay do you normally stay?**

Bressack: It really depends on the amount of time we have to shoot the movie as well as other variables. I try to stay as close as possible, but film is a living breathing entity and you have to be able to adapt or get left behind.

Joe: **What do you look for in a film editor?**

Bressack: Someone who can bring their expertise and show me things I wouldn't normally see or think of. Someone with more than standard editing skills with a bit of flair. Amazing things can be done in post. No dragnet editing ever!!!

Joe: **How, in your opinion, should a start-up film company go about promoting and distributing their films?**

Bressack: You need to contact as many distributors and websites as possible. Get the word out there with as much press as you possibly can. Normally, it takes three times being introduced to something to become familiar with it. Be sure to push the film. Also reach out to any distributor that put out similar films in the similar budget level of what you made that you like. Ask filmmaker friends if they have any distributors they would recommend, most can tell you who to work with and who to stear clear of.

THOMAS F. MONTELEONE

'VE PUBLISHED MORE than 100 short stories, 5 collections, 7 anthologies and 27 novels including the bestseller, *New York Times* Notable Book of the Year, *The Blood of the Lamb*. Four times I've won the Bram Stoker Award (for Novel, Collection, Anthology, and Non-Fiction). I've been known to write scripts for stage, screen, and TV, as well as the bestselling *The Complete Idiot's Guide to Writing a Novel* (now in a 2nd edition). My latest novel is a global thriller, *Submerged*. I live in Maryland with my beautiful wife, Elizabeth, and all the high taxes. I am also co-editor of the award-winning anthology series of imaginative fiction, *Borderlands*. It is said I am a great reader of my work, and it may be true because I routinely draw SRO at conventions. Despite being dragged kicking and screaming into my sixties and losing most of my hair, I still think I'm dashingly handsome—humor me.

Joe: **Are there any resources you can recommend to screenwriters? Online sites, workshops, books, or formatting programs?**

Monteleone: Not sure about online sites or workshops because I never consulted or attended any. I've read plenty of books about the process, and Goldman's *Adventures in the Screen Trade* and Tom Lazarus' *Secrets of Film Writing* are probably the best I've encountered for the sheer *understanding* of the industry they impart. I don't think books can teach you how to actually *write* a screenplay, but they can teach you how to comprehend the medium of film on paper.

Joe: **What made you write your very first screenplay, and can you still recall what it was?**

Monteleone: It was an adaptation of a stage play I'd written called *UFO!* And I did it because I ran into a local director who thought it would make a great small film.

Joe: **What legal pitfalls should a screenwriter watch out for when selling their scripts?**

Monteleone: There are so many that I cannot elaborate them in this limited space—that's why you MUST have a Hollywood agent (as opposed to some chooch in Kankakee) handling your scripts and why it's a good idea to register them with the WGA.

Joe: **Would you recommend writing collaborative scripts to beginner screenwriters?**

Monteleone: Sure, but only if it's with someone who's been around the block a few times and either has credentials or connections. It's a great way to learn from people who've made all the usual mistakes and probably won't make most of them second or third times.

Joe: **What would you say are the biggest pitfalls when writing a script?**

Monteleone: The failure to understand that a film is NOT a book or a play or short story. They are weird hybrids of sight, sound, music, dialogue, and unfortunately . . . actors. And many of these elements are *far* beyond your control when you are writing your script (and will remain so for the rest of your days on the planet).

Joe: **What kind of schedule do you keep when writing scripts on a deadline?**

Monteleone: If I can do between ten and twenty pages a day, I'm delirious.

Joe: **Do you have any advice for screenwriters or those interested in the field?**

INTERVIEWS

Monteleone: All you need is one to make yourself comfortable for a very long time . . . so take your best shot . . . and then take a few more.

Joe: **How involved do you think a screenwriter should be once production starts?**

Monteleone: Loaded question. Loaded answer: the operative word is **should** . . . and the truth is that people who make movies perceive screenwriters as the most necessary or the most evil of evils. Once they have your script in their greasy paws they want you—like a putrescent odor—to simply *go away*. So, yes, the screenwriter should be very involved in how his initial *vision* of the film ends up on the screen. But he rarely is.

Joe: **Tell us a bit about your biggest acting role to date.**

Monteleone: I'm not an actor . . . although I've been known to ham it up when I do readings of my short fiction at conventions. And years ago, when one of my plays was being performed in a One-Act Play Festival, I had to fill in after one of our actors became violently ill. I knew the lines (hey, I wrote them . . .) and I knew the part, so I killed it. My depiction of a dimwitted car mechanic won me the Festival Award for Best Supporting Actor. Something that did not go over well with the rest of our cast.

Joe: **If you could remake any movie, which one would it be and why?**

Monteleone: *The Keep.* Based off the great novel by my goombah, F. Paul Wilson, the celluloid abortion that made it to the screen needs to be scrubbed clean from our minds, and replaced by a film that actually captures the original brilliance and originality of the book.

Joe: **How has the horror movie genre evolved since you started out (content, theme, CGI)?**

Monteleone: Well, there's evolution and then there's evolution . . . Back in the Fifties and Sixties when I was a big moviegoer/fan of horror films, they were crude and simplistic and that was part of their charm and allure. They dealt with monsters—big and small, human or otherwise—and we always knew the Bad Guy was going down like a Friday night palooka by the end of the final reel. Things began to change as special effects improved, budgets swelled, and less predictable plotting started showing up in Seventies and Eighties films where anti-heroes and ambiguous endings became more and more common. A preponderance of serial killers and He's-Coming-To-Fuck-You-Up antagonists kind of took over the horror film industry during that time, and it became very boring to me. It was also a constant source of irritation for me to have to explain that the horror I wrote had nothing to do with ciphers like Jason and Freddie. There have also been lots of cyclic booms regarding iconic horror characters, or as the literary types like to say—tropes. Vampires, werewolves, ghosts, mummies, and zombies have all had their times to lurch and sway across the screens. I guess that's okay as long as writers and directors take the time and the care to create something new with any of those guys. I don't need to see the 87th iteration of *Dracula* or the *Living Dead*. When CGI became cheap and easy and the sy-fy channel discovered this, we got flooded with tsunamis of turgid, uninspired contests of can-you-top-this kinds of crapfests.

Boiled down and flensed of all the dross, I think there is a definite place for CGI in horror/SF films because there are certain visuals (like Velociraptors banging around in a stainless steel kitchen) you just can't do it with guys in rubber suits. Some of the big swarming battle scenes that used to employ "casts of thousands!" are certainly better served with computer simulations. For me, I will always prefer experiencing things as real as possible, but if the CGI is necessary and it's well done, I think it's just another tool in the box that makes a good film. Films that exist only for vehicles of SFX magic usually suck.

Joe: **Which horror scene haunts you the most?**

INTERVIEWS

Monteleone: I will never forget that moment in *The Invasion of the Body Snatchers* when Kevin McCarthy realizes his girlfriend has fallen asleep just for a moment while they were hiding in the cave . . .

Joe: What's your favorite book/author, and why?

Monteleone: *Atlas Shrugged* is my favorite book because it is a horror story that's coming true. Rand, for all her excesses and obsessions is terrifyingly prescient.

Joe: Which movie inspired you the most in your early career?

Monteleone: For the sheer power of its storytelling and characterizations, there's nothing like *The Godfather* for me. Let's just say it spoke to me on several levels.

Joe: What would you say is your biggest career or personal accomplishment?

Monteleone: I've probably had a few that should stand out, like making the *NY Times* bestseller list (even if just once) or selling a TV series to Columbia Tri-Star, or getting my books optioned by Jerry Bruckheimer . . . but I gotta tell you sometimes when I sit in my library at home and look up at an entire wall covered in bookshelves and realized that *every* book on that wall is either a novel I've written, or had translated into any of 18 languages, or a book I've edited, or an anthology to which I contributed a short story . . . and that I've been doing it for 40+ years . . . I think that in itself is enough accomplishment for anyone—especially a guy like me.

Joe: So what's next for you? Any future goals you're working on?

Monteleone: Always working on a bunch of things. The next novel, a YA trilogy, yet another screenplay based on one of my novellas, instructing at a writer's boot camp, trying to sell a mini-series . . . you know, just the usual stuff.

Joe: What's an average day like on set?

Monteleone: Only been on set a few times watching my stories get filmed and I was bored out of my ass because everything take 20 times longer than you thought it would.

Joe: Any advice for newbies, or perhaps a recap of how you got where you are now?

Monteleone: A few scraps: never stop believing in your talent and your desire and your need to succeed. I think I literally *willed* myself to make it as a writer because I refused to take no for an answer. More than 200 rejection slips before a sale didn't stop me, didn't even slow me down. I think I forced people to notice me by getting out there and putting my then-handsome face right in front of theirs. It's always better to make *some* kind of impression on people than none at all.

Joe: What was the scariest movie you watched as a child?

Monteleone: There were a few of them: *Creature from the Black Lagoon* really bothered me, but I think *The Curse of the Demon* absolutely freaked me out. I kept seeing that Demon outside my bedroom window for years.

Joe: Why do you think people enjoy the horror genre so much?

Monteleone: It's the age-old fascination with what's behind that Final Door, don't you think? Whistling past the graveyard is a universal pastime.

Joe: What is your favorite movie making slang, for instance Kensington Gore?

Monteleone: I like "MOS"—which is a motor-only shot without an audio track, but supposedly came from the German director Fritz Lang who used to say: "Vee Will shoot dis one mitt–out sound." I also like the "Martini Shot" which is the last shot of the day (any after that one come out of a bottle).

Joe: **What's the biggest piece of advice you can give anyone in your field?**

Monteleone: Love what you're doing . . . or simply don't do. There is no middle-ground.

WILLIAM STOUT

INTERVIEWED BY MICHAEL MCCARTY

WILLIAM STOUT IS a famously diverse artist of international renown in many fields: entertainment theme and motion picture design (specializing in science fiction/fantasy/horror films), comic book art, book illustration, poster design, CD covers, public murals and dynamic yet accurate reconstructions of prehistoric life. His endeavors in the fields of movies and comics have gained him a loyal following, making him a popular guest at comic book, science fiction and horror movie conventions around the world.

In 1978 Stout began his film career with the movie *Buck Rogers in the 25th Century*. He has worked on over 30 feature films including the original *Conan, First Blood, The Hitcher, Invaders From Mars*. The cult classic *The Return of the Living Dead* made Stout the youngest production designer in film history. Stout wrote *The Warrior and The Sorceress* for Roger Corman and a dinosaur feature for Jim Henson. He did production design for *Masters of the Universe* and was the key character designer for the Walt Disney computer animated feature, *Dinosaur* (2000). He designed "Edgar" (the big bug in *Men in Black*) for ILM in 1996. Stout's other work includes designs for Guillermo del Toro's horror classic *Pan Labyrinth*, Christopher Nolan's *The Prestige*, and Frank Darabont's *Stephen King's The Mist*.

Michael McCarty: **How did you go from underground comic book artist to working in cinema?**

William Stout: I accidentally fell into the film business. Ironically,

INTERVIEWS

I've found the more you want to work in film, the harder it is to get a job in that business.

My friend Bob Greenberg was working as a production assistant on *Conan the Barbarian*. I had no interest in making movies at that time; I was making a fortune advertising them. But I was a big Robert E. Howard/*Conan* fan. Bob told me Ron Cobb was the production designer. That blew my mind, because I only knew Cobb as a political cartoonist for the underground newspapers. I was intrigued. What would he do with *Conan*?

I wanted to come by the *Conan* offices to see what he was doing, but I just didn't have the time—I was too busy creating movie posters.

I finally got a break from my schedule—but instead of going to the *Conan* offices, I went to the ABA (American Booksellers Association) event at the Los Angeles Convention Center. The ABA was a great place for an illustrator to pick up work, as every single editor and publisher in America was there.

The first person I ran into at the ABA was, coincidentally, Ron Cobb. He told me that I was his first choice of whom to work with on *Conan*. But, he explained, he had a deal with John Milius, the film's director. John had veto-power over anyone Ron wanted to hire. Would I be so kind as to drop off my portfolio for John to see?

I went to the *Conan* offices the next day. Kathleen Kennedy was the receptionist. Milius happened to be there. I met with John. He flipped through my samples portfolio, recognized a *Heavy Metal* story I had done that he had liked and handed me back my book. As he walked out the door, he barked, "Hire him!"

I then had a meeting with Buzz Feitshans, the line producer. He told me what I would be making on *Conan*. I nearly fell off my chair laughing. It was 10% of what I was making in advertising! Nevertheless, I thought it might be fun to learn how films were made. Plus, the job was only for two weeks. Well, the two weeks turned into two years—and a film career. Oh, and whose office was opposite mine when I started on *Conan*?—Steven Spielberg. Cobb and I would work on *Conan* during the day and then at 6:00PM cross the hall into Steven's office where we would kick around ideas for Steven's next film project, *Raiders of the Lost Ark*.

McCarty: **You've done storyboards for such films as *First Blood, The Return of the Living Dead, Raiders of the Lost Ark* (uncredited) and other movies, too. Explain the process that goes into doing a storyboard.**

Stout: First, I read the script. Then, if possible, I talk to the director. I want to know what his vision is for the film. If he doesn't have one (some directors are just not very visual), then I feel it's my job (working in tandem with the production designer) to help create one. Then, I either board the entire film or, most commonly, board the key scenes of the movie, the action scenes, the effects scenes or the most difficult to visually understand scenes.

McCarty: **Is there anything cut from one of your storyboards, you wished they kept for any film?**

Stout: I wish they had kept the entrance I had designed for Evil-Lyn in *Masters of the Universe*. I think main character entrances and their design are very important. They can tell you so much about the character without anyone saying a word.

McCarty: **What are the things you are most proud of with your storyboards?**

Stout: Their strong composition and the clarity of their storytelling.

McCarty: **Do you think CGI has helped or hurt the artist in the film industry?**

Stout: Both. I really miss stop motion animation—although it seems to be making a bit of a comeback in some cinematic areas. I see CGI as just another tool among many.

McCarty: **I like to talk a little about the film *The Return of the Living Dead*, because I feel this is such a watershed film with zombie motion pictures. As far as I know, it is the first movie that featured fast moving zombies, which is done a lot nowadays. Why do you think this movie has**

INTERVIEWS

been such a hit with audiences for over three decades now?

Stout: It accomplished something that's very difficult to pull off: it was very scary AND very funny. And the humor didn't come from jokes—it was funny because (like the great beginnings of John Landis' *An American Werewolf in London* and *Twilight Zone: The Movie*) of the characters' natural, real life responses to horrific situations.

The characters also seem to be true friends with a real past together. That was mainly due to Dan O'Bannon's gift to the cast of two weeks of rehearsal prior to shooting.

McCarty: In *The Return of the Living Dead*, you play a bum towards the beginning of the movie. How was it to be on the other side of the camera for a change?

Stout: I loved it, but I also took my cameo very seriously. I never broke character that day—which upset a lot of people.

I was originally cast as the shopping cart bum but our line producer nixed that idea. He thought that as the film's production designer, I already had enough on my plate.

McCarty: In *The Return of the Living Dead*, there is this half lady corpse that is strapped onto a steel table and slapping her spinal chord around and she is leaking spinal fluid. Do you remember what they used for the spinal fluid? Did you also help with the production of that scene?

Stout: I'm a hands-on production designer. For that scene I was under the gurney, operating the mechanism that made the spine flop around and ooze spinal fluid, while Tony Gardner operated her arms and Brian Peck (Scuzz) puppeteered her head and mouth. Brian also spoke her lines for the temp track (which later got replaced with a female voice).

I don't know what was used for the spinal fluid. I would guess it was glycerin. You'll have to ask Tony Gardner for the definitive answer to that question.

McCarty: In *The Return of the Living Dead*, one of the characters is reading one of your comic books in the backseat of the car. Which comic book are they reading?

Stout: Scuzz is reading *Weird Trips*—the Ed Gein issue. Ed (the inspiration for *Psycho*'s Norman Bates) died during the making of our film. Dan O'Bannon and I had a moment of silence for old Ed when we got the news.

McCarty: Have any other of your comics ended up on the silver screen?

Stout: Not that I know of . . .

McCarty: You've done a number of famous movie posters, as well, including *The Wizards, House, Life of Brian, More American Graffiti*, and *Up From The Depths*. First of all, they are fantastic pop art. How do you go about capturing an entire film with just one image of artwork?

Stout: I either watch the movie, read the script or ask my advertising art director for some direction. Then, I make a list of what I consider all of the most important elements of the film. I then try combining some of them to create an arresting image that somehow captures the feeling of the movie at its most moving or exciting.

McCarty: You did a comic book of *King Kong*. King Kong is an iconic movie monster for over eighty years. What are some of your favorite Kong movies over the years?

Stout: The original 1933 classic is my favorite movie of all time. I have a soft spot for the rushed-to-the-screen sequel, *Son of Kong*, too. I think all the other *Kong* films are crap, quite honestly.

McCarty: Did you feel a lot of pressure in doing the *Kong* covers, because you were doing the artwork of one of the most famous monsters in cinema?

Stout: No; it was sheer, total pleasure on my part; I was in my element. I wanted to do *all* of the covers but they only let me do two.

McCarty: You also have connections with the *Godzilla* world. You wrote the episode "Why Is Thy Sting" for the animated *Godzilla: The Series*, which pits The King of the Monsters against a gigantic mutated scorpion called Ts-eh-go. How did you get that gig?

Stout: My animation agent, John Goldsmith, scored that gig for me. It was a tremendous experience. Animation writers are treated SO differently from movie screenwriters. It felt like I was living in Fantasyland.

McCarty: What did you think of the show?

Stout: I was very impressed. Except for me, they had top professional writers turning in scripts with terrific characters and dialogue. The writers were inspired by the quality of Joss Whedon's *Buffy The Vampire Slayer* TV series—and it showed. Nice look, too.

McCarty: Of all the Godzilla films, which are your favorites?

Stout: I know this sounds like sacrilege but, honestly, I'm not a real big fan of the *Godzilla* movies. I think the suits look hokey. They're baggy and you can always tell that there's a guy inside. The early ones in the series are painfully slow. There's a lot of unintentional humor in most Kaiju movies. I really like Toho's *Attack of the Mushroom People*, though. It pissed me off that the Matthew Broderick *Godzilla* movie kept repeating effects (a big no-no in the Stout filmmaking handbook). The new big budget *Godzilla* movie hardly had *Godzilla* in it at all.

My favorite is the one we didn't get to make.

McCarty: *Pan's Labyrinth*, you were a conceptual artist for the film. What did you contribute to the movie?

Stout: I created the first designs for the Faun (Pan), the exterior of the main set (the building that houses the general, the girl and her mother), the giant toad (originally it was going to be carved from stone. It had all kinds of runes and symbols covering its body), and something we called the Nerve Ghost, a creepy character that got cut from the film.

McCarty: **What was it like working with Guillermo del Toro?**

Stout: Guillermo gave me good direction and a lot of freedom. I wish he could have afforded me for the entire film.

McCarty: **On a related note, Guillermo del Toro was supposed to make a movie of H.P. Lovecraft's *At The Mountains of Madness*. What has ever happened to that project? Were you going to be involved with *Mountains* too?**

Stout: Guillermo told me he wanted the triumvirate of Mike Mignola, Wayne Barlowe and me to design the film. The project seemed like it was on the verge of being made a number of times. Then, something would come up (like *Pacific Rim*), and it would be postponed and kicked down the road for another chunk of time. Guillermo also was insistent that the film had to be a hard R-rated movie. The studios didn't think that would pencil out financially.

McCarty: **Do you do a series of studies before beginning a project?**

Stout: Always.
    My first advertising course at art school was taught by the Boston brothers. They were tough. I had them on Tuesdays and Thursdays. On Tuesday they would assign us two ads to do for Thursday. We were expected to show 200 thumbnail ideas for each ad. On Thursday, we were assigned four ads. Same thing: 200 thumbnails per ad. So, that resulted in my coming up with 1200 ideas and sketches—plus the six ads themselves—per week for that class—in addition to all the work I was assigned in my other classes. I'm glad

that class was in my first semester at art school. It made the rest of my four years seem like a piece of cake.

McCarty: **What mediums do you use?**

Stout: My favorite medium is oil on canvas. I rarely use that medium in film, however, as it is too slow for movie work (even though I use fast drying oils—alkyds—when I paint) and I need to work outside (because of the fumes).

I also enjoy pen & ink, watercolor, ink & watercolor and acrylic painting (somewhat; acrylics have several disadvantages, most notably that it dries about 10% darker than what you put down). I color my comics digitally now (I used to cut hand separations and then later used the European gouache-on-blue-line method). I'm a decent sculptor but I rarely sculpt because I am so damned slow at it—unlike when I work graphically.

McCarty: **How long does it take before you are satisfied with the results?**

Stout: That varies piece-to-piece. Complex works take longer for obvious reasons. Typically, though, a 24" x 18" oil painting takes me about three days. A comic book cover usually takes me a day to pencil (more if I'm doing all the cover lettering), two thirds of a day to ink and a day to color. My pen & ink convention sketches typically take an hour or two.

McCarty: **What advice would you give to someone who wants to be an artist?**

Stout: Do as much life (figure) drawing as possible and never stop (on the days you can't find a model, draw yourself in a good full length mirror). One day per week should be devoted to animal drawing from life (pets, zoo, neighborhood animals). If you want to be a painter, do some plain air painting (on-the-spot landscape painting) as much as you can. It will teach you color, design, composition and how to handle your paint. Always give 100%, no mater how much or how little you're being paid for the job. Your past will never come back to haunt you and you'll get better as an artist at a faster rate. Plus, your clients will be pleased.

McCarty: **What advice would you give to someone who wants to work in the film industry?**

Stout: Don't; it will break your heart.

The most often question I get asked now on films is, "Bill . . . you're a really nice guy. What are you doing in the film business?" That should tell you something.

It's a brutal business, especially on women. I have successfully persuaded many of my family members *not* to get into The Biz. I think they're much happier for taking my advice. If you're single and can't do anything else, then go for it. If you're in a relationship, however, expect it to be destroyed. The divorce rate on David Lynch's *Dune* was 95%. There were people on that picture who hadn't seen their families in six years.

If you're doing your job properly on a film, you should be working 18-hour days, seven days a week *minimum*. I promise you will dearly earn every penny that you make.

McCarty: **Of all the movies you've done, which ones are you the most satisfied with?**

Stout: *Return of the Living Dead, Conan the Barbarian*, the opening to Walt Disney's *Dinosaur* (before the dinosaurs talked), our unmade *Godzilla, Stephen King's The Mist, Pan's Labyrinth, The Prestige, The Muppets' Wizard of Oz* (before it was cast), *Men In Black, Predator* (but with the original ending that was never shot), *Rambling Rose, House, The Hitcher, First Blood, Raiders of the Lost Ark* and the Firesign Theatre movie *Everything You Know Is Wrong*. The trailer for the upcoming *Monster Roll* (with my creature design) is incredible. *Magic Kingdom* could have been incredible—but the Disney attorneys screwed that one up.

McCarty: **Which are you the least satisfied with?**

Stout: Easy: *Theodore Rex*, the most expensive direct-to-video movie ever made. To give you an idea how wrong this film was, it starred Whoopi Goldberg in a part written for Val Kilmer. I was the movie's production designer for the first nine months of pre-production. It was the only film I ever walked away from. Leaving that film is one of the reasons I'm still alive.

I was disappointed there weren't more differences between the scripts of *Invaders from Mars* and our remake.

I worked on three different versions of *John Carter of Mars*—but not the one that got made. There was one script I worked on that would have been a terrific film. I'm sorry that the Conran brothers didn't get their shot. We had a great vision for their movie.

Ant Bully could have been so much better. I was only on that film for about a week when Warners tried to negate our deal, so I left. Nevertheless, nearly everything I created during that one week made it to the screen.

McCarty: **Do you have a good behind-the-scenes story you'd like to share?**

Stout: I loved Billy Barty (Gwildor in *Masters of the Universe*). Every morning I'd feel a tug on my coat. I'd turn around and it was Billy. He had a new joke for me every single day on the set. He was such a sweet guy.

McCarty: **Last words?**

Stout: Find what you love to do and then endeavor to become the best at it. Be your own biggest fan. Give value to your time and work. Stand up for yourself. Expect the industries you work in (and their jobs) to change—because they will.

And be kind.

ENTERTAINING TIDBITS AND ANECDOTES

Since the opportunity to chat with some of my favorite authors and filmmakers presented itself, I couldn't just talk shop the entire time, right? Wouldn't you take the time to ask them every possible thing you ever thought about while watching their films?

Call me selfish, but I wanted to get to know these folks. A

It ended being so entertaining that I had to include some of it here. But, since space in the paperback is limited, I stuck to mainly informative answers.

If you pick up the two eBook editions, you'll find tons more questions and info, where we talk about favorite directors, horror characters, remakes, scariest scenes, favorite books and authors, inspiration, on-set moments, previous occupations, future goals, and so much more.

Joe Mynhardt

ENTERTAINING TIDBITS AND ANECDOTES

HOW HAS THE HORROR MOVIE GENRE EVOLVED SINCE YOU STARTED OUT?

Mark Steensland: I think the horror genre is less original now than it's ever been. I suspect this mostly has to do with wanting to make as much money as possible. So much of what I see feels like a rehash of something else. It's hard to believe there was a time when movies like *Suspiria* were being made.

Ed Naha: I don't think horror movies have evolved, exactly. I think they've found new tricks, new decorations for the tree. Unfortunately, now as always, many horror films have all the newest technological decorations but have forgotten the tree.

Graham Masterton: Enormously. In *The Manitou*, the most dramatic special effect was blowing up an IBM typewriter, and when the head of the reincarnated wonder worker rises out of the wood in the center of a table in the middle of a séance; this had to be done by making a wax model and gradually melting it and filming it in reverse. However, I don't think plots and ideas have made very much progress. There are still too many haunted houses (*Woman in Black,* etc.) and possessed children.

David Henson Greathouse: I joined the business when the make-up FX world was hot. Tons of FX-heavy horrorfests. Lot more micro budgets or bad CG these days. I do enjoy finding the diamonds though.

Harry Shannon: Atmosphere is still scarier than special effects. A good story works or it doesn't.

Jonathan Maberry: I'm not a fan of formula in horror flicks. Hollywood grabs an idea and then beats it to death, and in doing so they demonstrate a fearful reluctance to try new and innovative storytelling. For example, *Paranormal Activity* was riveting, but now there are dozens of movies like it. You see it too often. My gold standard for horror will always be *The Haunting*—the original BW version. It used suspense rather than shocks and cheap-shots to scare the bejeezus out of viewers. Modern Hollywood filmmakers (and more importantly the bean counters who interfere with the creatives) should be made to watch that movie before any meeting.

Mick Garris: When I started in the eighties, there weren't very many horror films aimed at adults; they were mostly slashers or teen horror exploitation films. But it started to turn the corner when Cronenberg's *The Fly* and others with intelligent themes and mainstream level actors and performances joined in. *Silence of the Lambs* really was the first horror film to perform extraordinarily at the Oscars in 1990. I think it won five.

The tools have changed, too, with CGI becoming affordable, allowing you to create believable imagery in ways you never could before. But perhaps the biggest earthquake has been the preponderance of horror on television: *Dexter, Penny Dreadful, American Horror Story,, The Strain, From Dusk 'till Dawn*, and so many others have achieved an amazing level of mainstream success. And in some ways—shockingly—a lot of the horror on television is better than horror in the cinema.

William F. Nolan: Splatterpunk came and went (thank God!) and now horror is much more subtle, with much less gore.

Jeff Strand: The height of my horror movie mania was in the 1980s, when films were less nihilistic. In the 80s, the remaining characters would usually solve the problem . . . and then, yeah, the killer would jump back out at the last moment. But there were way fewer endings where everything just turns to complete crap for everybody.

Stephen Volk: The first film I wrote was *Gothic* which was directed by Ken Russell just after he did *Altered States* and *Crimes of Passion*. It was a time when fantasy was being injected into British cinema with product like *Dream Demon*, Clive Barker's *Hellraiser* and Neil Jordan's *Company of Wolves*. There was a feeling that *Gothic* might be part of that renaissance but sadly the critics didn't get it and fairly attacked it—though I warm my hands on the fact that Harlan Ellison loves the film. (Thanks, Harlan!) Since then, entering the 90s it was all about teens being murdered by serial killers, and then the Scream franchise parodied that, then *The Sixth Sense* brought things back to classical suspense-horror, then *Blair Witch* reinvented everything. So a lot has changed between 1987 and 2015! I think the themes stay the same—fear of physical injury, fear of spiritual infestation, fear of psychological disempowerment or loss of identity—it's just that new ways emerge of trying to express that, whether it's *Repulsion* or *The Babadook*, or *Rosemary's Baby* or *Lovely Molly*. If anything, any evolution has been a path that has split in two—with effects laden and mainstream "entertainment horror" like *Van Helsing, The Mummy* or *Dracula Unborn* down one path, and the other path of more subtle and psychological tension and creepiness like *Absentia* or *The Devil's Backbone*. My own taste is for the latter.

Stephen Johnston: The horror genre went through the doldrums there for a while, and it was hard to get Hollywood types to even have a conversation about making a horror movie, but it's been enjoying a resurgence. The unfortunate thing is there are more than a few people operating within the genre for entirely cynical reasons, not because they have any respect for horror (and indeed, in some cases obvious disrespect). Going back to my mention of *Plan 9 from Outer Space*, there's a movie that may have been made badly, but it's also the product of a passionate filmmaker who loved what he was doing. How is that worse than the seventh sequel to a dreadful franchise, or remaking a movie that's ten years old?

Nancy Holder: Special effects have ratcheted up—so amazing! I think we're currently in a renaissance of storytelling and that horror films reflect this.

Jack Thomas Smith: When I started, the effects in most horror films were practical. And I love practical effects. Over the past twenty years, so many of the effects in horror films now are CGI and I'm not a fan. Sometimes it works and sometimes it doesn't. I completely understand the necessity for CGI . . . I just don't like when it's used incorrectly. I'm not a fan of the torture/porn genre. It's just not for me. I love good old fashioned horror films that have strong characters, suspense, and a storyline that keeps you guessing such as *The Conjuring* and *The Abandoned*. I love *The Walking Dead*, as well.

Jason V. Brock: CGI has been a blessing and (mostly) a curse. I am a fan of traditional filmmaking techniques, to include practical special and physical effects. There are times when CGI has been able to create the previously impossible—*Gravity* and the 2014 *Godzilla* remake are good examples—but in general the over-reliance on CGI has done nothing to advance the artform of cinema. It still comes down to the vision, the characters, and the story. Those are timeless elements, and CGI can be used to enhance them, but more often it undermines this process, and in the worst instances it disrupts it entirely, flinging the observers into the Uncanny Valley and thwarting the point of making a film to begin with, which is to connect with a sympathetic audience.

Denise Gossett: Things have changed so much since I founded Shriekfest in 2001! More women are directing/producing, the scripts are stronger with stronger female roles, CGI can be used for the good, but it isn't always and that is frustrating!

DO YOU THINK TODAY'S CGI CAPABILITIES IMPROVE OR IMPEDE ON THE QUALITY OF HORROR MOVIES?

Billy Hanson: I don't inherently hate the idea of CGI like a lot of people do, nor do I think it's a good idea to automatically dump every decision on the After Effects team. It's an amazing way to achieve things that we weren't able to fifteen years ago, which allows far more creativity from a director. Problem is, it also makes terrible ideas possible. I think we all remember the shot from *The Matrix Reloaded* where Neo starts spinning around a pole, kicking all of the Agent Smiths in the face. Bad idea, made possible by CGI. On the flipside, I doubt we would have any of the Marvel movies without CGI. I still remember being blown away by the wizard fight in *Harry Potter and the Order of the Phoenix*, and in reality, that's just two people waving sticks at each other. So while there are people out there who can and will misuse CGI, there are really great visionaries that understand how to wield it and create something amazing with it.

I don't have much experience with heavy CGI work myself, but the one time I did, it was for a shot of a seagull that gets hit with a rock and falls over, dead. Since we obviously couldn't kill a real seagull (not that we would want to do that, of course), we needed to use CGI. But, since we spoke with our graphics person before we shot, and had him as part of the production process and delivered to him exactly what he needed, we were able to make it seamless. He ended up getting an award for that effect.

Mark Steensland: I suppose they were asking the same question when sound was introduced, right? It's just another tool. Some artists use it well. Some don't. I know that's a matter of personal taste, but so is the use of sound, and music, and art direction, and so forth.

Ed Naha: Any movie that relies solely on CGI for any reason pretty much sucks. CGI, used sparingly, can really add to a film's fantastic aura. Too much CGI, however, reduces a film to Looney Tunes status. I really get bored with the mega destruction scenes that go on forever, where cars are hurled, buildings crumble and, after a while, you don't give a shit. I especially abhor giant CGI monsters that aren't insects. Any giant that has a mammalian mouth seems to always be missing its lower jawbone. When they open their mouths to roar the lower portion of the mouth seems to be as awesome as that of a herring. It's fluid and quivering. I don't know if the monster is dangerous or about to embark on a crying jag.

David Henson Greathouse: CG is a mixed bag. It has created many wonderful scenes and characters. However in the world of horror, many times the limitations are what make it scary. I would rather see a practical creature briefly shown than having a CG character bounce and jump around like an animated cartoon.

Harry Shannon: I don't like them when they literally intrude on the story, which is all too often.

Jonathan Maberry: Horror movies suffer from CGI. I love computer-generated graphics in science fiction and thrillers, but in horror they tend to knock me out of my suspension of disbelief. They remind me that this is a movie. This was most clearly seen in *The Wolfman*. They had brilliant makeup effects by Rick Baker, and then they slapped CGI over it. It's a bit like putting a drop-ceiling in the Sistine Chapel.

Mick Garris: It's all about using the best tool. You can do amazing, almost limitless, things with CGI, but if it looks fake, then it's just a cartoon or a videogame. To me, the very first elaborate use of CGI is still one of the best. *Jurassic Park* used it as the best tool to tell the story. You felt the weight of the beasts, they interacted completely convincingly with the actors and the surroundings. Technically, we may have come even further, but those still are just right; they tell the story. When you use effects just because you can, then it becomes a show reel, not an organic element of storytelling.

When the snake-tongue things come shooting out of the vampires' mouths in *The Strain*, they look remarkably realistic, even though nothing like it happens in real life. It's imaginative but organic, and you couldn't do it any other way.

William F. Nolan: Improve them.

Tim Lebbon: One of my favourite movies is *The Thing*. I think that's a perfect answer. Those effects have still never been beaten for their visceral, bloody impact.

Jeff Strand: I think that today's capabilities improve them. For much of the history of CGI, we got fakey-looking cartoons, but now they're sophisticated (and often invisible) enough that I think they do help the storytelling process. We all love practical effects, but a lot of that is nostalgia! What I *despise* is shaky-cam. That's where I become the old man shouting, "Movies were better back in my time, dammit!"

Stephen Volk: Overly CGI in horror for me doesn't work because "how did they do that?" takes me out of the moment and out of being involved with the reality of the piece. It basically stops me being scared and often stops me caring.

Stephen Johnston: CGI is just a tool, another paint for your pallet if you will. I do think it should be used far more sparingly than it is. No matter how seamless the technology may become, I think there's a part of the human brain that still reads it as false. Give me the guy in the giant rubber costume! It may appear as obviously fake, but your brain at least knows it's real.

Nancy Holder: I think that as long as they serve the story, they *can* improve movies. I'm thinking about *Mama*, which was mostly practical, but had some incredible CGI as well.

Jack Thomas Smith: I think it's a little of both depending on how it's used. I think if CGI is used to enhance a scene it works great. For example, *The Walking Dead* uses CGI to create hundreds of zombies in the distance. It's not practical to have hundreds of zombie extras with a TV show budget and tight shooting schedule. In my opinion, this is when CGI works. But I personally don't like CGI monsters or creatures. It takes me out of the film for some reason . . . I guess it just doesn't feel real, almost cartoonish. I don't mean any disrespect to the CGI artists, who work very hard on these effects . . . It's just my personal taste.

L.L. Soares: I think they have the potential to improve, but are more often used out of laziness. And even in some of the bigger budget movies, CGI often looks very fake to me, so that defeats the whole purpose of using it. Those big wolves in the *Twilight* movies, for example. Those aren't scary on any level, they aren't convincing as real creatures, and they're certainly not werewolves as I'd want to see them. It's like it's just expected at this point—"Well, if there's a monster, then it has to be CGI, because that's what people expect now."

CGI is just a tool. They don't make a movie good or bad. The story does that. CGI should always be secondary to the story.

Denise Gossett: It can do both. When well done, you have amazing creatures brought into the stories, when it's harmful is when blood splatter is added in after the fact . . . so fake looking.

Tim Waggoner: Impede, without a doubt. CGI, no matter how good, still doesn't have the weight, heft, and sheer presence—the *thereness*—of practical effects. It seems there's an almost irresistible need to show too much when CGI is used. Horror works best in the shadows, when things are left more to the viewer's imagination. If *Jaws* were made today with CGI effects, the shark would be shown a lot more, and it would suck so bad. This is one of the reasons I prefer low-budget, indie horror films. They're forced to rely on script, acting, direction, lighting, etc. to tell their stories instead of expensive SFX. The worst thing a studio can do is a give a horror filmmaker butt-loads of cash to make a film.

ANY ADVICE FOR NEWBIES, OR PERHAPS A RECAP OF HOW YOU GOT WHERE YOU ARE NOW?

Mark Steensland: Make 90 second films without dialogue that still tell interesting stories. Keep making them and testing them on people. Find out what they think the story is. Then make more films. Eventually, you'll come up with something really unique. That's the one you enter into film festivals.

Jonathan Winn: I'm still getting where I'm going, but, as for advice, how's this: work hard and then dig deep and work harder. Grow a thick skin and learn to take nothing personally even if it feels like it is. But more importantly, I'd urge people to be unique and never lose their Voice. That's where success truly lies. If you can offer professional work with a unique voice, you'll get noticed. But the Voice needs to sit in a script that's professional and predictable as far as formatting goes. A unique voice is good. Having to struggle through a "unique script" is not.

David Henson Greathouse: My advice to newbies is to work hard and be smart.

ENTERTAINING TIDBITS AND ANECDOTES

Harry Shannon: Be as versatile as you can, and polish up every talent you possess. You may need them all to survive.

Mick Garris: It really does seem that everyone follows a different route. For me, starting as a writer really put me in a good place, and being hired for the first time by Steven Spielberg gave me an even better opportunity. Some of these things you can't effect on your own; talent, timing, and being able to deliver what they are looking for are hard to control. But being able to deliver, to be cooperative without being a pushover, having a vision and being able to articulate it . . . those are the things that give you a good shot at it.

The careers go up and down; it's a rare artist or writer or actor or filmmaker or musician that hits their stride and stays there. It's feast or famine, but even in the down time, if you write, you can at least control a part of your destiny.

Tim Lebbon: Read a lot, work hard, write a lot, read a lot, take criticism on the chin, learn from rejections. Believe in yourself. I love the saying: 'Whether you think you can do something, or you think you can't, you're probably right.'

Stephen Volk: Since I was fifteen I always had a dream of writing for a living but never thought I'd achieve it—who does? I certainly never thought a Grammar School boy from the Welsh Valleys could be a Hollywood screenwriter. But I knew I wanted to write stories and I got this little book which was the script of *Westworld* and I started writing stories in that format, all the way through studying graphic design in college, then specializing in animation, then going to film school. I was still writing all the time, and even getting a job in an ad agency, writing in all my spare time, most of it crap but slowly getting better. Then I got a break and met a director and that didn't work out, and I constantly sent scripts out and got them back and finally got an agent through the director who didn't work out and—wham!—suddenly I sold three scripts in three months! Then it started, and a few years later I could give up the day job. All I'd say as advice to newbies is that successful people don't succeed more than other people . . . they FAIL more than other people. All that failure, failure, failure, it edges you forward and it's important to have faith in yourself and not seek their validation for what you do and not take no for an answer.

Stephen Johnston: Apply yourself to the craft, and don't get into it because you want to get famous or, God forbid, make money. Those people are a dime a dozen in this town. The only thing that will make you stand out is being as good as you can be at what you do.

Nancy Holder: Be flexible, be courteous, and always do your best. Be the easiest person to work with. Deliver with a smile. Network and be generous with praise. Never diss anyone in the industry. It will get back to them. Be a professional.

James Cullen Bressack: I've learned the worst thing isn't putting out a product that people may not like, but not putting out a product at all. If you never finish the film, how will you ever know if people would like your style? You won't. So you have to just go for it! Make the best movie you can and market the shit out of it. Make sure people know about your movies.

Lynne Hansen: Do all the prep work you can up front, but when it comes time to make your film, work fast enough that all you have time to do is listen to your gut. It'll help you make something that stays true to the creative spark that inspired the project in the first place.

L.L. Soares: Most of all, to stick with it. I had this silly idea when I was a kid, that I would sell stories right away and have a long career, and it just didn't work out that way. I started sending stories to magazine in high school, and for a long time, all I got were rejections. The one short story I sold in college, the magazine went under before they could publish it. But I kept writing. I went through years where I didn't even send anything out, I'd almost given up on getting published, but I never stopped writing. It was something I *had* to do.

But I never gave up. By their 30s, most people would think, *"Well, it hasn't worked out for me, so I guess this isn't worth it anymore."* But in *my* 30s, I finally made my first professional sale. And I didn't see my first novel published until I was in my 40s. So, instead of that child prodigy who had a long career, I became instead, more of a late bloomer. But I never gave up. I never stopped writing, and, despite years of almost mind-numbing frustration, I never lost the desire to be a published author.

Denise Gossett: If you really want something, then don't ever give up! Do something every day that gets you closer to your goals. Write out your goals—writing them out makes them real—then break them down into small goals that you can pursue on a daily basis.

WHAT'S AN AVERAGE DAY LIKE ON SET?

Jeffrey Reddick: There is no average day. But the surprising thing is there's a lot of waiting around if you're acting. You'll shoot a scene. But then you have to wait while the cameras and lights are re-set to shoot the scene from another angle.

Mark Steensland: Hurry up and wait. No other way to put it. There's never enough time, yet somehow people are standing around.

Jonathan Winn: Regardless who you are, actor, writer, director, grip, caterer, crew, you're there early. Like, REALLY early. And then you wait, sipping coffee, nibbling on donuts, chatting quietly, until they call you to the set and then you rush like mad to get there only to wait some more. Seems odd, this hurry up and wait thing, but there are so many moving pieces to the filmmaking puzzle and each piece has to be in place before the camera rolls. If not, it costs money. And eats up more time. So it makes sense to get all those ducks in a row before pulling the trigger.

David Henson Greathouse: For an FX technician it can be a waiting game. You have an effect to shoot. It gets pushed to the end of the day when now it is a mad rush to get the shot. Everyone else got four takes. You have one chance between action and cut to pull off the effect flawlessly.

Harry Shannon: From boredom to hysteria with no in between stages.

Mick Garris: It always changes. Sometimes it's eight pages of actors talking. Sometimes it's a half page of extraordinarily complicated practical or digital effects being worked out to great tedium. Or all stops in between. But it's always a good twelve hours, almost always in a city away from home, with travel time to and from a hotel, and almost always surrounded by an army of amazing, creative people all eager to do something special. You live on the glow of excitement and creative explosion. It's addictive, and you chomp at the bit when you're in between productions.

William F. Nolan: I'm never bored on set—and have been on the sets of many of my twenty scripts. It's always fun and I never stop learning.

Stephen Volk: Exciting for ten minutes. Then boring. But location catering is great. And I like to go because it might be my only chance to meet the actors, so that I can tell my mum!

Stephen Johnston: For me it usually just involves the occasional visit, in all honestly.

Nancy Holder: The standard work day on a TV series is twelve hours. I love production minutiae so I never tire of the endless setups, shoots from different angles, and set breakdown. I love learning my shows—watching all the episodes over and over until I know them backwards and forwards—and I love interviewing the writers and showrunners, who are smart, talented people.

Jack Thomas Smith: During pre-production, I normally storyboard every single shot . . . even cutaways. And then I write up a shot list, documenting every shot I need in the order I need it based on our lighting setups. I'm very detailed about the shots I need. If you miss something on set there's no going back. With that being said, during production, I'll start each day by focusing on the scenes we're going to shoot; I'll work with the actors and their performances; I'll discuss the blocking with the DP; and I'll deal with all of the other unforeseen issues that arise during a normal day of shooting. Something always comes out of left field that knocks you off your game, but you have to be quick on your feet and adjust to make sure you get everything you need. Every day presents new challenges that you need to push through.

Lynne Hansen: An "average" day on set doesn't exist. The only commonality is that no matter how well you plan, stuff will go wrong. Lots of it. And you'll have to go with it. But the beauty of filmmaking is that it's often in those moments of crisis that you and your team excel, and you end up with an end product that's even better than it would have been if you'd stuck with the plan.

Denise Gossett: Hurry up and wait. Lots of waiting. First you have breakfast, get into makeup/hair, wardrobe, they take you for a rehearsal, then they set up lights, camera, then you shoot. Repeat.

Tim Waggoner: It's not much different from working on original fiction, except from time to time I'll need to hit the Internet and consult Wikipedia, fan Wikis, or other sites for specific information on an IP, like what sort of vehicle does Nick from *Grimm* drive, how exactly is the Bunker in *Supernatural* laid out?

WHAT S THE BIGGEST PIECE OF ADVICE YOU CAN GIVE ANYONE IN YOUR FIELD?

Mark Steensland: Be yourself. It's the only thing Hollywood doesn't have. And it's really the only thing you've got. I think many people are too afraid to try something really unique or personal because they don't want to have something that close to their heart rejected. But you have to risk that. I think that's the only place where true happiness as an artist can be found.

Ed Naha: Get out of the field and use the sidewalk. You'll get there faster.

David Henson Greathouse: Keep creating. Don't obsess over money or a minute of fame. One day you are hot. One day you are not. Who cares. Keep writing, painting, composing, sculpting, performing.

Harry Shannon: Work harder.

Jonathan Maberry: Richard Matheson gave me great advice as a kid. He said: 'Be as good at the business of publishing as you are at the craft of writing. They're not the same thing, so you need to know them both top to bottom."

Mick Garris: Just do it. Don't talk about it. If you're a writer, write. It doesn't cost you anything but time. You're not a writer if you just talk about it and never finish anything. It's said that you're a writer when somebody else tells you you're a writer. I think you're a writer when somebody pays you for your writing.
Write. Make films; the tools are available to anyone. Play music. Just do it and keep getting better at it. Don't do it because you think it will make you rich. If that's why you do it, it ain't gonna happen for you. Do it because you love it, because you can't *not* do it. And just keep getting better until someone notices, someone who has the power to put it in front of an audience.

Tim Lebbon: Write for yourself.

Stephen Volk: Keep going. Write to what you love, constantly try to do it better, and don't be an asshole (I was going to say a c-word, but asshole will do).

Stephen Johnston: Treat people with the same respect you demand yourself. That applies to life in general.

Nancy Holder: Be industry literate. Know what's current but also know your genre. If you're a horror person, for example, know who Val Lewton is. And James Whale. And Robert Wise.

Jack Thomas Smith: Go to business school! The film business is exactly that . . . It's a business. We all get into the movie business because we love films. We want to tell a story and share our vision. But how do you do that? It takes money to make a movie. And you need to know how to convince an investor to invest in you and your project. So you need to know how to put together a budget, a business plan, a PowerPoint presentation, comps and projections. You need to understand the Section 181 Federal tax incentive and state tax credits. When you meet with an investor, you need to know how the investor will get their money back and make a profit. If you look like a deer caught in the headlights at one of these meetings, you'll lose your investor. It's very important to know the business side of filmmaking in order to make your vision a reality.

Lynne Hansen: Be kind and funny. Always take your work seriously, but don't ever take yourself too seriously. Help as many people as you can along the way.

Jason V. Brock: In any endeavor, I think perseverance is key. Also, ignore haters: People get jealous and act out. Forget them and focus on your goal. Begin with the end in mind, and, to quote the classic movie *Galaxy Quest*: "Never give up, never surrender."

L.L. Soares: Don't give up on yourself. Read everything you can—the more outside the genre you can, the better. As I get older I find myself reading less and less horror, but that exposes you to new ideas, new ways of doing things, and keeps you fresh. *And just keep doing it.*

And, now more than ever, there are so many distractions with the Internet and social media and the like, that it's tough to just sit down in a quiet place and write. Back before the Internet, writing was a very solitary business. You sat in a room and wrote. But now, there's much more social interaction, which makes being a writer less lonely, but creates an all new set of problems. You have to make the time to actually **do** the work, you have to acquire a degree of discipline, otherwise you'll get nothing done.

Denise Gossett: Be kind, work hard, never give up.

Tim Waggoner: These days, I'd tell writers to have patience and not be in a hurry to publish. It takes a while to hone your craft and learn to write at a professional level. Over the last several years, I've watched writers get one rejection on a novel, say to hell with it, and then self-publish it. They're too eager to experience the ego-boost of Being a REAL Writer, and less interested in learning to write well. Having your fiction "out there" (which is the phrase a lot of these writers use) is far less important than having your *best* fiction "out there." Far better to write one truly good story than publish a dozen inferior ones.

ALONE IN THE PACIFIC WITH PROJECTOR, SCREEN AND TEN BEST FILMS

RAMSEY CAMPBELL

EXCUSES, EXCUSES. I'm about to start a new novel, *The Influence*, and feel the need to relax. I've just bought a word processor and feel as above (though, to be truthful, I find working with the new technology enormous fun). *Shock Express* made me do it—that is, asked me to write about my ten favourite horror films. I'm hoping that my comments are stimulating enough to justify reprinting them here.

If I had to choose a single favourite, one candidate would be Carl Dreyer's *Vampyr* (1931). It is certainly one of the unique experiences offered by the cinema. It's only fair to warn anyone approaching the film for the first time that some of its odder elements look awfully like flaws: the hesitant performances of the almost entirely non-professional cast, in particular the glassy-eyed Baron Nicolas de Gunzburg, who backed the film and, under a pseudonym, acted the role of the hero; the inordinate amount of time spent by various characters (much as in Murnau's *Nosferatu*) in poring over a tome about vampirism; the extraordinary subtitles, where a character can't ask "Who are you?" without its being transformed into "How are you?" But on repeated viewings I find that even these elements blend into a unity, together with the film's attitude to the narrative, originally Sheridan Le Fanu's but now ungraspable as a dream. However, let me not fall into the trap of calling the film simply dreamlike, for I regard it as the cinema's greatest evocation of the supernatural in my experience, of a landscape where the extraordinary is almost commonplace. Shadows dance independent of their objects, a lake reflects a figure that isn't visible on the bank, the earth of a grave flies back onto a gravedigger's shovel, a face fills a window, the doctor who treats a vampire's victims is the vampire's vanguard, the mediaeval figure of Death who summons a ferry in the opening sequence (a ferry which is used only by the hero and heroine, and only at the end of the film) may be the disfigured old man who has a room above the hero's at the inn . . . All this takes place in the midst of dazzlingly bright natural locations, where the nominally normal characters seem entranced. Perhaps that explains, or is explained by, their fascination with the book, but as I've said, in *Vampyr* language shifts as alarmingly as the narrative: "Dou you hear?" people ask, and the visual continuum is broken by explanatory titles such as, "An atmosphere loaden with mystery keeps him avake." Tom Milne describes a press conference Dreyer gave after the premiere of *Gertrud,* his last film, where the director shifted from language to language in his answers until "his way was lost in a jumble of languages and the translators retired, baffled." So, I know, do many viewers of *Vampyr,* but I give you my word that it is a film worth getting to know intimately.[1]

It is the only vampire film on my list. I have to reserve judgment on Murnau's, since the only reasonably coherent print of *Nosferatu* that I've seen has to be projected at sound speed, making the dead travel even faster[2] (the use of natural locations, and Max Schreck's inimitably unlovely vampire, survive this treatment, though). Tod Browning's vampire films are vitiated either by stiff theatricality or strained last-minute rationalizations Christopher Lee's Dracula is the most authentic —aristocratic, brooding and seductive—but the direction of his various Dracula films lacks his intensity. A special mention to Klaus Kinski, both as an unexpectedly poignant (as well as expectedly frightening) Nosferatu and, in Jesus Franco's dull *Dracula,* a distressingly convincing Renfield. I also admire *Martin,* George Romero's film about the tedium of vampire life in Pittsburgh. The most beautiful vampire films since Dreyer's, though, are Mario Bava's *Black Sunday* and Harry Kumel's *Daughters of Darkness.*

Chronologically, the next film to make my list is Mamoulian's

---

1. Recent restorations—for instance, the Eureka Masters of Cinema DVD and Blu-ray—offer more rational subtitles and the most complete available version of the film

2Again, the Eureka version (among others) plays at the correct speed and restores footage missing from other cuts, demonstrating that it's a remarkable film.

ALONE IN THE PACIFIC

Doctor Jekyll and Mr Hyde (1932). A recent BBC television showing of the complete version demonstrated its superiority over all other cinema versions of the story (though I must note John Barrymore's remarkable, cumulatively terrifying, performance in the 1920 version). I was especially pleased to find how disturbing Mamoulian's film remains (so much for the alleged blunting of our sensibilities by the excesses of recent graphic horror movies): Fredric March's gradual slide from delight in his release from staidness to dependence on his sadistic relationship with Miriam Hopkins is both compelling and, I'd venture to suggest, as shocking now as it must have been in its day. Hyde's monstrousness is always presented as an aspect of humanity rather than a rejection of it, and so it's appropriate that when we look in the mirror in this film, we may see Hyde's face. Elaborate as the film's technique sometimes is, it is never meaninglessly so.

I find the film more rewarding than the werewolf movies to which it can be related. *The Wolf Man* is written and directed with intelligence (all of which I tried to respect when I wrote the novel of the film ten years ago), but Lon Chaney's transformation is both too literal for the context and insufficiently lupine (Curt Siodmak wanted the wolfman to be seen only in reflection, as he sees himself; Siodmak later took his subtlety to Val Lewton.) *The Curse of the Werewolf* is broken-backed, but I did like the elaborate Hollywood werewolf films of the early eighties, particularly *Wolfen*, despite its uncertainties. I also value *Company of Wolves*, not least for its willingness to leave some of its images unexplained.

King Kong (1933) is the next of my ten. I have no doubt that it is the greatest of all monster films. When I was nineteen years old I had, and said so stridently in an issue of the British fanzine *Alien*, antagonizing many of the readers, Ray Harryhausen for one. That was in the days when I often mistook controversy for criticism, but at least the film will be remembered long after my carping has crumbled to dust. The characterization of the giant ape is incomparable (and, as the remake demonstrated, inimitable), and the film is one of the very few monster movies that convey a sense of genuine terror. It's a pity that most copies tone down Kong's violence, rather as Sylvester Stallone originally did to Rambo (or they used to; the restorations now available are as uncensored as can be). At least no version gives Kong a final monologue to justify himself.

My list leapfrogs over the forties, to my surprise. I should certainly have expected to include a Val Lewton film: perhaps *The Body Snatcher* (for moral clarity) or *The Cat People* (for psychological subtlety and the delicacy of its scenes of terror)—*The Curse of the Cat People* and *I Walked with a Zombie* take the Lewton virtue of restraint so far that I feel justified in classing them as fantasy rather than horror, a classification which I tell myself lets me exclude Charles Laughton's extraordinary *Night of the Hunter*. Instead I'm listing the film I regard as the last great example of Lewton's influence: not *The Haunting,* which is almost Lovecraftian in the way it makes an issue of not showing its horrors, but *Night of the Demon,* Jacques Tourneur's 1958 film. It was heavily cut on its original release, but a restored print is now available. Both Tourneur and Charles Bennett, the screenwriter, complained that their work was interfered with by the producer, yet only the opening reel (in which, *pace* Marvin Kaye, the demon is shown in closeup in all three versions that I've seen) compromises the structure of the film. Without that scene, the audience would be guided as gradually as the Dana Andrews character from skepticism through doubt to reluctant agnosticism. For me it's the most intelligent film on this process, and the most frightening, and the horror film I most love. I first saw it when I was fourteen, and before the opening credits were over I was enthralled by the introductory voice-over accompanied by Clifton Parker's great score over shots of Stonehenge. I still think Maurice Denham's drive through the spectral night is one of the greatest first scenes in all horror film, and by the time he encountered the demon I knew it was a classic. I must have watched the film perhaps a dozen times by now, and I'll watch it again. I discuss it more fully in the Penguin encyclopaedia of horror.

No Hammer films in my list, I see. Lee and Cushing are fine actors, but Terence Fisher's remakes of Karloff films are otherwise inferior to the originals. Losey's *The Damned* is a considerable achievement but not, I think, a horror film, and Nigel Kneale's excellent Quatermass stories were never given as high a budget as they deserved, though the first two contain probably Val Guest's sharpest direction. To my great regret, *The Innocents* has been crowded out too, even though it is one of the very few genuine ghost stories in the cinema (far superior to the overrated *Uninvited*). So the fourth film on my list is *Psycho*.

A good deal of what's best about the film is Robert Bloch's, of course, including some of his neatest black jokes. But it is also Hitchcock's most densely constructed film in terms of images: the recurring journey into darkness (the opening track in from a cityscape into the darkness of a room leads to Janet Leigh's drive into night) becomes a plunge into darkness (the car into the swamp, Martin Balsam's down the stairs, Vera Miles' descent into the cellars; indeed, this recurrence seems to be the justification for the otherwise inexplicable unnerving track through the darkened hardware store toward Miles). The film shares with *Peeping Tom* a preoccupation with looking and with eyes, and the journeys into darkness lead into the black gaze (even blacker than the motorcycle cop's) of Mrs Bates, who stares at us out of Norman's eyes in the final seconds of the film (in the scene where, as Robin Wood points out, the audience has become "the cruel eyes studying you" which Norman earlier described as one of the horrors of being institutionalised). It is the most poetically organised of Hitchcock's films, and a triumphant vindication of genre.

If *Repulsion* rather than *Peeping Tom* joins it on my list, it was a difficult choice. *Peeping Tom* is Michael Powell's masterpiece, an especially witty and intelligent film, and disconcertingly gentle in its treatment of voyeurism and violence. I can only suggest rather lamely that its themes are dealt with in *Psycho,* and plump for *Repulsion*. Some of Polanski's images of schizophrenia may derive from his experiences with LSD (as I imagine is the case with the hieroglyphics that print themselves out on the lavatory wall in *The Tenant*) but I think that hardly matters. When I see the rooms of Catherine Deneuve's apartment growing cavernous, when the walls grow soft and hands burst out of them, these things aren't happening to an actress up there on the screen, they're happening directly to me, and to object that we aren't asked to feel sympathy for the character seems redundant. I take Polanski to be one of the cinema's most distinguished specialists in horror, and I'd like to put in a word for *Rosemary's Baby,* not least because Marvin Kaye recently dismissed the book, of which the film is an exceptionally faithful (if sinuous) adaptation. "Try to find anything the least bit ambiguous about its sweet-young-thing-brutalised-by-the-bogeyman plot," Kaye challenges, but I don't think the ambiguity he seems to want is necessary: of course Rosemary's predicament isn't "solely in her mind", any more than is Irena's in *Cat People,* but surely by the time either of these films becomes unambiguously supernatural the psychological aspects have been explored—in Rosemary's case, the expectant mother's sense of losing control of her own pregnancy and confinement (eloquent word!), of becoming the property of experts, self-styled or otherwise. I'd suggest that if either film turned out not to be supernatural it would be much less of a film.

Hour of the Wolf is next on my list, for a variety of reasons. It uses generic conventions for deeply personal ends, yet it is one of the very few truly Gothic films (another being *The Saragossa Manuscript*), even using a possibly unreliable narrator; it is the culmination of the scenes of terror in Bergman's work—the opening of *Wild Strawberries,* the finale of *The Face,* various images in *The Seventh Seal* . . . For different but equally powerful reasons I might have chosen *The Shame,* except that I'm restricting myself to one film per director.

There was never any doubt that the next two films would be on my list—*Taxi Driver* and *Eraserhead.* If anyone wants to argue that *Taxi Driver* isn't a horror film, I'd be interested to hear their reasons. Travis Bickle is one of the cinema's most persuasively terrifying creations, and seems to me to underlie Scorsese's subsequent collaborations with de Niro, so that I continually expect the mask of Jimmy Doyle or Rupert Pupkin, already somewhat askew, to slip and reveal Bickle, eager for another crusade. Friends of mine have wanted the film to end as soon as the carnage is over, but I think the contentious ending adds to the film's power: Bickle is still on the streets, and the media's sanitised version of what he did even allows his lost love to admire him. "I'm over that now," he tells her, but his eyes in the rear-view mirror suggest otherwise.

As for *Eraserhead,* it is the most nightmarish film I know. There are films that deal explicitly with nightmare (*Los Olvidados,* for instance, or that admirable moment in *Tristana* where the clapper of the bell turns out to be something else, leaving the audience groping in their memories for the point at which the dream must have begun); there are films whose illogic comes to seem nightmarish (*The Brain Eaters,* allegedly related in some way to Heinlein, makes no sense whatsoever, and I found my inability to predict its narrative appealingly disconcerting); the nightmarishness of some may or may not be inadvertent (for instance, Corman's *Attack of the Crab Monsters* works surprisingly well for me, perhaps because it traps its characters on a constantly shrinking island with its defiantly unlikely monsters). The last films to trouble my sleep were *Los Olvidados* and *Onibaba.* But in my experience, no film other than *Eraserhead* records nightmare in such detail—the textures, the lighting, the meanings that flicker out of reach, the utter casualness of the outrageous. *Eraserhead* can be read as a metaphor about fears of birth, but I don't find that makes the experience of the film any more manageable. The only other films that affect me similarly these days are some of the work of Andrei Tarkovsky; for whatever reason, I was unable to watch a videocassette of *Stalker* for more than half an hour at a time.

One more film to go. I was tempted to include *The Shining,* not only for polemical reasons: I find it frightening, and Jack Nicholson's controversial performance (which some detractors have suggested, incredibly, was indulged against Kubrick's wishes) seems to me wholly convincing and impressively detailed. I see the objection that in the film, unlike the book, Jack Torrance starts out pretty deranged, but so did quite a few of Poe's characters, and after all, the novel specifically invokes Poe. However, on balance the film (which I discuss at length in the Penguin encyclopaedia of horror) just falls short of my list, from which it is ousted by *Videodrome.*

I'll own up to a personal interest in Cronenberg's film. On my first viewing it seemed more like a dream that was taking place in my own head, or rather one that already had taken place, for the film's narrative methods reminded me uncannily of those I'd used in my novel *Incarnate*—the moment when we see that James Woods and Debbie Harry are already in the Videodrome set, which throws into question the reality of all that has gone before; Woods slapping his secretary under the impression that he's slapping Debbie Harry, only to realise that he hasn't touched the secretary either . . . I've admired Cronenberg ever since *Shivers,* though I thought misogyny flawed *The Brood,* the horror film's equivalent of *Stanley and the*

Women, unless one justifies Amis's novel as a study of a deranged narrator. *Videodrome* is Cronenberg's most adventurous film, and if the ending isn't totally satisfying, I take that to be a measure of his ambition. It is also the most verbally witty horror film I can think of; in some scenes there's hardly a line without resonance. A flawed masterpiece, perhaps, but nonetheless a masterpiece, and I see that my list ends as it began, with a film that refuses its audience the reassurance of conventional narrative. Here's to fiction that isn't reassuring—here's to the innovators.

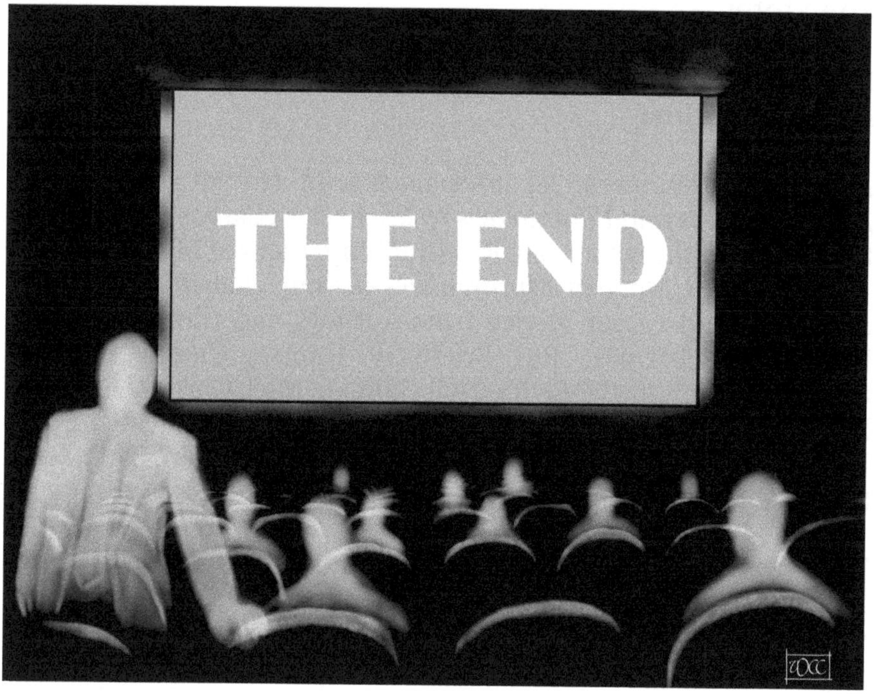
THE END

THE END?

NOT AT ALL.

Be sure to check out the two eBook versions of *Horror 201*, which includes a lot more entertaining tidbits and anecdotes.

If you enjoyed this book, I'm sure you'll also like the following titles:

Modern Mythmakers: 35 interviews with Horror and Science Fiction Writers and Filmmakers by Michael McCarty—Ever wanted to hang out with legends like Ray Bradbury, Richard Matheson, and Dean Koontz? *Modern Mythmakers* is your chance to hear fun anecdotes and career advice from authors and filmmakers like Forrest J. Ackerman, Ray Bradbury, Ramsey Campbell, John Carpenter, Dan Curtis, Elvira, Neil Gaiman, Mick Garris, Laurell K. Hamilton, Jack Ketchum, Dean Koontz, Graham Masterton, Richard Matheson, John Russo, William F. Nolan, John Saul, Peter Straub, and many more.

Tales from The Lake Vol.1—Remember those dark and scary nights spent telling ghost stories and other campfire stories? With the *Tales from The Lake* horror anthologies, you can relive some of those memories by reading the best Dark Fiction stories around. Includes Dark Fiction stories and poems by horror greats such as Graham Masterton, Bev Vincent, Tim Curran, Tim Waggoner, Elizabeth Massie, and many more. Be sure to check out our website for future *Tales from The Lake* volumes.

If you ever thought of becoming an author, I'd also like to recommend these non-fiction titles:

Horror 101: The Way Forward—a comprehensive overview of the Horror fiction genre and career opportunities available to established and aspiring authors, including Jack Ketchum, Graham Masterton, Tim Waggoner, Armand Rosamilia, Edward Lee, Lisa Morton, Ellen Datlow, Ramsey Campbell, and many more.

Writers On Writing: An Author's Guide—Your favorite authors share their secrets in the ultimate guide to becoming and being and author. With your support, *Writers On Writing* will become an ongoing eBook series with original 'On Writing' essays by writing professionals. A new edition will be launched every few months, featuring four or five essays per edition, so be sure to check out the webpage regularly for updates.

A SPECIAL THANKS TO . . .

Wes Craven, Adrian Roe, Emma Audsley, Michael McCarty, E.C. McMullen Jr., Johnny Mcculloch, Scott Montgomery, Stuart Morriss, Joshua L. Hood, Hal Bodner, Tim Waggoner, William C. Cope, Ben Baldwin, Jason V. Brock, Jonathan Maberry, and every person who took time out of their lives and careers to contribute to this project.

BIOGRAPHIES

Bursting upon the indie horror scene at the age of eighteen with his first feature My Pure Joy, **James Cullen Bressack** *has been called "horror's new hope" (StudioCity Patch—Mike Szymanski) and "a talent to watch out for" (H.S.T.- Ben John Smith), as well as garnering rave reviews on almost every horror web site. Released by Media Blasters on their Fresh Meat Shriek Show label in 2012, the film quickly rose to the top of the best sellers list on Amazon.com in the horror category. His second feature, a real shocker,* Hate Crime, *was a festival favorite and garnered many awards. Bressack then made history with his next feature,* To Jennifer, *which was the first feature film shot entirely on an Iphone 5. The prolific filmmaker then made* Pernicious, *filmed in Thailand and due to be released later this year. His film,* 13-13-13 *followed and his most recent feature,* Blood Lake, *which aired on Animal Planet, was a top ratings getter. A winner of multiple Best Picture and Best director awards on the film festival circuit, James has become one of the few indie filmmakers Verified on twitter, where he has 100,000 + loyal fans.*

Jason V Brock *is an award-winning writer, editor, filmmaker, composer, and artist, and has been widely-published online, in comic books, magazines, and anthologies, such as* Qualia Nous, Disorders of Magnitude *(a Bram Stoker and Rondo Hatton Award-nominated nonfiction collection),* Simulacrum and Other Possible Realities *(an illustrated fiction/poetry collection),* Fungi, Weird Fiction Review, Fangoria, *S. T. Joshi's* Black Wings *series, and many others.*

He was Art Director/Managing Editor for Dark Discoveries *magazine for more than four years, and publishes a pro journal called* [NameL3ss], *which can be found on Twitter:* @NamelessMag, *and on the Interwebs at www.NamelessDigest.com. He and his wife, Sunni, also run*

Cycatrix Press (their books include he Bram Stoker Award nominated A Darke Phantastique, *and* The Bleeding Edge, *to name just two), and have a technology consulting business.*

As a filmmaker, his work includes the critically-acclaimed documentaries Charles Beaumont: The Life of Twilight Zone's Magic Man, The AckerMonster Chronicles! *(winner of the 2014 Rondo Hatton Award for Best Documentary), and* Image, Reflection, Shadow: Artists of the Fantastic (due in late 2016). *He is the primary composer and instrumentalist/singer for his band,* ChiaroscurO. *Brock loves his wife, their family of reptiles/amphibians, travel, and vegan/vegetarianism.*

He is active on social sites such as Facebook and Twitter (@JaSunni_JasonVB), and their personal website/blog, www.JaSunni.com.

Ramsey Campbell *is one of the most respected, lauded, awarded writers in fantasy. He has won multiple British Fantasy and World Fantasy Awards and several Bram Stoker and International Horror Guild Awards. He is the author of such classic works of horror and dark fantasy as* Obsession,The Face Must Die, The Nameless, Incarnate *and* The Influence, *and, more recently,* The Darkest Part of the Woods, The Overnight *and* The Grin of the Dark.

Nick Cato *is the author of the novel* Don of the Dead, *the novellas* The Apocalypse of Peter, The Last Porno Theater, The Atrocity Vendor, *and* Uptown Death Squad, *as well as the short story collection* Antibacterial Pope and Other Incongruous Stories. *He writes the Suburban Grindhouse Memories column for the acclaimed website,* Cinema Knife Fight. *A collection of this column in book form is forthcoming. Visit nickyakcato.blogspot.com and the usual sites for more info.*

Richard Chizmar *has edited more than 20 anthologies and his fiction has appeared in dozens of publications, including* Ellery Queen's Mystery Magazine *and* The Year's 25 Finest Crime and Mystery Stories. *A new collection,* A Long December, *will be released in 2016 from Subterranean Press.*

Chizmar and Johnathon Schaech have also written screenplays and teleplays for United Artists, Sony Screen Gems, Lions Gate, Showtime, NBC, and many other companies.

Wesley Earl "Wes " Craven *(August 2, 1939 – August 30, 2015) was an American film director, writer, producer, and actor known for his work on horror films, particularly slasher films.*

He was best known for creating the A Nightmare on Elm Street *franchise featuring the Freddy Krueger character, directing the first installment and* Wes Craven's New Nightmare, *and co-writing* A Nightmare on Elm Street 3: Dream Warriors *with Bruce Wagner.*

Craven also directed all four films in the Scream *series, and co-created the Ghostface character. Some of his other films include* The Hills Have Eyes, The Last House on the Left, The People Under the Stairs, Red Eye, The Serpent and the Rainbow, *and* Vampire in Brooklyn.

On August 30, 2015, Craven died of brain cancer, at the age of 76, at his home in Los Angeles.

Award-winning filmmaker **Mick Garris** *began writing fiction at the age of twelve. By the time he was in high school, he was writing music and film journalism for various local and national publications, and during college, edited and published his own pop culture magazine. He spent seven years as lead vocalist with the acclaimed tongue-in-cheek progressive art-rock band, Horsefeathers.*

His first movie business job was as a receptionist for George Lucas's Star Wars Corporation, where he worked his way up to running the remote-controlled R2-D2 robot at personal appearances, including that year's Academy Awards ceremony. Garris hosted and produced "The Fantasy Film Festival" for nearly three years on Los Angeles television, and later began work in film publicity at Avco Embassy and Universal Pictures. It was there that he created "Making of . . . " documentaries for various feature films.

Steven Spielberg hired Garris as story editor on the Amazing Stories *series for NBC, where he wrote or co-wrote 10 of the 44 episodes. Since then, he has written or co-authored several feature films (*Riding the Bullet, *Batteries Not Included, The Fly II, Hocus Pocus, Critters 2, Riding the Bullet) and teleplays (*Amazing Stories,

Quicksilver Highway, Virtual Obsession, The Others, Desperation, Nightmares & Dreamscapes, Masters of Horror, Fear Itself), *as well as directing and producing in many media: cable* (Psycho IV: The Beginning, Tales from The Crypt, Masters of Horror, Pretty Little Liars, *its spinoff,* Ravenswood, *and* Witches of East End), *features* (Critters 2, Sleepwalkers, Riding the Bullet), *television films* (Quicksilver Highway, Virtual Obsession, Desperation), *series pilots* (The Others, Lost in Oz), *network miniseries* (The Stand, The Shining, Steve Martini's The Judge, Bag of Bones), *and series* (She-Wolf of London, Masters of Horror, Fear Itself).

He is Creator and Executive Producer of Showtime's Masters of Horror *series, as well as creator of the NBC series,* Fear Itself, *both anthology series of one-hour horror films written and directed by the most famous names in the fear-film genre: John Carpenter, Tobe Hooper, George Romero, John Landis, Dario Argento, and several others. Garris is also a writer and director on both series. Garris was also Executive Producer and Director of Stephen King's* Bag of Bones *miniseries for A&E. He is currently developing three series.*

Garris is also Executive Producer of the Universal feature, Unbroken, *based on the life of Louis Zamperini and the book by Laura Hillenbrand. It was directed by Angelina Jolie, and has proven to be an international box office hit.*

Mick is also known for his FEARnet television interview series Post-Mortem, *where he sits down with some of the most revered filmmakers in the horror and fantasy genre for one-on-one discussions.*

A Life in The Cinema, *his first book, was a collection of short stories and a screenplay based on one of the included stories, published by Gauntlet Press. Garris' first novel,* Development Hell, *was published by Cemetery Dance, who are also publishers of his novellas,* Snot Shadows *and* Tyler's Third Act, *his second novel,* Salome, *and next year's novella,* Ugly. *He has also had many works of short fiction published in numerous books and magazines.*

Denise Gossett *is the founder and director of Shriekfest Horror Film Festival, currently in its 15th year! Shriekfest is the longest running horror film festival in Los Angeles! Denise has also been* an actress in Television & Feature Films for over 20 years! She can most recently be seen in the Tom Hiddleston movie I Saw the Light, the Mel Gibson starring Feature Film Get The Gringo and the Morris Chestnut movie When the Bough Breaks.

Taylor Grant is a Bram Stoker Award-nominated author, Hollywood screenwriter and award-winning filmmaker. His short films, Sticks and Stones and The Vanished, both premiered at the prestigious Cannes Film Festival. His work has been seen on network television, the big screen, the stage, the Web, as well as in comic books, newspapers, national magazines, anthologies, and heard on the radio.

Several of Taylor's screenplays have sold or been optioned by major Hollywood film studios such as Imagine Entertainment, Universal Studios, and Lions Gate Films. He created the horror/comedy series Monster Farm, which aired on the Fox Family Channel, and sold pitches and scripts to a host of children's TV series. His fiction has appeared in two Bram Stoker Award nominated anthologies, and his collection The Dark at the End of the Tunnel, was just released by Cemetery Dance Publications (eBook) and Crystal Lake Publishing (print).

Taylor is currently working with a successful video game company to bring one of his stories to life as an exciting RPG game.

David Henson Greathouse is a make-up effects artist, actor, director, writer, cameraman, and editor. Highly regarded by his peers for his work creating special make-up effects for over 50 movies such as The Usual Suspects, Late Phases, Tales from the Crypt, All Cheerleader Die, John Dies in the End, The Rage, Freaked, Mighty Morphin' Power Rangers, Necronomicon, and Buried Alive.

Greathouse developed his skills as a kid in Cleveland Ohio, where he shot movies with his friends, built a FX portfolio of prosthetics, and performed and managed multiple haunted attractions throughout the country.

In 1991, David relocated to Los Angeles to work as an artist in the movie industry. He has since contributed special make-up effects for many feature films and television shows.

He returned to Cleveland every October to shoot his debut film,

Legion of Terror. *A feature length documentary on a dedicated and demented ensemble of haunted house actors. The film explores the distinctive personalities, the complexities of a seasonal haunted attraction and the rise and fall of a very weird family over a thirteen year period.*

In 2001 Greathouse became involved with the heavy metal band, Mushroomhead. He would design and create the band's signature masked appearance and tour the world with them as a roadie and documentarian.

Greathouse directed the band's music video for "12 Hundred," earning them the MTV's Headbangers Ball 2007 Video of the Year.

Since 2001 Greathouse is now part of Robert Kurtzman's Creature Corps in Crestline, Ohio with a dozen other relocated Hollywood film artists and technicians working toward ushering in their own brand of imagination.

In 2013 House *was seen as a make-up artist contestant on* Syfy⬚ Faceoff *Season 4.*

Lynne Hansen *is the award-winning filmmaker of the horror-comedy* Chomp. *Her film has been nominated for over a dozen awards and screened at over 50 film festivals worldwide, including Ireland, Scotland, Belgium, and Spain. She was nominated twice for Best Director of a Short Film, and was honored as Buffalo Dreams Fantastic Film Festival's 2014 "Filmmaker to Watch." Her current projects include a feature-length horror comedy and* Filmmaking is for Girls, *an inspirational how-to guide to help young filmmakers find their voice and creative spark. To find out what she's up to next, visit WithoutWarningMedia.com.*

James Hart *is an independent filmmaker raised watching* Star Wars, Labyrinth *and* The Dark Crystal *with his parents and* Alien, American Werewolf *and* Carpenter's The Thing *when left to his own devises. Watching movies inspired him to make them. Hart is a proponent of Tarantino's 'no film school' ethic and considers this to be intrinsic to his style of organic film making.*

Hart has worked on six independent short films, producing and directing five and trying his hand at cinematography on three since making his first film in 2013.

His first film, Ascension, *has been shown around the world, translated into Spanish and won him the Best Director Award at The Bram Stoker International Film Festival as well as a Best Film Award at The Worcester Film Festival.*

David C. Hayes *is an author, performer and filmmaker. His films, like* A Man Called Nereus, Bloody Bloody Bible Camp, Dark Places, The Frankenstein Syndrome, Vampeggedon, Machined, Reborn, Back Woods *(and approximately 60 more) can be seen worldwide. He is the author of several novels, collections and graphic novels including* The Midnight Creature Feature Picture Show, Cherub, Cannibal Fat Camp, Pegged, American Guignol, Scorn *and* Muddled Mind: The Complete Works of Ed Wood, Jr. *As a playwright, David's full-length and one-act plays have been produced from coast to coast with a run Off-Broadway for the comedy* Swamp Ho *and sell-out performances in Phoenix for* Dial P for Peanuts. *He is a voting member of The Horror Writers Association, The Dramatist's Guild and the Great Lakes Association of Horror Writers.*

Nancy Holder *is the New York Times bestselling author of the Wicked Saga (with coauthor Debbie Viguié.) She has sold over ninety books and two hundred short stories. She has received 5 Bram Stoker Awards from the Horror Writers Association, of which she is vice-president. She has also received awards for her young adult and tie-in work, which includes tie-in prose for properties such as Guillermo del Toro's* Crimson Peak, Buffy the Vampire Slayer, Teen Wolf, Beauty and the Beast, *and many others. Her books have appeared on recommendation lists from the Horror Writers Association, the American Library Association, the American Reading Association, New York Public Library's Stuff for the Teen Age, and many others. She teaches for the Stonecoast MFA in Creative Writing program at the University of Southern Maine and lives in San Diego with her partner, the writer Mark Mandell, and her Corgi, Tater. Socialize with her @nancyholder and https://www.facebook.com/nancyholderfans*

Tom Holland *is an American director and screenwriter of horror* *and thriller films. His early writing projects include* Class of 1984 *(1982) and the Robert Bloch-inspired* Psycho II *(1983), the latter starring Anthony Perkins as the menacing psychopath, Norman Bates.*

Tom gained more notoriety, however, as a director. His directorial debut was the popular 1980s Vampire film, Fright Night *(1985) which, at the time, was said to have been responsible for redefining the sub-genre, influencing later films like* The Lost Boys *(1987) and* Near Dark *(1987). The film was a box office hit and garnered three Saturn Awards and one Dario Argento Award.*

For his next project, Child's Play *(1988), Tom again cast Chris Sarandon. The film was a Number One box-office hit in America and a worldwide success, despite controversy over its thematic content. It, like* Fright Night *(1985) has since gathered a cult following amongst horror fans. Tom then went onto direct two films based upon adaptations of Stephen King's novels:* The Langoliers *(1995) and* Thinner *(1996). He also took a cameo role in the Stephen King miniseries* The Stand *(1994).*

Tom's other projects have included The Incredible Hulk *episode "Another Path," Steven Spielberg's* Amazing Stories *(1985), three episodes of* Tales from the Crypt *(1989), and the prestigious* Masters of Horror *(2005) anthology. He starred in* A Walk in the Spring Rain *(1970) with Ingrid Bergman.*

Dave Jeffery *is a screenwriter and producer for Venomous Little Man Productions. The short film* Ascension *(adapted from his own short story) has garnered two awards. To date Jeffery has written and co-written three feature screenplays and several short films.*

As an established writer, Jeffery is perhaps best known for his zombie novel Necropolis Rising *which has gone on to be a UK #1 bestseller. His Young Adult work includes the critically acclaimed* Beatrice Beecham *Series, BBC: Headroom endorsed* Finding Jericho *and the 2012 Edge Hill Prize Long-listed* Campfire Chillers *short story collection.*

Dave has contributed to several anthologies from a variety of publishers including Dark Continents Publishing, Inc., Wild Wolf Publishing, Imprint Phoenix, Hersham Horror Books, Wicked East Press, Western Legends, and Hidden Thoughts Press. His work has featured alongside many zombie impresarios including John Russo (Night of the Living Dead), *Tony Burgess* (Pontypool) *and Joe McKinney* (Flesh Eaters). *His short story "Daddy Dearest" features in the award-winning* Holiday of the Dead *anthology (This is Horror Awards, Best Anthology, 2012).*

In August 2014, his Necropolis Rising *series was acquired by award winning publishing house, Severed Press in a five book deal.* Dead Empire *is slated for release in 2016.*

VLM Productions website: www.venomouslittleman.co.uk
Author Website: www.davejeffery.webs.com

Lee Karr *is a devoted fan of the films of George Romero, in particular* Day of the Dead, *having authored the 2014 book* The Making of George A. Romero's Day of the Dead. *He has contributed photos and liner notes for DVD and Blu-Ray releases in both the U.S. and Japan for* Day of the Dead *and* Dawn of the Dead *and has written for magazines such as* Horrorhound *and* Famous Monsters of Filmland. *He has penned set reports for* Land of the Dead, Diary of the Dead, *and* Survival of the Dead *for homepageofthedead.com, as well as interviewing George Romero in his Toronto home for the website. Born and raised in Savannah, Georgia (filming locale for Lucio Fulci's* City of the Living Dead) *he currently lives in the zombie capital of the world: Pittsburgh, Pennsylvania.*

Tim Lebbon *is a New York Times-bestselling writer from South Wales. He's had over thirty novels published to date, as well as hundreds of novellas and short stories. His latest novel is the thriller* The Hunt, *and other recent releases include* The Silence *and* Alien: Out of the Shadows. *He has won four British Fantasy Awards, a Bram Stoker Award, and a Scribe Award, and has been a finalist for World Fantasy, International Horror Guild and Shirley Jackson Awards. Future books include* The Rage War *(an Alien/Predator trilogy), and the* Relics *trilogy from Titan.*

The movie of his story Pay the Ghost, *starring Nicolas Cage, is out now, and other projects in development include* Playtime *(an original script with Stephen Volk),* My Haunted House *with Gravy Media,* The Hunt, Exorcising Angels *(based on a novella with Simon Clark), and a TV Series proposal of* The Silence.

Patrick Lussier *is a genre writer, editor and director, who has mastered the art and craft of directing live action 3D. Most recently, he co-wrote* Terminator: Genisys *with Laeta Kalogridis for Skydance Productions and Paramount Pictures, released in 2015. He has collaborated on several projects with Ms. Kalogridis, dating back to 1999 when Laeta was hired to rewrite Scream 3 which Lussier was film editing. His previous motion picture credits include directing both* Drive Angry 3D *and* My Bloody Valentine: 3D, *released by Summit Entertainment and Lionsgate, respectively (MBV3D, made for 16 million, made over 50 million domestic on 1003 screens over just 3 weekends, and over 50 million foreign in its initial release. It is currently the 11th highest grossing slasher film of all time). Lussier directed and edited* White Noise: The Light *(aka White* Noise 2*), and directed and co-wrote the vampire trilogy* Wes Craven Presents Dracula 2000 *notable for Gerard Butler's feature debut in a starring role,* Dracula II: Ascension *and* Dracula III: Legacy. *He made his directorial debut with the horror fantasy* The Prophecy 3: The Ascent, *the Prophecy series' final installment with Christopher Walken as the Archangel Gabriel.*

Lussier edited the lion's share of Wes Craven's movies through the 1990s and early 2000s, including Wes Craven's New Nightmare, Vampire in Brooklyn, Music of the Heart, *the original* Scream *trilogy,* Cursed *and* Red Eye. *Additional editorial credits include Gonzalo Lopez-Gallego's* Apollo 18, *Guillermo del Toro's* Mimic, *Steve Miner's* Halloween: H20 *and the comedies* My Boss's Daughter *and* D3: The Mighty Ducks, *directed by David Zucker and Rob Lieberman respectively. Prior to a career in features, Lussier edited* MacGyver *for three seasons and the* Doctor Who: TV Movie *in 1996. Lussier has also worked as a visual consultant on* Darkness Falls, 54, Brothers Grimm, Exorcist: The Beginning/Dominion, The Return *and* Whisper, *and as a music consultant on* Reindeer Games *and* Equilibrium.

Graham Masterton *was born in Edinburgh in 1946, the grandson of John Masterton, the chief inspector mines for Scotland, and Thomas Thorne Baker, a world-renowned scientist who was the first man to send news pictures by radio.*

After joining his local newspaper at the age of 17 as a junior reporter, Graham was appointed deputy editor of Mayfair the men's magazine at the age of 21. At 24 he became executive editor of Penthouse.

His career at Penthouse led him to write a series of best-selling sexual advice books, including How To Drive Your Man Wild In Bed, which sold 2 million copies worldwide and 250,000 in Poland alone, where it has recently been reprinted.

After leaving Penthouse he wrote The Manitou, a horror novel about the vengeful reincarnation of a Native American spirit, which was filmed with Tony Curtis in the lead role, and also starred Susan Strasberg, Burgess Meredith and Stella Stevens. Three of Graham's horror stories were adapted by the late Tony Scott for his TV series The Hunger. Over the years he has published five collections of short stories, several of which have won awards.

Graham has also written historical sagas like Rich, Maiden Voyage and Solitaire, as well as thrillers and disaster novels such as Plague and Famine. The newest disaster novel Drought will be published in May, 2014.

In 1989 Graham's Polish wife Wiescka was instrumental in his becoming the first Western horror novelist to be published in Poland since World War Two, and his sex books have not only won popular success in Poland but acclaim from the medical profession.

He was a regular contributor of humorous articles to the satire magazine Punch, as well as scores of articles on sexual happiness to American women's magazines.

He has encouraged younger writers in several countries, including France, Germany and the Baltic States. For the past 13 years, he has given his name to the prestigious Prix Masterton, which is awarded annually for best French-language horror novel. He was the only non-French winner of Le Prix Julia Verlanger for best-selling horror novel and he has also been given recognition by Mystery Writers of America, the British Fantasy Society and many others.

He edited an anthology of short stories by leading horror writers, Scare Care, in aid of children's charities, and has been honoured by the Irish Society for the Prevention of Cruelty to Children for his fund-raising.

Recently he has very successfully turned his hand to crime

writing, although his murder scenes are as stirring as anything he has written in the horror genre.

Drawing on the five years in which he and his late wife Wiescka lived in Cork, in southern Ireland, he has created a series of novels featuring Katie Maguire, the first woman detective superintendent in An Garda Siochána, the Irish police force—White Bones, Broken Angels and Red Light.

He currently lives in Surrey, England.

Michael McCarty has been a professional writer since 1983 and the author of over thirty-five books of fiction and nonfiction, including I Kissed A Ghoul, Laughing In The Dark, A Hell of A Job, A Little Help From My Fiends, Dark Duets, Monster Behind The Wheel (co-written with Mark McLaughlin), Lost Girl of the Lake (co-written with Joe McKinney), Conversations With Kreskin (co-written with The Amazing Kreskin), Night of the Scream Queen (co-written with Linnea Quigley), Bloodless (co-written with Jody LaGreca) and Liquid Diet & Midnight Snack: 2 Vampire Satires. He is a five-time Bram Stoker Finalist and in 2008 David R. Collins' Literary Achievement Award from the Midwest Writing Center. He lives in Rock Island, Illinois with his wife Cindy and pet rabbit Latte.

He is also the author of the mega book of interviews Modern Mythmakers: 35 Interviews With Horror And Science Fiction Writers And Filmmakers and an essay for Horror 101: The Way Forward, both published by Crystal Lake Publishing.

Michael McCarty is on Twitter as michaelmccarty6.

His blog site is at:
http://monstermikcyaauthor.wordpress.com
Facebook! Like him on his official page:
http://www.facebook.com/michaelmccarty.horror.
Or snail mail him at:
 Michael McCarty
 Fan Mail
 P.O. Box 4441
 Rock Island, IL 61204-4441

Mark McLaughlin's fiction, nonfiction, and poetry have

appeared in more than 1,000 magazines, newspapers, websites, and anthologies, including Galaxy, Living Dead 2, The Best Of All Flesh, Writer's Digest, Cemetery Dance, Spectral Realms, Midnight Premiere, Dark Arts, and two volumes each of The Best Of Horrorfind and The Year's Best Horror Stories (DAW Books).

Trade paperback collections of his fiction include Best Little Witch-House In Arkham, Beach Blanket Zombie and Hideous Faces, Beautiful Skulls. His Kindle collections include Drunk On The Wine That Pours From My Wicked Eyes and The Slime Of Our Lives. He also wrote the novel Monster Behind the Wheel with collaborator Michael McCarty.

McLaughlin and McCarty and the co-authors of the poetry collections, Revenge Of The Two-Headed Poetry Monster, and Bride Of The Two-Headed Poetry Monster. Also, McLaughlin once won the Bram Stoker Award for Excellence in Poetry, along with co-authors Rain Graves and David Niall Wilson, for The Gossamer Eye.

Eric Miller has been working in the movie business for over twenty years as a screenwriter, producer, and many other fun-filled, low-stress jobs. He has worked on numerous horror films and is proud of the untold gallons of fake blood he has helped spill. His produced horror scripts include Ice Spiders, Night Skies and Mask Maker. When not playing on set, Miller is the Bram Stoker Award nominated editor of the movie-themed horror anthology series Hell Comes To Hollywood and the trucking horror anthology 18 Wheels of Horror. He is slowly—very slowly—working on The No Bullshit Guide To Screenwriting. Find out more at www.BigTimeBooks.com.

Joe Mynhardt is a HWA nominated South African horror writer, publisher, editor, and teacher.

Joe is the owner of Crystal Lake Publishing (Publisher of the Year in the 2013 This Is Horror Awards), which he started in August, 2012. Since then he's published and edited short stories, novellas, interviews and essays by the likes of Neil Gaiman, Clive Barker, Ramsey Campbell, Jack Ketchum, Graham Masterton, Adam Nevill, Lisa Morton, Elizabeth Massie, Joe McKinney,

Edward Lee, Wes Craven, John Carpenter, George A. Romero, Mick Garris, and hundreds more.

Just like Crystal Lake Publishing, Joe believes in reaching out to all authors, new and experienced, and being a beacon of friendship and guidance in the Dark Fiction field.

Joe's influences stretch from Poe, Doyle and Lovecraft to King, Connolly and Gaiman. His collection of short stories, Lost in the Dark, is available through Amazon. You can read more about Joe and Crystal Lake Publishing at www.crystallakepub.com or find him on Facebook.

Joe is also an Associate member of the HWA.

Ed Naha began his professional writing career while still in college, selling an article to Rolling Stone magazine. In the 1970s, he established himself as a rock critic, film columnists and author. He has written and published over 30 books in his career in both the fiction and non-fiction categories. His novel, Cracking Up, was nominated for an Edgar Award. Moving to California, he turned his attention to both screen and television, selling over twenty screenplays and executive producing two TV series. He is kind to animals, children and large people with guns.

Jeffrey Reddick is best known for creating the Final Destination (2000) film franchise. He also co-wrote the story for, and executive produced, Final Destination 2 (2003). Jeffrey lives in Los Angeles. He grew up in Eastern Kentucky and attended Berea College. Jeffrey made his first connection to the film industry at age 14, when he wrote a prequel to A Nightmare on Elm Street (1984) and mailed it Bob Shaye, the President of New Line Cinema. Bob returned the material for being unsolicited. But the young man wrote Bob an aggressive reply, which won him over. Bob read the treatment and got back to Jeffrey. Bob, and his assistant, Joy Mann, stayed in contact with Jeffrey for over five years. When he went to The American Academy of Dramatic Arts in New York at age 19, Bob offered him an internship at New Line Cinema. This internship turned into an 11-year stint at the studio.

Aside from Final Destination (2000), which spawned four successful sequels, Jeffrey's other credits include Lions Gate's *thriller,* Tamara *(2005) and the remake of George Romero's classic,* Day of the Dead *(2008).*

Jeffrey has several feature and TV projects in development and he directed his first short, Good Samaritan *in 2014.*

George A. Romero *never set out to become a Hollywood figure; however, by all indications, he was very successful. The director of the groundbreaking "Dead" pentalogy was born February 4, 1940, in New York City. He grew up there until attending the renowned Carnegie-Mellon University in Pittsburgh, Pennsylvania.*

After graduation, he began shooting mostly short films and commercials. He and his friends formed "Image Ten Productions" in the late 1960s and they all chipped in roughly US$10,000 a piece to produce what became one of the most celebrated American horror films of all time: Night of the Living Dead *(1968). Shot in black-and-white on a budget of just over US$100,000, Romero's vision, combined with a solid script written by him and his "Image" co-founder John A. Russo enabled the film to earn back far more than what it cost, became a cult classic by the early 1970s and was inducted into the National Film Registry of the Library of Congress of the United States in 1999.*

In 1978, Romero returned to the zombie genre with the one film of his that would top the success of Night of the Living Dead *(1968):* Dawn of the Dead *(1978). Shot on a budget of just $1.5 million, the film earned over US$40 million worldwide and was named one of the top cult films by Entertainment Weekly magazine in 2003. The film also marked Romero's first work with brilliant make-up and effects artist Tom Savini. After 1978, Romero and Savini teamed up many times.* Dawn of the Dead *(1978)'s success led to bigger budgets and better casts for the filmmaker. First was* Knightriders *(1981), where he first worked with an up-and-coming Ed Harris. Then came perhaps his most Hollywood-like film,* Creepshow *(1982), which marked the first, but not the last, time Romero adapted a work by famed horror novelist Stephen King. With many major stars and big-studio distribution,* Creepshow *(1982) was a moderate success and spawned a sequel, which was also written by Romero.*

Harry Shannon is the author of fourteen novels, dozens of short stories and several screenplays. He is a former music supervisor for major motion pictures. He has also been employed as an actor, a professional songwriter, a music publisher and a recording artist. He has been a counselor in private practice since 1988.

John Shirley won the Bram Stoker Award from the Horror Writers Association for his story collection Black Butterflies. His novels Demons and Bleak History *have come close to being movies—and who knows? He wrote the first four drafts of the movie* The Crow, *and shares co-writing credit for that film with David Schow. His newest novel is* Doyle After Death.

Jack Thomas Smith *made his feature film-directing debut with the psychological thriller* Disorder. *He was also the writer and producer of that film.* Disorder *opened in select theaters in the U.S. and was then released on DVD by Universal/Vivendi and New Light Entertainment. It was later released on Pay-Per-View and Video-On-Demand by Warner Brothers. Overseas, it screened at the Cannes Film Festival and the Raindance Film Festival in London. Curb Entertainment represented* Disorder *for foreign sales and secured distribution deals around the world.*

Smith's current project he calls Infliction, *is a dark and disturbing assembled footage film that documents two brothers' 2011 murder spree in NC and the horrific truth behind their actions.* Infliction *opened in select theaters in 2014 and is now available on DVD, VOD, and Digital HD in the U.S. and Canada by Virgil Films & Entertainment.*

Infliction *is now being represented for international distribution by the foreign sales agency Cardinal XD and will be available at all of the major film markets around the world, including the Toronto Film Festival; the American Film Market in Santa Monica, CA; Sundance; the Berlin Film Festival; and Cannes.*

Smith's production company, Fox Trail Productions, Inc., is currently developing the action/horror film In the Dark.

Armand Rosamilia *is a New Jersey boy currently living in* *sunny Florida, where he writes all day until his back hurts and then gets doted on by his wife Shelly. Who yells at him to get out of the chair every once in awhile. He has over 150 releases to date, has two successful podcasts on Project iRadio (Arm Cast: Dead Sexy Horror Podcast and Arm N Toof's Dead Time Podcast with co-host Mark Tufo) as well as runs the Authors Supporting Our Troops event, collecting author-signed books for the soldiers in remote areas. He is a firm believer in karma and helps fellow authors as much as he can. http://armandrosamilia.com for more information.*

*With twenty books published internationally and nineteen feature movies in worldwide distribution, **John A. Russo** has been called a "living legend." He began by co-authoring the screenplay for* Night of the Living Dead, *which has become recognized as a "horror classic."*

His three books on the art and craft of movie making have become bibles of independent production, and one of them, Scare Tactics, *won a national award for Superior Nonfiction. Quentin Tarantino and many other noted filmmakers have stated that Russo's books helped them launch their careers.*

John Russo wants people to know he's "just a nice guy who likes to scare people"—and he's done it with novels and films such as Return of The Living Dead, Midnight, The Majorettes, The Awakening, and Heartstopper. *He has had a long, rewarding career, and he shows no signs of slowing down. Recently his screenplay for* Escape of The Living Dead *was made into a five-part comic book released by Avatar to great acclaim; it made the Top Ten of Horror Comics nationally and spawned two graphic novels and ten sequels.*

Russo's recent novel, The Hungry Dead, *was published by Kensington Books. He is also slated to direct two movies: a remake of his cult hit,* Midnight, *and a brand new take on the "zombie phenomenon" entitled* Spawn of The Dead.

Russo's latest novel Dealey Plaza *was published by Burning Bulb Publishing. His short story "Channel 666" appears in* The Big Book of Bizarro.

Aaron Sterns *is the co-writer of* Wolf Creek 2 *(best screenplay, Madrid International Fantastic Film Festival 2014) and author of the Australian Shadows Award-winning prequel novel* Wolf Creek: Origin, *described by Jack Ketchum simply as "brutal." As well as being the author of various Aurealis Award-nominated and Year's Best Fantasy & Horror recommended short stories, Sterns is a former lecturer in Gothic & Subversive Fiction, editor of* The Journal of the Australian Horror Writers, *and Ph.D. student in postmodern horror. He served as a script-editor on Greg McLean's* Rogue, *and appeared as Bazza's Mate in* Wolf Creek *and a police officer in the last scene of* Wolf Creek 2. *His latest work is a Lovecraftian-action novella 'Vanguard', opening the anthology* Cthulhu: Deep Down Under.

He lives in Melbourne, Australia, and can be found on *www.aaronsterns.com, via* Facebook at /aaronsternsauthor, and on Twitter @aaronsterns.

L.L. Soares *is the Bram Stoker Award-winning author of the novels* Life Rage, Rock 'n' Roll *and* Hard. *His other books include the short story collection* In Sickness *and the novella* Green Tsunami *(both with Laura Cooney). His fiction has appeared in such magazines as* Cemetery Dance, Horror Garage, Bare Bone, Shroud, *and* Gothic.Net, *as well as the anthologies* The Best of Horrorfind 2, Zippered Flesh: Tales of Body Enhancements Gone Bad! Volumes 1 & 2, Someone Wicked, *and* Insidious Assassins.

He also co-writes the Stoker-nominated horror movie review column Cinema Knife Fight, *which can be found at:* cinemaknifefight.com.

To keep up on his endeavors, go to www.llsoares.com.

Stephen Volk *is best known as creator of the infamous BBCTV "Hallowe'en hoax"* Ghostwatch *and the drama series* Afterlife. *His other screenplays include* The Awakening *(2011), Ken Russell's* Gothic, *William Friedkin's* The Guardian, *and, most recently, a 3-part adaptation of Phil Rickman's novel* Midwinter of the Spirit *for ITV. His short stories have been chosen for* Year's Best Fantasy and Horror, Mammoth Book of Best New Horror, Best British Mysteries, *and* Best British Horror, *he has been a Bram Stoker and Shirley*

Jackson Award finalist, and his second collection, Monsters in the Heart, *won the British Fantasy Award in 2014. He wrote the highly-acclaimed novella "Whitstable," which featured revered Hammer horror star Peter Cushing, while the follow-up, "Leytonstone," takes as its subject matter the childhood of Alfred Hitchcock. He is planning the third in the trilogy, as well as developing several feature film and TV projects.*

Kevin Wetmore *is an actor, director, writer and professor. He has appeared in numerous horror plays and low budget films. He is the author of* Post-9/11 Horror in American Cinema *and* Back from the Dead: Reading Remakes of Romero's Zombie Films as Markers of their Time, *as well as numerous short stories, included in such anthologies as* Midian Unmade, Enter at Your Own Risk: The End is the Beginning *and* Moonshadows, *as well as such magazines as* Mothership Zeta, Devolution Z *and* Odd Tree Quarterly. *He lives with his family in Los Angeles.*

Jonathan Winn *is a screenwriter as well as the author of* Eidolon Avenue: The First Feast *(Crystal Lake Publishing, 2016), the full-length novels* Martuk . . . the Holy *(A Highlight of the Year, 2012 Papyrus Independent Fiction Awards),* Martuk . . . the Holy: Proseuche *(Top Twenty Horror Novels of 2014, Preditors & Editors Readers Poll),* Martuk . . . the Holy: Shayateen *(2016) and* The Martuk Series, *an ongoing collection of short fiction inspired by* Martuk . . .

In addition to his work in Horror 201: The Silver Scream *and his essay* Do Your Worst *in* Writers on Writing, Vol. 2., *Jonathan's award-winning short story* Forever Dark *can also be seen in Crystal Lake's* Tales from the Lake, Vol. 2.

We hope you enjoyed this title. If so, we'd be grateful if you could leave a review on your blog or any of the other websites and outlets open to book reviews. Reviews are like gold to writers and publishers, since word-of-mouth is and will always be the best way to market a great book. And remember to keep an eye out for more of Crystal Lake Publishing's books.

CONNECT WITH CRYSTAL LAKE PUBLISHING:

Website:
www.crystallakepub.com
(and receive a free eBook by joining our newsletter)
Facebook:
www.facebook.com/Crystallakepublishing
Twitter:
https://twitter.com/crystallakepub

With unmatched success since 2012, Crystal Lake Publishing has quickly become one of the world's leading indie publishers of Mystery, Thriller, and Suspense books with a Dark Fiction edge.

Crystal Lake Publishing puts integrity, honor and respect at the forefront of our operations.

We strive for each book and outreach program that's launched to not only entertain and touch or comment on issues that affect our readers, but also to strengthen and support the Dark Fiction field and its authors.

Not only do we publish authors who are legends in the field and as hardworking as us, but we look for men and women who care about their readers and fellow human beings. We only publish the very best Dark Fiction, and look forward to launching many new careers.

We strive to know each and every one of our readers, while building personal relationships with our authors, reviewers, bloggers, pod-casters, bookstores and libraries.

Crystal Lake Publishing is and will always be a beacon of what passion and dedication, combined with overwhelming teamwork and respect, can accomplish: Unique fiction you can't find anywhere else.

We do not just publish books, we present you worlds within your world, doors within your mind, from talented authors who sacrifice so much for a moment of your time.

This is what we believe in. What we stand for. This will be our legacy.

Welcome to Crystal Lake Publishing.